DRAGONS

In addition to
novels, including
Angel Eyes, Lustbader spent fifteen influential
years in the music industry. The author, who
travels worldwide when researching his novels,
lives in Southampton, New York, with his wife
Victoria.

Voyager

ERIC LUSTBADER

DRAGONS ON THE SEA OF NIGHT

The fifth novel in the Sunset Warrior Cycle

HarperCollins*Publishers*

Voyager
An Imprint of HarperCollins*Publishers*
77 – 85 Fulham Palace Road,
Hammersmith, London W6 8JB

The *Voyager* World Wide Web site address is
http://www.harpercollins.co.uk/voyager

This paperback edition 1998
1 3 5 7 9 8 6 4 2

First published in Great Britain by *Voyager* 1997

Copyright © Eric Lustbader 1997

The Author asserts the moral right to
be identified as the author of this work

ISBN 0 00 649027 1

Set in PostScript Photina by
Rowland Phototypesetting Ltd,
Bury St Edmunds, Suffolk

Printed and bound in Great Britain by
Caledonian International Book Manufacturing Ltd, Glasgow

CONTENTS

This is for my father,
Who asked for more tales.

The world is more —
Once we understand there is
Only this, we have woken
From the Dark.

From the Tablets of the Iskamen

That which is known as Magic
Was once the progeny of ignorance.

Ancient Shinju saying

KILL RHYTHM

'He is coming!'

Qaylinn, the chief Rosh'hi of the Bujun, gripped the wooden balustrade of the terrace that ran the entire length of the top floor of the temple of which he was the master. His old, lined face shone in the deep russet glow of the huge, oblate sun as it began to sink over the marshes where geese rose and alit as they had from time immemorial.

'I told you he would come!'

'Yes,' the voice said from behind him, 'but will he listen to what we have to say?'

Qaylinn, who had been trained since infancy to intuit intent from the nuances of the human voice, turned to face the other man – a tall, stately figure with a halo of steel-gray hair. Even so long from the battlefield, he is still the soldier inside, Qaylinn told himself. 'You are afraid,' he said quietly.

'Are you not?'

Qaylinn shook his head. 'You forget. I have met the Dai-San. I know him.'

The tall man shook his head. 'I, too, have met the Dai-San in the presence of the Kunshin, our sovereign, and my private opinion is that he is allowed too near the Dragon Throne,' he said. 'I think it is foolish to delude oneself into believing that he is knowable. Can one know a god? I think not.'

'Whatever he may be now, he was a man, once,' Qaylinn said steadily. 'And I assure you he has no designs on the Dragon Throne. He has bonded with the Kunshin; they are closer than brothers.' It was important to keep the minister's fear in check. Should it spread to the other members of the council . . . In any event, their faith in the Dai-San must not be shaken. His work was not yet done, and he was their only hope. 'From the womb of woman he came and so in his mind – whatever he has now become, whatever magic has been worked on him – he remains at his core a man.'

High Minister Ojime grunted. 'Would that I had your faith, sayann.' Sayann, a Bujun term for extreme respect, was not often used, and even less by Ojime. 'I, too, know that our fate – and the fate of the entire world of man – rests in the hands of the Dai-San.'

A wind was rising, unnatural and unsettling. It caused Qaylinn's deep saffron robe to swirl about his bare feet, ruffled Ojime's oiled cotton and cured leather coat which was the color of indigo, connoting his senior rank within the Sekkan, the council of Bujun.

Of course Ojime is frightened, Qaylinn thought. He is a political animal; he has been taught to fear and covet power that is greater than his own. It is how he came to don the cloth of indigo. Qaylinn wondered how many of the other high ministers feared and envied the Dai-San his godlike powers. His bald pate tingled. There was danger here, he knew, over and above the pressing reason he had summoned the Dai-San to Shinsei na-ke Temple in Haneda, Ama-no-mori's capital. It was a danger closer to home, the viper hidden in the breast of those who would have you believe they were friends. Ojime – and, indeed, all the high ministers – would need constant surveillance.

2

He looked to the west, where it seemed the lavender clouds were parting and, if he squinted, he could just make out a black speck near the horizon. The wind blew in his face and he felt the kind of electricity in the air one experiences during a lightning storm.

'I see him,' Ojime whispered from just behind Qaylinn. 'He answered your call, after all.'

'As I knew he would,' Qaylinn said without inflection. 'He is the Dai-San.'

'Even so,' Ojime said, 'he is not going to like what you have to tell him.'

'What the snow-hare's feet have told me!'

The Rosh'hi had whirled around, his voice uncharacteristically tense. 'When I speak to the Dai-San — when I tell him what I must — I will merely be a messenger of the kami, the spirits who reside in Ama-no-mori and protect it from harm.'

'Let us hope the Dai-San believes that, eh?' the high minister said darkly.

The wind whipped their cloaks around them with a fiery turbulence. The speck, illumined by the setting sun, was now an identifiable object. As he stared, Ojime's bowels threatened to turn to water, for he found that he was facing the great triple-horned head of a Kaer'n, one of the ancient beasts all Bujun warriors rode in the days of fire, ice and necromancy which, even for the Bujun, were becoming a thing of legend.

Where once they had been plentiful, living in harmony with the Bujun, the huge winged Kaer'n were now vastly reduced in number, living in a valley protected by the icy alpine regions of the northernmost of Ama-no-mori's three islands.

What I would give to get my hands on one of those beasts, the minister thought, shifting from one foot to the other. *My power would increase tenfold if I was seen directing one*

3

of the legendary Kaer'n. My drive to become head of the Sekkan would be assured, and I could then begin my assault on the Kunshin himself. But, by the gods, this creature makes my knees weak!

Qaylinn's thoughts were also filled with the Kaer'n, but they were tinged with nostalgia and regret that the Bujun had somehow lost their abilities to nurture and interact with the Kaer'n. He looked upon the beast with awe and veneration.

The flapping of the Kaer'n's wings filled the men's ears just as it caused the curling and blowing of the cloud formations high above. There was a certain rhythm, a kind of pulsing that seemed to invade the entire body. It was said, though Ojime had never seen documentation, that when the Kaer'n killed, their wings beat the air with a rhythm that slowly aligned itself with the victim's heartbeat. When synchronicity was achieved, the victim somehow died.

Astride the beast was the last person on the planet able to control and speak to the Kaer'n – the Dai-San, the Sunset Warrior.

Qaylinn felt a fire on his face as the Kaer'n's golden talons extruded through flesh, horned and armored to grip the highest parapet of the temple. Its iridescent wings folded in upon themselves, its long scaled neck bent, the large-boned, trapezoidal head almost touching the stone flooring, the amber intelligent eyes impaling the minister and the Rosh'hi in their unwavering gaze.

The two men stood transfixed as the Dai-San dismounted over the arch of the Kaer'n's neck. He was impossibly tall, wrapped in a cape of an unidentifiable material the color of night. His high curious helm was studded with gems that gave off a lambent illumination not unlike starlight. His faceted armor was unlike anything Ojime had ever dreamed of. A veritable galaxy of mythical beasts was embossed into the metal with such consummate skill that they appeared to be alive. What unknown artisans had fashioned this fantastic second skin he had no idea, but he longed to touch it, to don it, to investigate for himself its efficacy, the heady sense of invulnerability it must surely engender. Oh, what he could do with such armor!

The Dai-San's face was human-like, but in a multitude of ways it was vastly different. For one thing, his hooded eyes were faceted. It was almost as if one were being scanned by a company of people all with different personalities, differing points of view. His prominent nose seemed sculpted out of granite, his cheeks to have been scraped from the depths of the howling deserts. His mouth was like a dagger of ice, slashed horizontally across the lower half of his face. He was, in short, like no other creature either man had ever met.

'Dai-San,' Qaylinn said softly, with a small, ceremonial bow. 'It was good of you to come.'

The Dai-San's terrifying mouth split into what might, in others, have been a smile. 'It is good to see you again, my friend.'

Qaylinn lifted a hand briefly in Ojime's direction. 'May I introduce High Minister Ojime. He represents the lay portion of Bujun society.'

When the Dai-San fixed Ojime in the glare of those inhuman orbs, the minister blanched. He was adept at reading people; this was, after all, a talent that had served him well in his climb up the political ladder. But this was another story. He tried to fix his sights into the depths of those eerie eyes, because he knew that the soul of each man and woman was written in those individual depths. What he saw now appalled him. Rather than the blank wall he had imagined, he encountered a hall of mirrors which threw back on him the excesses and sins of his own

5

soul, so that he felt a line of sweat creep down his spine and his stomach turned to ice. He bowed deeply, if only to free himself of the terrible images that had danced before his gaze. He felt sick to his stomach, but he hid his distaste deep down as Qaylinn ushered the Dai-San into the sanctuary of the temple. Through the Hall of Secrets they went with its peculiar curved walls and massive thousand-year cedar columns, down the Corridor of Remembrance where the scrolls of the founding Rosh'hi hung in hand-carved niches, until at length they came to the Chamber of Prayer.

The last dying rays of the sun touched the thick stone sill of the high narrow west windows so that slices of crimson stained the tea-green walls, illuminating in electric fashion the raised platform from which hung a vertical scroll in stark black and white. The running calligraphy upon it had been written by Qaylinn's great-grandfather, who had founded this temple long ago.

'Please excuse us for not offering you hot tea, Dai-San,' Qaylinn said, bowing again, 'but our purpose is urgent and time is very short.' He went to the platform and, kneeling at the spot directly beneath the scroll, pressed two of the short wooden boards. Ojime, almost morbidly fascinated by the Dai-San, switched his gaze momentarily to the Rosh'hi. Lifting aside the boards, Qaylinn reached into the space beneath and, a moment later, lifted out an object swathed in layers of sueded leather. He rose, holding it away from him as if he would become contaminated by it. Without a word of explanation, he slowly unwrapped the cloth until all the layers had fallen away. He offered it up for the Dai-San's inspection.

Ojime caught the quick reaction in the Dai-San's face before he bent down, sniffing the thick gray object. To Ojime's surprise, the Dai-San's head jerked quickly back.

'It is fresh!' His voice, though a whisper, thundered in Ojime's ears.

6

'Fresh.' Qaylinn nodded. 'Yes.'

The Dai-San took a step backward. It happened so quickly that Ojime missed the motion. One instant, the Dai-San was in one place, the next he was in another. Astonishing!

With a whisper of polished leather and beaded silk, the Dai-San drew his enormous sword, *Aka-i-tsuchi*. Its long blue-green blade shone in the last of the day's light just as if it were noon outside instead of dusk. The Dai-San held the blade horizontally, the point almost touching the layers of sueded leather as they lay open like the petals of some alien flower. Slowly, the tip slid along the leather, then beneath the gray object until it rested on the blade. Then the Dai-San lifted it away. Was it his imagination, Ojime wondered, or did the Rosh'hi heave a sigh of relief?

The Dai-San regarded the thing with intense interest. 'It is the tongue of a Makkon.'

'A Makkon, yes.' Qaylinn nodded. 'One of the Chaos beasts that were the outriders for the Dolman.' The Dolman, ruler of the creatures of Chaos, had attempted to take control of the world some years ago. A pitched battle had been fought, culminating with the Kai-feng at the citadel of Kamado. The Dai-San was intimately familiar with the Dolman. They were linked in a curious and particular manner, since it had been the Dolman's decision to invade this world which led to the creation of the Dai-San, the savior of mankind, he who had defeated the Dolman.

'But all the Makkon are dead,' the Dai-San said. 'There were four and they all died.'

Qaylinn shook his head. 'What you hold on your sword, Dai-San, is a Makkon's tongue. It is fresh, unpreserved. It is proof that either one Makkon lived somehow or . . .' His voice petered out, his words hanging in the air.

'Or there are more than four.'

'Yes.' The Rosh'hi refolded the layers of leather, set them aside. From the pocket of his robe he threw five small items across the floor. 'I have cast the foot bones of the snow-hare, Dai-San, and they tell of a new attempt by the forces of Chaos to enslave our world.'

'The Dolman—'

'Exists no more,' Qaylinn said. 'You made certain of that when you sundered it with your magic dai-katana. But Chaos did not die when the Dolman ceased to exist. It was thrown into disarray and torment, and we wished to assume that it would remain leaderless and, therefore, without threat to us. Now the bones of the snow-hare have told us the truth. There is a new leader in Chaos, and it means to succeed where the Dolman failed.'

'I knew my work was not yet done,' the Dai-San said.

'I wonder whether it ever will be, my friend,' Qaylinn said.

The Dai-San flipped the tongue into the air, caught it on the talons of the scaled, six-fingered glove, made from the hide of a Makkon. 'Where was this tongue found?'

'On a Kintai clipper during a routine inspection,' Ojime said, pleased that the tactical phase of the discussion had begun. Since the Dai-San's return to Ama-no-mori, the islands had been opened up to trade. 'A keen-eyed tariff assessor spotted a nervous crewman and ordered the ship searched from stem to stern. The tongue was found secreted within the crewman's sea-chest.'

'I would question this crewman,' the Dai-San said.

Even being asked questions by him was painful, and Ojime sucked in his breath before he said, 'I am afraid that is impossible. The crewman took his own life.'

'Are you certain this is the way it happened?' the Dai-San asked. 'Your men are still unused to outsiders. They are notorious for over-reacting.'

8

Ojime noticed the Dai-San's gaze meet Qaylinn's, and he found himself deeply envious of their relationship. 'Absolutely certain,' he said stiffly. 'There are half a dozen witnesses.'

'All men under the tariff assessor's command, I will warrant,' the Dai-San said.

'Why the Makkon's tongue was being brought here we have no idea,' Ojime said, desperately trying to deflect the Sunset Warrior's wrath. 'But we did discover where it came from: the Great Rift.'

'That is a long way from here,' the Dai-San said. 'Beyond the Mu'ad desert of Iskael, the country of my bond-brother, Moichi Annai-Nin.'

'Upon the summit of the sacred mountain of Sin'hai,' Ojime affirmed. 'We need you to beat back this new threat, Dai-San. We believe that something *or someone* is using the depths of the Great Rift to break through from the dimension of Chaos.'

The Dai-San nodded. 'Who knows, perhaps the Great Rift itself is the tunnel built by the new forces of Chaos. I will go there immediately.'

He turned to depart but Qaylinn's voice stopped him in his tracks. 'There is something else the snow-hare revealed.'

The Dai-San turned his baleful gaze upon the two men. 'Tell me.'

'Yes, Dai-San.' Qaylinn recognized an order as well as did the minister. 'There is an agent – a human agent whom the Chaos forces are using to help them gain a foothold in our world.'

'Have you a name?'

'Yes.' Now, to Ojime's astonishment, the Rosh'hi actually appeared to quail beneath the burden of his message. In the face of his cowardice, Ojime spoke.

'The bones of the snow-hare were cast and there can

be no mistake,' he said quickly, before he, too, lost his nerve. 'The agent, the traitor, Dai-San, is your bond-brother, Moichi Annai-Nin.'

PART ONE

ISKAEL

ONE

SEA-CHANGE

The ship heeled over and Moichi Annai-Nin shouted, 'Haul away! By the Oruboros, haul away now, lads!'

All the sheets were being struck, coming down in fluted columns as the howling wind tore at them in great clawing gusts. But the mainsail, larger than the others and therefore more vulnerable, was caught out of position. The carefully tied rigging gave way beneath the violent storm's startlingly sudden fist. It tore the fittings like corks out of a line of bottles: pop! pop! pop!, the highest end of the triangular sail a serpentine banner, slapping wetly against the rain-slick mast before shredding into ragged tongues.

Moichi, his great brawny dusky-skinned body fighting aft toward the terrified tillerman, felt rather than saw the heightened agitation of the sea. The diamond set into the flesh of his right nostril flashed blue light as he drew in the sharp, charged scents of the storm, and he thought, damn this Bujun vessel and its delicate construction – unless I can straighten our course we'll go under for sure. He unsheathed one of the pair of copper-handled dirks that were his trademark, cutting through ratlines that had broken free and were whipping about the halyard.

Outwardly, he grinned hugely as he urged his men on with his immense confidence. But inwardly he cursed each and every one of their grimy souls, for he recognized the

13

panic that had gripped them all on the *Tsubasa*'s decks at the storm's initial onslaught. Well, he told himself resignedly as he went from group to group, hauling hawsers here, lashing down wildly swinging spars there, what can you expect from a crew dredged up from Sha'angh'sei's bituminous waterfront dens but drunken ex-sailors and drugged-out petty criminals whose dreams had been faded by time and evil incidence? He should never have allowed himself to cobble together such a crew, but the urge to return to his native Iskael with his love, Aufeya Seguillas y Oriwara, had been too much for him. He had been on dry land far too long.

This morning, six-and-a-half weeks out from Sha'angh'sei, the principal port on the southern face of the continent of man, he had been belowdeck with Aufeya, having already tested the wind thrice during the cormorant watch and learning nothing for his efforts. Or else he had been distracted by Aufeya. He had asked her to marry him when they reached his home in Iskael and she had accepted, her joy igniting the copper of her eyes.

A gray-green wave, opaque in its turbulence, sprang over the taffrail, soaking Moichi where he labored with a tangle of loose and shattered tackle. On his knees, he shouted a warning to those down below as the water roared across the mid-deck. It was then that Moichi felt the underlying power of the storm, and he knew that this was no ordinary tempest that periodically whirled through the eastern stretches of the Iskael Sea. For an instant, his mind seemed aware of something beyond the storm, yet quite a part of it, almost – and this was almost laughable – a kind of malevolent presence, as if the typhoon itself were alive. But that was quite impossible, he told himself, and went on with his frantic duties.

To make matters worse, the *Tsubasa* was no ordinary ship on which he had learned the art of navigation and sailing; it was a Bujun vessel – a gift from Moichi's bond-brother, the legendary Dai-San, who had saved the world of man from the Dolman and the invading forces of Chaos in the Kai-feng, the final cataclysmic battle that signaled the end of the Ages of Darkness and Necromancy.

The *Tsubasa* was like all things Bujun – that remote island chain the Dai-San had visited – delicate and mysterious as the mist that enshrouded its shores. The Bujun were reclusive, master warriors who preferred their own company. Many tales existed regarding the Bujun. One such insisted that they rode through the skies astride great horned and winged dragons called Kaer'n.

Though Moichi was a master navigator, he had yet to fully grasp the intricacies and peculiarities of this magnificent, superbly constructed Bujun vessel. As he rose, dizzy, blowing seawater from his nostrils, he cursed the impatience that had led him to set out for home too soon and with an improper crew. He staggered down the companionway to the mid-deck like an over-confident wrestler who, having stepped into the ring, was only now realizing the hidden reserves that lay behind the obvious strength of sinew of his opponent.

He risked a glance upward. There was no horizon. Instead, scudding clouds like angry bruises dipped to meet the rising sea, creating an almost seamless whole, a vast, writhing beast within whose belly the ship rocked and yawed dangerously. In every groan from the seasoned *kyoki*-wood timbers, from every pitch the ship took in the ever darkening swells, from the precarious bowing of the masts before the shrieking, gyring winds, his senses picked up the beginnings of the *Tsubasa*'s death throes.

God bear witness, he berated himself, this would not have happened if I'd not been so involved belowdecks. Aufeya! Even now his thoughts betrayed him, straying to the silkiness of her creamy skin, the look of longing and

15

love filling her copper eyes, the pleasure – sometimes gentle, other times fierce – of their nights together in the captain's cabin.

Dammit, no! Moichi had been born to be master of the seas: a navigator. And now, as captain of his own ship, he had at last achieved a lifelong dream. No storm, unnatural or no, would rip his new charge from beneath his bootsoles. Oh no, he vowed, gripping the railing to regain his balance. By the Oruboros, the great sea spirit who guides all mariners, I will not allow it!

The roiling clouds above his head mangled the murky periwinkle daylight into patches of shifting, menacing shadow that raced across the ship's foundering flanks as if they were working in concert with the angry sea in trying to pull it under.

The fittings howled in protest and the *Tsubasa* again shipped water dangerously. On Moichi's shouted orders men ran, stumbling, toward the bilges, manning over-worked emergency pumps. But the wind was rising, sudden violent gusts like the claws of some evil-tempered beast making the tying off of the sails almost impossible. Moichi tried to shout further instructions to his crew but the storm cried him down hysterically.

The ship canted over, almost capsizing, and Moichi turned, heading back aft to the tiller. He was halfway up the companionway when he heard a cracking from over his head like the sundering of a roofbeam. He did not have to look up to know that the mizzen mast – the thinnest of the clipper's three masts – had been bent past its breaking point and had splintered.

He launched himself up the companionway and raced across the shuddering deck. Unmindful of the treacherous footing, he shoved men out of the way of the hardwood as it came crashing down in a bird's nest of rigging and tackle. Nevertheless, one of the crosstrees struck the first

16

mate across his face, his flesh gashed open as he reeled backward, arms flailing in a vain attempt to right himself.

Moichi lunged after him, stretching to his full limit, slipping, then catching himself. His powerful fingers encircled the mate's wrist as a combination of his own momentum and the violent motion of the ship sent the man arcing over the side rail.

With a shriek, he disappeared, and Moichi was dragged several heart-stopping feet after him across the deck. He fetched up against the side with a rib-jolting blow. Half-dazed he held on, gritting his teeth with the effort, his muscles bulging, veins popping in lightning streaks.

He peered over the side, his face filled with seafoam and rain. He saw the mate's mouth twisted in terror, his eyes staring wildly. Blood ran off him like pink rain.

'Hold on! I have you now!' Moichi shouted into the storm as he gathered his strength to bring the mate up onto the deck. But just then, the *Tsubasa* lurched sickeningly, sending the side they were on plummeting downward into the thrashing sea. My God, Moichi thought, it's dark down here. Like the underside of the world.

And with just an indifferent flick of its bulk the ocean took his mate from him, tearing his hand from Moichi's. The man's mouth opened in a silent shriek as the water in great black swirls lifted him into its embrace, up, up, and then, quite suddenly, sucking him into itself, down and away.

There had been absolutely no sensation of him slipping away, no intimation of what was to come. One moment Moichi had him firmly in tow, the next instant there was nothing to hold on to, just the chill wetness all around, moaning and pitching as if in agony.

God of my father, Moichi thought, I have never seen the sea like this.

His head came up and he squinted through the typhoon, thinking, No! By the Oruboros, this is too much!

But in truth his ears had not deceived him. They were picking up a vibration rather than a true sound – a horrid, bone-chilling rumbling that reverberated through his body and buzzed evilly in his brain.

With a bellow of rage, Moichi stormed the high poop deck and, shouting mingled instructions and encouragements to the young, petrified tillerman, brought his own brawny weight to bear on the protesting steering mechanism. It would not budge.

He raced to the railing, leaped down onto the mid-deck, gesticulating as he picked himself up and ran for the mainmast. 'Raise the mains'l!' he cried. 'Raise the mains'l!'

No one reacted. The best of them knew only to trim all sail, batten down all hatches and tackle in order to ride out a storm. Raising sail in the face of foul weather was unthinkable. What their captain was asking of them was sheer madness.

'Move,' Moichi shouted, 'or we'll all be dead men, lying at the bottom of the sea and food for the big fish!'

As if to underscore his words all light left the world. In the unnatural blackness the men turned aft. There came a shriek among them; or perhaps it was the infernal typhoon itself, laughing at its height, at the puny creatures who dared ride its coruscating back.

No matter. They all saw it at once: the *tsunami*. The towering wavefront, black and purple, had risen up behind them, traveling at a fast rate, growing and curling with every split second until it had formed a massive fortress wall threatening to engulf them. The pressure drop was palpable, a great rushing in their ears, a pounding in the heads. The crew stood paralyzed, staring helplessly at the advent of their doom.

Only Moichi was in motion, striding among them,

18

screaming in their ears, shoving them this way and that. And still the building *tsunami* transfixed them. Then one among them came to life, moving to the mainmast, hauling with all his slight weight, his dark almond eyes sliding from Moichi's face to the rapidly unfurling sheet. It was the lone Bujun among them, a man who had kept to himself so completely throughout the voyage that Moichi could not even recall his name.

'The Oruboros curse you!' Moichi shouted as he and the Bujun struggled with the mainsail. 'You'll do as I say or die!'

Perhaps they felt the proximity of their deaths or perhaps it was the example of the grim-faced Bujun hauling mightily on the rigging that galvanized them. In any event, they threw off their stupor and bent to their task, moving as one to deploy the flapping mainsail, which moaned in protest as it was raised into the brunt of the storm.

Now Moichi left the Bujun to work them, and he returned to the high poop deck, bounding toward the ashen-faced tillerman. 'Into the wind!' he shouted into the man's tense face. 'By God and all that's holy, we'll be swamped in a moment if you can't do it!'

Moichi would not turn around, but he could feel the approach of the *tsunami*, feeling its vibrations, dark and deadly, rushing closer as each precious second raced by.

Bug-eyed in terror, the tillerman cried, 'You're mad! You'll turn us right into the path of the wavefront! We'll be sucked down for sure!'

In desperation, Moichi threw the tillerman aside and, lifting his head, called for the Bujun. The mainsail was up and bowed, catching the lashing wind. If only the Bujun cloth would not rip in the typhoon's violence.

The small, almond-eyed man bounded up the companionway, and the instant his hands gripped the tiller, Moichi could feel the ship respond. He looked hard into the Bujun's eyes, saw only mute concentration as the man fought with him to turn the *Tsubasa* fully into the wind before the filled mainsail capsized them.

Behind them, the *tsunami* was rushing at them, building even higher, creaming and bubbling like a cauldron at its serpentine crest. Moichi risked a glance over his shoulder. The wavefront was the deepest black within the enormous cradle of its rising bulk.

Sweating like beasts of burden, digging their heels into the slick deck boards, Moichi and the slim Bujun dragged on the recalcitrant tiller. The violent sea had the *Tsubasa* and it did not want to give her up. Grunting with their effort, their lungs hot bellows, they heaved on the tiller, and slowly, agonizingly slowly the craft began to give grudging way, shifting through the water, fighting the wind, the wildly fluctuating cross-currents and the relentless tide. Turning to port, always to port, the two men struggled, their teeth ground together, their shoulder muscles bunched, their chests expanding like sails full out.

But now their world was filled with the rumble of the *tsunami* over and above the wail of the storm, and Moichi knew that it was possible they had left it too late, that the mainsail full out would not now provide enough extra speed to allow them to cleave the wavefront, that they would all go down, broken like the timbers that would splinter all around them. He did not want to end up like seaweed, adrift on the tides.

'By God, put your soul into it, lad!' he cried into the Bujun's ear. 'Everything you have now! Everything!'

The Bujun trembled with the vehemence of the typhoon and the words spat out by this great bearlike demon at his side. He had signed on to the *Tsubasa* to escape the endless gloom of Sha'angh'sei's narrow crooked streets, its double-dealing, lice-ridden merchants, its evil-eyed provocateurs, its sleazy arms dealers. It had been a mistake

20

to leave his island home, to come to the seething continent of man. To sail a Bujun vessel had seemed the perfect escape from Sha'angh'sei's madness. Now he was trapped in this sea-drenched coffin! As he hauled on the tiller his white lips trembled in a prayer that had, until this moment, been only half-remembered.

But no prayer could dispel the terrible onrush of the *tsunami*. It rode triumphantly above the siren shriek of the typhoon, a sound out of all nature, a vibration rattling his clenched teeth, causing the short hairs to stand on the back of his neck, making his drenched flesh crawl. Still, his half-numbed brain registered the exhortations of his captain who stood side by side with him, who needed his strength to turn the ship fully into the wind. This sense of intimacy, of comradeship was new to the Bujun, and he felt it a pleasurable and compelling sensation. No one had ever needed him before, and he was bound and determined to deliver up his very soul to his captain if that were what was asked of him. Shoulder to the groaning tiller, he redoubled his efforts, grunting like a rutting animal.

The *tsunami* was a living being pursuing them like the hand of God, rolling and roaring like a giant in agony, an unstoppable mailed fist bent on demolishing them all.

Down on the mid-deck, men tying off the last of the mainsail's singing lines felt cold sweat snaking down their rigid spines. They fell to their knees where they were, vomiting and urinating without volition. Others cried or simply prayed to gods they no longer believed in, returning unconsciously to the ways of their forebears that they had once ridiculed for their piousness. They cried for succor, no longer believing in their innate power as men, pleading with these long-dead gods to deliver them by a miracle.

Above them, Moichi shouted, 'Now!' in the Bujun's ear. 'Now, now, now, by the Oruboros!' And they fought the

21

tiller, fought the raging seas and gusting gale as Moichi willed them further to port, bending his mind as well as his muscles to the near impossible task.

Now that special bond between captain and ship was springing up between them, and he called upon the *Tsubasa*, his ship, speaking silently to her in the universal language of the sea. He cajoled her, cursed her, caressed her and beat her, threatening her with an eternity of rot at the bottom of the sea.

And all the while he could feel the presence of the onrushing *tsunami*, its crest widening, higher now than the tallest buildings of his memory, even those great arcane pyramids he and the Dai-San, when he had been called Ronin, had ascended in the land of the Majapan.

I survived the horror of Xich Chich, Moichi thought, defeating gods more powerful than any one element. I fought in the Kai-feng, the war against Chaos's agent, the dreaded Dolman. I destroyed the monster Diablura in the land of the Opal Moon, resisted the deadly magical lure of the Firemask, I outfoxed the sorceress Sardonyx, defeating her at her own diabolical game. I survived it all. I will not die here, so close to home, in my own element! By God, I own the seas!

He raised his head to the lightning-flecked clouds. He felt the proximity of another spirit, the conjunction of their power, battling the howling elements all around them, and he grinned, loving the whip of the wind, the briny smell of the sea, and always the titanic struggle the ocean put to you in order to prove your ultimate worth.

His heart beat fast and strong, and his spirit expanded, directing itself along the sleek flanks of his new ship, pointing its sharp upswept prow toward the wall of water that was now almost upon them. And, for the first time, he appreciated the Bujun craft's design. His own ships would have wallowed in a wave trough but the *Tsubasa*'s sleek shape sliced through the waves. The mainsail was almost full out and he could feel a corresponding quickening of their speed. They were almost there. But the wavefront had also picked up momentum as it drew strength from the heart of the typhoon, the flailing arms of the gale, the deepening surge of the sea itself deep down where light itself was forever banished.

The *tsunami* was all they could see now, their entire universe, and Moichi knew that the ship still had several meters to go. It had been a desperate gamble, trying to cleave through the wavefront on speed and nerve, a long-odds bet at best. They had run out of time.

The Bujun was trembling in fear and effort beside him. Moichi felt it almost as if it were his own, and he murmured, 'Come on, lad, don't fail me now! It's just the two of us and the *Tsubasa* against this leviathan!'

Inwardly, for just a moment as he stared into the heart of the *tsunami*, Moichi felt his resolve begin to crumble, for surely there was no way through this cyclopean madness. He had been a fool to attempt this run at it.

Then he felt movement beside him, heard the Bujun's call like a distant sea bird's in his ear, 'She's coming to, Captain. Helm's answering fully. The wind's directly aft!'

All doubts vanished. 'Double and redouble!' Moichi shouted, immensely grateful for the Bujun's courage and resolve. 'Keep the helm steady, mate! If we're blown off course even a few degrees we'll be lost! Our bow must strike the wavefront dead on!'

The sound of the *tsunami* was like the rending of the earth's mantle. It shuddered the decks, chattered the men's teeth, making them weep with fear and loathing.

'Bastard!' Moichi called at the curling black wall of water. 'I'll beat you yet! My time's not come and surely not by your evil hand!' And with immeasurable effort, the two men held the helm steady as they met the onrushing wavefront, towering over them to an impossible height so that even Moichi, his soul expanded to its limits, felt the chill tendrils of fear writhing in his belly. 'The time of truth's come, lad!'

The *Tsubasa* sliced into the wavefront. Walls of wind-whipped water rose above them until they seemed a part of the raging sky, replacing it altogether. They were within the *tsunami*, their fate now linked with its elemental and unpredictable power. Its energy was unendurable – it was like being inside a massive hive of bees stirred by an intruder to a frenzy. Then the sides of the wavebody seemed to glass over, to deepen in color and depth. What was happening?

God of my father, Moichi prayed. This is truly the face of death. For within the *tsunami*'s very heart he discerned what could only be termed a female face, elemental, to be sure, its features shifting like currents, sliding away into shadow and reappearing slightly altered as if each heart-beat, each moment in time brought it a new aspect.

It was like looking into the face of a god. It was domi-nated by great lidless eyes and a lipless mouth. It was a face of unmitigated rage, so shocking in its intensity that Moichi felt the breath sucked from him as if all the air had been withdrawn from this place. He also had the impression of immeasurable age, so that for the first time in his life the concept of eternity was given form and substance.

Then he felt the bosom of the sea buck and judder beneath their tortured keel as if a gigantic hand from the depths had risen and grasped it. The ship, as if possessed, shot forward, as the howling winds filled the mainsail to bursting. The *Tsubasa*'s high bow lifted upward to meet the creaming crest of the wavefront now beginning to tumble over them with an ominous tearing sound. Moichi and the Bujun almost had their arms torn out of their

24

sockets as the helm tried to pull this way and that. But the two men held the *Tsubasa* fast to its course, and with an astonishing burst of speed, the Bujun craft continued to slice through the whirling maelstrom before them.

Moichi felt rather than heard the Bujun praying as the clipper, trembling, dipped precipitously into the trough of terrifying depth. For long breathless moments their world was stark green and obsidian black, the curve of the vast wavebody filled their ears, their heads and bodies with an alien din.

Gargantuan shapes slid through the depths on either side of them, far from the surface high above, moving and twisting in a silent display none had ever seen before or could even have imagined.

How long they plowed through the aqueous gorge was impossible to judge, and at last, directly ahead of them, the first patch of deep blue appeared, so small at first that many took it to be a part of the roaring sea. Gradually, it widened, seeming to bring them out of their watery tomb, and at length they felt the ship rising to meet it, as if in concert with the changing tide below them.

Grinning hugely, Moichi spared an instant to clap the Bujun on the back. Then he swiftly returned both hands to the helm as the *Tsubasa* wavered a bit in the still treacherous cross-currents, the aftermath of the ferocious typhoon.

'Softly, now,' Moichi whispered in the Bujun's ear, 'the *tsunami*'s behind us but this gale can still do us in.' Between them they kept a tight rein on the ship's course. 'Listen to the wind in the sheets and take care to read the pattern of its changes. If we get broadside to it with the mains'l filled, we'll go down like a stone.'

The Bujun's grip on the helm remained firm, his knuckles white with the pressure. He concentrated on the job given him, tracking the gusty wind expertly, making

25

incremental course corrections as needed. In no time at all, he was nearly anticipating the gale.

Seeing this, Moichi nodded to himself. That Bujun had more guts in the crunch than all of the scurvy crew combined. Glancing upward, he noticed that the blue sky was gone. In its place, thick glowering thunderheads, dark with rain, rippled across the clogged sky, dipping down to meet the gray-green ocean. Lightning forked and licked, yellow-pink, blinding him momentarily.

With that the downpour began anew. Moichi glanced around. The *Tsubasa* was already lying low in the water, her scuppers blocked with twisted masses of sea grape and wrack.

'What do you think,' he asked the Bujun, 'if I ask for all sail to be set will this ship take it?'

The Bujun looked into his face and nodded. 'She'll take anything you put her to, Captain. Of that you can be assured.'

Moichi nodded and, turning toward the crew on the deck below, called for all sail to be set. They needed all speed now in order not to ship more water and risk a high wave pulling them under.

One of the mates, a glum-faced giant with an oily drooping mustache and some years' sea experience, mounted the companionway.

'You're not thinkin' o' fillin' the yards in this foul weather, Cap'n,' he growled. It was not a question.

'We'll go under if we don't raise the sails,' Moichi said, not bothering to look at the mate as he directed the crew to clear the last of the debris over the side.

'You're wrong, Cap'n. We'll surely go under if we do set sail.' He was close enough now to smell the rum on his breath. 'That god-rotting demon wave was an omen. We'll do nothing now but ride out the storm.'

Moichi swung at him. 'Look at how low we sit. With

26

this heavy rain and the scuppers clogged we'll be sunk inside a watch. You'll follow my orders, by God!'

'I warn you,' the mate said, 'do not tempt the gods further.'

'I said set all sail,' Moichi said in a menacing tone.

The mate did not back down, but pulled agitatedly at his oily mustache. He nodded his head in the Bujun's direction. 'It's he who gave the order, isn't it? That Bujun bastard. I heard stories of how they sail their damned ships.' The mate spat, a heavy yellow gob of saliva. 'This is no time t'be takin' the advice of a rotting Bujun.'

'I am the captain of this vessel,' Moichi said, knowing he had to restore his sovereignty immediately, 'and you will obey my orders.'

'But why should I, Cap'n?' The mate raised his arms wide. 'Why should any of us? You saw it as well as anyone, I reckon.'

'Shut up!' Moichi thundered. 'Or I'll give your job to the Bujun!'

The big mate spat again and tried to laugh; it came out as a moan. 'Well, who cares a whit now, eh? This is a damned voyage and you've murdered us all, in any case.' Unable to tolerate the heat from Moichi's glare, he turned to the men, his voice raised in a hoarse shout. 'Ye all saw it plain as day, I'll warrant. The face in the wave. All gods curse the day I set foot on this miserable alien ship!'

'I told you to shut your yap!' Moichi shouted, hauling the big man all the way up the companionway.

'Too late, Cap'n, it's happened. The moment all seafaring men dread. We've all looked into Miira's Mirror! We're all dead men now! You can't deny the legend! We're doomed!'

Moichi slammed his huge fist into the mate's greasy face, sending him reeling down the companionway, tumbling head over heels. He was about to descend after him when he saw that the door to his cabin was open. Aufeya had emerged. Unused to the rigors of the sea, she should have been white-faced and weak, but she seemed to have weathered the typhoon without ill effect. How long had she been standing there? Moichi wondered. Long enough to have heard the rantings of the mate? By God, he prayed not. She looked at him, making the sign of the Palliate. She was Daluzan – a people whose culture, like Moichi's, was intimately bound up with their religion.

'Set all sail!' Moichi bellowed. 'Snap to it, mates! All those thinking otherwise will find a watery grave, this I swear, for I'll tolerate no mutiny aboard the *Tsubasa*!'

The crew snapped to, breaking out the sheets as quickly as they could. But while all about him was frenzied activity, Aufeya stood her ground, her long red hair whipping her shoulders and cheeks, her copper-colored eyes glancing back and forth from the supine mate to Moichi's stern gaze.

He could see the curiosity in her face, and the fear. Aufeya came from a people who were overly superstitious. And she had witnessed her own demon – the Diablura – come to vivid and terrifying life, almost destroying her. To her, the world of sorcery and devils had not entirely passed into oblivion. Moichi knew now that she had overheard the mate's warning regarding Miira's Mirror, and he cursed the man all over again.

He was descending toward her, when a sudden burst of rain obscured his vision. The wind howled and the ship heeled dizzyingly to port. Moichi was knocked over the railing of the stair, crashing to the mid-deck. He was up on his feet in an instant, shaking off the sparks behind his eyes, the pain in his shoulder and hip. He shouted instructions to the men tying down the mainsail. It was then that he realized he did not see Aufeya.

He broke off his tirade, rushing to the port rail. He could just see a hand, small and pale, the white knuckles gripping hard the lower wooden railing. He reached down, saw Aufeya's face, pinched with fear, her eyes wide and staring, her long copper hair whipping around her face and neck.

'Aufeya! Hold on, I have you!'

As his fingers closed over her wrist, the ship lurched again to port and the angry sea rose up as if it were a beast with a will of its own. It smashed against the hull of the Bujun ship, inundating Aufeya completely.

At that instant, Moichi felt a tugging, an added weight that almost pulled his arm from its socket. He knew that it was impossible, but it was as if something from the deep was trying to pull Aufeya under.

Then the ship rose upward on the breast of a swell and the wave receded, bringing Aufeya back to him. She was drenched and gasping, her thick hair clinging to her like sea grape. She coughed, spewing seawater, and reaching down with his other hand, he began to haul her upward.

The ship dove down again into a trough, the rain beating at them like hail and it was as if a kind of shadow fell over them as the sea rose up her hips, chest and shoulders until it appeared to tower over them. It was then that some inner tingling caused Moichi to look up into the blue-gray underside of the wave. In its shifting depths he saw again the eerie primordial face, filled with rage. The slash of a mouth appeared to open and he heard a rumbling as of distant thunder.

He shook his head as if to clear his ears of water, but it did no good. He heard the rumbling again, breaking apart and re-forming into what could only be construed as words:

I WANT HER. I MUST HAVE HER.

What, he thought wildly, *am I hearing?*

IT IS MIIRA'S WISH.

29

Miira!

DEFY ME AT YOUR PERIL!

The water was rising, lapping up over Aufeya's mouth and nose. She was struggling now, clearly terrified. And with good reason. In a moment, she would drown.

With an extreme effort of will, Moichi looked away from the sorcerous face, concentrating on the task at hand. He was Aufeya's only chance at life, and he had only moments within which to act. Already a larger wave was forming, heading toward them. The ship was beginning to climb the next crest and Moichi knew this was his last shot at saving Aufeya from a watery grave.

He pressed his knees against the side timbers, hauled upwards, using all the strength in his legs, back and arms. Muscles popped, corded tendons pulled his skin this way and that. He could feel Miira dragging against him, fierce in her determination. But Moichi was more determined. He called upon the strength of his bond-brother, the Dai-San, and slowly, painfully slowly, he drew Aufeya toward him, until as the ship crested the wave, he brought her, gasping and shivering over the rail to his side.

He had one last glimpse of that rage-stained face in the sea, then it broke apart into ten thousand shards, the wave crashed harmlessly against the hull of the ship, and was gone in white plumes along the ship's wake.

TWO

MIIRA'S MIRROR

Of course, Aufeya had heard the voice.

And, of course, he had to tell her about Miira's Mirror. He had no choice. They had come too close to Miira – or something that called itself Miira – for him to be able to do otherwise.

He had spent several hours seeing to the ship, but in truth the magnificent prowess of the Bujun ensured that what damage had occurred was minor. Again, he marveled that such a slight-looking vessel could so courageously weather such an evil storm, and he thanked the Dai-San all over again for his gift, for he was certain that no ordinary ship would have survived.

In the end, he left what remained to be done to the tillerman, whose name was Arasomu, and who he had now elevated to first mate. He climbed the crosstrees of the mainmast like a monkey. At its tip, he tested the wind and tasted the sweet smell of the ocean's marker that meant fair winds. Back on deck, he broke out his navigator's instruments and, fixing on the shining constellations of the stars, calculated their position. He relayed all this information and his instructions to Arasomu. Confident that the weather had turned for good and that within hours they would be back on course for Iskael, he went belowdeck to his cabin, where Aufeya was waiting for him.

31

He told her the legend of Miira's Mirror as she lay in their berth, swathed in warming blankets, while the *Tsubasa* rode a tranquil sea and lightly gusting trade winds beneath a star-filled night sky toward Iskael. Just her nose and eyes peeped out from beneath the blankets and she seemed, with her wild hair and copper eyes, to be no more than a small child readying herself to hear a night-time tale before sleep.

Miira, it is said by seamen the world over, was a woman of exceeding grace and beauty (Moichi began). She lived in Syrinx, a land far, far away on the other side of the Mountain Sin'hai, on the edge, it is said, of a stony abyss that plunged into the very heart of this planet. Her people, I think, must have died out long ago.

These people were political animals. Power meant everything, and intrigue was second nature to them. Miira's husband was a vice-minister in a government rife with internecine warfare.

At the time of the birth of Miira's son, her husband, Bnak, was engaged in a potentially explosive power struggle with the leader of the main opposition movement. He was a staunch loyalist, and had dedicated himself to battling those who sought to overthrow the reform-minded regime.

Again and again Bnak would uncover plots against the highest government officials and he would take measures to thwart them because his sources were numerous and he was as exceedingly clever as Miira was beautiful.

Now you may well ask, if Bnak was so clever and possessed of so much power in a power-oriented society why had he not risen to full ministerial rank? The answer is as simple as it is distressing.

Miira was Shinju.

The Shinju were the indigenous people of this land. Centuries before, Bnak's people had swept across a vast, turbulent ocean on a mission of expansion. They found the Shinju's land and had straightaway sought to colonize it. In the process, they decimated the Shinju, driving what was left of them into the bleak, desolate highlands. There Bnak's people left them, to die of starvation and the elements, or so they thought. The Shinju were as tough as they were resourceful and they survived like the sure-footed mountain goats, whose thick winter coats they sheared, processed and wove into fantastic garments that were as light as air and as warm as a blazing fire.

As a young man Bnak had a penchant for anthropology and he spent two years in the highlands among the Shinju conducting his studies. It was here that he met Miira and fell in love with her. Her people would never have allowed her to court him, let alone marry outside her race had they not come to know Bnak and to appreciate his special qualities. For his part, Bnak had never shared nor even understood his people's abiding antipathy and scorn for the Shinju. He knew they were not inferior. Quite the contrary, in fact. He discovered that in many ways his own people would never fathom, the Shinju possessed far more knowledge and wisdom. They were simply not a warlike race.

Though it would have been far easier for Bnak to have stayed with Miira among the Shinju, he was no coward. He chose to return to the capital and to work from within to change the laws regarding the Shinju, to help educate his people about Miira's people. The reformers were his best hope. No other faction would even have given him a minor post. And Miira, at her intuitive best, agreed to help him in any way she could.

That Miira was beautiful beyond compare or as graceful as a lark descending from the heart of the sun, that she was cleverer than most men, meant nothing to the ministers who ruled the land; in their minds, Miira and all her people were inferior. Though they readily admitted Bnak's cleverness and exploited it and all his assets to their benefit, yet they mocked him behind his back, made disparaging remarks about Miira and refused every promotion that was his due. In short, they made pretense of listening to his impassioned treatises on the Shinju and then dismissed them as if they were the ravings of a lunatic.

Still, Bnak, loyal to the end, continued on their behalf.

As for Miira, she went about her life as if the scorn of these men and their high-born wives meant nothing to her. That is, on the outside. On the inside, (here Moichi shrugged) who can say? Though she was by no means a vain woman, Miira used her Shinju mirror to make up her face each morning. Now, it was her husband's habit to sit with her and watch her at it. The very early morning was their quiet time, and because Bnak often did not return from his work until midnight or later it was here that the peace of those deeply and truly in love descended over them.

'You are the most beautiful,' Bnak would tell Miira in a voice filled with wonder. 'Each morning you grow more so. And do you know that your reflection is beautiful . . . and different. There is, somehow, a purity of image I can see that comes from the deepest part of you. It is as if when I stare at you in the mirror I see you as a young girl, untouched and unmarked by time, care or worry.'

Bnak would tell her this so often that quite soon it had become a ritual. But no matter how often he said it Miira made no reply. She would merely smile the soft and dreamy smile she allowed only him to see, the smile he had seen while he was on his sojourn among the Shinju.

Three months after a son was born to Miira, Bnak's enemies invaded their villa in the gray and dismal hour before dawn. They slew the guards Bnak had posted and stole the infant from his crib in the small room adjacent to where his parents slept.

They offered Bnak a choice. Either he could resign his post and leave the capital with his son safe in his arms or he could have the infant delivered blue-faced and lifeless at his doorstep.

Now Bnak knew what would happen to the government should he be forced to flee the city. The plots would multiply until those who sought to take his place would be overwhelmed. The governmental leaders would be slain, the city – the entire nation for that matter – would be thrown into turmoil and confusion. Rivers of blood would run through the capital and the gods only knew where or when they would stop.

To stay and fight for reform or to flee and see all that he had worked for crumble to dust and blood. This was no decision that he could make on his own. So he did what he always did with questions knotty and of high import: he consulted Miira.

Though she was beside herself with grief, still she counseled him to follow the dictates of his heart. ('I often wonder,' Moichi said, interrupting the tale briefly, 'whether she was intuitive enough to have known that Bnak's goal of a united country was but an unattainable dream of a man of good heart and soul.') 'My heart and your heart are one, Miira,' Bnak said with tears in his eyes. 'Tell me what I should do.'

'What does your heart say?' she asked, holding his hands. She looked deep into his eyes now with that purity he had come to know so well. 'The truth now.'

'Loyalty is everything to me. That's the truth of it, beloved,' he said. 'If I betray them, if I betray my loyalty, then I am no man. I am nothing.'

Miira was unsurprised. This purity of purpose was what she loved best about him, what reminded her most of the

35

best of her own people. 'Do as you will, husband,' she said with a voice like the tolling of a bell, 'for I fear either way our son is lost to us for ever.'

She meant, of course, that their son's abductors had no intention of letting him live. They were desperate men, desiring power above all else. What was the life of one infant – especially a half-breed – to them? Less than nothing. They would, Miira feared, simply take pleasure in his death.

Bnak clapped his fists over his ears but it was too late – the bitter truth was branded into his brain and he could do naught else but to follow Miira's advice and do what he would. He had to forget his son ever existed, wipe all the precious memories away. Start over.

Could he carry out such a heinous but requisite task?

He knew he must.

He defied his enemies, the enemies of the state. He remained loyal, he remained a man. But at what price?

The next morning, as they had threatened, their son appeared at the gateway to their villa, strangled with a blue cord.

After the requisite three day mourning period, Bnak returned to his duties at the ministry. He pulled in all the favors he had been hoarding for years and the directive went out across the length and breadth of the capital: find the abductors, the murderers.

But on his way home that night he was ambushed, his guards slain, and he was brutally murdered. At almost the same instant life was seeping out of him, men invaded his villa, looking for Miira. They found only empty rooms.

In another quarter of the capital, the chief ministers were assaulted in their bed chambers. Blood flowed in the streets, as Bnak had feared. Chaos reigned as the old was destroyed and the new sought to solidify its power in the

36

corridors of the ministry and in the streets. Thousands died; the capital was turned into an abattoir as the loyalists battled the insurgents.

During those dark weeks of brutal warfare and death, Miira rose each morning in the cave at the northernmost outskirts of the city to tend to the wounded men and the women who had been beaten and raped. She no longer had the time nor the desire to make up her face, and yet, out of habit, she continued to look at her reflection in her Shinju mirror. She did this mainly to keep the memory of Bnak alive. In the moment just before he was ambushed, she had been pulled out of sleep by a harsh shriek that, upon awakening, she knew existed only in her Shinju mind. In that shriek was carried the crosstown assault and imminent death of her husband. Also, the hastening bootsoles on the street along which their villa was set. She had leapt out of bed, grabbed clothes, money and her mirror and had fled the villa by a secret passage just moments before it was invaded by those sent to kill her.

Now, in the cave of war, she looked daily upon her reflection. It was a wholly different image that greeted her. It had been frequently said that there was a kind of magic running through the Shinju. Rumors still surfaced, now and again, but no civilized man believed them, of course. Why would they? If the Shinju actually possessed magical powers would Bnak's people have been able to invade their land, slaughter them, take what had once been theirs?

And yet had anyone else been present to gaze into Miira's mirror they might have had grave second thoughts. For her reflection no longer bore the imprimatur of her husband's love. Bnak was dead; their son, as well. Miira's heart was cold, gray ash. Her normally calm and flexible spirit had become the dark adamantine jewel of fury.

Even as she tended the wounded and dying, counseled the psychologically battered, she burned for vengeance. And, staring into her mirror at what was reflected there, she knew what she must do to dissolve that dark jewel, though she had vowed never to do so and to break the vow meant certainly that she must die.

As Bnak's enemies had done so cleverly before her, Miira now made a comprehensive diary of the new regime's comings and goings. She listed all the key ministers and, after their names, the times of the day when they were inside the ministry building.

After a month of this diligent detective work, she sat down to evaluate her copious notes. By this time the worst of the fighting had subsided to sporadic outbreaks among the last remnants of the die-hard loyalists. The stranglehold of the new regime was all but complete. There was, she discovered, the hour of midnight when all the ministers met in council. Midnight, she thought, putting aside her diary. The hour of Bnak's death.

How she slipped past the phalanxes of guards is anyone's guess. In any event, no one saw her enter the ministry; no one saw her inside until she appeared within the central chamber of state and by then it was too late.

She passed around the great oval table at which her enemies sat, sleek and self-satisfied. Those murderers. There was still time to turn back, to forego vengeance. But her mind was filled with memories of Bnak and of her baby. And she broke her sacred vow.

She used her power; the power of the Shinju, for all the rumors were quite correct. As she passed behind each minister, she placed her mirror before them, and each had no choice but to look at his image reflected there.

What they saw no man, perhaps, can say. But I suspect it was different for each of them. One by one, they clawed the air as if phantasms were assailing them. Their faces twisted grotesquely in horror and dread. They fouled themselves abysmally; some wept uncontrollably in their death throes.

And when the last of the ministers had died, Miira too, looked deep into her mirror and, it is said, died on the spot (Moichi concluded).

Aufeya, who had been sitting up in the berth for some time now, her own aches and fears forgotten as she became more and more enthralled with the tale, said, 'Is this story true? It is so fantastic. Terrible and fantastic.'

'Aye, it is that, but though it makes a gripping tale I doubt its veracity.'

Aufeya seemed lost in thought for some time. Then she threw the bedclothes off and, padding about the cabin, began to dress. 'I want to go on deck,' she said. 'I'm stifling in here and dawn is breaking over the water. I want to see it. It has been a long, fearful night.'

Even in this early hour there was much activity on deck. Arasomu checked in briefly with Moichi. He had made two slight course corrections during his watch. According to the information that Moichi had provided him he believed they would sight the shore of Iskael before noon. The skies were fair, with scattered ribbons of high wispy cloud, and the wind was freshening out of the northwest quarter. It was ideal weather.

'I find it curious,' Aufeya said when they were alone, 'that you hold no truck with superstition yet you are a mariner and mariners are a powerfully superstitious lot.' She tossed her head, glad to be abovedeck in fine weather. 'In fact, I've heard you call upon the Oruboros even though you believe in the One God.'

Moichi shook his head. 'I call upon him, no. I curse him on occasion because one does not speak of the God of my people in that way. Just as one does not call upon Him to change the wind or ensure success in business. He is not

39

like the tiny gods of smoke and stone other people kneel before. He is the universe; He is everything. He lives; He provides for His people. But He does not grant petty favors like some desert jinn out of legend.'

Aufeya smiled. 'And the Oruboros does.'

He noted the mocking tone in her voice. 'The Oruboros, the great ancient sea serpent, once lived, Aufeya. In another time his power was great, indeed.'

'You talk about him as if he no longer exists.'

Moichi looked down at her, not knowing whether this was some game she was playing, needling him with her disbelief. Not for the first time, he was struck by how little he really knew her. 'Ronin slew the Oruboros when he was transformed into the Dai-San.'

At the mention of Moichi's bond-brother Aufeya dropped her amused look. She knew full well how important this already mythical figure was to him. 'But I don't really understand who – or what – the Dai-San is,' she said.

Now Moichi smiled. 'Does anyone, really?' His tawny eyes were misty with remembrance. 'Ah, Aufeya, what adventures we two shared.' His eyes cleared as he tried to explain the unexplainable. 'He was once a man, not unlike me, perhaps. But his fate lay in another direction. On Ama-no-mori, he was transformed by ancient Bujun sorcery that was part of a grand design. Pulled apart, then reassembled, he was compelled to ride the back of the Oruboros, to slay this venerable creature who he held dear so that he might be reborn as the Dai-San.'

'Dai-San,' Aufeya repeated. 'That name is of a language unfamiliar to me.'

'As it is to most. It is Bujun.'

'But the Dai-San is not Bujun.'

Moichi shrugged. 'Ama-no-mori has become his adoptive country. It was there that his transformation began.'

Aufeya's eyes were huge. 'Is he really more than mortal man?'

'In the time of magic from which he was born anything is possible.'

'Even the legend of Miira's Mirror?'

She had him and he knew it. For a moment his brows knit darkly, then he burst out into deep, booming laughter. 'Perhaps. But I believe the age of magic died when the Dai-San defeated the Dolman. This is the age of mankind.'

'And what of Sardonyx?' Aufeya demanded. 'Was she not the most powerful sorceress?'

Moichi considered this highly charged topic carefully, as he always did with her. Sardonyx, who had been born Adenese, had been sold into slavery. Eventually, she had killed her master and had been thrown into jail for her crime. Eventually, she managed to escape, bribing her way out with her body. The rest of her history was a mystery – he was not even certain of the veracity of what she had told him. She was a consummate liar; she actually enjoyed spinning tales, changing personalities as readily and effort-lessly as others breathed air.

Sardonyx had become fixated on Aufeya, and when Moichi had prevented her from getting her, she had returned to Daluzia from her castle in the land of the Opal Moon and had murdered Aufeya's mother Tsuki by somehow using Aufeya's body, thus wreaking a diabolical revenge on mother and daughter both. One was dead and the other could never forgive herself for what her body had done.

'As far as Sardonyx is concerned,' Moichi said, keeping one eye on the wind and the other on Aufeya's face, 'it is my considered opinion that she was more prestidigitator than thaumaturgist. To put it in its simplest terms she was a highly accomplished illusionist.'

41

'Then everything that happened to us in the land of the Opal Moon was a hallucination?'

'Ah, no. You know it was not. But the Firemask, the artifact of power, that Sardonyx so desired, was real enough. And it was from the time of magic; its power was awesome.' Seeing her shudder and make the sign of the Palliate, he put his arm around her and kissed her cheek. 'I think we'd both do best in forgetting all about Sardonyx. After I took the Firemask from her, her only thought was to avenge herself on your mother. Having, unhappily, accomplished that, she is now, I have no doubt, far away from here, back in her castle in the land of the Opal Moon.'

Together, they went to the rail, stared out at the rising sun.

Aufeya turned to Moichi. 'You miss him, don't you?'

'Who?'

'Your love for the Dai-San runs very deep.'

'He is my bond-brother.'

'He's much more, I warrant.'

Moichi was silent for some time, as if he were wrestling with a thorny problem. 'In some unfathomable way we are one. I cannot explain it further. He was created to defeat the Dolman and the forces of Chaos who threatened to claim this world and to put an end to the races of man for all time. My fate was to be at his side. He is the greatest warrior of all time; together we journeyed to the Kai-feng, the last great battle of mankind.'

'Yet you were not with him in Ama-no-mori for the beginning of his transformation.'

He sighed. 'Ah, Aufeya, all journeys have an end. My fate dictated that I return to Sha'angh'sei. I had my own role to play.' He chuckled. 'And lucky for me that I did. I never would have met you otherwise.'

'Or come to grips with Sardonyx.'

'I am no longer interested in her or the land of the Opal Moon. They belong to our past, nothing more.'

'Speaking of the moon,' Aufeya said excitedly as she pointed overhead, 'it is out here during the day! Look, Moichi! Look!'

THREE

THE HOUSE OF
ANNAI-NIN

The pure white buildings of Ala'arat glowed in the tropical sunlight. The city was strategically situated on a series of nine clawlike hills which rose around the sweeping crescent of a generous and sheltering bay. In all ways, the city was the direct opposite of Sha'angh'sei, the main port of the continent of man. Beyond the bustling quays, the streets, avenues and alleyways of Ala'arat radiated out in a precise star-shaped pattern. Instead of a massive jumble of hodgepodge shapes, the buildings were neat squares or rectangles, or as the city rose up the slopes to where, inevitably, the wealthy and politically connected families lived, other more complex but no less methodical geometric shapes.

Standing on deck as the *Tsubasa* hove to and, with all sails furled, dropped anchor, Aufeya clapped her hands delightedly, crying, 'How beautiful! The city looks like it was made of sugar cubes!'

Moichi, standing beside her with his arm around her slender waist, found his eyes wet with tears. How marvelous his home looked to him after long years traveling to the far ends of the earth with the Sunset Warrior.

But his joy was short-lived. A well-armed lighter rode the gentle waves out to meet them as he was ordering a

44

boat into the water so that he could pay a call on the harbor-master and secure a mooring license. Even though he could see that the port was far too busy to allow him a berth at one of the quays, which were full of massive four-masted freighters loading and off-loading all manner of fruits, vegetables and grains, bolts of hand-dyed silks, voile cottons, tightly-woven linen, and raw materials such as cypress, ebony, precious marble and glossy obsidian, he had no doubt he could buy a mooring further out on either side of the main channel.

He was surprised to see a contingent of Iskamen naval-men boarding his ship. The leader was a very young man, bald but for a long tongue of thick hair growing from the top of his head. He swaggered across the deck, calling for the captain. When Moichi stepped forward, he was momentarily taken aback to see a fellow Iskaman.

'Where are you from?' the officer asked, and when Moichi told him, he nodded, adding, 'You make any stops along the way? Were you boarded at sea or did you make a rendezvous with any other vessel?'

'No on all counts,' Moichi said, somewhat bewildered. 'Is there a problem?'

'Not if you've told the truth,' the officer said, eyeing Aufeya. 'What is your business here?'

'I am coming home,' Moichi said. 'I intend to marry.'

The officer watched him for some time. 'Your vessel will have to be searched.'

'What for?'

The officer took a step forward, his eyes narrowed. 'Have you anything to hide?'

'Certainly not,' Moichi said. 'But I must have an explanation for this extraordinary action.'

'In fact it is quite ordinary,' the officer said. 'You are Iskaman, but I see you have been away from Iskael for a long time. Much has changed in your absence. For some

45

time now our intelligence sources have reported ... disturbances in the desert settlements. Deaths and ... disappearances under mysterious and suspicious circumstances. Enemy spies have been discovered in Ala'arat. How are they delivered here? They die before they will tell us, so now all vessels seeking to moor must be searched.' He waited a beat. 'Now may we begin, *Captain?*'

Moichi nodded, abruptly uneasy. 'Do what you must. I want Ala'arat as secure as you do.' As the officer turned away to instruct his men, Moichi said, 'This almost feels like war footing.'

The officer turned back to him and, despite his youth, Moichi could see the bleakness of premature age in his eyes. 'A most astute assessment, Captain,' he said.

The villa of the Annai-Nin was as he remembered it: whitewashed stucco walls drenched in brilliant sunlight, jade-green glazed tile roofs glinting like faceted jewels at every angle.

In a land filled with fragrant cedar groves and thickly fruited date palms, it was perhaps surprising to see the great slabs of tiger-grain oak intricately carved and handsomely worked which opened inward, on clever hinges, the imposing front doors to the compound. But Moichi explained that his forefathers had been world merchants even when it had been dangerous and inadvisable to seek trade with the continent of man, and they had fallen in love with many of the foreign products for which they hammered out long-term deals.

The villa was situated atop the highest of the nine hills that overlooked the great curving bay that was one of Iskael's few natural assets. Far below them, the crescent city of Ala'arat spread like the frond of a date palm. It had taken them all day to file the necessary papers with the harbor authorities. For a bustling port, Ala'arat was crawling with security in the unwieldy guise of bureaucratic red tape. Now, in the twilight, the city shone like a jewel, lights twinkling, changing colors in the twists of smoke rising from myriad cooking fires. The air was perfumed by the sounds, distant and haunting, of voices raised in ululating prayer. The cobbled streets of the city's vast markets, choked since dawn, were almost deserted as the sacred hour of chaat, the weekly holy evening approached. Moichi hoped to reach his villa before the beginning of the ritual feast.

'Once, many years ago, all of Ala'arat was as bare and bleached as desert bones,' he told Aufeya as they walked up the snaking drive. 'In the space of a generation, the Iskamen made lush landscape out of rock and wind-blown sand.'

'Why did you settle here, if it was so inhospitable?'

Moichi paused, pointing over the roofs of the villa. 'Out there is the Mu'ad, the Great Desert. The Iskamen traveled half a year in the Mu'ad wastes. Any other people wandering in the Mu'ad for so long would have died of thirst or exposure. But God was with us. He showed us that we had no choice – the Mu'ad was our destiny.' They began to walk again, toward the villa's great oaken gates. 'You see, Aufeya, the Iskamen had spent eight generations enslaved by a race called the Adenese, who live on the far side of the Mu'ad. God spoke to the Iskamen elders. He told them they would be safest across the Great Desert.'

'But even though your people are free, Moichi, there are so many armed guards, so many suspicious eyes at the port and in the streets.'

'Old fears die hard, and the bitter truth is that the persecution of the Iskamen has never really ceased.'

She cocked her head quizzically. 'You knew this, and yet you chose to turn your back on it.'

'I chose to become a navigator.'

'To take to the seas. To leave your homeland and your people's fight far behind.'

He rounded on her angrily. 'Are you questioning my courage?'

She felt the searing heat from his eyes and put her hand gently on his arm, feeling the muscles tense and rippling. 'Not your courage, Moichi, never that. I owe you my life – more than I could ever know how to repay in one lifetime.' Her voice softened as she kissed him passionately. 'And I love you as I've loved no other man. It's your commitment to the ancient struggle of your people I'm talking of.'

Moichi was silent for some time. The swirling palm fronds seemed to bend the last of the sunlight, making of it something living and aqueous, like a creature from the sea-bottom slithering out of its coral den. A kestrel cried suddenly, a predator from the desert.

'"Man the ramparts, the Adenese are coming!" That was my brother's battle cry. It was the rationale for the entire Fe'edjinn, our virulently militant sect. Freedom fighters, they called themselves, but in my mind they were no more than assassins, bent on circumventing the laws of Iskael to achieve power and their fanatical objective: a holy war of retribution against the Adenese. His *commitment* to the cause was more than enough for one family.'

'Do you really believe that your brother is an assassin?' Aufeya asked.

'Jesah is . . .' Moichi bit his lip and turned partially away from her. In a softer voice, he said, 'I would believe anything of Jesah Annai-Nin.'

'Moichi–'

'No, no!' He swung around, his face afire with anger. 'You would not understand.'

Aufeya opened her mouth to speak, then thought better of it. Instead, she said, 'At least you must be looking for-

48

ward to seeing your sister Sanda. You have spoken of her often.'

'Sanda, yes.' They were almost at the gates. In contrast to the bustle of the packed streets and alleys below, the courtyard of the villa was still and deserted. But there were lights on within the main building itself. 'I miss her very much. If there was a pain in my heart over leaving Ala'arat, it was that I would not see her for a very long time.' He turned his face to the lights of the villa as he pushed open the gates. 'How long it's been! How much has happened in her life! When I left she was just a young girl.'

They crossed the courtyard, their bootsoles crackling against the bed of crushed sea shells. As they climbed the enormous steps to the front door, Moichi was aware of a bittersweet swirl of mixed emotions, dragging up memories – some of which he would have preferred not to re-examine.

He was thinking of his father and painful feasts of chaats past when the great doors opened inward and they stepped across the threshold of the villa of the Annai-Nin.

Torches were thrust in their faces and strong fingers gripped their biceps and forearms. Moichi smelled strong body odors, the stench of fear and long waiting.

'Moichi!'

He took a step toward her, but a sword-blade at his throat stopped him. Through the blinding torchlight he could see bits and pieces of rugged faces creased by wind and weapon. Then a flash of a uniform sleeve set his mind to racing. 'I am Moichi Annai-Nin, eldest son of Jud'ae Annai-Nin. Who dares hold me hostage in my own house?'

'*Your* house?' The voice was sharp, as quick as the flick of a whip. 'Make way!'

The uniformed men moved aside, but kept their grip firmly on Moichi and Aufeya. In the shifting light Moichi made out a tall, rangy figure, impeccably dressed in a finely woven uniform of silk and cloth-of-gold. 'If you are the eldest son of the patriarch Jud'ae you had better be able to prove it. You've been gone a long time.'

The tall officer had thick black hair and a full curling beard. His coffee-colored eyes were deep-set in a hawk-nosed face the color of burnt almonds. It was a face that gave away nothing but which saw everything.

All of these things Moichi absorbed in the space of a split second and they would have gone toward defining the man had he not spotted something that made his stomach turn to ice. Around the officer's neck and over the top of his head he wore the green and brown striped cowl of the Fe'edjinn.

'I don't understand. Are you state militia or Fe'edjinn?' Moichi asked in a hoarse voice.

The tall officer smiled. 'I see that you *have* been away a long time. The Fe'edjinn *are* the state militia of Iskael.'

'But how is this possible?' Moichi asked. 'The state can-not sponsor murderers and assassins.'

One of the men delivered a heavy blow to the side of his head. 'Hold your tongue, lout!' he growled. 'Or I'll cut it out!'

The tall officer cocked his head to one side, said nothing while blood seeped from a cut opened on Moichi's cheek. 'Bitch of a homecoming,' he said at last.

'What are you doing in my home?' Moichi said.

The same man lifted a fist to strike Moichi again but the officer signed to him. 'If you, indeed, are the eldest son of the Annai-Nin then you have a legitimate right to know.'

'Shall I take you through the villa?' Moichi asked. 'Shall I show you where my brother Jesah and I hid when we were eight and our father was blind with rage at what we had done? Shall I show you where I found my sister Sanda

50

sitting and crying over a bone she broke in her left wrist? Shall I show you the spot where my mother is buried? And my father?'

The tall officer nodded. 'All this and more you shall show me. As much as I ask of you.'

'Let us go, then, so we may walk unbound through the villa of my family.'

After a moment, the officer nodded. 'This much I can do. But my men will accompany us with weapons drawn.'

'It is a sacrilege to draw weapons on chaat.'

The officer shrugged, held out a hand to indicate that Moichi should lead the way.

They went slowly through the villa of the Annai-Nin, and at every turn shadows and ghosts assailed Moichi. Memories, long buried beneath carefully woven cobwebs, reappeared, thrusting their snouts rudely into his consciousness. He saw himself again as a child, the dour, lanky Jesah, the beautiful blue-eyed Sanda, and everywhere the world of the Annai-Nin as it had been – his father's world, full of prestige and accolades, riches beyond a child's limited scope of understanding. The parade of dinner guests from the worlds of politics, philosophy and religion had been endless, then, with lavish, glittering parties each week welcoming the most famous into the sumptuous villa of the Annai-Nin. It was a world against which Jesah had chosen to rebel. The great successes of their father in business meant nothing to him, the contacts Jud'ae had managed to forge, the respect he had labored to build with the peoples of the continent of man across the sea, had no meaning for him. He had early come under the spell of the fanatic Fe'edjinn, finding in their strict interpretation of the Tablets of the Iskamen, their obsession to avenge themselves on the Adenese, a lightning rod for his own inner rage.

Had he and Moichi ever found reason to offer one

another a kind word or even the most rudimentary sign of affection? Hadn't they hidden together in this spot behind the larder that Moichi was now showing to the Fe'edjinn officer? And hadn't they fought each other bloody in the blackness of the hidey-hole?

Better by far to recall Sanda and how she'd cling to his waist, how he protected her from the bullies at school, how he taught her the fundamentals of religion – how to interpret the sacred scriptures writ on the Tablets that had been brought down from the summit of that holiest place of the Iskamen, the Mountain Sin'hai.

But it was impossible to get away from Jesah's treachery for long. Dark, snakelike memories continued to intrude into his consciousness. Hadn't it been Jesah who had abandoned the family, leaving for the Fe'edjinn boot camps in the wilds of the sere Mu'ad wastes? Yes, but it had been Moichi who had been berated by Jud'ae and Sanda for taking to the seas, for forsaking not only the Annai-Nin but all of Iskael.

'For my part, I can never forgive you,' Jud'ae had said only months before his death. 'As eldest, you have a sacred responsibility to me and to the family. Who will run the business after I am gone? Jesah? He has only blood-lust in his eyes. Sanda? She is a woman. Soon she will marry, yes, but I will not take a stranger into my confidence. Blood is blood, Moichi. You of all people must know this and abide by the covenants.'

What Sanda thought of all this Moichi did not know. She had been witness to his humiliation, but her silence had been absolute.

It had been dark two hours by the time Moichi completed his tour to the satisfaction of the Fe'edjinn officer. At that point, the officer dismissed his men to other parts of the villa, nodded almost imperceptibly. 'Moichi Annai-Nin, I, Tamuk, First Darman of the Fe'edjinn, welcome you home.' He did not extend his wrist to be grasped in the Iskamen manner and Moichi marked this well.

'Where is everyone?' Moichi asked. 'And why are you here?'

Tamuk offered a hand. 'Please sit down.'

Aufeya sat, nervously glancing at Moichi, who remained standing. His eyes had never left those of the Fe'edjinn officer. They were in Jud'ae's study, a smallish room in the rear of the villa, filled with scrolls and books and the mementoes of a lifetime. The air was thick with imaginings of what might have been. Moichi had brought them here to show Tamuk the hidden recess that held his father's most precious possession: a hand-writ copy of the Tablets of the Iskamen which had taken five years to create. Oil lamps had been lit, their perfume triggering yet more memories.

Tamuk sighed. 'You are making this more difficult for yourself.'

'I have done nothing, First Darman, but come home for chaat.'

Tamuk remained silent for some time. The only sound came from the whip of the palm fronds beyond the windows and a slow drip of water from the scullery nearby. Tamuk took a breath, laced his fingers together and said, 'First, it is my duty to tell you that your sister is dead.'

'Sanda!'

Aufeya gave a tiny cry as Moichi staggered backward just as if Tamuk had driven a blade through his chest. She rose and held him as he stood, trembling.

'What . . . How?'

'She was murdered most brutally. It happened three nights ago as she lay sleeping in her bed.'

Moichi's head came up. 'You said brutally.'

'I beg you not to make me detail it,' Tamuk said, glancing at Aufeya.

'Tell me!' Moichi almost screamed it.

'All right.' Tamuk sighed. 'The front of her torso was – well, for lack of a better word – shredded. All her ribs were shattered, as if pulled outward, and her intestines had been ripped from her abdomen.'

'Oh, Lord!' Aufeya clutched Moichi's arm. A cold chill was creeping down his spine, but he stopped it, admonishing himself. It cannot be true, he thought. There must be some other explanation.

Tamuk gave him a withering look before continuing, 'Her husband–'

'Husband?'

Tamuk raised his black eyebrows. 'Yes, your sister married last year. Did you not know?'

Moichi's mind seemed frozen. There was the past, when Sanda had been alive, and then there was the present, when she was not. A sharp and evil demarcation separated the two like a pane of glass. Moichi saw himself locked on the wrong side of that glass.

'Who . . . ?' His mouth was dry. All of a sudden he was overcome with guilt. If only he had not abandoned his family for the lure of the sea. If only he had been here . . .

Aufeya left his side long enough to pour out a dark, thick liquor from a glass decanter. She handed him a metal cup, half filled. Moichi looked at it blankly. The cup was inscribed with runes from the Tablets. It was the ritual cup his father had always used for the toast to usher in the chaat feast. He found that his knuckles were white and, in a convulsive gesture, he knocked back the date wine. His eyes watered slightly as he licked his lips. Then his eyes once again focused on the Fe'edjinn officer and he said, 'Who did Sanda marry?'

'A merchant from the near slopes of the Mountain Sin'hai. A man named Yesquz.'

'What is known about him?'

'Almost nothing at all. He deals in the spices, herbs and medicinal roots found only at the foot of the Mountain Sin'hai. He apparently makes quite a good living of it – he has cornered the market. Your sister did not want for money.'

'He was not . . . murdered too?'

'He is not at this time in Ala'arat. Nor was he on the night your sister was murdered. He travels often.'

'Where is he?'

'In the Mu'ad. Trading his goods.'

'Bring him back,' Moichi said. 'I want to question him.'

Tamuk looked at him curiously. 'That was our thought, as well. Your brother, Hamaan, has departed with a detachment to do just that.'

'Hamaan? My brother's name is Jesah.'

Tamuk waited a moment before adding, 'No more. He is Qa'tach now, one of the five leaders of the Fe'edjinn, and as such he has taken a Qa'tach name.'

'I had no idea,' Moichi said after a time.

Tamuk seemed disgusted.

'Why are my other sisters not here?' Moichi asked.

'They moved with their families to the Mu'ad settlements,' Tamuk said, 'when their husbands joined the Fe'edjinn.'

'God of my fathers,' Moichi whispered.

'Much has changed here since you left,' Tamuk said, echoing the words of the naval officer who had boarded his ship. 'This murder, terrible as it is, is far from the first. But your sister is different. She was an Annai-Nin, and her death has galvanized the people. Even the peace party has been silenced, and now all Iskamen are of one mind.'

'One mind?' Moichi echoed.

'It is war, man,' Tamuk said. 'The holy war against Aden.'

'But how can this be?' Moichi was stunned. 'Thousands,

perhaps millions will die. We are speaking now not merely of war but of genocide.'

'You had better get used to it. This is the reality you have come home to. Now, if there are no more questions to answer . . .' Tamuk glanced briefly at Aufeya. 'So ends my night.' He gave a perfunctory bow that seemed to exclude Moichi. 'I regret your homecoming is under such tragic circumstances. I will post two men at the front gates.'

'That won't be necessary, First Darman,' Moichi said.

Tamuk smiled thinly. 'I am afraid it is. Security policy. The excruciating and inhuman nature of your sister's murder makes it all too likely that the Adenese were responsible. A blow to the Qa'tach, a personal sort of revenge. A typical Adenese message of terrorism.'

Moichi thought of his conversation with the young naval officer. 'So at last there are Adenese in Ala'arat.'

Tamuk nodded. 'Agents of their Al Rafaar, their infiltration and assassination organization. They have been quite active of late.' His grin was lupine and mirthless. 'You see now the necessity of the Fe'edjinn's rise to power. Perhaps you will despise us a little less now. Iskael needs our mailed fist more than ever these days.' He turned to Aufeya. 'Good evening, madam.' Then he left them without another word.

FOUR

SHADOWS

In the half-darkened villa, Aufeya made them dinner. It was very late. The calls to prayer were long gone and, down the steep slope of the hill, the lights of Ala'arat flickered and died – all but brightly lit sentry posts where the fanatic guards of the Fe'edjinn patrolled in ceaseless vigilance. Still, violence and murder had visited itself upon the capital city and no one slept easily.

Placing the food upon the long elaborately carved Macasser ebony table, Aufeya called to Moichi then, hearing no reply, went in search of him. She heard noises as of a fight echoing down the hall, and she flew down it, calling his name over and over. Her heart was in her mouth. What if the murderer had returned to the scene of the crime as Tamuk and his Fe'edjinn obviously suspected?

'Moichi!' she cried.

And, rounding a corner, found him in his father's vast library, overturning furniture, using his dirks to smash everything in sight. He was alone and in a fury. She shuddered, making the sign of the Palliate, but as was becoming usual these days it did nothing to calm her.

She stood in the doorway, watching the wanton destruction, knowing that she must not stop him, must not interfere in any way, but let the blood madness run its course. She well knew what was ailing him now.

At last it was done, the destruction of his father's carefully mapped-out library complete. He stood in the middle, panting and sweating, his eyes wide and staring like a mad animal. At length, his breathing slowed, his head swung around and his eyes came back into focus.

'How long have you been standing there?'

'Does that matter? You haven't eaten since early in the day. Food is on the table.'

The return to the mundane snapped him out of it completely. He nodded, then taking her hand, said, 'I want to show you something.'

He took her into a room filled with fabrics, brocaded and woven of bright desert colors, all obviously by the same fine hand. He crouched beside the wooden-posted bed, its linens thrown back and crumpled as if the occupant had left in some haste. He lit a single thick candle, setting it atop the bed in its waxy porcelain dish.

He moved aside and she saw the dark irregular stain upon the floor. So this was where Sanda had been slain. There had been no one left in the villa to clean it up or, just as likely, Tamuk and his Fe'edjinn had not allowed anyone in here during their investigation.

'I miss her and that is so ironic for me, the wanderer, to feel.' She heard the bitterness in his voice. 'I could have saved her, Aufeya.'

Her heart went out to him. 'Oh, Moichi, how can you say that?'

'Because I know,' he said fiercely. 'Her husband left her here, alone, unprotected.'

'But this is Ala'arat.'

He shook away her words. 'If I had been here instead of on the seas . . .'

'Your life – *our* lives – would be very different, yes.' She caressed him. 'But that is a dream, nothing more. She's dead, my darling, but I promise you, you are not to blame.'

He looked down at her, then kissed her forehead. Time, she thought. It will take time.

As she went to the door, he said, 'There is something I have to do here. No. Please stay.'

He knelt by the side of the bed. His fingertips brushed the dark stain, then lifted away. In a moment, she could hear his voice chanting softly in what she knew to be the Iskamen prayer for the dead. His head was covered by a small piece of fabric and his massive shoulders were hunched as if he carried upon them an enormous burden.

He completed his prayer, and still she waited patiently, her head bowed. At last, she took a step forward and, placing her hand gently upon his shoulder, said, 'You must eat something now. Then we will sleep. It has been a very long day.'

But after the meal there was to be no sleep for them. Moichi, silent while they ate, went out onto the veranda. A moment later, Aufeya followed him. She knew he had heard her because he said, 'On the sea these hours just before dawn are my favorites, because they are always the most peaceful. A single frigate bird or gull, perhaps, is the only creature stirring. Even the lookout high in his nest is often dozing lightly. On deck, I can feel . . .' He threw out his arms wide. 'It is as if my entire being has been attuned to the world, the slow spin, the cosmic clock whirring unheard, unseen, but felt now by me alone.'

'Can you feel it now?' Aufeya asked softly. 'It is the time.'

'I don't know.' He shook his head. 'Feel like a fish out of water.'

'On land?'

'No, here in Iskael I am a stranger . . . nothing is as I remember it.'

She came and stood by him, her hand on his forearm. 'Then you should remember that you are not the same, either. Nothing remains, like a fly stuck in amber. Everything is mutable, and change is inevitable.'

'But war is coming, Aufeya. Oh, not merely war. Now the Iskamen and the Adenese will have at each other until only one race is left alive. It is a nightmare, perhaps the very one that led me to sail the seas. Yet, as you see, I have not escaped. I have returned home on the eve of the holy war. Perhaps, then, it is my fate. And now I am faced with the question I have lived with all my life: how does one stop the inevitable?'

A bird rustled in the underbrush. All around them, the date palms rattled and clattered in the dawn wind that had just begun rising. 'When I was young, I never came out here on my own. I was too busy down at the port, watching the seamen tramping up and down the quays, and looking out to sea to catch a glimpse of my destiny. Or so I thought. Now I think I did it simply because my father had forbidden it to me. Always with him it was a question of the law and of obeying.'

'The sea is a harsh master,' Aufeya said. 'Perhaps you only traded one for the other.'

'But it was *my* choice,' he said harshly. 'Not his.' Then he put his head down and gripped her hand in his own. 'How Sanda wept when I left. She ran all the way down to the port in order to beg me to stay. "I shall die without you," she said, and I kissed her and laughed at such childish sentiments.'

Aufeya turned and gently kissed away the tears on his cheeks. 'Perhaps one day,' she whispered, 'you will realize that you miss your father as much as you now miss Sanda.'

The moon, bluish-white and full to bursting, broke from behind a cloudbank. Behind Aufeya and Moichi, shadows appeared, so faintly that they were like ghosts or angels, seen only intermittently in the corners of the eyes.

Moichi raised his arm and pointed into the moonlight. 'There, across Mu'ad, the Great Desert, lies Aden.'

But Aufeya was looking to their left where, past the thousands of hectares of Iskael's famed cedar groves, beyond the blackened volcanic steppes that led upward in unsteady increments to the lowest reaches of what, even as far away as the horizon, appeared to be a towering mountain. It was impossible to judge its size, since its crown was obscured by billowing cloud, mist and what might have been ice veils.

She stared at the mountain, transfixed by something she could neither name nor imagine. The mist that clung to its ragged upper reaches appeared, in places, almost translucent. Once or twice she started, convinced that she had seen a flash of indescribable color, diffused and expanded by the curious, curling mist.

What she could see of its slopes convinced her that she had never come across a natural formation like it. In her time she had seen many kinds of hills and crags, those humped and rounded by age, others sharp-edged, deep-gorged and in their adolescence. But the formidable ridges and rills of this mountain defied category.

It was as if she were staring at a formation that had just now, in the darkness of the night, emerged from the molten core of the earth, raw and bleeding as Moichi's emotions, and still full of primeval, fulminating energy. The fluted rills were disquieting, like great ebon rifts in the crust of the earth, the ridges plumed and spiky. She felt her scalp constrict, and she wiped her eyes which had unaccountably begun to water as they had done when as a child, she had stared too long into the noonday sun. She was about to make the sign of the Palliate but shuddered instead, knowing it no longer calmed her.

'Moichi,' she said in a hoarse voice, 'tell me about the mountain to the north.'

'I am afraid that would take years,' he said. 'That is the Mountain Sin'hai, the place of God.'

'The Iskamen God.'

'The *only* God.'

And still she could not take her eyes off the terrifying and exhilarating sight of the Mountain Sin'hai. 'Do you think that somewhere beyond it lies Syrinx, the land of Miira and her people?'

'Only God knows,' Moichi said. 'So far as I know, none has ventured there for centuries.'

'The only God.' Aufeya turned to him briefly. 'How can you say that? You who have encountered mages, beasts beyond imagining, sorceresses. You whose best friend is akin to a god.'

'Because, Aufeya, there are gods and pretenders to be gods – and then there is the God who dwells there atop the Mountain Sin'hai.'

'Have you ever seen this God?'

'No. No one has. But the Mountain is his manifestation. Our archaeologists tell us that the Mountain Sin'hai is unimaginably ancient. Ages have passed. Wind storms, rains, hail and ice. It is impervious to all. And that is as it should be. God led our people out of Aden and into the Mu'ad. The Adenese laughed at us and let us go. They were convinced we were dead men, anyway, because that is what the Great Desert does best: kill. But our faith in the God of our fathers was absolute and He led us through the searing heat and out the other side to Iskael. We survived the Mu'ad where no other men could.'

Aufeya, entranced, said, 'In fine weather what does Sin'hai's summit look like?'

'No one knows. The mists and cloud swirl there perpetually.'

'You mean no Iskaman has climbed the Mountain to see what is up there?'

'We *know* what is up there, Aufeya. Besides, the Tablets forbid it, and with good reason. The Mountain Sin'hai goes on forever, rising upward into the realm of God. Mortal man cannot conceive of such a height let alone contemplate scaling it.'

In Ama-no-mori night was coming on, the shadows lengthening across the cryptomeria and carefully groomed red pines. In one of the myriad great halls of the Kunshin's castle, the Dai-San sat eating his last meal before setting out for his trans-oceanic journey on the armored back of his Kaer'n.

His high helm cast dark and light across every corner of the hall, which was empty save for himself. At the other end, bathed in an ethereal light that appeared to have no visible source, was the Dragon Throne, the ceremonial seat of power on which only the Kunshin sat. It was carved of a single piece of Fu-chui jade, the rarest of its kind, a luminescent, translucent green the color of spring leaves just as they unfold from their winter buds.

There were few who were allowed into the Dai-San's presence – or who could bear to be scrutinized by those eerie faceted eyes. Only those few who knew him well understood what went on behind those alien orbs and weren't intimidated by their gaze.

One of these now appeared from out of the shadows, a beautiful woman, to be sure, with slanting almond eyes and an unusually wide and sensual mouth. But she wore her hair in the long, traditional warrior's queue as, indeed, did the Dai-San beneath his high helm. Also, she was armored in the layered steel of Bujun manufacture that was the finest of its kind, both strong and supple so that it would not split beneath even the most ferocious sword blows. Each section of her armor was imprinted with the

63

platinum seal of the Kunshin: three plovers on the wing within the circle of the world.

'Chiisai,' the Dai-San said even before she had fully emerged from the shadows, 'would you join me for supper?'

The Kunshin's only daughter looked at the platinum ring on the index finger of his left hand. In its center was a blue pearl, the rarest of all, that she herself had plucked from a prized Kray oyster half-hidden on the bottom of Haneda bay. This oyster, which was now well over five feet in diameter, had been introduced into the bay by Chiisai's great-great grandmother. All the women in the Kunshin's direct line were exceptional divers, and part of their fortune had been amassed through the sale of pearls.

As Chiisai came and sat next to the Dai-San, she took his hand, her fingertips closing over the familiar warmth of the extraordinary pearl. She had been delivered of the secret knowledge of the pearl's properties by her mother before she had died, and one day, after she had taught her own daughter how to dive, she would divulge the secrets of the Kray oyster's blue pearl. Her father, the Kunshin, did not know these secrets, and neither did the Dai-San. She saw it as a symbol of the depth of her love for him that she had given him this gift of such hidden power.

'Must you go?' she said, although of course she knew the answer.

'I was created for war, Chiisai. Not for me home or hearth, family or love.'

She leaned forward, her face creased with worry. 'But we love one another.'

His high helm flashed darkly as he turned his head. 'We have been one, and when we couple I see your heart. That is very special to me.'

She wanted him to continue but she knew that he had

already said more than he would to almost anyone else. Only Moichi Annai-Nin, his bond-brother, meant as much to him as she did. 'I would go with you,' she said in an almost defiant voice.

The Dai-San wiped his mouth, pushed his plate away. 'Why do you desire this?'

'You know why,' she said. 'It is because I desire you.'

'That is not enough,' he said in his enigmatic way. 'Besides, there are compelling reasons for you to stay.'

'Do you believe Ojime?' she asked. 'Are the forces of Chaos massing once again beneath a new banner? Is there really a successor to the Dolman?'

'I believe the roll of the snow-hare bones,' the Dai-San said. He rose and, with him, Chiisai. They crossed to the slitted windows, staring out at the geese flying in formation above Haneda's fields and paddies, and beyond the dark, rising slopes of Fujiwara. 'But as for High Minister Ojime, he is why I want you here in the capital. He has plans far and above those which he publicly espouses.'

'Have you heard something? How do you—?' She gave a tiny gasp as those baleful eyes were turned upon her. Was it her imagination or did they glow with a febrile, unearthly light? What *was* he? Neither man nor god, but something in between, a creature for which there was no current definition.

'Ojime fears me,' the Dai-San said, ignoring her questions for which there were no answers – at least no rational ones. 'Perhaps he hates me as well. I daresay I would if I were him. But he bears close watching. He is a liar and a cheat. Also, he harbors grandiose ambitions. I am a stumbling block to those ambitions – as is your father.'

'But what if this mission he has sent you on is false? What if he means only to get you as far away from Amano-mori as possible?'

The Dai-San regarded Chiisai's exquisite face. 'Then

your reasons for remaining here are all the more compelling.' He lifted her chin with one huge knuckle. 'You are a warrior in your own right, Chiisai. It is not your karma to be either my concubine or my assistant.'

She nodded and sighed. 'I returned from Sha'angh'sei and the continent of man to be with you. I had thought to stay there a long time.'

'And you will go there again,' he said. 'But your instincts are solid. I can assure you that you did not return home simply to be with me. There is danger here – serious peril. And it is your destiny to confront it.'

He stared again out the slitted window and she could feel his desire to be lifted into the clouds, to begin his long journey. It was as if a third entity had slipped into the hall and now stood, silent as a shadow, between them.

Chiisai shivered a little, despite herself. It was impossible to grow enured to his other selves, as she had come to think of his enormous energy. 'Do you ever miss him?'

'Who?'

'Ronin. The human being you used to be.'

For a long time, the Dai-San said nothing, and Chiisai thought she had made a serious mistake. At last, the shadow between them stirred, and he said, 'You cannot miss what you do not remember.'

'You don't remember your former life?'

The Dai-San's fingers caressed the scaly hide of the six-fingered Makkon glove he wore. 'I remember it as you would a dream.'

'Oh, but that is so sad.'

He presented her with the smile he reserved only for her. 'I never said I didn't dream.' He drew on the Makkon glove. 'Red, green, blue. He is still here inside me, along with the tragic man-beast, Setsoru, and the female spirits, the essence of my old life, which I shed like the sere skin of a snake. Red, green, blue. Facets of a gem, parts of a whole.'

'I do not understand.'

'You were not meant to,' he said. 'That is why I do not speak of it.'

'Hold me,' she whispered, and with his arms around her, she felt better.

'Are you afraid?'

'Not for myself,' she answered, 'but for mankind. I thought when you killed the Dolman at Kamado we had defeated Chaos for all time.'

'Evil has one mind,' the Dai-San said like the tolling of a bell, 'one lung and one heart. It is monolithic in its thinking and in its progress. Its influence waxes and wanes, but always it has many devotees who succumb to its siren call. Nothing can be defeated for all time. We won a battle at Kamado, nothing more. The War continues.'

The tea-green walls of the Chamber of Prayer were brocaded with shadow. The Shinsei na-ke Temple within whose heart the chamber lay was no more than a block from the moated castle of the Kunshin where Chiisai and the Dai-San were, at that moment, saying their farewells.

The chamber which, but a moment ago, had been deserted, was now inhabited by what appeared to be one more shadow. Its ebon length remained motionless for some time, then it detached itself from the spiderweb darkness and swiftly, silently crossed to the raised platform and, in its exact center, just below the calligraphied scroll which Qaylinn's great-grandfather had written, the shadow knelt as if in prayer.

The long agile fingers of High Minister Ojime reached out and, emulating those of the chief Rosh'hi, pulled up the polished boards. Inside, within the hidden compartment, he pulled out the lumped, sueded cloth. His hands shook as he opened the package. Inside was the tongue sliced from the Makkon.

Power! thought Ojime in a fever of excitement.

He had managed to position himself during the interview with the Dai-San so that he could duplicate the movements the Rosh'hi had used to open the secret compartment. Then he had waited in a delirium of anticipation for the right moment. He knew he could not wait too long, for the power of the Makkon's flesh was ephemeral, and if it was allowed to dry out, it would dissipate uselessly. Ojime was determined not to allow that to occur.

Instead, he had formulated a plan and, arranging to be in the temple for some hours, had detailed the comings and goings of all the priests and Rosh'his. Then, at the time he had selected, he had stolen through the Corridor of Remembrance and, secreting himself within the thick shadows, had made certain that he was alone.

Now all his preparation had paid off. He had his prize!

Power! his mind screamed, as he carefully re-wrapped the Makkon's tongue and placed it within an inside pocket. He rose to steal away. But as he turned, he became aware that he was not alone.

'What are you doing, High Minister?' Qaylinn said. His face was dark with suspicion and anger. 'I doubt I need remind you that the Chamber of Prayer is a holy place. And I am hardly naive enough to believe you stumbled into it by error.'

'Oh, there was no error, sayann,' Ojime said, walking slowly and methodically toward the Rosh'hi. 'I am here for an important and profound reason.'

'And that is?'

The high minister was so close to Qaylinn when he pulled the knife that Qaylinn had no time to react. His mind afire, Ojime plunged the blade into the Rosh'hi's chest and, when Qaylinn did not fall, stabbed him again and again while he ground his teeth with the effort of splitting tissue, gristle and bone.

Death filled Qaylinn's eyes and he fell without a sound to the polished floor, a fountain of blood pumping with the last beats of his heart. The blood spread in a black, pristine pool at his feet. In it was reflected both slayer and victim.

Staring down at the dead man, his chest heaving, the high minister said, 'Not every question deserves an answer, sayann.' Then, throwing the bloody knife into a corner of the chamber, he strode swiftly and purposefully out of the temple.

A frenzied knocking came upon the villa's front door in the hour of false dawn. Moichi, half-dozing with his arm around Aufeya, started up. As he strode down the dark hallway his knuckles rubbed the sleep from his eyes. It seemed weeks since he had had a decent night's repose.

He opened the door to see one of his crew and, just behind him, one of the Fe'edjinn guards Tamuk had promised to post along the perimeter of the property.

'Cap'n!–'

'Is this one of your men?' the guard asked crossly. 'He claims–'

'He's mine,' Moichi said, directing his gaze to the crewman whose face was white with anxiety. 'What brings you here?'

'It is Arasomu, Cap'n. He went ashore on leave and was supposed to return to the ship for Rat Watch.'

'Four hours ago,' Moichi said, as Aufeya came up behind him.

'And he hasn't returned yet,' the mate said. 'With you ashore and–'

Moichi cut him short. 'Where was he headed, do you know?'

The crewman nodded. 'The Shadow Warrior.'

'A bad place,' the Fe'edjinn said darkly. 'We only go there in pairs, and then only when it is necessary. It opens at midnight and closes at dawn. Women and sometimes, for the right customer, men sell themselves for an hour of bliss. It is also rumored that almost any illicit substance can be had there for a price.'

'Where is it?' Moichi barked.

'At the head of Red Spice Quay,' the Fe'edjinn said. 'But I wouldn't recommend–'

But by that time Moichi had pulled the door shut and, with Aufeya at his heels, was hurrying toward the front gates.

'Don't say I didn't warn you!' the guard called. 'There's a murder there so often we no longer bother investigating.' But he was just as happy. With the occupants of the villa gone he sought out a soft spot beneath a date palm and slept until his relief arrived.

At the far end of Red Spice Quay, a sleek, four-masted schooner was being loaded with bolts of wool and flax, crates of livestock to be taken into the far reaches of Kintai to the north. But the head or landward end of the quay was deserted. The Shadow Warrior crouched sullenly in a narrow space between two gargantuan warehouses, shuttered and black-faced.

A single red lantern creaked as it swayed above the narrow door. The crewman, who had hurried after them huffing and puffing to keep up, cowered against the façade of one warehouse. Moichi sent him back to the *Tsubasa* with a curt order. Then, grasping the brass knob, patinated green by the salt air, he pushed roughly into the interior.

It was overly hot inside the place, as if a blast oven's white iron doors had been left open. They found themselves in a single great room with a low beamed ceiling, black with years of smoke and soot. Red lanterns lit the room in a rubiate monochrome. A scarred, metal-topped bar ran along the rear and dark mirrors everywhere reflected their moving images. But the mirrors were in shards, flecks littered across the blackened wood floor. There were great dents in the bar, as if a giant had smashed his fists upon it. The room gave onto a small, cramped dining room, littered with overturned chairs, cracked tables and splinters of crusted dishes. Behind were a filthy kitchen and toilet facilities. All were deserted. But the ovens were very hot, and the stove was lit and had obviously been on for hours. A pot of stew was burning, and Moichi took it off the flame. A flat loaf of unleavened chestnut-flour bread lay on a nearby wooden cutting board, which was otherwise dusted with crumbs.

'By the Oruboros, what happened here? It's as if a legion of berserkers was let loose in here,' Moichi said. 'And where is everyone?'

Aufeya looked around. 'It's as if they all disappeared in the blink of an eye.'

'Passing strange.' Moichi's nostrils dilated as he poked his head out of the kitchen. 'Perhaps there is more to the Shadow Warrior than meets the eye. After all, hiding contraband would be a primary goal of any such establishment.'

But an hour's futile search revealed nothing. He returned to the toilet to relieve himself. It was a particularly squalid place that stank so badly he was convinced the privy had never been cleaned out. He held his breath while he urinated, and that was when he saw the faint outline on the wall. At first, he thought it was another crack in the soiled stucco, but as he rebuttoned his trousers he saw that the line was perfectly vertical. He stepped away from the privy and, putting the flat of one hand to one side of the line, pushed hard. Nothing happened. He pushed on the other side and part of the wall swung inward and he saw the first treads of a steep and well-worn flight of stairs.

He called for Aufeya and told her to bring a lantern. Together, they went up the stairs. On the second floor, the stink of sweat and stale sex was everywhere. They went down a narrow hallway off which were doors on either side. Peering briefly into the tiny cubicles, they observed insensate couples or, in some cases, triads, naked, sprawled together. A peculiar sweet stench filled their nostrils.

'Opayne,' Moichi whispered. 'I thought I caught a whiff of it downstairs.'

'Opayne?'

'A powerful hallucinogen that purports to transport those in the throes of sexual bliss.'

'Now that sounds interesting,' Aufeya said.

But Moichi shook his head. 'It is highly addictive, and sometimes fatal. The effect on the brain is highly unpredictable.'

Aufeya shuddered as they proceeded from room to room. 'All of these people have used the drug?'

'Undoubtedly. You or I could kick them to a pulp and they would not awaken.'

By this time, they were almost at the end of the hall. Moichi opened the door on his left.

'But they will awaken sometime today?' Aufeya asked uneasily.

'Chill take it!' Moichi cried, standing stiffly in the doorway.

Aufeya pushed against him to gain a look at the shadow-shrouded room, and gasped. 'Arasomu.'

Moichi's First Mate was spread-eagled across a bed that had become a viscous lake of glistening innards that still seemed to crawl. The fecal stench was overpowering.

'This just happened!' Moichi said hoarsely as he drew one of his twin jewel-handled dirks.

'What happened to him?' Aufeya whispered.

It was a legitimate question. That Arasomu was dead was beyond dispute, but the method of his murder was almost beyond comprehension. Great ragged slashes had been scored vertically down his chest and abdomen so that all his ribs, fractured into shards, stuck out pinkly from the ribbons of his excoriated flesh. And, below, his viscera had been pulled out of him in a frenzy of death-lust.

'I've seen this before,' Moichi said with such fierce emotion in his voice that Aufeya became even more alarmed.

'Seen what before?' she said, clearly terrified.

'He has been killed by a Makkon,' Moichi said in a voice that indicated that he could not believe what he was saying or seeing. And now he could not stop the crawling down his spine because his worst fears had been confirmed.

A horrific howling filled the room, and the shadows shuddered, dying and coming alive all at once. Moichi caught a brief glimpse of a pair of baleful eyes, their orange lambent in the semi-darkness of the quivering torchlight.

The flame was almost extinguished as the Makkon flew through the room, its bulk filling it now. Its great taloned feet crushed the bed and Arasomu with it. The thick, spiked tail thrashed from side to side, and the claws on its upper extremities were fully extended, black as obsidian, catching light and holding it, as if it could suck the living energy out of the atmosphere.

The howling came again, like a physical presence, as Moichi thrust Aufeya behind him, back toward the doorway. 'Get out!' he shouted, as the Makkon's beak opened. Where its thick tongue should have been, ululating its unearthly battle cries, was nothing but a repulsive black stump, quivering and pulsing in mute rage.

The Makkon's forepaw shot out, grazing Moichi, spinning him around, sprawling Aufeya onto her back. Moichi spun, simultaneously slashing with the blade of his dirk. But the blade merely skidded harmlessly off the Makkon's skin, plated like armor.

The Chaos beast thrust his claw at Moichi's chest, the ebon talons shearing cured leather and metal alike. The talons closed and the Makkon pulled Moichi toward its open beak.

Moichi could sense the chill, fetid breath of the beast, and he felt as if all the oxygen were being pulled from the air. As if he were underwater, he could not breathe. Still, he struggled to gain a foothold, a place of purchase upon the plated chest of the Makkon. The beast was vulnerable in its mouth, as attested to by its lack of a tongue. Someone or something had cut it out, and even through the terror of the situation Moichi found himself wanting to meet whoever had mutilated the Makkon. He fought to bring his dirk up and over, so that he could plunge its point into the soft tissue of the Makkon's throat.

The edge of the blade caught the Makkon's lower beak, sliding along the surface, and the Makkon staggered backward, smashing a hole in the outer wall of the building. In rage, it began to squeeze the life out of Moichi, slowly, inexorably, agonizingly, its orange eyes gaining in intensity with the escalation of Moichi's pain.

Through the rent in the wall blue moonlight fused with the yellow-red torchlight tumbling over the antagonists, bathing Aufeya, and in so doing, revealing a remarkable transformation.

Where an instant before Aufeya had been, now lay a tall slender woman with the head of an ibis. She was dressed in cloth-of-gold with wings of feathers protruding from her shoulderblades. Then the light changed subtly or perhaps it was the lurching of the antagonists throwing shadows against the still-melding light sources. Whatever the case, in another instant she had become a statuesque woman with the coolly glowing skin of pearls. Her thick, twining hair was platinum flex and her eyes were cabochon rubies. Her long, curving nails were translucent sapphires and her partially revealed breasts were fire opals. Then, the light shifted again, and she was revealed as a far smaller woman with a flat face and high cheekbones. Her skin was as dusky as Moichi's, as any Iskaman or Adenese. Her eyes were the color of cobalt chips and her long hair, plaited into a single braid was the color of freshly scrubbed copper. She was clad in a curious mirrored corselet over which was a black doeskin vest. Trousers of the same material were tucked into well-worn hunting boots that came to just above her knees.

She twisted her torso so that one mirrored facet on her breasts caught the moonlight and, reaching out her hand, her long, slender fingers closed over the resulting flash of reflected light. When they opened, she was holding an odd weapon that looked like nothing more than an icicle, so clear and glistening was it. She drew back her arm and hurled it at the Makkon's shoulder. It pierced hardened skin and flesh, disappeared completely inside the beast.

The Makkon roared, arching back and, simultaneously, letting go of Moichi, who swiped at it with his dirk. Black viscous fluid, sticky as glue, drooled from the wound. Still howling, it drove through the rent in the wall, disappearing instantly into the shadows of the massed warehouses.

Moichi, head bowed, hands on his knees, gasped air into his lungs. When at last he was able to rise, he turned to Aufeya, who stood, looking as she had always looked to him. She stood with the torch raised high, far back in the doorway, safe where the moonlight could not reach her.

'Are you all right?' she asked.

He nodded. 'With perhaps the aid of God.'

'The God of the Iskamen,' she said. 'How I envy you that.'

It was an odd thing for her to say, but given the circumstances he thought no more of it. But the memory stayed and when, much later, it surfaced, he knew who had said it before: the sorceress, Sardonyx.

But by then it was far too late.

The Dai-San speaks:

If only I could make Chiisai understand, but she is only human, after all, though Bujun. I have a great and abiding kinship with the Bujun. It was their sorcery that created me; it is their secrets which invigorate me. But these are not secrets which can be passed on, like the lore of a people, from one generation to the next. I am enmeshed in secrets, now. That is my karma. But it is wearisome, sometimes, because, as with Chiisai, they distance me from all others save the Kaer'n.

I look deep into Chiisai's eyes and I know her heart. She has joined with me many times and those couplings have been as much fierce physical contests as they have been tender mercies for her. She is the Kunshin's daughter, after all, and by definition untouchable. But I know her. She is fierce and proud and not a little bit sad. I know, too, that she is the less sad for knowing me. That is not a boast, merely fact which I can read at every moment in her eyes.

In other times and circumstances surely I would take Chiisai as my wife. Surely, the Kunshin would wish it, but I have spoken to him as the Kaer'n have spoken to me and he is resigned. He is, after all, more used to the Kaer'n than even I. I have lived with them, it is true, for some years, but he has known them all his adult life.

He knows the inevitability of what must happen, but he does not know everything. His mind is human, after all, and can absorb only so much at a time. The Kaer'n are most cognizant of this. They are, I fear, more understanding than I would be. I find, over time, that I lose patience with this slowness of human thought, the sheer linearity of it.

I must guard against such tendencies. The Kaer'n say that I must hold close the shreds of humanity still remaining to me, that I must not lose them. They are as important to my make-up – and therefore my power – as my own sorcerous dai-katana.

I know the Kaer'n are right. They always are . . .

PART TWO
MU'AD

FIVE

SPIRITS RISING

The white sun, crystalline as diamonds, heavy as a mailed fist, beat down upon Mu'ad, the Great Desert. Moichi, lampblack smeared on his cheeks, his head covered with a capacious Fe'edjinn cowl, squinted into the rolling nothingness of white dune and wind-whipped sand. The heat penetrated even the sturdy oil-hardened leather of his seaboots. The soles of his feet were on fire and there was a distinct wetness between his toes, whether from burst blisters or blood and sweat he did not know.

Four days out into the Mu'ad and already it felt like a month. Tamuk had warned them of this. In fact, the First Darman had used every form of persuasion he could think of to talk Moichi out of his desire to go to the settlements in the Mu'ad. But Moichi remained resolved and, at last, Tamuk had acceded. Moichi was an Annai-Nin, after all, and brother to the Qa'tach.

Aufeya, lighter and thinner than he, seemed to be faring a bit better. Her entire face had disappeared within the Fe'edjinn's cowl and she wore the d'alb, the traditional desert robes as if she had been born to them. Being Daluzan that was, of course, impossible. Still, there was no doubt that she took to the desert life like a native, and for that Moichi was grateful.

In the hottest portions of the day she used small sticks

to tent out the cowl, giving more shade, even a millimeter of which was priceless, and she caught herself as she nodded in her saddle.

Other times, she ignored Tamuk's instruction to ride single-file and came up beside Moichi. They spoke of many things but, oddly, never distant Daluzia, her home. She seemed fascinated by the Mu'ad, and when Moichi told her how the Iskamen had learned to terraform parts of the Great Desert, she seemed to know about it already. He should have marked this moment, and others like it, but perhaps still his need not to face the truth was too pressing.

Moichi would tell neither Tamuk nor Aufeya why he was so adamant about going to the Mu'ad. In truth, he was not sure himself. He only knew he was being drawn here like a lodestone to north. He wanted to mourn for Sanda and for his mate Arasomu, but his mind kept returning to the Makkon. Surely the Chaos beast had slaughtered them both. The manner of their deaths was identical. Over and above Moichi's shock at seeing another Makkon when he had been certain that the Dai-San had destroyed them all was the question: why? Why had the Makkon murdered these two people? Was there a connection or was it random mayhem? But, chillingly, his knowledge of the Makkon told him that they were a kind of harbinger – outriders for a more highly developed, more powerful Chaos force. In the time of the Kai-feng, it had been the Dolman. But the Sunset Warrior had slain the Dolman, of that Moichi was certain. What, then, was this Makkon's liege lord?

The Makkon never killed randomly. There was always a purpose. Chaos's purpose. But this Makkon was slightly different than all the others Moichi had encountered. Those had never been able to fully integrate themselves into the world of man and so their outlines pulsed and changed with every beat of their twin hearts. This one had not; it was fully in this world.

It was also without its tongue and filled with such a rage as Moichi had never felt before. There was a mystery here he knew needed solving. In the morning of Arasomu's murder he had walked the jam-packed streets of Ala'arat and was certain that the Makkon had fled the city. Where had it gone?

There was a spoor. Whereas its former brethren had left none, being only partially in this world, this one was all here, and Moichi could smell it. Not with his nose, but with his mind.

He could say nothing of these things to Tamuk, who would immediately dismiss him as a madman – the First Darman had his own agenda which dictated the murders had been committed by Al Rafaar, the Adenese terrorists. As for Aufeya, Moichi did not want to alarm her, as he himself was alarmed by the Makkon's malevolent presence.

Across the Mu'ad they rode, on dun-colored co'chyn, long-legged desert beasts with knobby knees, horned, triangular heads with sorrowful eyes and a curling trunk for sucking up water from the most unlikely places. Co'chyn also had three stomachs, two of which apparently stored fluids in the stifling heat and the long migratory marches of the species. Both the Iskamen and the Adenese had found ways to train these animals, using them exclusively for desert travel.

Tamuk, ever security-minded, had brought two of his Fe'edjinn warriors with him. They invariably rode at the front and rear of the single-file line. Normally, desert travel was accomplished at night, when the worst heat of the furnace day had dissipated somewhat, but in the Mu'ad this would have been a mistake and, in fact, had claimed the lives of many travelers unaccustomed to its peculiarities. Here, it was imperative that you keep moving during the bulk of the day, otherwise you could quite literally fry. In fact, sleep was only possible in those few hours on either side of midnight when the Mu'ad was merely hot, rather than unbearable.

Sleep, then, was often dreamless and absolute, the mind and body so exhausted that you would drift off before the evening meal was over. Not so for Moichi.

Each night he dreamed, and it was more or less the same dream – at least, it was the same person who came to him as if she were an angel in the cindery dark.

He dreamt of Sanda, slaughtered like a beast in her own bed. But they were like no dreams he had ever had before. Rather, they were like fevered visions or hallucinations that, in some cultures, were still called visitations.

Aufeya's mother Tsuki had claimed to have experienced such phenomena. Poor dead Tsuki, killed by the vengeful Sardonyx.

Sanda came to him in many guises. At first, she appeared as a teenager, bursting with life and energy, her eyes laughing even when he teased her or her face dark and flushed after witnessing one of his epic fights with Jesah. In these dreams she never spoke, merely guided him through flashes of memory which electrified him like lightning on a stormy night. At last, she led him to the deathbed of Jud'ae, a scene, finally, of forgiveness between father and son. At once, Moichi was again on the deck of his ship, scenting the imminence of death. He had returned home to find his father dying.

Then, Sanda came to him as a woman with the head of a bird – a snowy egret with downy feathers glistening of beaded water. Her long black beak hooked downward and there was a flopping fish impaled on its sharp tip, its flat golden eye staring at Moichi as if with a singular purpose. With a sudden flip of her head she swallowed the fish whole. Then her beak opened and she spoke:

> 'Time is of the essence/When the spirit flies above marsh and chasm Take care to bury past heart/And seek out the bear in the stone Not to possess/But to be possessed.'

The voice was high, like a peacock's harsh and grating cry, and the dreaming Moichi was obliged to strain mightily to hear all the words. They made no sense to him, but he remembered them when he awoke and wrote them in charcoal in his stained leather-bound captain's logbook.

In the last of the dreams the night before they reached the first oasis encampment, deep within the Mu'ad, Sanda appeared as she must have on her blood-stained bed. It was appalling to see her face blue-white instead of flushed with color as he remembered her. She moved as if she were still in pain. Only (he thought in his dream) dead people cannot feel pain. She shuffled and cupped her hands at her lower belly to keep her innards from slithering to her feet. Her shattered chest was opened up like the skeleton of a wrecked vessel, rotting at the bottom of the sea. Ribbons of skin hung from her like sea grape.

Moichi tried to look into her eyes, to see any semblance of the beloved sister he had once known but, as in many dreams, his eyes refused to focus or, again, perhaps she had no eyes at all, for he was aware only of a yawning and terrifying void, as if whatever had once been Sanda – her spirit – had been torn from her along with her insides.

Sanda! he cried soundlessly. *My sister!* His heart was beating so fast it seemed it might fly out of his chest or break into ten thousand pieces. He wanted only to talk with her – to *her* – not all these manifestations. He ached for reassurance that this was indeed a nightmare – everything she had ever been had been taken from her in the manner of her death.

Then she opened her mouth and, to his horror, blood spilled out. There was a horrid gurgling sound that eventually resolved itself into two words repeated over and over, and even when he awakened, bathed in sweat, trembling, his pulse pounding and his heart constricted with grief, he heard it still, echoing in the utter silence of the desert dawn:

Save me!

A blood-condor screamed, its iridescent purple plumage swooping just beyond the top of a dune. Tamuk called for the column to halt, and swinging his co'chyn around, rode back to where Moichi had reined in.

'The settlement is on the far side of that dune,' he said tensely. 'But you know as well as I do what the presence of the carrion eater augurs.'

'Why have we stopped?' Aufeya asked, coming up on her co'chyn. 'I see no sign of a settlement.'

'I fear for them, lady,' Tamuk said, wheeling his mount round. 'There were twenty settlers and Fe'edjinn.'

'But there are no palms, no signs at all that we are near an oasis,' Aufeya insisted. 'Even the Fe'edjinn could not have pitched camp without a steady supply of water nearby.'

'She's right,' Moichi said. 'Are you certain we are in the right place, First Darman?'

Tamuk snorted derisively, then, signalling to his men, who drew their scimitar-shaped weapons, he spurred his co'chyn toward the long rise of the dune beyond which the blood-condor continued to circle and swoop. Moichi and Aufeya followed the Fe'edjinn at a distance.

One of the Fe'edjinn, fed up with the bird's grating cry

or perhaps nervous at what was waiting for them, loosed an arrow which struck the blood-condor in its breast. It plummeted straight down, disappearing behind the dune.

Moichi stood in his stirrups, urging his steed slowly forward as he scanned the horizon. There was naught to see in any direction but an endless sea of gently rolling dunes, here and there tufted with powdery sand as gusts of fiercely hot wind swirled.

Tamuk and his men crested the dune and began their descent of the far side. In a moment, they had disappeared, and Moichi urged his co'chyn up the slope. At the dune's crest he paused, waiting for Aufeya.

'Where are they?' she asked, staring down at the waad, the deep depression below. It was devoid of all life. 'It's as if the desert itself swallowed them whole.'

At that moment, they felt a rumbling. Their co'chyn snorted and skittered nervously as rivulets of sand began to stream down the far side of the dune into the waad. The rivulets soon became rills and streams that plumed into the air like rapids and waterfalls. The co'chyn screamed and bucked as their footing was eroded and they began to slide down the dune into the waad, which itself had changed radically. It was now an evil-looking swirl of sand that seemed to have turned molten, to be revolving, expanding before their eyes.

'Quick!' Moichi shouted. 'Off the co'chyn!'

He slid off his terrified mount, only to see it shoot past him, tumbling into the waad, which sucked it down like a gigantic maw. He turned, slipping in the cascading sand, pulling Aufeya off her co'chyn, as it slipped to its knobby knees, then tumbled trunk over tail into the maelstrom of the shifting waad.

'Let's get out of here!' Moichi shouted, keeping hold of her as he tried to struggle up the slope of the dune. The two were reduced to crawling on all fours, but for every step up, the cascading rivers of sand took them down the equivalent of three.

Moichi glanced over his shoulder, saw how appallingly close they were to the sucking, swirling base of the waad and redoubled his efforts. He was rewarded by a heavy cascade of sand in his face, and he and Aufeya tumbled further down the dune.

The bottom of the bowl-shaped waad was sucked abruptly down, and from out of this hole rose a slithery thick shape, like a primeval serpent, huge and either covered by sand or made of sand itself. A beast. Could it be? Moichi wondered. A beast that lived below the surface of the Mu'ad.

The shape arched – far too large for the bowl of the waad to contain – and then, with a great thrashing, plunged into the center of the waad. It was now very close, and abruptly they heard the rumbling again, but this time it seemed to resolve itself into a voice that echoed off the dunes and the distant, uncaring white sky high above.

'FE'EDJINN!' In an eerie, hissing attempt at pronunciation. *'FE'EDJINN!'*

Just above them, an avalanche of sand was forming, shaking itself from what once had been the crest of the dune. It was coming and Moichi knew there was nothing they could do to avoid it. But the rumbling echoed still in his brain and he fought for one last hope, to understand.

Think! he berated himself. *Think!*

The avalanche of sand now drowned out all sun. The blessed shade inundated them and for an instant it seemed utterly delicious. Then Moichi was scrabbling at his Fe'edjinn cowled robe, clawing at it to get it off.

'What are you doing?' Aufeya screamed.

'Take off your d'alb!' Moichi shouted, throwing his aside in a knot and pulling Aufeya's over her head.

'Are you mad? You–'

The avalanche took them, tumbling them down, down into the maw of the rumbling waad. Had he gotten the d'alb all the way off Aufeya? He couldn't be certain. Then a huge fistful of clotted sand struck him full in the face and he began to suffocate. He struggled but a weight, growing heavier, lay upon his chest. The blood rushed to his head as he was flung upside down; the world went black and he lost consciousness.

Blood was still on High Minister Ojime's hands, metaphorically speaking, as he hurried through the city of Haneda. He could feel the lumped package of the Makkon's tongue burning like a live coal against his lower belly.

He could not mourn the Rosh'hi's death because from the first he had seen Qaylinn as an enemy. Not that that was necessarily immutable. Over the years, by dint of bribe or other less savory coercion, Ojime had proselytized many enemies to his cause. But not Qaylinn. He was a stubborn man, some might say a righteous man, though that term left a bitter taste in Ojime's mouth. Ojime's father had thought of himself as righteous. He had beaten Ojime mercilessly when his 'righteousness' was in full flower. Ojime had no idea why his father beat him, and the fact he was never given the reason made it all the more terrifying. The randomness, the pure irrationality of it, scarred Ojime more deeply than any laying on of the chain his father had used on him.

As a result, Ojime was properly skeptical of those who characterized themselves as righteous, divining in their strict rectitude the bud of evil and twisted psychosis.

And yet there was another reason, just as compelling, why he could not mourn the Rosh'hi's passing: he had enjoyed plunging the blade into Qaylinn's breast. This vertiginous rapture was what made him stab the Rosh'hi over and over. He could not stop, did not want to stop.

Deep down, his delight in death appalled him, turned his belly to ice, but it had also turned his heart to stone and, these days, he found it ever more difficult to understand what he had found appalling in the first place.

Ojime crossed a narrow and rotting bridge into the Hinin, the area of the city that lay in the lowest section of the capital's terrain. It was to this place that all of Haneda's sewage flowed on its way to the bay, and it was here that the garbage of Bujun society had been dumped, eking out of the wet, clayey earth the semblance of an existence.

Down alleys dark and slimy even at noon-time Ojime hurried, following a convoluted path that he had devised days ago. He paused frequently to check whether he was being observed, and he altered his pace, doubling back often to ensure that no one was following him. And with each clever detour he made, as he advanced further into the squalid and dangerous depths of the Hinin, he felt increasingly secure.

At length, he came upon a packed dirt-lane that even for the Hinin was putrid. He ducked into this and, holding his breath down its entire length, knocked upon a thatch and willow door. He was just becoming slightly light-headed when the door opened a crack. It was unnaturally dark in the interior, and, gasping for breath, Ojime breathed in an odor from the gap so fetid that he was certain he would faint.

'Who sent you?' said a rough voice. The reek of foul breath sent Ojime back a pace.

'Tokagé.' Ojime uttered the forbidden word as softly as he could. Even within the Hinin the name of the arch-collaborator with the forces of Chaos should not be used.

'Inside,' the voice commanded harshly, raising Ojime's anger. But he had been warned repeatedly about the ill-mannered creature who dwelled within this mud and thatch hovel, and he held his tongue.

The door banged shut behind him and immediately his eyes began to water. *What is the floor made of,* he wondered, *feces?* For that was precisely what it smelled like.

Some hump-like thing shuffled just ahead of him, leading him through room after room, until Ojime began to distrust his senses. Surely, something was amiss. From the outside, the house at the end of the evil-smelling lane looked as if it could contain no more than four rooms, and yet he had already counted three times that.

Alarmed that he had been entrapped, his hand crept to the long-bladed dirk sheathed on the inside of his left boot.

'Violence in any form will get you dead.'

Ojime started erect at the sound of the voice. He looked ahead, saw a shadowy figure sitting in a fan-backed chair in what could only be called a solarium. Sunlight flooded through the highly polished panes of glass, illuminating a bewildering array of dwarf potted plants, herbs, ferns, mushrooms and curious flowers, none of which Ojime had ever seen before.

Ojime, blinking heavily after the long journey in darkness, looked around for his humped guide but it appeared that, for the moment at least, he was alone with the figure in the fan-backed chair.

'Who sent you?' the shadowy figure asked.

And Ojime gave the same answer: 'Tokagé.'

'Present yourself,' the figure said as imperiously as if they were in the Kunshin's opulent castle instead of here in the village of the pariahs.

Ojime stepped forward. As he crossed the threshold into the solarium, the evil odors vanished as if they had never existed. Instead, the sweet scents of new-mown grass and packed hay mingled with the pleasant spices and nectars of the unknown herbs and flowers.

Light fell upon him in a steady stream, like waves upon a shore, until Ojime felt himself to be in the center of a celestial spotlight, singled out, chosen.

'What have you for me?' the voice rustled.

Ojime hesitated for just an instant. Instinctively, he trusted nothing and no one, but he also understood that great risk was a necessary part of his plan. The Makkon's tongue meant nothing to him in its present state. He had been assured that this creature was the only one in Ama-no-mori – perhaps in the entire world – who knew what to do with this piece of otherworldly flesh. And so, long before he would steal the Makkon's tongue, he had schemed and connived, cajoled and threatened and, lastly, had given up lordly sums of jewels, mother-of-pearl and platinum to arrive, untouched and unknown, at this place at the far end of Haneda.

'Have you come this far only to be ruled by your fear?' the voice rustled crossly.

'I *have* no fear,' Ojime said, believing this to be so.

'Then give it to me.' An impossibly long-fingered hand extended out of the shadows, and Ojime found himself wondering, not for the first time, what foul and perverted creature would lock itself away in such a gilded cage surrounded by a moat of stinking excrement.

His fingers trembled slightly as he dug inside his robe and placed the lump of sueded cloth into the outstretched hand.

'*Ahhhh!*' It was like a long-drawn sigh. The fingers were trembling as they unwrapped the flaps of cloth, revealing the grayish-blue lump of otherworldly flesh. 'It is true, then!' she cried. 'Damn his soul to a thousand hells unknown!

'But have I a revelation for him!' The figure rose and stepped out of the shadows. Though Ojime had steeled himself for the worst his imagination could conjure up still he was unprepared for the sight that greeted him. For he found himself standing face to face with the most ethereally exquisite female he had ever seen.

She was as delicate as a butterfly and when she moved she seemed to float like a fairy on a current of fragrant air. Her skin was the color of the first snow and her long hair was jet black, floating about her face in a style alien to the Bujun. The perfect bow of lips was a scarlet so intense it seemed to sear his retinas, and the heavy lids of her enormous eyes were powdered in silver dust. Her long, graceful neck was girdled by a chain of perfectly matched pearls the color of sea-foam. Her slim frame was cloaked in a kimono of white, on which were brocaded egrets in cloth-of-platinum. It was cinched tightly with a wide sash of white silk studded with seed pearls. They looked like stars flung into the ocean.

Ojime, his face flushed, whispered, 'You are magnificent!'

The woman smiled with the innocence of a child. 'You are kind to say so.' Her long fingers closed over the Makkon's tongue, and her voice changed, momentarily chilling him, 'You did not touch this?'

'No.'

'Did anyone else?'

He heard the tenseness in her voice but did not understand it. 'Not to my knowledge. Except for the Dai-San.'

Her head swiveled. 'The Dai-San knows.'

'Yes. He held it. But he was wearing that hideous six-fingered glove of his.'

'The Makkon's skin.' She nodded. 'But he knows nothing. No harm done, then.' She looked at him. 'I can do it, then, what you wish, what you have paid handsomely for. I can make the potion that will make you immortal.'

He hesitated but a moment as she turned and led him now to the rear of the solarium where there were fires

93

burning from an unknown source. She thrust the Makkon's tongue unceremoniously into a blocky stone and ceramic square not unlike a forge. The orange flames turned immediately black and a cloud of chokingly thick smoke rose into the air. The stench made Ojime forget about all the dark rooms he had passed through. He fell to his knees and gagged.

The fairy-like woman stood motionless, staring down at him until the flames returned to their original color. Then, astonishingly, she slid her right hand into the forge's opening, into the flames and the incredible heat. Ojime gasped but she did not so much as flinch. A moment later her hand, blue with cinder, emerged in a fist. She walked over to a zinc-topped table filled with the implements of gardening and grinding.

She opened her fist over a large marble mortar and Ojime watched a colorless ash sparkle down in a thin stream. What she added to this residue of the Makkon's tongue he could not even begin to say. An hour after she had first beckoned him into the solarium, she announced that she was done.

'I will take possession of it now,' Ojime said.

She turned and, smiling that innocent childlike smile, said, 'You must meet my price.'

Ojime's face darkened. 'Why, I have paid you more than a score of men and their sons will earn in their lifetimes. I have met your price.'

'That you have,' she affirmed still smiling sweetly. 'That was my price for making the potion. What you have asked for, after all, is unique, highly dangerous.' She held a small glass phial aloft. It contained a thick liquid that seemed to flash and fluoresce. 'You could hardly have gone anywhere else to get this.'

'Damn you,' Ojime said menacingly, taking a step toward her. 'We struck a bargain. We have a deal.'

The woman appeared unperturbed. 'My price for delivery is simple. You will grant me your allegiance *after* you have become immortal.'

Ojime, who had no intention of honoring any promise he made to this witch, laughed out loud. 'Is that all?'

'I warn you.' She lifted a long finger. 'There will be dire consequences should you refuse to grant my wish.'

Ojime, his mind aflame only with the consequences of what she held in her hand, knew he had no reason to heed her counsel. 'I agree to your price for delivery,' he said.

Power! his mind cried, transfixed by this moment. *Power!*

The woman nodded, and he stepped forward, took the glass phial out of her hand and, with a quick flick of his wrist, upended it over his open mouth. He swallowed convulsively, and felt a peculiar burning in his gullet, working its way down to his stomach. Any liquid that was powerful enough to raise the dead, he had reasoned, would make of him, a living human being, something akin to a god. Someone to challenge and defeat even the great Dai-San.

It is working! he thought, gripped by exhilaration. He began to laugh. 'I've tricked you, witch,' he said, looking at the ethereal woman through eyes that had begun to water.

That angelic smile. 'Have you, Chief Minister Ojime?'

'No names!' he cried. 'How do you know my name?'

The woman began to laugh. 'Why, you fool, I know *everything.*' She spread her arms wide. 'Did you think I didn't know that you lied to me?' She leaned forward and now – though Ojime could not be sure because his eyes were streaming tears – her aspect did not seem quite so angelic. In fact, she did not appear benign at all. '*Power*, Ojime. That is your ambition. And now that you have it, tell me whether it meets with your expectations.'

Ojime had fully intended to do just that, to tell her that despite her gloating he still maintained the upper hand. He was Chief Minister, after all, and a Bujun warrior. What was she? He opened his mouth to utter these things and more but at that moment the liquid cascaded into his stomach.

The pain hit him like a swordsmith's hammer. Every cell in his body seemed on fire, bleeding, imploding, the agony feeding on itself, until . . .

Ojime kept right on screaming all the way through the transformation.

SIX

BELLY OF
THE BEAST

Moichi awoke into musty darkness. It was warm, but far from the broiling heat of the Mu'ad.

'Aufeya?'

He reached out, but could not find her. He rolled over and groaned, holding his head steady until the waves of vertigo subsided. He got up on his hands and knees, felt for his dirks. They were gone; he had been disarmed. He began to move, but almost immediately paused. Didn't the floor feel spongy? Didn't it feel moist and almost sticky?

He heard the eerie sibilance in his mind again: '*Fe'edjinn! Fe'edjinn!*'

A cold chill swept through him. Could it be that he was in the belly of the beast? Swallowed but not ingested. And where was Aufeya?

He began to move again, but it wasn't long before he felt the hard steel edge of a weapon at his throat.

'Don't move!' a voice hissed.

A light appeared, a small brass lamp with a tiny flame rising from its wick. By its mean light Moichi saw a moon face the color of suet. It seemed to be stuck directly onto a body of gross weight with no intervening neck.

'You're not dead,' the moon face said with some surprise.

'Should I be?'

The blade of the weapon – one of Moichi's own dirks, he saw – softly caressed the skin on his throat. 'Everyone else is who comes here,' the moon face said. Black round button eyes blinked below a beetling brow, and the cherry bow of feminine lips made a moue.

'You're not.'

The button eyes blinked again. 'Turn over.'

'What?'

The point of the dirk drew blood. 'You heard me. Turn over, I'm hungry.'

Moichi was obliged to move. As he turned on his side, he said, 'Where are we?' And then, on his back, 'What are you going to do?'

A tiny pink tongue worked its way around the bow of his lips. 'Hungry. I'm going to open you up and feast on –'

Perhaps it was the hunger or the anticipation of satiation, but his concentration wavered for an instant. Moichi slammed his fist into the side of the hand that held the dirk. At the same time he used the edge of his other hand on the nerve plexus in moon face's shoulder. There was so much flesh he had to lift himself off the floor in order to find it.

Moon face cried out and the dirk fell to the floor. Moichi scooped it up and, placing it at the fat man's throat, felt around for its twin. When he had both dirks in his possession he said, 'Who are you?'

'Dujuk'kan's my name,' the moon face wailed. 'And for the love of God have pity on me. I've been incarcerated here for . . .' His head swung around in disbelief. 'Assan, I don't know how long I've been here!'

'Assan!' Moichi repeated. 'You're Adenese!'

'What of it?' Dujuk'kan said. 'Are you an Iskaman?'

'As it happens, I am.'

The fat man stared at him open-mouthed. 'Assan, you can't be Fe'edjinn.'

Now we're getting somewhere, Moichi thought. 'Why can't I?'

'Because . . . because . . .' Dujuk'kan looked away. He yelped, jumped as Moichi pricked him with the dirk, and his head turned back. His eyes, squinting, made him look sad like a child's forgotten toy, thrown in a corner to gather dust instead of love. 'You're hurting me,' he said mournfully.

Moichi laughed mirthlessly. 'That isn't the half of what I'll do unless you cooperate. You were going to eat me for dinner!'

'That was necessity. I am hungry. What choice did I have? But you're just being cruel.'

Moichi pricked him again and he squealed like an animal. 'The . . . thing here . . . eats Fe'edjinn. Like everything else in the Mu'ad its survival instincts are honed to a sharp edge.'

'But why only Fe'edjinn. Why didn't it eat you?'

Dujuk'kan shrugged. 'I don't know I – oww!' He stared at the rivulet of his own blood and Moichi felt sure he was on the verge of tears. 'Now look what you've done!' he wailed like a woman.

'If you tell me the truth no more blood will be spilled.'

Those black button eyes stared at Moichi. 'Promise?' And when Moichi nodded, he sighed. His expression was very sad. 'I'm a trader, you see. I've lived in the Mu'ad all my life. Don't ask me why except it is my home and I find it impossible to leave. Like this . . . thing's, my survival instincts are formidable. When it sucked me in I knew I had to make a deal fast.'

'So you bartered your knowledge of the Mu'ad for your life.'

The fat man nodded. 'It's true. I'm guilty. I led it to

99

Fe'edjinn settlements in return for my life. But the bargain backfired. I became too useful; it refused to let me go, so I've been imprisoned down here for Assan only knows how long.'

'But *where* are we? In the belly of the thing?'

'Oh, no! We're in one of the underground tunnels it digs out for itself wherever it goes. It's somewhere –' he looked to either side – 'around here.'

'But it didn't eat me.'

'No.'

'And the woman I was with?'

'What woman?' Dujuk'kan said. 'I saw no one else.'

Then where is Aufeya? Moichi asked himself frantically. *Could the thing have . . . ?* But he stopped himself. That way led madness. 'We have to find her,' he said to the fat man. 'How extensive are the tunnels?'

'We've been here quite some time while it . . . feasted. If she's still alive, she could be anywhere. We'd never find her in time.'

'In time? What do you mean?'

'The thing has just gorged itself on . . . the three Fe'edjinn. It's in a period of stasis now while it digests. It–'

Stasis! That was it! 'Quick!' Moichi said, pulling the fat man to his feet with a grunt. 'Take me to the thing.'

Those button eyes nearly popped out of Dujuk'kan's head. 'Are you mad? What this thing is . . .' He shuddered. 'You don't want to go near it. Trust me, you don't even want to see it.'

'Take me there! Now!' Moichi pushed the lamp into the fat man's trembling hands, then shoved him along the tunnel. 'If it is still in stasis we have a chance to kill it before it awakes.'

'Kill it?' The fat man's tongue licked his lips as if he needed to taste the concept.

'It's the only way you will get out of here,' Moichi said.

Dujuk'kan's eyes lit up. 'Kill it! Yes!' He ducked his massive head as he began to lead Moichi down a twisting tunnel. The lamp illuminated the curving walls, carved with corkscrew markings, as if they had been routed out with a gigantic drill.

'Just what is this thing?' Moichi asked as Dujuk'kan led him down a left-hand branching.

'Assan knows,' the fat man said. 'A misshapen monster bred in this desert of wonders. Perhaps it is the last of its kind.' He shuddered again, his shoulders and sides wobbling like Daluzan custard. 'I pray to Assan it is so.'

Moichi was aware that Dujuk'kan was leading him along a series of tunnels that led deeper into the desert floor. There seemed to be no rock here, but sand compressed into the density of stone. Still, it was sand, moist and almost springy to the touch as he had discovered.

Ever downward they went until they were enveloped by a wet coolness that seemed as stifling as that of an ocean's floor. The air seemed as thick as honey and Moichi's lungs began to labor with each breath. When he felt a wave of dizziness, he pulled the fat man around. 'How much farther?'

'Not far.' The button eyes squinted. 'Are you all right?'

'Fine,' Moichi said, indicating that they should push on.

They hardly needed the lamp now, for the walls of the drilled out tunnels spiralled with crawling things, insects of some sort, which emitted a pulsing greenish-yellow light. The moving lights served to further disorient him so that he staggered and, at one point, fell against the wall. Huge insects began to crawl all over him, turning him phosphorescent.

Seeing this, Dujuk'kan turned and brushed the creatures off him. 'The light will waken the thing prematurely.' His voice was now a whisper, a sign that they were close to the stasis lair. But so close to the wall Moichi saw thick, dark veins running through the hard-packed sand. He touched them with his fingertips. They seemed metallic and Dujuk'kan confirmed this.

'There is no real rock bed until you get much further down,' he said. 'But there are veins of metal ore – tin, lead and antimony – hard as diamond.'

The route now turned so steep they were obliged to slide part of the way down. Moichi wondered how they would ever get back up for there were no handholds and the floor of the tunnels, smooth and giving, would be impossible to climb.

At the bottom of what was almost a chimney of sand the tunnel narrowed down. Moichi could see immediately that the Adenese would never fit through. There were no insects here and it was dark and dank, save for the pitifully small circle of light from the lamp's flame.

'There,' Dujuk'kan whispered, pointing directly through the narrow defile. 'That is the neck of the lair.' He crouched down, lifting the lamp as he did so. 'It is still curled in stasis.' He looked at Moichi. 'You will have to go in there.'

Moichi drew one dirk, put it crosswise between his teeth. He held the other in his left hand and, pushing the Adenese aside, took the lamp from him and began to crawl through the narrow neck. He was immediately aware of the walls closing in on him until he could feel them on all sides. Still, he pushed on, though he could feel the compressed sand dragging at his clothes. How much narrower could the neck become?

He squirmed his way onward. Now he was obliged to curl his shoulders toward one another in order to keep going. The narrow tunnel seemed to stretch onward. He had supposed, going by Dujuk'kan's description of a 'neck,' that he would have to pass through only a short distance.

Still, the tunnel narrowed. There was no space to turn

102

around. Moichi could hear the thunder of his heartbeat, the wheezing of his breathing. He could not even lift his head anymore. He was like a worm, heading downward into darkness, into an unknown fate, to confront . . . what? Some monstrous beast that ate human beings as naturally as he drank water.

He pressed on, knowing instinctively that to stop would be a mistake, for that respite would allow doubts, fears and even panic to assail him, crushing courage underfoot. But it was now so narrow that it was all he could do to inch painfully along. His skin beneath his clothes felt rubbed raw by the constant contact with the compressed sand.

Abruptly a fetid whiff came to him. The neck had ceased to narrow and, with a great effort, he wriggled forward. The air, though somewhat foul, ceased to be moist, and his grateful lungs sucked it in. Then, all at once, his head and shoulders were through and, squirming, he used his elbows against the wall of the lair to lever himself all the way out.

He found himself in a small chamber. It was empty. He went back to the neck he had climbed through, shouted, 'Dujuk'kan, the thing is no longer here. What–'

His voice was drowned out by a deep rumble, and he leaped back from the opening a moment before a torrent of sand came rushing through. It spewed into the chamber, filling it by a third. His heart sinking, he lifted the lamp, kicked at the sand. It was solid enough. He pushed it away from the opening and more gushed through. There was no doubt that sand filled the neck completely. He was cut off. Which, he saw now, was precisely the Adenese's plan.

Chill take him! Moichi thought. He has buried me alive here. Too late, it occurred to him that Dujuk'kan must have lied about almost everything, that he knew where

Aufeya was, that he wanted her for himself or, just as likely, to sell in the infamous and illicit Mu'ad flesh markets. With her red hair and copper eyes she was an exotic type in this part of the world; she'd no doubt fetch a fortune for the fat Adenese.

Holding the lamp high, he walked around the chamber. It was devoid of anything except sand, and it was small enough so that with the one opening blocked it could not be long before he ran out of air. In fact, the lamp's flame was using precious oxygen. He could douse it, of course, but he lacked a means to relight it.

He stood in the middle of the chamber, overly conscious of his breath going in and out. He knew he shouldn't concentrate on it, he should think of other . . . Wait! Maybe he *should* concentrate on his breathing – or at least the air he was taking in. Because it wasn't musty and, this far down, in a chamber with one egress that was now blocked, it should have been. But, except for that faint fetid scent, the air was clear and, as he had noted earlier, drier than that of the tunnels above. This could mean only one thing.

He looked upward, searching for the place where fresh air was filtering into the chamber. He went around the room four times, slowly examining the high walls and ceiling of the chamber. It had to be there, he just knew it.

And, at last, he found what appeared to be a crease in the near featureless wall. It was appallingly high up, almost at the ceiling but . . . He stood beneath it, sniffing lightly and then more deeply. Yes, the air was marginally drier and fresher here. His spirits lifted. Then there was at least a chance of another way out. But how to reach it? The walls of the chamber, though grooved lightly like all the other tunnels, rose straight up without so much as a hint of hand- or footholds. And what good was a way out if he couldn't reach it? The irony of it threatened to overwhelm him.

Then he went over to the wall, put the flat of his hand against it. It was harder, drier than those in the moist, heavy atmosphere above. He took one dirk, drove it horizontally hilt deep into the wall three feet up. He put his weight on it, straining. It did not give.

His heart beating fast, he climbed on it then, reaching up, drove the second dirk into the wall, three feet above that. He stepped up, carefully putting his weight onto the higher dirk. It held. He took his weight off the lower dirk and, leaning down, pulled it free. It was tough work, and he resolved to make the subsequent steps up shallower. It would slow his progress but he would be assured of pulling the lower dirk out of the wall.

Thus he made his painful way up the chamber toward the breath of air seeping in. He was sweating heavily from the exertion and the delicate balancing act he was obliged to perform simultaneously. Once, he was sure the lower dirk would not shift, and he spent an agonizing ten minutes working on it, using patience as well as muscle to inch it out of the wall. When it finally came free, he paused, crouching on one bent leg like some exotic avian, letting his heartbeat return to a semblance of normalcy.

He went on, rising until he was within three feet of the ceiling. He could see the rift in the wall now, a dark ruffled scar in the sand. Carefully, he reached up until his fingertips closed over the top of the rift.

It was a ledge of some sort!

God of my fathers, he breathed silently, thank You!

He had one dirk sheathed, and now he put the flat of both hands onto the ledge and, with a massive effort, pulled himself up. It was very tight. The rift itself ran for more than eight feet horizontally, but it was only about eighteen inches in height, and that was in its center. It tapered off on either side so narrowly it seemed that no one could squirm through. Moichi turned around and, reaching down, pulled the dirk out of the wall. Then he turned his attention to the rift.

He could feel clean fresh air blowing on his face, and there was a dim illumination some way in the distance. That was good news indeed, since he had been forced to leave the lamp behind on the chamber's floor.

He examined the rift and calculated that if he went headfirst into the center of it he could just about make it through. In any case, he had no choice. He had to try.

The way was somewhat easier going than he had expected. The sand here was so dry it was like shale, cracking off in thin layers so that he could work the aperture wider in spots. Also, the rift was shallow, so that he was through it in just over two body lengths.

He sat for a moment on the other side, bathed in the eerie bluish glow and wiped the sweat from his forehead. I'm still not out of this, he had to remind himself.

And that was when he saw the six red eyes staring at him from the shadows. It was a moment before the image resolved itself and he understood that all six eyes belonged to one entity.

God of my fathers, he thought, so Dujuk'kan wasn't lying about everything after all.

Slowly, he took one dirk, held it point first in front of him. He crouched in the gloom, his muscles tense, his nerves singing with adrenaline.

'Fe'edjinn.' It was the voice he had heard just before he and Aufeya had tumbled into the swirling waad. 'Fe'edjinn.'

'I am *not* Fe'edjinn,' he said emphatically. He thought of the fate of Tamuk and his men and his stomach turned over in revulsion. 'Who are you?'

'I am I.' The thing shifted in the shadows but Moichi

still had no clear idea of its shape or size. He knew only that it was blocking his sole path out of this underground prison. As if it had read his thoughts, the thing said, 'I am Jailor. I mete out punishment.'

'Is that why you swallow Fe'edjinn whole? To punish them?'

'I only punish one. The others are sustenance. I must live; I must eat.'

Moichi crept a little forward, willing his gorge not to rise. What was it about this creature that caused such absolute antipathy? Was it simply its gruesome diet?

'Your prisoner?'

Those horrific red eyes staring at him. 'Yes. The Adenese Dujuk'kan. He is criminal. His cruelty is boundless. Incarcerated, he was here for a purpose. Now you have disturbed that purpose.'

'Dujuk'kan told me he was a merchant.' The Adenese had told Moichi many things. Which ones were the truth and which the lies?

'As is usual with him he lied and truthed all at once,' Jailor said. 'Merchant he is, but in only one specific way: he is a slaver. For years, he ran an Adenese slave camp in the Mu'ad. Iskamen settlers – mostly children and adolescents – were his prey. Cruel he was to them. Inhuman he was.' An odd, chilling sound filled the cavern, rolling and echoing. It was only after a time that Moichi understood that the thing was snickering. It had used the word 'inhuman' ironically. It was at this moment that it came to Moichi that this was no unthinking monster as Dujuk'kan had led him to believe.

'Oh, yes, he is merchant. He sold his contraband or himself tortured them until he laughed hard and long.'

'But someone must have put an end to it,' Moichi said. 'Someone put him down here with you as his guardian. Who?'

'Bjork.'

'Who is Bjork?' Moichi asked.

'Bjork made me with his magic. With his magic he set Dujuk'kan's poor livestock free. He caused Dujuk'kan's prison to be made. I am prison and guard, yes, one and same.' The eyes wavered and seemed to glow more brightly. 'There was a plan. Bjork's plan. Now you have disturbed it all.'

'I? How?'

'Dujuk'kan has escaped. Because of you.' Those six eyes were like fiery coals blasting the shadows, and Moichi could feel an animus rising, dark and dangerous. 'You and the woman have my attention diverted.'

Moichi's heart leapt. 'The woman. Aufeya is alive?'

'Dujuk'kan clever is,' the creature continued. 'Taken the woman he has. Gone he is.'

Moichi shifted forward. 'Then I must go after them. Is Aufeya all right?'

'Unconscious she is. All I know.'

'You must let me go. You–'

'NO!' The shriek filled Moichi's ears, overflowing the cavern, echoing on and on without end. The eyes grew as the thing slithered forward until it blocked the way completely. In a moment it would emerge from the shadows and Moichi would see. 'You will go nowhere. Here is where you will stay in place of Dujuk'kan.'

Moichi flicked the blade of his dirk. 'But I am no criminal. You have no cause to keep me against my will.'

'Best cause,' the thing said, and that odd, chilling snicker came again. 'My life, my existence, depends on prisoner. I told you of Bjork's plan. He created me to guard. When Dujuk'kan dies, I cease to exist. But while Dujuk'kan lives, so must I. Without someone to guard I will perish. Happen I will not let that.' The six eyes seemed to expand exponentially as it came straight for Moichi. 'You are my prisoner now for all your days until the moment of your death.'

When Chiisai knocked on the thatch and willow door of the mean house at the end of the foul-smelling lane in Hinin, she was clad in the rags of a street urchin. She had made it her business to follow High Minister Ojime to the Shinsei na-ke Temple where, unbeknownst to her, Ojime had stolen the Makkon's tongue and had callously murdered the chief Rosh'hi. She had hunkered down in the shadows, waiting patiently for him to emerge, and so she had observed him at length slip out of the temple and hurry away. He had led her a merry paranoid chase through crowded shops and teeming marketplaces, beneath arching bridges, down cobbled thoroughfares thick with produce carts and itinerant calligraphers and fortune-tellers, and along narrow alleyways, some of which he had furtively doubled back on. But she had persevered, shadowing him all the way to the Hinin bridge where she quickly slathered her clothes with mud and hurried after him. Seeing where he was headed, she rent her already filthy clothes and, to make the picture perfect, had rolled around on the packed-dirt lane until she had acquired the right degree of ripeness. Then she had boldly knocked upon the thatch and willow door.

'We have no food to spare,' the humped figure muttered from the open doorway. 'Be gone with you. Weeee–'

The voice turned into a screech as Chiisai put a knife to the hunchback's throat. 'Where is he?' she said.

'Who?' The screech came again as she drew the edge of the blade lightly across his curiously hairless skin.

'Do you think I am joking?' she hissed in the hunchback's ear. 'Do you think I am unaware of the treasonous activities attributed to the owner of this place?' She tightened her grip upon the figure. 'Ojime. Where is he?'

'You will wish you never came here,' the hunchback said as Chiisai propelled him through one evil-smelling chamber after another.

'I am already wishing that,' she said, her nose wrinkling.

'My mistress will kill you,' the hunchback whined. 'She guards her privacy most jealously.'

'Don't we all.'

'Not like her,' the hunchback said, racing along as fast as his short, misshapen legs could carry him. 'She is fanatic. You'll see.' He tried to twist his head around to look at her and she rapped him smartly on the temple. He made a low gurgling sound, like a cud-chewer, and hurried on. She was almost climbing his back as she urged him on.

'No matter how quickly we get there, you will not unnerve her. She knows everything. It is her business.'

'And what business might that be?' Chiisai said.

'She is Kaijikan, the Keeper of Souls.'

Chiisai grabbed at the shell-like back, hurling the figure against one filthy wall. He bounced off with a grunt and she slammed the heel of her hand into his chest. She put her face up against his, pale, sickly and worn, as if he were centuries old instead of decades. 'What nonsense are you promoting? Kaijikan is a myth, an ugly creation to frighten young children into behaving. Kaijikan does not exist.'

'Then you will be slain by a myth,' the hunchback said through thick lips the color of freshly seeping blood.

'Go on,' Chiisai said, hurling him forward, 'show me where she is.'

'No need,' said a soft but commanding voice. 'I am here.'

The hunchback gave a little moan as the tall figure reached out, enfolding him in an embrace of sorts. In a moment, he was no longer there.

Chiisai squinted through the gloom. 'Who are you? And where is High Minister Ojime?'

110

'I am as Te-te said. Kaijikan, the Keeper of Souls.'

Chiisai laughed, but she was uneasy. She could not make out a single feature in the gloom.

'But you have already met one,' Kaijikan said. 'A soul, I mean. Isn't that right, Te-te.' And just like that the hunchback reappeared, cowering and shivering.

'I hate when you do that,' he said. 'It hurts.'

With a yowl he disappeared again.

'Spiritually, he means,' Kaijikan said. 'Of course he is beyond feeling any form of physical pain.' She lifted one long arm. 'Come. You wanted to see the High Minister. This way.'

She turned and went through the doorway. Chiisai had no choice but to follow. She did not for a minute believe that this creature, whoever she might be, was the mythical Kaijikan, Keeper of Souls. She was a madwoman, but no doubt cunning and dangerous for all that.

The brightness of the solarium was almost blinding for the first few moments. As Chiisai adjusted to the flood of light, she saw Kaijikan's features emerging, one by one. She saw the long black hair first, in its asymmetrical, non-Bujun style, then the enormous eyes, the bright bow of a mouth, the long, elegant neck, and the slim, firm body wrapped in the magnificent white and cloth-of-platinum kimono.

She was taken aback, though she struggled mightily not to show it. The eyes, for instance, told her that this woman was clever, yes, but not mad. Madness, she had come to learn, had its own spectrum of toxins that dissolved the color of the irises, causing them to become nothing more than lenses beyond which could be glimpsed the dark void of insanity. These eyes glittered with life, with energy beyond understanding.

On the other hand, the snowy skin was like nothing she had seen on a human. It was without line or blemish and, when she looked more closely, was without pores as well.

'You are wearing a mask,' Chiisai said.

'Do you think so?' Kaijikan pouted, then opened her mouth wide, making certain Chiisai saw there was no possibility of a mask. She put impossibly long fingers up to her cheek. 'Do you think I need one? So many men – and women – have fallen in love with me it never occurred to me that I might need one.'

'Where is Ojime?'

'Oh, yes,' Kaijikan said sweetly. 'I almost forgot.' She turned toward the rear of the solarium, where it was damnably hot from a squat kiln and a roaring fire. 'It seems as if the Chief Minister doesn't feel himself today – to say the least!'

Chiisai looked in the direction Kaijikan indicated and her heart thudded so heavily in her breast it seemed to skip a beat. There, stood a huge, dark-bearded man, immense and powerful, dressed in full battle armor of a manufacture unfamiliar to her. His square face was heavy-jowled, with slanting cheekbones and thick, almost alien, brows over heavy-lidded black eyes that were all glittering iris. Upon his helm was soldered a golden, writhing reptile that Chiisai recognized as a salamander, the creature of eternal life, and the same signal creature was depicted in a clasp at his throat carved from a single ruby with onyx eyes. It was surrounded by onyx flames which reached up into its open mouth.

'Tokagé!' she intoned. 'But that is impossible!' She turned to Kaijikan. 'What trickery have you conjured? What illusion? This beast – this traitor to mankind – was killed by the Dai-San in the Kai-feng.'

'True enough,' Kaijikan said. 'But I won't try to convince you this is indeed Tokagé. Illusion, do you think? By all means, go to him. Touch him. See for yourself.'

Chiisai went hesitantly across the solarium. As she

passed Kaijikan a scent came to her nostrils of rose petals and silver sage, and she gasped, for these odors were associated with the mythical Keeper of Souls. She paused for a moment, staring at Kaijikan, who merely smiled back at her. Then she turned and went up to Tokagé. As she did, his glittering eyes followed her, but when she reached out to touch him – he was indeed solid enough – he did not move.

'Satisfied now?' Kaijikan asked.

'No. He could be anyone,' Chiisai said. But she was staring into his eyes and she recognized that look and knew, despite what she might rationally believe impossible, that this was indeed the arch-traitor of mankind. 'Besides, he hardly seems alive.'

'In that you have some justification,' Kaijikan said. 'He is but halfway back from the dead.' And when Chiisai turned to look at her that smile was still in place. 'You see, I needed two things to reanimate him. The tongue of the Makkon and someone living ambitious enough so that when Tokagé's soul re-entered the physical realm the body – and mind – would not be torn apart. High Minister Ojime fit the bill perfectly.'

'*This* is Ojime?'

'Not anymore,' Kaijikan said. 'Oh, parts of him still exist, I would imagine, here and there. But he has become what he dreamed of, something more.'

'So that is what Ojime was doing hanging around Shin-sei na-ke Temple. He wanted to steal the Makkon's tongue.'

'And steal it he did,' Kaijikan said, 'spilling the Rosh'hi's blood in the process.'

'He murdered Qaylinn?'

'In cold blood, I am pleased to say.' She was beaming. 'Such a perfect host for Tokagé!'

Chiisai whirled. 'I will kill him!'

She drove at the huge, armored figure, her blade drawn.

But behind her, Kaijikan made a series of complex signs in the air, a circle of talismans, and just as the point of Chiisai's blade was about to pierce a seam in his armor, Tokagé moved.

The point glanced off metal, shrieking in protest, and a huge mailed fist chopped down, making her whole arm go numb. The blade clattered to the solarium floor, and Tokagé grabbed her in an iron grip, spun her around.

'His soul was mine from the very moment of his violent death,' Kaijikan said. 'I have plans for him now. Plans so sweeping you could not even imagine them. And I have no intention of allowing you, or anyone else, to interfere with them.'

SEVEN

DUK FADAT

The jailor with six eyes came crawling out of the shadows and Moichi thought he would faint. The thing was so hideous the reaction was instinctive. It had a long, flat insectoid head. A double slit like a cross with four thin lips served as a mouth. It was surmounted on either side by black, beetle-like mandibles. Its bloated, misshapen body, blotched and mottled with patches of clotted wiry hair, wound around and around, ending in a wickedly barbed tail, segmented like that of a scorpion. It had a multitude of short legs, each ending in four powerful talons, on which it scuttled crabwise. A viscous white foam ebbed and flowed from the corners of the ghastly mouth. The eyes, however, were alive with interest.

'You thought me ugly before you even saw me,' the creature said. 'Now have I fulfilled your fear.' The flat shell-like head bounced up and down. 'That is how Bjork made me. A Jailor should be hideous, yes, and I was the only creature Dujuk'kan was meant to see.'

'Then Aufeya and I got sucked in,' Moichi said, swallowing hard. 'How was it you didn't eat us as you did the Fe'edjinn?'

'Came they first. Full was I when you appeared. You were sucked down in the aftermath of my great hunger.

115

No need had I for you while I slept, while full was my belly.'

'So we were meant to stock your larder.'

'I understand not.'

It was hard to look at the creature but Moichi forced himself. 'You were saving us until you were hungry again.'

'That will be long time. I liked woman.'

'Liked Aufeya?' Moichi cocked his head. 'In what way?'

'Dujuk'kan saw her. Saw I him drooling and thought I, if I keep her and he can't have her, sweet torture for him then and I am fulfilling Bjork's purpose even more.'

Moichi considered this a moment. 'Do you understand what is happening? Something Bjork obviously did not anticipate.'

Jailor sniffed. 'Bjork anticipated everything.'

'Not the fact that his jailor would begin to take on the characteristics of his prisoner.'

'Understand I not.'

'Look. You were created to keep Dujuk'kan incarcerated, away from his own kind so he could not harm them as he had for so many years.'

'I do so.'

'Yes,' Moichi said. 'And then you decided to do more. To torture him as he tortured the children he had stolen. What is the difference then between jailor and prisoner?'

It seemed as if Jailor was humming as it got down to work. Using its mandibles, it collected the viscous white liquid and rapidly began to spin out strands of shining filaments. These it strung from the walls of the low grotto which it was guarding.

'What are you doing?' Moichi asked uneasily.

The humming continued as the web became more complex. 'One prisoner escapes, another can do. This will prevent further escapes.'

Moichi stepped forward, slashed at the strands with the

dirk. To his consternation, the strands mended themselves even as they were being sliced. He hacked and hacked at the web with the same result. There was never enough time to break free before the strands coalesced.

'You see,' Jailor snickered, 'told you I that Bjork thought of all.'

Moichi stepped back, wiping the sweat from his face. What would it be like to spend the rest of his life in captivity? he wondered. Each day like stepping into a pool of quicksand, sucking you down into nothingness. Time would become meaningless; so too, eventually, responsibility and thought. Just a slow drifting away like a tiny boat on a vast night-time sea. He could not allow that to happen.

'What now of Dujuk'kan?' he asked. 'Won't you go after him? He's your real prisoner. I am only a stand-in.'

'Go nowhere but tunnels I,' Jailor said. 'Made me Bjork for this. Here stay I.'

'But you *must* go after Dujuk'kan. He's a criminal. Surely Bjork could not have meant this to happen?'

The beast rose up, its mandibles clutching and opening in extreme agitation. 'You see not. Leaving the tunnels I die. End of story.' Then the humming came again as it continued to spin its maddening web.

'Do you know where Dujuk'kan went?'

'Yes. But no use to you.'

Moichi had his eye on several spots where the strands were not yet woven close together.

'I want to know where he is taking Aufeya.'

He moved as Jailor did, waiting for the angle he needed, patient until the beast was very close.

'Ah, Aufeya it is that interests you. Like Dujuk'kan.' Its mandibles clicked in admonishment or incomprehension. 'So much interest in one creature. Well, takes her he to depths of Mu'ad: the Mas'jahan.'

117

Inching forward, calculating vectors. 'Are you sure?'

Jailor continued its clicking as it spun. 'An evil place. Very wild. Business interests has he in the citadel. Of course go there he.'

Moichi lunged with the tip of the dirk, angling it through the space between the strands. The blade shot through the diamond-shaped opening, straight into the beast's head. A great cloud of purple dust shot upward as Jailor shrieked. It bucked upward, almost dislodging the dirk from Moichi's grip. But he had been prepared and he threw himself against the web. As he suspected, it gave, enough for him to follow Jailor's movements and shove the blade further into the carapaced skull. He twisted the blade as he buried it hilt-deep.

All Jailor's short legs began to tremble as it collapsed. Its long talons scored deep gouges in the packed sand. The purple dust continued to spew from the rent Moichi had made in its head. It writhed on the ground, in agony, jaws working spastically. Its eyes, four of them dark and ruined, stared up at Moichi.

'So, Jailor, it comes to this. In order to catch Dujuk'kan, I must kill you.'

'Not my wish,' the beast said, 'but my nature.'

Moichi nodded. 'Unfortunately, I understand.'

The mandibles, covered with purple dust, leaked white viscous fluid. 'Understand nothing you. Pain am I. Born into misery, asked not for this I. How often wished I for death but Bjork's magic would not let me. Dujuk'kan must be guarded.'

'But now that he has escaped you are vulnerable?' Moichi said pressing down with the blade. 'Is that what you are saying?'

The jaws worked, but no sound came out. A moment later, they were filled with purple dust.

'Don't die yet, Jailor,' Moichi said. He withdrew the dirk,

slashed again at the strands with the same result as before. 'Tell me how to get past this damnable web you have spun. Tell me!'

'Want to know I,' Jailor said, his voice weak and half-strangled now, 'what makes this woman you and Dujuk'kan think of worth saving?'

'Chill take you, how do I get out of here?' Moichi thundered.

'What do if not tell you I? Kill I?' Jailor tried to laugh, but there was too much of his own substance choking his throat. The body gave a great shiver and the two working eyes bulged as if a great pressure were building up. 'That woman . . . you think of . . .' The voice was so soft Moichi had to push against the web to hear it. 'At my release from bondage give you her I.'

'What do you . . . ?' The light was dying in its eyes. A musty smell filled the grotto. And then into Moichi's mind popped Aufeya. She was strapped across the back of a co'chyn that was speeding across the Mu'ad beneath Dujuk'kan's black whip. He knew it was Aufeya as one identifies people in a dream – by the feel of her. But how could this be his Aufeya? For the woman in his mind had the head and neck of a snowy ibis.

Moichi blinked and the vision was gone. He looked down at Jailor who was stone dead. He had kept his promise to Moichi – or was he playing some cruel joke? Had the vision been an image of reality? If so how had Dujuk'kan come upon a saddled co'chyn, and how had he altered Aufeya?

Moichi realized that neither of these questions would matter a whit if he could not break free of Jailor's web. How was he going to . . . ?

And then he noticed that down low one strand had been sliced in two and had remained cut. What had been able to do that? And then he saw: Jailor's own talon!

Quickly, Moichi bent down and, using his dirk, carved

off a foot. He brought it back through one of the larger spaces between the strands and, reversing it, began slicing through the web with a wickedly curved talon.

He ducked through the circular hole he had made and stepped over the hideous beast's carcass. Then, he turned back, hunkered down next to it. Somehow, Jailor seemed more pitiable than ugly now. That odd animosity had passed and in its place was a kind of gratitude at being human, prey to all the joys and sorrows attendant on the condition.

'Sleep well, Jailor,' Moichi said, rising. 'It seems to me you've earned it.'

The warren of tunnels was riddled with the kind of vertical chimney Moichi and Dujuk'kan had used on the way down to what was supposed to have been Jailor's stasis chamber. These, Moichi worked out, were short-cuts Jailor had carved out of the Mu'ad's sandbed in order to better keep an eye on its charge.

He was near exhaustion and racked by dehydration by the time he came upon one that provided a surprising way up – and the answer to the question of how Dujuk'kan had managed to escape.

The clever Adenese had sunk chunks of the metal ore that ran in veins throughout much of the tunnels, making a series of foot- and hand-holds in the chimney. He looked up seeing, far away, a tiny oval of clear blue. Sky! As dizzy with relief as with exhaustion, Moichi began his long ascent.

He had to stop many times, as a blackness that swam at the periphery of his vision threatened to overwhelm him. Increasingly, he crouched against the side of the chimney, shivering as if with the ague, his clawed finger-tips digging frantically into the packed sand to stop from toppling backward into extinction. He knew this was dangerous, that he must continue upward at even the slowest pace, that the longer he kept motionless the more difficult it would be to get going again, both physically and mentally. His muscles were cramping and he was losing strength exponentially as he ascended.

At first, the smell of the fresh air quickening all around him was enough to keep him at it, but when that proved insufficient he set small goals for himself. He thought of Aufeya, and the vision the Jailor had provided for him of her strapped to a co'chyn ridden by Dujuk'kan on the way to Mas'jahan. Then, when he had reached his goal, he turned his mind to Sanda, and the stream of dreams or, alternatively, presentiments he had had in the Mu'ad when she came to him. He recited from memory the enigmatic words she had spoken. *Seek out the bear in the stone,* she had chanted. *Not to possess but to be possessed.* He pondered the riddle for some time until the image of his ravaged sister would not be denied and he heard again her heartfelt plea: *Save me!* From what? What had the Makkon done to her soul at the moment of her death? During the Kai-feng he had heard outlandish stories about the Makkon's predilection for drinking the souls from the eyes of their victims, but he had dismissed such whispered stories as psychological propaganda sown by the forces of Chaos to dishearten their enemy.

Save me!

Was Sanda – or some part of her essence – somehow still alive?

Reaching his next goal, he turned his thoughts to the tongueless Makkon. What had happened to it? Who or what had made it mute? Who had power enough besides the Dai-San? Moichi knew of no one else. While trapped in Jailor's lair he had lost all scent of the thing, and now he wondered whether he would be able to pick it up. Didn't such things have a specific afterlife? His experience in tracking both man and beast told him that there was. But the Makkon was not of this world, and perhaps different laws applied to it.

Reaching his goal, he crouched panting, on the outcrop of metal ore. Because of Dujuk'kan's girth and weight these were quite generous by Moichi's standards so that he was able to get both feet on at once. However, he was so near total exhaustion that his muscles jumped and shuddered so that he shook almost uncontrollably. He closed his eyes for a moment, but that was a mistake as he almost toppled off his perch. To distract himself, he looked upward and was immediately cheered by the size of the oval of blue sky. He was almost there!

But, oh, it was hard to raise himself off his haunches, and when he reached up toward the next outcrop pain streaked through his left hamstring, making him pant out loud. He put his forehead against the rough sand wall and massaged the muscle until the agony was reduced to a deep ache. He continued upward, his nails torn, his fingers bloody, half-unconscious, continuing now by sheer effort of will. But when he reached the next – the penultimate chunk of ore – his left leg gave out and he slipped off his perch.

He caught himself, held on by his linked fingers, his body swinging precariously over an abyss he had overtly refused to acknowledge. Painfully and laboriously he levered himself up onto the perch then, without stopping, climbed onto the next one. Only one more to go.

But now he became aware of a soft ululation. As the echo filtered down from the opening above his head, his blood turned to ice. He knew that eerie, almost bestial, sound from his childhood. Duk Fadat. A sandstorm was brewing in the Mu'ad. Moichi wondered whether he was safer here at the edge of the Jailor's world than up there where the wind-whipped sand could flay the d'alb and skin off a man.

Then, with a whoosh, a great swirl of sand spilled through the opening, nearly detaching him from the outcrop and he knew he had to take his chances in the Duk Fadat. It was certain death to stay in the chimney; it was not a question of if but of when some gust of blasted sand would take him down.

He stretched upward, gaining purchase with his elbows, since the shifting sand outside the mouth of the chimney would provide no certain ground for his fingers. With a mixture of a groan and a gasp, he drew his torso, then his legs, up and out of the chimney. He was free at last, but into what nightmare world had he been thrust?

Tokagé, reanimated, wanted to break Chiisai's neck.

'She is the Kunshin's daughter,' he said in a curious metallic rumble like dangerously nearby thunder. 'She should be dead.' It seemed to emanate not from the voice box of his diaphragm but from some distant and unrecognizable shore, some pale land beyond Chiisai's imagining. She looked at Kaijikan – for she had no doubt now that this ethereal woman was the legendary Keeper of Souls – for deliverance. Strange thing! She knew she would get none from Tokagé.

'It is because she is the Kunshin's daughter that we will keep her alive,' Kaijikan said reasonably. 'She is far more valuable to us as a means of extortion.'

'I say extortion be damned,' Tokagé said, tightening his grip of Chiisai and enjoying it. 'The wreckage of this body flung down at the Kunshin's doorstep will strike terror into every Bujun warrior's heart.'

Kaijikan seemed not to exert herself at all as she came across the solarium to stand a hand's span from the huge and intimidating figure. As she did so, she appeared to become taller so that she was now the equal of his extraordinary height.

'But you know so little about the Bujun heart,' she said. The rebuke was like a slap across his great square face and his onyx eyes glittered in anger. Noting this, she said, 'Why do you think I had you reanimated here in Ama-no-mori? Why do you think I endured years of squalid life in this putrid swamp? Why I slunk undetected into this island Kunshindom in the first place? To complete your education. You will never rule this world until you learn to master the secrets of the Bujun heart, for the Bujun are the protectors of this world. It was their magic that created the Dai-San, your arch-nemesis.'

The mention of the Sunset Warrior's name stung him deeply. Chiisai felt his muscles twitch in involuntary spasm, heard the horrific sound of his gray tombstone teeth grinding together.

Kaijikan held out her hand. 'Now, give her over to me, Tokagé. I know how to use her best.'

'Tell me,' he said, his eyes canny slits. 'Then you can have her.'

For a long moment, Chiisai listened to the silence that had sprung up between them because it was an unquiet silence, one rife with emotional sparks. If not quite a full-blown contest of wills, she recognized in the sizzling tension a psychological maneuvering unusual in allies. It was a matter of power, of course. Both were used to absolute obedience and one would have to give way each time a decision was made.

'I had a sister once,' Kaijikan said. 'A twin, my mother once told me, though I could never see the resemblance.' She squared her shoulders but, curiously, Chiisai could detect no sign in her that she had ceded power to him. 'My sister was a mute from birth. She was very smart, very clever, but her muteness was her weakness and it proved her undoing. As a young warlord the Kunshin took a fancy to her and took her as his concubine. He used her when it was his will and it was gratifying to him that at other times she could not use her voice to complain or to ask for favors, for my sister was too ashamed of her disability to use writing as a substitute.' She stared unblinkingly at Tokagé. 'I do not know whether you will understand this, but the emotions on her face were her sole form of communication. The future Kunshin had neither the time nor, apparently, the inclination for emotion. He was driven by lust: power and hormones were his sustenance and the devil take those who interfered with his unholy feedings.

'One night, my sister got in his way. She was frightened in one way or another most of the time she was with him. My sister was used to fear and she could manage it, but when she became lonely for her family she was inconsolable. And when she refused to perform when her warlord demanded it, he had her beheaded.' Her eyes, which had been locked on Tokagé's, swung abruptly to Chiisai. 'This is your father I am speaking of, my dear, so my advice is for you to pay close attention.'

'It is a story, that is all,' Chiisai said. 'An uncorroborated story.'

A flicker of raw emotion passed across Kaijikan's usually imperturbable countenance. 'Are you foolish enough to think the Kunshin a saint, then?' she said.

'No, he is but a man,' Chiisai said. 'But a good man for all that.'

'*Good,*' Tokagé spat, as if it were a filthy expletive.

Kaijikan smiled, having found common ground. 'Good and evil are not immutable, my dear. They are not laws of nature, but concepts dreamed up by mankind. How typically naive of you to cling to notions without true meaning.'

'You are wrong,' Chiisai said hotly. 'Morality *is* as immutable as any law – as gravity.'

'Really?' Kaijikan cocked her head and, with a complex weaving of her hand, began to rise off the floor. '*Nothing* is immutable, not gravity, not death. And here with your own eyes you witness the proof.'

Chiisai said nothing. What *could* she say? With a grunt, Tokagé flung her away from him and she was caught by silken fingers, preternaturally long, that closed around her slender wrists.

'You are a warrior, and I admire that,' Kaijikan said. 'Be assured that when you die – and you *will* die, my dear – it will not be a warrior's death. That would bring a modicum of solace to your father and I cannot have that. I have waited a long time for this moment. My sister's soul cries out for vengeance, and vengeance she shall have.'

Moichi was too hungry to sleep. As he crouched, slumped over, breathing hard, he saw an iridescent blue-black shape in the lee of a dune. Above it, great plumes of sand were gyring like Catechist dervishes, the fanatic sect who had carved the Mas'jahan out of the unforgiving bones and flesh of the Mu'ad.

Moichi crawled painfully toward the shape. As he did so, his tongue licked lips that were cracked and dry, bleeding now as the sand scoured them. He crawled gratefully into the lee of the dune and, ducking his head below the shrouds of sand, could not believe his luck. It was the blood-condor the Fe'edjinn had shot down. It was still fresh. How long had he been in the Jailor's enchanted lair? He had no way of knowing, but this evidence indicated it had been a shorter time than he had imagined.

He pulled the arrow from its breast. The desert sun had already half-baked it and, though Iskamen law forbade the eating of carrion predators, he tore into its flesh with his teeth, spitting out some of the feathers, swallowing others. The taste of food in his mouth overshadowed the pain in his raw lips as he gnawed at the bloody meat, sinew and bones. He sucked the blood out of those parts he did not eat, then cracked the bones, digging out the rich marrow. Finished with his meal, he threw what remained of the carcass into the wind. Then, abruptly, he lay back in the dune. His starved stomach, unused to food, let alone half-raw blood-condor, threatened to revolt on him. He gagged once, then willed his stomach into quiescence. He could not afford to vomit up the only thing that would keep him alive.

He turned over and, closing his eyes, plunged into a slumber so profound that only the scent of the Makkon could have driven him awake.

Later he started awake. In that instant between sleep and consciousness he thought the Makkon was here. His hand pulled free a dirk, then he snapped fully awake and, looking about him, laughed mirthlessly. Even the unearthly Makkon would think twice about venturing into the Mu'ad during Duk Fadat.

He was about to crawl along the lee of the dune when he saw a shape emerging over the crest and begin a remarkably steady descent out of the gusting wind and sand.

A co'chyn!

And, upon further inspection, he discovered that it wasn't a wild one, but one of the group on which he had come into the Mu'ad. How had it escaped the sand whirlpool? Then he remembered the vision Jailor had set in his mind of Dujuk'kan and Aufeya on a co'chyn. His heart leapt. As he took hold of the co'chyn's reins he was more inclined to accept the vision as the truth, for this was Tamuk's mount. He recognized the weapons-laden saddlebags. A shame it was not one of the others that held their supply of food and water. He had just feasted on the blood-condor but that sustenance would last no more than

127

two days before his body required more. Otherwise, lassitude, extreme muscle weakness, dehydration and death would be his fate.

He patted the co'chyn's neck, stroked its trunk as he swung up onto its back. He pulled on the reins and its head swung around, dipping once before it took off, loping from dune to dune, always in the lee, exposing itself to the swirling sand as briefly as it could. Still, those bursts were painful, like a severe lashing with a multi-tailed whip. Moichi knew from the sun which direction to head in, and he kept it always over his left shoulder. Mas'jahan was in the extreme north-western section of the Mu'ad, in a wide sandstone waad that bordered a desolate and uninhabitable section of Aden.

The Catechists were strict political neutralists, and had remained aloof from overtures of an alliance with either the Adenese or the Iskamen. Even the Adenese Al Rafaar were leery of inciting these brutal and utterly fearless warrior-zealots. The Catechist dervishes believed in a living god who chose to walk among them anonymously. Their search for him was constant and eternal because to look upon his face meant beatification, a shedding of the mortal coil and an end to all suffering. They were devout mystics about whom other races knew little, yet because they condoned slave trading and sexual promiscuity – their peculiar religious rites had a distinct sexual edge – Mas'jahan drew a steady stream of intrepid and evil-minded infidels. Because they were rabid proselytizers the Catechists accepted – even, stories insisted, encouraged – such travelers. As far as they were concerned every evil-minded criminal they came in contact with was a potential acolyte. And, by all accounts, they were surprisingly successful in their conversions.

Moichi, hunched over the saddle in a combination of exhaustion and self-preservation, could scent the Makkon in his mind. Beyond his left shoulder, the slowly setting sun was largely obscured now by the sand devils sent aloft by the Duk Fadat. He had consulted Tamuk's maps, still rolled securely in one saddlebag, and knew that the oasis the Jailor inhaled was two-thirds of the way toward the settlement to which Hamaan had gone to bring Sanda's husband Yesquz back to Ala'arat. As it happened, this settlement was not far from Mas'jahan, but Moichi knew that in Duk Fadat with no food or water the distance might as well be that of the ocean that separated Iskael from the continent of man.

He had been elated to find the co'chyn alive but now this might prove to be a cruel jest – merely a prolongation of misery and slow death.

Time was his most precious commodity and he determined to make the most of it. Accordingly, he pressed the co'chyn to its limits and past it as he headed ever northwest. The pace he chose was not the swiftest, for the intensifying Duk Fadat obliged him to make less frequent directional sightings than he was comfortable with. He resisted the temptation to spur his mount on faster for he knew well the worst fate that could befall him was to become lost, only to find that he had chased his co'chyn's tail in a circle for days. Sun and stars were only visible sporadically through the thickening hail of sand and, as the days progressed, they became ever more faint, until at last he could have believed he was back in Jailor's underground lair.

Still, he urged his mount on a steady pace day and night. He fell asleep, swaying, slumped over his saddle, remaining there only because he tied his wrists tightly to the pommel with the reins. Once, his co'chyn found water, using its trunk to burrow in the sand where a patch of dune grass clung precariously, but Moichi was unable to find it with fingers and dirk.

129

He pushed on, dehydration draining him of energy and, finally, of consciousness. He awoke, choking on sand and knew that if his journey continued in this manner he would perish in less than a day.

With the utmost reluctance, he drew his dirk and slew his mount with a swift, merciful slash across its throat. He drank its blood but that merely made him more thirsty, so sprawled in the lee of a dune, half-covered in cascading sand, he carefully made an incision along the skin of its underside. He slid out the three ovals of its stomachs, opened the third one and drank the fluid inside. He made a bladder of the second one, also filled with precious fluid, then set about butchering the beast as best he could.

He ate slowly, mindful of his last meal. After he had eaten his fill, he threw out everything in Tamuk's saddle-bags, loaded one side with the bladder, the other with choice slabs of co'chyn meat wrapped in skin. He slapped it over his shoulder and continued his trek northwestward. The spoor of the Makkon was stronger in his mind and this drove him on, past even his tolerance for pain and fatigue.

Pain-racked days passed and he pressed on, into the Mu'ad, into the teeth of the Duk Fadat, measuring out rations of water and meat until both were gone. Still, he put one unsteady foot in front of another, his eyes all but plastered shut against the stinging sand.

But, at length, even his mind and iron will gave out and he collapsed upon the breast of the Mu'ad. Soon, in the height of the Duk Fadat, his form was layered with whispering sand until only a creature indigenous to the vast, shifting wasteland would recognize the cairn upon the dune as something alive.

EIGHT

RED VEIL

One bright spark in the darkness danced, its gyrations expanding into a recognizable pattern that was speech:

'The Black Angel is shut away. Evil is as evil does. Darkness is as Darkness will. The living testament of Zarathus, of He Who Walks Alone, shall be done.'

Scrims of sand resolved themselves into swirling arcs of brightly patterned fabrics. Blue, green, yellow, the turquoise of a bay, the jade of a storm-tossed ocean, the amber of the sea at sunset, all these shades and more spun by him like wheels on fantastic vehicles.

He opened eyes which seemed to him to have been glued shut for weeks and saw the robes and skirts billowing and whirling past him. At once, he grew dizzy and he shifted his gaze overhead. He was in an enormous tent of some thick natural muslin. Tentpoles of polished wood rose up like a copse of trees wherever he looked. He became aware of odors next: the strong scents of broiling meat and stewing fruit, rich and astringent all at once. Now and again, through these mouth-watering smells came the acrid stench of unwashed bodies.

Moichi closed his eyes. Perhaps he was dreaming. Perhaps he was dead, having been buried in the Duk Fadat and this was some afterlife the Iskamen had not imagined. Then the swirl of color, motion and fabric became recognizable for what they were: dancing. He was among the Catechist dervishes.

He groaned a little as he tried to rise up from the pallet of soft goatskins upon which he lay and immediately a heavy woman was at his side, squatting, smiling down at him benevolently. She looked oddly familiar despite the fact that he had never before met a Catechist. She was quite beautiful.

'You have healed magnificently,' she said in a heavily accented voice that was nonetheless pleasant. 'Your warrior spirit has impressed the Fianarantsoa.'

'The what?' he managed through cracked lips.

She laughed, her jowls shaking, her long earrings swinging, her myriad bracelets clacking together. Her bosom heaved with her laughter. 'The elders, dear one. The religious teachers. The word, literally translated, means seeker after truth.' Her clear blue eyes regarded him with some mirth. 'Yes, you are truly back from the dead. You were but a burial mound in the Duk Fadat when we found you.'

Moichi licked his lips and she gave him liquid to drink from a hollow gourd. It was sweet and citrusy and he drank it all down.

'What were you doing out in this weather?' he asked, gingerly feeling his lips with his fingertips.

'Keep them clean,' she said, taking his hand in hers. 'They were infected, but the salve I have been using is taking care of that.'

'My name is Moichi Annai-Nin,' he said.

'And mine is Ambositra. I am a healer.'

Moichi struggled to sit up, grateful that she made no move to help him. 'I must thank you for your kindness. I would be dead without you and your people. But what *were* you doing out in the Duk Fadat?'

'Why, looking for you, dear one. The dervishes dance

in order to follow Zarathus's living testament and we divined your presence in the Mu'ad.' She smiled. 'We found the saddlebags with the remnants of the co'chyn's innards. You are an ingenious man.'

'All my ingenuity would not have stopped me from dying.' Moichi held his head. 'Where am I? In Mas'jahan?'

Ambositra shook her head. 'Still the desert. But our band is on its way there. We will reach the citadel tomorrow evening.'

Moichi stared at the dervishes, whirling and spinning, faster and faster in concert to an inner rhythm old as time.

'They are synchronizing themselves to the cosmic pulse of Zarathus.'

'Entering into a mystic state,' Moichi said, fascinated.

'Exactly. In this way they can hear the words of his living testament and carry them out.'

Was it his imagination or did he feel a kind of heavy pulse in the air timed with the dervishes' movements? He was very conscious of Ambositra's proximity: her heat, the scents of her that were not all displeasing. She jangled as she moved closer, hunkering next to him. She leaned over so that her sun-streaked hair brushed his cheek. 'I am your nurse, dear one. I have seen your body. I have put my hands upon it, lovingly healing your flayed flesh.' He saw her smile broaden and she squeezed his arm. 'While the Fianarantsoa were impressed with your spirit I was impressed with your warrior's body.'

'Ambositra,' he said softly, 'I am grateful to you for all you have done, but . . .'

She cast down her eyes. 'It is my size. Like most infidels you find me too fat, too gross.'

'On the contrary, I find you desirable, but the truth is my heart belongs to a woman who has been abducted by a criminal, an Adenese named Dujuk'kan. I was told he was headed to Mas'jahan. A terrible murderous beast called a Makkon is also on its way there – I can tell from its spoor.' He looked at her. 'Now that I am feeling better I would speak to the members of the Fianarantsoa to determine if they know anything of the criminal or the beast.'

'In time,' Ambositra said gently. 'The elders dance now, and later they will rest. Tomorrow morning, before we set out for Mas'jahan, I will arrange an interview.' She turned, brought bowls into his lap. 'Now you must eat. Build up your strength for the journey tomorrow. We travel very fast.' She rose with a soft jangling of jewelry. 'When it is time for sleep I will return to check your wounds.'

It was quiet and deserted by the time he saw her re-enter the tent. He had been staring at the thousands of footprints left in the sand by the dervishes. Like clouds, he thought he could make out the shapes of fantastic buildings and beasts, one flowing into another. All the gourd bowls had been scrubbed with sand and packed away in preparation for the morning's journey. The tent was filled with shifting shadows, the lone light source a torch that had been left flickering near the tent flap. He could hear the occasional snort and pawing of the band's co'chyn that had been tethered somewhere outside. And, once or twice, he heard soft voices as the guards passed each other. He had had a glimpse of the Catechist weapons: wicked double-bladed push-daggers which, when held properly, were magnificent for hand-to-hand combat. The blades seemed to emanate from between the second and third fingers so that the entire force of wrist, arm and shoulder could be brought to bear in the strike. He assumed they possessed long-range weapons as well.

'How do you feel?' Ambositra asked as she knelt beside him. 'I thought you would be drowsing by now.'

'I am tired but sleep will not come,' Moichi admitted. He winced slightly as she peeled bandages off still tender skin. The Duk Fadat had done an admirable job in almost flaying him alive, but whatever was in the salve she was applying was healing him with astonishing speed. 'I am anxious to continue my search.'

'You are healing more quickly than I had anticipated.' Her clear blue eyes met his and again he was struck by a profound sense of déjà vu. Had he met this woman before? Impossible, and yet . . .

Ambositra smiled. 'I am happy you are attracted to me despite my size.' She wrapped fresh bandages around his wounds. 'It proves a point I have been longing to make.'

Moichi looked at her. 'And what is that?'

He gasped, his heart turning over heavily as he saw the outline of her body flicker like the flame of the torch, then begin to melt like hot wax. And as it did so, her face began to change ever so subtly. Only the eyes remained constant, regarding him covetously through this transformation.

And when it was over, he understood everything: Aufeya's strange behavior, her remarking on the moon, her knowledge of the Mu'ad, her use of the phrase *The God of the Iskamen – How I envy you that*. Everything. His mind was whirling with ten thousand questions, but only one escaped his lips.

'Where is she?' His voice was dry and harsh.

'Aufeya, dear one?' the sorceress Sardonyx said softly. She moistened her lips. 'She never came with us on our journey to Iskael. It was always me.'

'God of my fathers!' he cried in anguish. 'How could I have been so duped?'

'You weren't duped, dear one.'

'Stop calling me that!' he shouted so violently that the tent flap parted and a guard peered in.

Sardonyx, in her guise as the Catechist Ambositra, put her finger to her lips. 'It is his wounds,' she said. 'They pain him.'

When the guard nodded and disappeared, she returned

135

to her form as Sardonyx. She appeared as she had the first time he had encountered her in her castle in the land of the Opal Moon, all glittering metallic skin, heavy-lidded eyes, hair of twisted platinum strands. She lay down beside him, stroked his chest softly. 'I lied a little when I told you that Zarathus had revealed your existence to the dervishes. I put you in their minds while they danced. How they interpreted the vision was up to them.' Her stroking continued. 'I couldn't let you die, dear one.'

'Why not?'

'Because you love me. You are the only one who ever has.'

'You are out of your mind.'

'Am I? Who was it you made love to all across the ocean?'

'It was Aufeya, chill take you! I thought –'

'That I was your betrothed? Truthfully? But wasn't there something in the back of your mind, some sure knowledge you chose to ignore?'

'No, I–'

'And in Ala'arat? Tell me you did not suspect. Tell me the doubt did not come crowding home. No, no, dear one, you ignored them all because . . . Because you loved me from the moment we first met.'

'I admit I was intrigued, like a moth to a flame, but–'

'Yes, you were all that, but there was something more. I felt it and so did you.'

He felt rage trembling his muscles, but he lay back, staring at the star-shaped top of the tent. 'How did you escape from Dujuk'kan?'

'He came upon some of his former cronies – flesh peddlers unafraid of the Duk Fadat. While they sat at camp eating, drinking and fornicating I slipped away. The fat Adenese was lucky. Were he alone I would have turned him into a co'chyn so I could ride him into Mas'jahan.'

It was an amusing thought but Moichi was in no mood for wit or levity. 'Tell me about Aufeya. Is she alive?'

'The story is complex and goes far back in time.'

'I will have no more of your lies, Sardonyx.'

'No lies,' she said softly. 'I promise.'

He rose up on one elbow. 'What is the worth of the promise of a pirate, a freebooter and a murderess?'

'Perhaps we should both stop lying to one another.'

'This isn't about me,' he hissed, doubly angry at her cleverness. 'It's about you!'

She stared at him for some time, her clear blue eyes searching every millimeter of his face as if trying to memorize a long-cherished possession. 'What would you demand as proof?'

'I want the truth,' Moichi said firmly. 'I want to know what you really look like. No more masks, animations or transformations. Forget the sorceress.'

'You once called me a prestidigitator, a highly accomplished illusionist. Do you believe that now?'

He ignored that. 'Show me the woman.'

'I don't know.' She looked away for a moment. 'She has been in hiding for so long even I have forgotten what she looks like.'

'No you haven't,' Moichi said. 'Not by a long shot.'

'I am afraid.'

He said nothing.

'You *do* love me, don't you. Just a little bit.'

Moichi, ready with a sharp rebuke, found that he did not want to look inside himself, and in a sense that was answer enough.

Her head bent so that the platinum strands fell across her face. Then they began to run together, pulsing and shifting, flowing like a stream gathering speed as it runs downhill. Her body shimmered, becoming less slender than it had been but not as heavy as it had been when she was

Ambositra. The metallic arms and legs became flesh and blood, garbed in ebon leggings, suede waistcoat over a silk shirt open at the collar. The outfit accentuated the swell of her full breasts while hiding the flare of her hips, the roundness of her belly. The hollow of her throat was filled with an oval star sapphire that emitted an eerie, milky light. Her hair was the color of cinnamon, streaked by the sun. She wore it as short as a man. And when she lifted her head he saw revealed, at last, the woman Sardonyx.

She had been born beautiful, with a heart-shaped face, finely sculpted cheekbones, a strong nose and wide full lips, but then life had intervened. There was a scar running down the left side of her face from just beneath one blue eye to the point of her chin. It had been a deep cut; worse, it had not been taken care of and so had healed badly.

'So now you know.' There was a kind of defiance in her voice, born of vulnerability. 'And now you will never acknowledge your love for me. The truth!' She almost spat out the words. 'How I despise the truth. I have lost you for ever.'

He lay for a long time, staring at her face which she thought of as ruined. It was like looking at a lifetime, the ebb and flow of each year etched upon her countenance, the sorrow and the suffering; he could not deny recognizing them there. She reminded him of Licah, the woman written of in the Tablets of the Iskamen, who had borne the scorn of her people for her faith in God. They had taken her children from her, had stoned her unto death, but still she would not renounce her faith in God. And God had lifted her up, had healed all her wounds, had restored to her her children, and had taken her to dwell on the wooded slopes of the Mountain Sin'hai, where she lived for 999 years. And on the eve of her thousandth year God had summoned her to the summit, welcoming her into His House.

But then Moichi's heart hardened. 'She is dead, isn't she?' he said, already knowing the answer in his heart. 'Aufeya–'

'Yes. Dead like Tsuki, her bitch mother.'

Reality fell upon him like snow upon the icy upper reaches of the Mountain Sin'hai. But, surprisingly, he was beyond anguish, beyond even tears. He felt nothing at all.

'You wished for the truth,' Sardonyx said, her warm hand still upon him, 'so now you will have it. But the Catechists have a saying, "Beware for what you wish because one day you will be delivered unto it."'

She watched the rise and fall of his chest and, with it, the sheath of years peeled away until she was very young again, the unmarked girl who had been sold into slavery by her destitute and crippled mother, the girl who had murdered her master and had then been thrown into an Adenese jail for the crime of wanting to be free of abuse, the girl who had used her primary assets – her face and her body – to bribe her way to freedom.

'I left Aden as quickly as I was able,' she said. 'I had no clear idea of where to go or what I would do. I only knew that I had to get away from Aden and that I wanted never to return.

'Inevitably, I found myself in the Mu'ad. But I was in luck. I stumbled into a caravan of spice traders bound for Mas'jahan. Once there, I predictably came under the influence of the Catechist religion. I was drawn by the mysticism; I had no center, no sense of life or, more importantly, of myself. But quite soon I became skeptical of their main tenet: that God was living among them, speaking in tongues only the Fianarantsoa could hear and interpret. The ecstatic state of dervishing is indisputable – the feeling, believe me, is supremely exquisite – but I, at least, felt no closer to God when I danced, and within a year I had drifted from the faith.'

As she spoke, Moichi could see her words as if they were pictures moving in the air, montages of her early life into which he was now drawn as inextricably as any of the personages she was describing.

'One member of the Fianarantsoa liked me especially. Vato-mandry. It was he who supervised my training, who danced with me in order not to lose me. But, though he was as much a fanatic proselytizer as the others, he was the only one who treated me as someone, not just another piece of meat for the Catechists to mold. Vato-mandry was an ancient man with a long, bearded face and eyes that had surely glimpsed God. He offered to take me into his household, to be made one of his daughters, and had I accepted I have little doubt that my faith would have been restored. No matter. I declined. Curiously, he seemed to understand.

' "God comes to us in His own time," he told me. "Your time has yet to come. You *will* return to us, of that I have no doubt." And, in a sense, he was right because here I am.'

She was so still for some time that Moichi glanced over at her. Then she spoke again and the images swam before his eyes.

'Vato-mandry took me to meet a man. "Since your path leads you to the secular world I must ensure that it starts auspiciously." The man was a trader, only temporarily in Mas'jahan. In fact, I soon learned that he was scheduled to depart the next morning. Vato-mandry had arranged for him to transport me through the Mu'ad and, furthermore, for me to become his apprentice.

'This man was well-known in Mas'jahan, and to Vato-mandry in particular. And, with the perfect vision that comes with hindsight, I believe that everything that subsequently transpired was, in some way, anticipated by him. You see, it is my belief that Vato-mandry wanted me to learn all the lessons of the secular world, for he believed with all his heart and soul that I belonged to the Catechists. He often spoke of the possibility of my becoming the first female member of the Fianarantsoa. And when even that potent inducement would not keep me at his side, he threw me at once and totally to the wolves.'

Through the bridge of her hand on his chest Moichi became aware of a tension filling her and he concentrated more fully on the images.

'He was a tall, handsome man with clear, ruddy skin, green eyes and blond hair. It did not take me long to discover that he was a brilliant trader. His skill at negotiation, at obfuscation and deceit were mind-opening to me. To say that I was a quick study would be to understate the case. He was astonished at how completely I grasped the psychology of the con. People are gullible. They are your most potent ally simply because they want to believe and, curiously, the more outlandish the lie you spin, the greater the gain for them, the more eager they are to put themselves in your hands.

'I found in the con what I believed then was the same form of ecstatic liberation I had discovered with the dervishes. But I was young and foolish and wrong. The truth was, I was addicted to the adrenaline rush.

'As we traveled from province to province, from land to land, so I grew in skill and cunning. And as I made more and more money for this trader, he began to look at me differently. Utterly predictable. I went from being his paid-for pupil to his apprentice to his co-conspirator to, finally, his equal. By that time we were nearing his home and I noticed a curious change in him. The closer we drew to our destination the more ill at ease he became. It was as if he had lost all sense of home; that he cared only for being in distant lands, plying his trade with the greatest of skill – as if the game, of which he was a grandmaster, was all that mattered to him.

141

'And now he had created someone who was his equal. Again, with the benefit of hindsight, I can see that he was at once intimidated and impassioned. He wanted me – badly. At first, I would awake in the middle of the night to find him standing over me, staring at me. When I asked him what was the matter he turned away mutely and, naively, I assumed that so close to home he was missing his wife. This went on for three nights. Then I found him in my bed. I have a history of using my body and, further-more, I am a highly sexed creature. He was not only hand-some but charismatic. He had also been my teacher, had become my mentor and best friend. We had shared inti-macies in the heat of battle – and dangers, surely, from authorities who had sought to stop and imprison us had they ever caught us.

'It was a mistake to bed him. I think even then I under-stood that somewhere deep inside me. But the lure was too great. There were too many reasons for us to couple, and only one to abstain, and that got lost in the whirlpool of our lust.

'We enjoyed each other in that manner for four days and, during that time, made no attempt to travel further toward his home. By then, of course, it was too late. He told me what should have been obvious to me all along, that he no longer thought of home, that since meeting me all he wanted was for us to be together. Our couplings had been wonderful, even spectacular at times, but that was all they were, couplings. I was not in love with this man and I had no intention of spending the rest of my life with him. With the directness of youth I told him so.

'He tried to reason with me, talking of the fortune we would amass together, the life we could live as one. When that didn't work, he tried to have sex with me, as if that sweet oblivion could wipe out reality. Angrily, I pushed him off me. He fell to his knees and, pressing his head into my lap, professed his undying love for me. A little afraid of his intensity, I wanted to hurt him. I told him I was sure he had said the same thing to his wife and now look what was happening. What was to stop a man like him from doing the same thing to me a year from now?

'He seemed to go mad. Straddling me, he hit me again and again and when I tried to claw his eyes out he hit me so hard I passed out. When I came to I found myself bound to stakes he had pounded into the ground. When I began to cry out he gagged me. Then he raped me, brutally and without mercy. Why was I so surprised? I had seen this side of him many times when we worked the con, I had even admired it, tried to emulate it to the best of my abilities. My one failure.

'How many times he raped me I cannot remember. I am sure I will never want to. And each time he was more brutal and uncaring. He did things to me . . . Perhaps these were things he had dreamed of doing for years, and now that he had his chance he held nothing back.

'In between, he got drunk, because he could not face the future, which he blamed entirely on me. I choose to think it was because he could not face what he had become. In time, he passed out so completely that I had time to work my way free of the bonds.

'I was weak with the obscenities he had forced on me, shaking with rage and terror. I stanched the blood as best I could. I ate a little food, vomited it up and tried again. When I could get some to stay down I dressed myself with shaking hands. Then I stood over him. I can recall the moment as if it happened yesterday. I wanted to kill him, I admit it. God knows I had killed before. But this was somehow different. This man had been like a father, raising me, so to speak, in my new life, teaching me everything I needed to survive. How could I murder him in cold blood even after what he had done to me? I thought of Vato-mandry and the Catechists, and the utter purity of their dervishes sang like a haunting melody in my head. I felt the pull of Mas'jahan and knew that, for the time being, at least, I had had my fill of the secular life. So I took some money – only what I had earned – and I left him there.'

Her tension had risen to such a pitch that Moichi could feel the vibrations emanating from her fingers. There was a heat like the Mu'ad at noon penetrating him from the center of her palm.

'I was only a day and a half away from him when I was picked up by a patrol. They asked me if I had been the trader's companion and by the manner of their questions I knew they knew. If I lied I knew it would go bad for me so I told the truth.

'They took me into the trader's hometown, through the crowded streets where I was gawked at as if I were a circus freak. I was expecting them to take me to prison, but instead I wound up at a sumptuous private house. They forced me to kneel in front of a beautiful woman, a green-eyed witch with hair of silver.'

Moichi took her hand in his as he sat up. 'What are you saying?'

'You know what I am saying,' she said softly.

'You were in the Daluzan capital of Corruña. This woman was Tsuki Seguillas y Oriwara. Her husband was the trader who took you in.'

'Yes.'

'Aufeya's parents. God of my fathers!' He ran a hand through his hair. 'But I was told the Senhor died in a duel.'

'That would be an altogether honorable death, would it not?'

'But–'

144

'You wanted the truth,' Sardonyx said. 'Now you must accept it. Sometimes we are better off–'

'No, no. I want to hear it all.'

Sardonyx nodded. 'As you wish.' She pushed him down. 'Now lie back so that the pictures can come to you clearly.'

When he had done as she bade, she continued:

'Senhora Seguillas y Oriwara wore a long brocaded dress the color of dried ox-blood, and across her face was the traditional Daluzan red veil of mourning. "Is this the bitch?" she said. "The animal who murdered my husband?"

' "It is, my lady," the captain of the guard replied with such conviction that I knew I had been tried and convicted without having stepped into a courtroom.

'I gasped when I heard that Narris Seguillas y Oriwara had been killed, and supposed he had been set upon by brigands seeing, in his drunken stupor, an easy mark. I wept for him, but Tsuki bent over and slapped my face so hard I was thrown upon the marble floor.

' "How dare you!" she cried, her voice shaking. "How dare you!"

'I told her that I did not kill her husband.

' "And I suppose you did not fornicate with him either!" She bent over me, her face twisted evilly. "Liar! You were observed! There are witnesses!"

' "No one could have seen me kill him because I did not," I protested.

' "The blood, Senhora," the captain said dutifully. "Look at her. She is covered with blood."

' "My husband's blood!"

' "No! It is mine! You don't know what he did to me. He–"

'But the captain bent over me, shoved a rag down my throat. "You will not defame Senhor Seguillas y Oriwara."

He turned his face up to Tsuki's. "Should I kill her now, Senhora, and be done with such filth?"

'"No," Aufeya's mother said. "I have a better idea." And commanding the captain to hand over his dirk, she took it in her hand as if she had been born to it. "Hold her down," she commanded.'

Sardonyx put her fingertips up to her scar, running them down its entire length from top to bottom, and Moichi could see the tip of the blade do its deft work.

'She was an expert on carving. She knew just how deep to go and where to mark me. Then, she commanded the captain to keep custody of me until I was healed of my own accord. On no account, she said, was I to be allowed medical attention. If the cut became infected, so be it. God would decide my fate.

'"If she lives, let her be scarred from this time forward," she said. "So that everyone she meets will know what she is and what she has done."'

Outside the Catechist tent, Moichi could hear the co'chyn, restless now for a time. Perhaps they were in need of a feeding. After a while they calmed down, and only the sound of the fitful wind, the last feeble gasps of the Duk Fadat, could be heard.

'Now you have squeezed me dry,' Sardonyx said, getting up. 'I hope you are satisfied.'

But she stopped as he reached up and took her hand. She responded as he pulled her down to him. 'Somewhere,' he whispered, 'there is an end to this story.'

'I did not kill Aufeya, if that is what you mean.'

'Right now I don't know what it is I mean.' He touched her shoulder. 'What happened to her? How did she die?'

'It happened on the mountainside when we fought for the Firemask – when you had it on, when you were closing the door between our world and the dimension of Chaos.

146

She slipped and fell. Even with all my magic I could not save her. Nothing could.'

'So it was you I had the idyll with all the way back to Corruña.'

'Yes. I became Aufeya because that was what I thought you wanted. And what I wanted was to be close to you, to be loved by you. But very quickly the lie began to pall. I did not want to be Aufeya; I did not want you loving her. I ached to be me. But I was trapped in her skin. And I was terrified of what you would do if you learned the truth. I resolved then never to let you know. I was willing to become another person if that meant you would be mine. Or so I thought.

'All across the ocean voyage to Iskael my own personality fought to be free, and each time it rose up you knew, even though you will never admit it. You knew I could not be Aufeya.'

Sardonyx was done now, but though her words had died, the ghosts of the images she had conjured from out of the past still floated in the shadows. In a way, she had done the impossible: she had caused time to reverse itself. She had, for a little while, called upon the great spiral of time to open its iris so that they could peer across the gulf of the years to what had been, and what very well might be again. He was all too aware of the painful repetition. Was what Narris Seguillas y Oriwara visited upon her different from what she had suffered at the hands of her former slave-master? He did not believe so, and yet she had chosen a different resolution the second time.

Moichi looked into her clear blue eyes and, in doing so, peered into his own heart. 'Yes,' he said. 'You are right in what you say. I fought you in every way I knew how.'

'Not only me,' she said. 'Yourself.'

He sat, simply breathing for a time, trying out the air

147

in this brave new world he was discovering. At last, he said, 'Will you tell me about the scar? Why do you still have it? Surely someone with your sorceress powers could excise it, restore yourself to the way you once were.'

'But I am no longer what I once was. I am something else now.'

'Is it a form of self-inflicted punishment, then?'

Sardonyx was quiet for some time and he found he had no desire to intrude because he felt that silence involved him.

'Once I was beautiful,' Sardonyx whispered. 'I knew it and everyone around me did, too. They acted appropriately. They reacted to my face and I learned to use my body to get what I wanted. But, you know what, I discovered those things weren't what I craved. And then I understood the inadvertent grace that the bitch of Corruña had bestowed upon me. She had set me free – free of the prison of my beauty. And so I became a freebooter – independent – a city-state unto myself in the land of the Opal Moon. And like a city-state that is required to fortify itself against unwanted intrusion I cloaked myself, masked and armored in my own enchantments until I could no longer remember the woman beneath. Then you came and I found that I was afraid of everything that lay beneath the masks.'

Her hand lifted to her face briefly, then fell to her side. 'I can, if you ask me, make it disappear.'

He knew just what she was asking of him, saw in her face how profoundly his wrong answer would cut her. He reached out, touched her cheek. 'The scar means a great deal to me,' he said, taking her in his arms. 'But not in the way you feared.'

And when his lips closed over hers, when he felt her hot tongue meeting his, he also felt her tears burning his skin like the images from her past, embers lifted by emotion, like time, swirling around and around in a spiral without end.

NINE

SATELLITE

There was a place in Ama-no-mori where, it was said, the wind made no sound as it blew through the cryptomeria. These sentinel pines climbed a steep and ugly scree overlooking the ocean. At the summit, a dizzying height, so the tales went, lay a forbidden cavern.

In ages long past, it was said, the ancient ancestors of the Bujun were in possession of weapons of mass destruction and in the cavern were buried the remnants that survived the holocaust that had consumed nine-tenths of mankind. This alone was incredible enough but the stories were more specific. It was said that the cavern was guarded by evil kami who glowed, emitting invisible energy that sapped human strength, a kind of vicious borer that, once in the body, ate it away from the inside out.

Chiisai ascended the sparsely vegetated scree in the company of the magus, Kaijikan, and the reanimated Tokagé. The terrifying warlord was in possession of her dai-katana, her longsword, along with her wakizashi, the long-bladed Bujun dirk.

It had taken them three days to get here, riding astride swift luma. Always, Chiisai was between her two captors, her luma tethered to their mounts, her wrists bound tightly and painfully behind her back, with no chance to escape.

The weather had turned bitter, with icy winds whipping

the mottled underbrush on the scree. As she scrambled along, Chiisai glanced up at the boughs of the cryptomeria swaying in the wind. No sound came from them and her heart was chilled.

Half-way up the scree it began to snow, drifting white skeins heading in from the ocean that had all but disappeared in the front. The brightness of the day devolved to an unnatural milky twilight. A conch shell foghorn sounded every now and again, melancholy and remote, increasing her sense of isolation. Tokagé had unbound Chiisai's wrists so she could climb without undue difficulty, but he had tethered her around the neck as he had her luma on the journey here. It took some time for full feeling to return to her numb fingers.

At length, they rested in the lee of a copse of cryptomeria. Chiisai had never been to a place that was so utterly still. The powdery snow filtered through the boughs and needles, piling up quickly. While she watched, Kaijikan fed Tokagé as if he were a child. What she put in his mouth Chiisai had no idea, lumps like coal from an inner pocket of her robe. He drank no water nor liquid of any kind. The living dead, for certain. She thought of Kaijikan's manservant, the hunchback Te-te, and wondered. She had been able to frighten him, but when she had pricked his throat with her blade what had run out? Surely not blood.

As for herself, Kaijikan ate nothing. Even the Dai-San ate, so what kind of creature was she? Even magi must ingest sustenance. Chiisai shoved the last of her fish paste and cold sticky rice into her mouth while she pondered the imponderable. Then they continued their assault up the scree.

Clearly, their goal was the summit, and Chiisai approached it with an increasing sense of trepidation and fear. What if the stories were true? Magi and the living dead might not be susceptible to evil kami and their invisible energy but humans surely would be.

They reached the summit at the height of the snowstorm. It was impossible to see much further than a pace in any direction. Still, Kaijikan did not hesitate, but guided them unerringly across rock-strewn ground bearded with pale and efflorescing mushrooms. These, when trod underfoot, gave off a sickly sweet odor not unlike the stench of death.

All too soon an unnatural darkness loomed before them, and Chiisai knew that they were approaching the cavern. It was blown out of a matte-black massif unlike anything she had ever seen. The rock seemed to have a powdery surface which clung like sweat to a warrior's muscles, and there was a peculiar odor which invaded her nostrils, making her throat and lungs prickle as if with ten thousand minute insects.

'I will not go in there,' Chiisai said, standing her ground. 'It is forbidden.'

Kaijikan turned and smiled. 'Are you afraid, Chiisai? But I will protect you. My magic is stronger than the ancients' mistakes.'

'So the stories are true. There are guardian kami in there.'

'Not a bit of it,' Kaijikan said. 'But beware, the earth of the cavern floor is highly toxic.'

'Earth poisoned by the ancients?'

'As inimical to life as anything on this planet can be,' Kaijikan affirmed with an almost erotic pleasure.

'I will not take another step,' Chiisai said, digging her heels into the ground.

'I am afraid that decision is not yours to make.' Kaijikan gestured at Tokagé, a runic swipe in the air, and he jerked upon her leash so hard that she was pulled off her feet. He advanced toward the cavern mouth and immediately she began to choke on the noose. He dragged her along the hard-packed earth, making a wide runnel in the drifting snow.

He stopped at the mouth of the cavern as if by some pre-arranged signal. Kaijikan knelt, one knee pressed painfully on Chiisai's chest. 'If you fail to obey me it will go ill with you, this I promise. And do not mistake me. Death will not be your punishment. No, for what I do to you, you will cry out for death, believing it your only salvation.' She gave a quick meaningful glance at the reanimated Tokagé. 'But I shall see that it never comes to you. To bring him back I required the Makkon's tongue. This is because he made a blood-pact with Chaos. But I will not have so much trouble with you. Remember Te-te?'

Pulling the noose from her throat, Chiisai looked at Tokagé through watering eyes. She could not imagine what it must be like to be undead and under Kaijikan's spell. The very thought unnerved her, and she nodded meekly.

'Excellent,' Kaijikan said, rising. She reached down and, with surprising strength, helped Chiisai to her feet. 'Once we are inside remember one thing: while you are with me you are perfectly safe. But if you are thinking of escaping, don't. Without my protection the poison buried in the soil will claim you.'

Chiisai nodded, her heart a block of ice.

The cavern had no smell at all, and Chiisai was aware of being neither cold nor warm. There were no sounds, none of the dripping or small crackings one associated with deep caverns. And this one was deep. It was as if they had entered a void, a zone of nothingness.

Kaijikan had lit the tarred top of a reed torch, and by its flickering light Chiisai stared with morbid fascination at the ground upon which they walked. It was dark, but here and there it appeared streaked with a substance that seemed whitely metallic, faintly glowing. Could this be the source of the invisible death?

Far back in the cavern a wall rose up. In the center of it was a jagged streak of black, as if some primitive tribesman had crudely rendered a bolt of lightning. But, on closer inspection, Chiisai saw that it was no daub of paint but a fissure in the living rock.

As she stood before the fissure, Tokagé came up behind her. She could feel his massive armor plate at her back, his curious breathing on the nape of her neck. Kaijikan took Chiisai's dai-katana from him and placed it in Chiisai's hand. At once, Tokagé's heavy mailed fist closed over hers.

'Now,' Kaijikan said, 'I want you to direct the blade into the fissure.'

'What is going to happen?' Chiisai asked.

'Do as I say, child.' The warning in her voice was unmistakable.

'No.'

Kaijikan sighed. 'This was unavoidable, I suppose. Such a strong will would be applauded in other circumstances.' She made a series of signs in the air and Chiisai screamed. There was a pain inside her so intense, so terrible there was no name for it. It was as if Kaijikan had opened her flesh and was scraping raw one nerve at a time.

Chiisai, her eyes streaming tears, would have fallen to her knees, save for Tokagé's hold on her. She could not breathe, could not think, and, yes, she wished for death, anything to escape the unendurable pain.

Then all at once it was gone and she felt whole again.

'Now do as I ask, child,' Kaijikan said softly.

Chiisai's mind was blank with the intense sensory overload. Without conscious thought she lifted the blade and, flat side up, slipped it into the fissure.

Nothing happened.

'No, no,' Kaijikan said, irritably. 'You must *think*. You must want to do it.'

'But I *don't* want to do it,' Chiisai said.

'Then you choose the alternative?'

Chiisai closed her eyes. *I am weak*, she thought. *I am not worthy to be a Bujun warrior.* But she knew this to be untrue. Now she regretted bitterly not finding an opportunity during their journey here to use the slim, pearl-gripped tanto she had secreted inside her right boot. But there had been no opportunity and she had failed to make one. She had erred on the side of caution, knowing that she would have only one chance. She thought the undead Tokagé might be vulnerable but what about Kaijikan. The magus was the one Chiisai feared, and so far she had detected no weakness in her. Further, she did not know the extent of her powers. How then to fight her and prevail with only a tanto and limited knowledge of the enemy? She would have no more than an instant before Kaijikan reacted and brought her magic to bear. The odds had been untenable, and so she had chosen to do nothing. *Inaction, her sendai had once told her, is equal to action in its consequence.* Now she understood fully the meaning of that lesson.

But that was the past. Here, now, she was presented with another choice. Action or inaction, which would it be? Passivity would only get her more mind-bending pain that would continue until she either acquiesced or her mind snapped. Then, Kaijikan would surely do as she promised – she would kill Chiisai and reanimate her. Like Te-te, she would be Kaijikan's slave for ever. If she chose action, she would still be strong and clear of mind. There was at least a chance, no matter what the magus thought to the contrary.

Therefore, Chiisai raised the dai-katana and slid it into the jagged fissure. At first, nothing happened. Then, so gradually it took some time for her to become aware of it, a certain vibration was transmitted from the forged steel to her arm and, thence, into her body. It jarred her senses, rattling her teeth and making her heartbeat erratic. She nearly passed out, but Tokagé's strong right arm held her fast.

'Yes,' Kaijikan said. 'It is happening.'

When Chiisai became aware that her eyes were closed, she opened them. She could hardly breathe. In fact, if she did not know that it was impossible she would swear that she was absorbing something other than oxygen from the air, as if she had turned into another form of creature altogether.

And then her eyes locked on the blade of her dai-katana, which seemed to shimmer darkly in the torchlight. And then she blinked, for she saw that what she had mistaken for refraction was, instead, a substance crawling out of the fissure along the center of the blade.

It was orange-red and flowed like molten lava or mercury, travelling at first painfully slowly, then more swiftly along the blade. Chiisai's erratic heartbeat was making her ill. Black spots danced in front of her eyes and each breath caught in her throat, becoming a heroic labor.

'Almost there,' Kaijikan cried in triumph.

And then Chiisai's breathing became less labored, her heart rate descended. The orange-red substance flowed, coating the entire length of the blade and then began to drip off it onto the floor of the cavern. As it pooled it became more viscous, then solid, pouring upward – if such a thing were possible.

It became denser, darker, like the fall of a sea of night. And, to Chiisai's dismay, it began to take a form. At first, there were but hints – an appendage here, what appeared to be a tentacle or a tail there. The brief bulge of a head,

156

ballooning out, then as quickly deflating, forming in another place.

And all the time the thing was growing, expanding exponentially. Like a horribly deformed fetus it grew arms, legs, tail and head. Then the details began to be imprinted upon the living substance. Until, at last it rose up, and trembling in its birth pains, towered over even Tokagé.

Chiisai gasped and her nerveless fingers fell from the hilt of her dai-katana, which nevertheless remained securely inserted in the fissure. For standing in front of her was a beast at least seven feet in height. It stood upon sturdy hind legs with taloned feet and a scaled tail with a multi-spiked end. It had a humanoid torso, though horribly distorted, but its head was truly hideous: that of a predator owl – all enormous, circular eyes and a wickedly curved beak. The luminous yellow eyes gazed in rapt attention at the being it found confronting it. It turned its neck in small birdlike increments and when it spoke its voice filled the cavern. It was so grating Chiisai found it painful to listen to.

'So you have fulfilled your promise.'

'Yes, Phaidan. You are in the world of man.'

'Then the Bridge has been made constant.'

'It has, indeed,' Kaijikan said.

'No more maiming of my people; no more extinguishing of their spirit as they make the Leap from one dimension to another.'

'No,' Kaijikan assured him. 'The sword and this brave one make the Bridge absolutely reliable.'

And Chiisai screamed inside, cursing herself, because now she knew the consequences of all the wrong choices she had made. She should have chosen to act during their journey here, no matter the odds against her. She should have chosen passivity now, anything rather than place her dai-katana in the fissure, creating the Bridge from this world to . . .

'Many will follow me,' said Phaidan, the Chaos creature. 'This time there will be no error. Our retribution will be complete.'

The Dai-San speaks:

I wanted to stay with her but I could not. The world does not work that way; even the Dai-San cannot have everything he wants. In a profound way there is a kind of solace in that. Our universe tolerates no absolute power, but this is no time to debate the concept of God. No one – not even I, not even the Kaer'n – knows the truth about how the Mountain Sin'hai was born and what exists upon its summit. There are still some mysteries beyond our grasp; enigmas yet to be born.

Here I admit my love for Chiisai. Why not? It is part of my remaining humanity and, as I have said, the Kaer'n have taught me the importance of this. I will not think about her being taken away from me; my Kaer'n forbids me to think such thoughts and I must realize it is for a good reason. The Kaer'n nurture me and protect me and I still have much to learn about them. In many ways, they remain the greatest mystery left for me to unfold.

They are like origami – that complex Bujun art of making paper creatures – unfolding in so many layers the process itself becomes dizzying. The Kaer'n exist on many levels at once. Well, what can you expect, considering their origin. And it is this very thing which keeps them hewn to the shadows. Fear is still the easiest emotion to evoke in humans, and there is no telling what kind of panic common knowledge of the Kaer'n would set off – even in the Bujun.

But I must continue to learn about them for I have come to understand that this is the only way I will ever fathom the key to my own existence.

PART THREE

SYRINX

TEN

WHITE LOTUS

Unlike other desert communities, notable chiefly for their impermanence, Mas'jahan was a fortress. To the eye of the weary traveler its brooding brown-black sandstone walls, beetling with the weapons-filled crenellations of a citadel eternally at war, said *sanctuary*. This was no doubt because the vast majority of those who passed through its lion gates were considered, at least in other parts of the world, criminals. Not in Mas'jahan. The sacred Mahatsin'jo, the fiercely visaged lion with the plumed wings of the phoenix, was the protector of all who lived beneath his benevolent wingspan.

Mas'jahan sat at the extreme northwest corner of the Mu'ad. It was a desolate tract of land, even by the standards of the Great Desert, streaked with a curious dark sandstone the Catechists alone knew how to work. But over its ramparts one could see looming the Mountain Sin-hai, its summit perpetually obscured by fulminating clouds and severe ice storms. Occasionally, a kind of reddish lightning illuminated those clouds and the citizens of Mas'jahan lifted their heads to stare, standing with their legs far apart as the ground beneath them shuddered as if in great racking sobs. These not infrequent quakes were the overt signs, so the Fianarantsoa told its constituency, that Zarathus was, indeed, among them, striding across the snow-encrusted summit of the Mountain Sin-hai, his sacred site of meditation.

Near the base of the Mountain Sin'hai's blue-black flank, legend had it, lay the ancient land of Syrinx. But none in Mas'jahan had ever ventured there or, at the least, returned to tell of it.

This was what the members of the Fianarantsoa had told Moichi in the pre-dawn interview Sardonyx had promised him. As they tore rough chunks from rounds of unleavened bread and popped dried dates in their mouths, they told him the dogma of Catechism – the ecstatic side was not yet for him, an infidel. But as for Dujuk'kan and the Makkon, they had no knowledge and no recommendations. They had been in the Mu'ad for forty days and forty nights, as the Living God, Zarathus, had bade them. As for recent events in Mas'jahan they were deaf, dumb and blind. But they gave him a gift, just the same: a magnificent push-dagger with double blades of an almost black Damascus steel, a gold-veined bronze guard and a carved mahogany grip.

'I did not believe they could help. But no matter,' Sardonyx had said blithely.

'How can you say that?' Moichi had asked. 'When I get to Mas'jahan I will need help.'

'And you shall have it,' she told him with such conviction he had no other choice but to believe her.

Mas'jahan possessed a formidable presence, abetted no doubt by its reputation. No people had ever been successful in extraditing one of their own from this Catechist stronghold by diplomatic means and none were foolish enough to attempt such a thing by force. 'God has brought him to our bosom,' the Catechists invariably said. 'Sooner or later, he will find the Path.'

This was the Catechists' most profound belief: that in every human being lies the seed of good from which God would manufacture His magic: redemption. It spoke to the very heart of the faith which, with its other face, both condoned the trading in human life and encouraged sexual exploration as a furtherance to attaining the ecstatic state required to hear and interpret the testament of the Living God.

'We accept the trade in human flesh because it is part of the natural order, part of God's design,' Vato-mandry had told Sardonyx when she had been under his tutelage. *'We do not believe in equality for all people, for we have found that breeds anarchy and discontent. When people are given a free-dom they cannot handle, the wildness that is buried inside them erupts and disturbs the ongoing process of goodness that will lead them onto the Path. This is not mere speculation or religious dogma but proven fact.'*

'But how can you or anyone else make the decision of who will be free and who will be enslaved?' Sardonyx had asked. *'The Iskamen were enslaved in Aden and they rose up against it and became free.'*

'We are the chosen of Zarathus,' Vato-mandry had said, *'God chooses. As for the Iskamen, it is our belief that their freedom is illusory. They are still tied to Aden in ways hidden from normal sight. Their battle for freedom is not yet done.'*

Sardonyx related this disturbing conversation as they walked down the narrow streets of Mas'jahan. Everything was made from the same indigenous sandstone, so that it seemed somber and austere for a place with such a repu-tation for carnal and venal pleasures.

Above them, the harsh desert sun, the color of a ripening fig, hung brutally in the hard, cloudless sky. Moichi began to appreciate the cleverness of Mas'jahan's plan. The cita-del's high walls cut off all wind, and the narrow, plaza-less streets, made for a minimum of blown sand. The central market made a slightly crooked X through streets jam-packed with cowled and robed religious leaders and brigands and cut-throat traders alike. These people appeared to live in, if not quite perfect harmony, then a state astonishingly close to it. What minor incidents Moichi witnessed – petty larceny, disputes over prices – were swiftly resolved by a member of the Fianarantsoa. These elders moved through the throngs, faced drawn weapons and razor-thin tempers with the admirable sang-froid of seasoned politicians. Not one of the disputations that Moichi witnessed was allowed to get out of hand.

Sardonyx bought them a concoction of ripe black figs and a tangy yellow cream that she said was made from co'chyn mares in heat. They ate this with their fingers as they walked through the market. Below the colorfully striped awnings they passed merchants selling all manner of spices, dried fruits and meats suitable for desert journeys. Coppersmiths and artisans in pewter, silver filigree and gold wire watched them from behind their magnifying loupes. The air reeked of so many scents it was often impossible to identify them all.

Up ahead, Moichi saw a wizened old woman, her back in the shape of a comma. She sat upon a well-worn stool tooled with complex and indecipherable runes. Before her gnarled hands were the skulls of a half-dozen small animals – rodents, no doubt – in shades of white, cream and ivory. They had been bleached by the sun, patinated by being constantly handled. In this way, they had taken on a character all their own – almost another life – one might say.

Seeing her dressed in Catechist robes, Moichi asked about her.

'She is a Tsihombe, a kind of Catechist oracle.'

'I did not know the Catechists believed in divination.'

'It is often surprising what their religion embraces.' She looked at him cannily. 'Do you wish to petition her?'

Moichi nodded. Though he was anxious to get on with his search for Dujuk'kan, Sanda's merchant husband Yesquz, and the Makkon, he knew he had business here. 'I had a dream in the Mu'ad when Sanda came to me. *"Save me!"* she implored me. And then she recited what seemed a riddle to me.'

As they approached, the Tsihombe raised her cronish head and, licking her lips, took her handful of tiny skulls off her baize table and rolled them around in her palm. They made a curious clacking sound, as musical as a row of hollow gourds.

'The future, good sir?' she cried in her cracked voice. 'But no.' She lifted a gnarly forefinger. 'The future is not your immediate concern, though it should be. You seek an answer to a question.'

She cackled a little, rolling the skulls out before Moichi could tell her what question he wanted answered. She stared down at the result for not more than a tenth of a second. Then her watery eyes lifted to Moichi's expectant face. 'The bear you seek is not what you expect. It lies northwest of here.'

'Northwest lie the slopes of the Mountain Sin'hai,' Moichi said.

The Tsihombe nodded. 'But before the Mountain lie the great fens and marshes, the Barrier. Within them waits the bear.'

'What barrier?' Moichi asked.

'Why, the Barrier God created between the world and Syrinx.' There was a sly smile on her face. 'The moment His servant Miira passed her Mirror around the chamber of state He formed from the great marshes and fens the Barrier, expanding it a thousand-fold and populating it with all manner of strange and wondrous life. All this in the moment death and retribution were visited upon Syrinx.' The spread of her sly smile made of her face an eerie

167

mask. 'You know the tale of Miira's Mirror, do you not, good sir?'

'That I do,' Moichi said. He gestured to Sardonyx. 'Pay the Tsihombe for her service.'

The crone raised her hand. 'This oracle was not for sale, good sir.' She nodded her head, her rheumy eyes hooded. 'Continue on your way to the house of Vato-mandry, and may God look you in the eye.'

'How did she know where we were headed?' Moichi said as they hurried down the street.

'Vato-mandry's house is just down this block.' She shrugged. 'Then again how did she know what question you wanted answered?'

'I did not even know it was a question,' Moichi said, repeating for her in total the poem Sanda had recited in his dream.

The Fianarantsoa's dwelling was unremarkable. In fact, it looked much like the brown-black sandstone buildings on either side of it. Only a lone fig tree out front, gnarled and bent as the Tsihombe's back, marked it. Sardonyx used the brass knocker which sand and wind had blasted to a dull, rough finish.

A heavy cedar door opened inward and Sardonyx said, 'Bes-abas, is that you? I have returned.'

'Child!' A large turbaned woman with great red cheeks and frizzy strands of black hair flying free stepped out of the doorway, her arms open wide. She embraced Sardonyx with whole-hearted delight. 'Husband was right. The prodigal has returned at last!'

Sardonyx kissed her cheeks with tenderness. 'Sadder and wiser, as he no doubt foresaw.'

'Come in, come in!' Bes-abas said as Sardonyx introduced Moichi. 'No doubt you both are famished from your long journey.'

The interior was dark, candle-lit, blessedly cool. The

168

atmosphere was thick with the smells and humidity of boiling stew and vegetables. This moisture, Moichi soon saw, suited well the myriad small plants, flowers and ferns set in beautifully wrought metal and ceramic pots throughout the house. In the steaming kitchen, three burly women were at work. All stopped to hug Sardonyx in turn and ask her a non-stop flow of questions: Where had she gone? How far had she traveled? What sights had she seen? What adventures? Did men in faraway lands have different sexual proclivities? All eyes were on Moichi as the last question was asked. But before Sardonyx could answer, Bes-abas shooed them back to work.

She brought back plates piled high with food, and metal steins filled with a fizzy alcoholic beverage that was thick, thirst-quenching and delicious.

'You have a large kitchen staff here,' Moichi said. He saw Bes-abas give Sardonyx a quick glance.

'Those women aren't staff,' Sardonyx told him. 'They are Vato-mandry's other wives.'

'Other wives?' he said, dumbfounded.

'Precisely,' Bes-abas said, urging them on to eat and drink their fill. 'I am First Wife. These others – my sisters now in this family – well, Vato-mandry must produce progeny.'

'For the members of the Fianarantsoa it is a sacred duty,' Sardonyx explained.

Moichi thought of a horrifying possibility. 'So if you were to become the first female member of the Fianarantsoa . . .'

'I would be required to have many husbands,' she said with a twinkle in her eye, 'to ensure I bore many children.'

Seeing the expression on his face Bes-abas laughed until the tears came to her eyes. Then she slapped her thighs and, leaning over Moichi, kissed him hard on both cheeks. 'You are a good boy,' she said with obvious pleasure. 'I am glad Sardonyx brought you here.' Then she stood up.

She had made no mention of Sardonyx's scar; even her eyes had not betrayed her. 'I will tell Husband that you are here.' She smiled at them both. 'Though I have little doubt he already knows. He awoke earlier than usual, at dawn, already restless and glancing out the window over the ramparts and into the Mu'ad.'

They finished their food, washed it down with the last of the drink. Moichi looked at Sardonyx, who seemed nervous. He could well understand how she might be. More than anyone else, perhaps, this one man had helped shape her life. And he would not blame her if she felt conflicted toward Vato-mandry. If the Catechist had not himself visited ills on her, then he had been their facilitator. He had been so certain of her ultimate fate that he had allowed – encouraged, even – the worst scars of life to settle upon her flesh like carrion birds. He had done her no good service that Moichi could see, and so he was not disposed to liking this old mystic.

The man who eventually arrived down a staircase of polished ebony was not at all what Moichi had expected. If he was a man of extreme age, only his long gray beard and his lined face disclosed it. Otherwise, he was as straight-backed and nimble-limbed as any young man Moichi had come across.

'So, little sister, I see life has caught you by the throat,' he said from the foot of the stairs.

'Caught me and shaken me,' Sardonyx said. 'But I still have all my teeth.'

He had soft brown eyes, a hawk-like nose, cheeks sunken by a lack of body fat rather than age. He had the look of an outdoorsman rather than that of a philosopher; the squint lines at the corners of his eyes were the result of practical experience rather than chronically poor light. He wore a long, fur-trimmed robe and a tanned leather brimless hat, like all the Fianarantsoa, that hugged his skull. And he was so tall he was obliged to duck his head while navigating certain areas of the house.

He grinned, showing enormous square white teeth. 'Yes,' he said in his deep commanding voice, 'it is good to see you.'

'This is Moichi Annai-Nin, Reverend Father,' Sardonyx said, taking Moichi's hand.

'So,' Vato-mandry said with an enigmatic look, 'you have found him.'

'You know of me?' Moichi said.

'Who has not heard tales of the Kai-feng?' He regarded Moichi for a long time before returning his attention to Sardonyx. 'It is as I hoped, little sister, when I set you on your path outside Mas'jahan. God has tested you; He has prepared you for what is to come. You have proven my vision; you are, indeed, His handmaiden.' He stretched out a long arm. 'Now, come upstairs into my study. There must be no delay. Our very existence depends upon you both.'

The steps were like glass and made no sound as the three of them ascended to the top floor of Vato-mandry's house. The Catechist's study overlooked the Mountain Sin'hai and the swirling clouds that shrouded its summit. Moichi had never been so close to the sacred mountain, and the feelings engendered in him were more ambivalent than he had imagined. The God of the Iskamen was known for His fearful temper and for His code of revenge. And even those He loved He sorely tested in the crucible of life.

The study was a bright, circular room, unique in a citadel of squares and rectangles. It had white stucco walls covered with shelves of glassy petrified wood, streaked with green and carmine. These shelves were filled with scrolls, books and manuscripts, some, Moichi saw, unfinished. One such lay open upon the large desk carved from a single block of onyx. The stone floor was covered with a rug of Catechist manufacture. Primitive colors swirled and danced in eerily accurate representation of the dervish.

All of these things were quite fantastic, but they faded from Moichi's consciousness a moment after he stepped into the room because his attention was riveted on the tall dark man standing in the center of the study. He turned as they entered and his liquid brown eyes fixed on Moichi's.

Smiling without warmth, he held open his arms and said, 'Brother.'

'Hamaan!'

Hamaan nodded. 'A little older, a little wiser, but the same.' He opened his arms wider. 'Are you too long away from Iskael to greet your brother in the traditional manner?'

Moichi stepped forward, was embraced by his brother, and embraced him in turn. Then they both stepped back as if an unpleasant shock had gone through them.

'Apparently, Vato-mandry was expecting you,' Hamaan said. 'But I was not.'

'I returned to Ala'arat to find that Sanda had been murdered and the villa deserted save for a Fe'edjinn contingent led by a First Darman named Tamuk.'

'A good man, Tamuk, loyal and brave,' Hamaan said. 'I have been grooming him for advancement. He is here with you, I take it.'

'He was killed in the Mu'ad, along with two of his men.'

'I see.' Only a small twitch at the outer corner of Hamaan's left eye betrayed his emotionless façade. But then Moichi knew what to look for; he had seen that flicker before.

'Were you ambushed by the Al Rafaar? These days they act as if they own the Mu'ad.'

'We saw no Adenese. The desert itself did them in,'

Moichi said, not wanting to get into the magical aspects of the Jailor.

'And you survived. Along with the woman.'

'That's right.' Moichi took the opportunity to introduce Sardonyx.

Hamaan, taking her hand, said, 'I am used to meeting my brother's women,' in his most ungracious manner. To Moichi, he said, 'Well, brother, your record is intact. One way or the other you always manage to survive.'

'I think we should all sit,' Vato-mandry said, coming between them in order to defuse the tension. He poured them all Vash't, the deep yellow liquor of the Catechists. He turned to Moichi. 'Your brother has had quite a shock. Tamuk was like a brother to him. I am certain you understand.'

Moichi gazed at the Catechist with interest. Implicit in what he said was his knowledge of the difficulties these two brothers were struggling with. Just how much did he know of the Annai-Nin history? Moichi wondered.

Hamaan, who had tossed off his drink in one fiery swallow, put aside his glass. 'As Tamuk may have told you, I came here to bring Sanda's husband back for questioning in her murder.'

'Yes. Tamuk told me Yesquz is a spice trader.'

Hamaan nodded. 'That was as much as he knew – as much as we all knew. I have found Yesquz and I have discovered that along with the spices which are harvested on the lower slopes of the Mountain Sin'hai he is a dealer of the White Lotus.'

The atmosphere in the study abruptly became so thick one could choke on it.

'I have heard of the White Lotus but I had assumed it only legend,' Sardonyx said. 'I knew a man once who believed in its existence. He spent most of his life in a vain attempt at finding it.'

'It exists, all right,' Hamaan affirmed.

'The White Lotus is a powder of the Black Angel; a root with hellish properties,' Vato-mandry said. 'The strength and stamina ingesting it provides is otherworldly. A man possesses the power of a hundred and, with it, the mind-set to do battle night and day until blood runs in the streets, fills the gutters and gluts even the thirsty desert. White Lotus is anathema to us, for a man who has tasted it but once will have no desire for the dervish with which we serve the Living God, and will turn his face from Zarathus's eye.

'But White Lotus is treacherous in less spiritual ways, as well. It must be prepared correctly and ingested in the right dose, otherwise it proves fatal.' He, too, set his liquor aside, although he had failed to touch his. 'Its flower is white and, indeed, lotus-like, hence its name. It floats upon the black waters of the Khashm, a form of fen found in only one place: Syrinx.'

'But the Syrinxians are a dead race,' Moichi said. 'If they once harvested the White Lotus, who would do it nowadays?'

'The Khashm is an exceedingly dangerous place,' Vato-mandry said. 'The Syrinxians never possessed the knowledge to navigate it, let alone to harvest its most well-protected flora. No, only a people indigenous to the Khashm would be able to do that.'

'The Shinju?' Moichi said incredulously. 'But we are speaking of a people extinct for millennia.'

'It must be remarkable to have such absolute knowledge,' Hamaan said.

'But it is common knowledge.' Moichi turned to Vato-mandry.

'Exactly,' the Catechist said. 'But is it the truth? This trader Yesquz was in possession of White Lotus, properly harvested and correctly dosaged. This fact alone would tend to refute the common knowledge.'

174

'The Shinju, alive?' Moichi turned this over in his mind. 'It would be a fantastic discovery, if it were true.' He looked at his brother. 'What will you do with Yesquz?'

'Use him to lead us to his source,' Hamaan said. 'It is imperative we wrest control of the White Lotus trade from the Adenese.'

'The Adenese?'

Hamaan nodded soberly. 'My sources tell me that Al Rafaar has obtained from the Shinju the ultimate weapon. Can you imagine those fanatics stoked on the root? They would overrun Iskael in a fortnight, slaughtering us all.'

'Do you condone this?' Moichi asked Vato-mandry. 'I thought the Catechists were neutralists.'

'Indeed we are,' Vato-mandry said. 'Hamaan has pledged to hand over the White Lotus to us to destroy.'

Moichi looked at the Catechist for some time. Was he naive enough to believe that Hamaan, a fanatic himself, a warrior, would ever hand over such a military advantage to a third party? Perhaps so. But Moichi was not fooled. He knew what his brother had in mind: the way to ensure an Iskamen victory in its full-scale assault on Aden. There was no doubt that White Lotus in sufficient quantities would tip the balance of power in the Mu'ad. The destruction of the Adenese was all that Hamaan lived for. And now that Iskael was primed for war he saw a way to ensure its victory.

'My only regret,' Hamaan was saying now, 'was that I am convinced that Yesquz did not kill Sanda. Her murderer is still unknown.'

'I know who it is,' Moichi said. 'I have encountered it in Ala'arat, where it killed my first mate. I have tracked it across the Mu'ad, and now its spoor tells me it is here in Mas'jahan.'

At Moichi's first words, Hamaan had jumped up. 'You

know? Then tell me. Tell me, by the God of our fathers, so that I may have my revenge!'

'You said "it,"' Vato-mandry astutely pointed out. 'Not "he" or "she."'

'That's right,' Moichi told them. 'Sanda was ravaged by a Makkon, a Chaos beast.'

Moichi was looking at Vato-mandry when he mentioned the Makkon, and he saw to his astonishment that the Catechist's face went pale. He tugged at his beard and his eyes turned inward.

'Vato-mandry?' Sardonyx said. She, too, was aware of his distress.

Only Hamaan, rage spewing out of him, was oblivious. 'Tell me!' he cried. 'Chill take you, brother!'

'Keep still,' Moichi snapped.

'Why here?' Vato-mandry was saying. 'Why now?'

Down on one knee before the Catechist, Moichi said softly, 'Vato-mandry, what do you know of the Makkon?'

'The Chaos beast?' His eyes were still turned inward, veiled as they would have been at the height of the dervish. 'The Makkon is loose, killing, and now it is here where the White Lotus is, the White Lotus harvested by the Shinju.'

'There must be a connection,' Moichi said. 'I encountered the Makkon at an after-hours bar on the waterfront. The place looked as if it had been ripped apart by a legion of berserkers.'

'Or a single man on White Lotus,' Hamaan said.

Vato-mandry nodded. 'That, too, is possible.'

Moichi turned to his brother. 'What are you saying?'

'Al Rafaar has White Lotus. Selected agents, infiltrating Ala'arat have used it.' His eyes were filled with the fanatic's peculiar fire. 'Don't you see? It is a pilot project, to gauge the root's effects, an experiment. Al Rafaar murdered Sanda, just as we suspected, a berserker on White Lotus, a

176

madman. This is what we can expect when war is declared, brother, on a far, far larger scale.' His eyes fairly spit flames. 'Ironic, isn't it? This is the madness from which you sought so hard to flee. And now you are imprisoned within its very heart.'

Phaidan could not remain in its present form for long, and so began the last phase of Tokagé's reanimation. He held out his mailed hands and Phaidan's upper appendages flowed over his, creeping like tree roots run riot, like serpents in a frenzy of anticipation, like the corded veins on a strongman.

Tokagé's head was thrown back, his spine arched, as if a bolt of lightning were running through him. And all the while, the features, contours and the outline of the Chaos satellite beast were collapsing into rivulets, streams and, finally, a torrent of energy pouring itself into Tokagé at the point where his breastplate ended and his throatguard began.

'At last!' Kaijikan cried. 'At last!'

It was the moment Chiisai had been waiting for. She recognized it without thinking and, bending down, drew out the slim tanto concealed within her right boot. In the same movement, she thrust the point of the blade into the very spot where Phaidan was flowing into the warlord.

'Nooo!' Kaijikan screamed, as Chiisai rammed the blade home its entire length.

Tokagé staggered backward, his hands scrabbling for the blade. A nimbus of energy – Chaos energy – swirled around him, ballooning outward rather than flowing seamlessly into him. A thunderous rattling as of the bones of ten thousand skeletons filled the cavern. Tokagé, sounding as if he were choking, slammed into the cavern wall, bounced off and hit again. The nimbus, spreading darkly like the squirt of a squid's ink in water, followed him, thwarted in its goal of entering him completely.

Chiisai had no time to follow this drama, however. She had turned and was reaching to yank her dai-katana out of the fissure and, thus, abrogate the Bridge from her world to the dimension of Chaos, when she was whirled violently around.

She stared up into the raging face of Kaijikan.

'Bitch!' Kaijikan screamed. 'Stupid, stupid bitch!'

Kaijikan reached out slender, ephemeral arms and threw Chiisai so violently against the rock wall that she almost lost consciousness. She felt her knees buckle and she slipped to the packed dirt floor. Her head lolled on a neck that had turned to rubber. She tried to get up but she lacked both strength and coordination and she fell back.

Then Kaijikan was astride her. Spittle flew from the magus's mouth and, as Chiisai watched, horrified, her right hand elongated, the nails extruding brightly as if they were made of forged steel.

Kaijikan was spewing obscenities as her talon-like nails struck downward, puncturing Chiisai's skin and flesh. Chiisai cried out in pain, trying to twist away, but the nails were so long, penetrating so deeply that Chiisai, panicked, felt them at her very core.

'Die!' Kaijikan cried. 'Die!'

And, withdrawing her nails to slash them lengthwise across Chiisai's face, she turned away from the blood gurgling from the multiple wounds, and rushed to tend to her charge.

Through eyes slitted by shock and pain, Chiisai saw Kaijikan grab Tokagé and drag him, stumbling and still clawing at his neck, out of the cavern. She tried to rise, leaning hard against the wall to lever herself to her feet. Her hands were red and, when she looked down at her chest, it was covered in blood. There was no pain now, as the endorphins pumped into her system, shut down the pain receptors. She was filled with a warmth, a lassitude that made her forget why it was she had wanted to move.

With a little sigh, she slid back down to the packed earth and sat staring at her own blood leaking into the veins of metallic white which, like lightning trapped beneath glass, now seemed to flush with an almost feral light.

'Hamaan is quite correct,' Vato-mandry said. 'White Lotus had tipped the delicate balance of power along the Mu'ad. As long as the Adenese possess the White Lotus we Catechists must ally ourselves with Iskael.'

'But that is in contravention of your beliefs,' Moichi said. 'If you take sides what is to stop all the neighboring countries from doing so?'

'Perhaps they should,' Hamaan said heatedly. 'If the Adenese successfully overrun Iskael do you think they will stop at its borders? Once they taste such power they will be unable to stop. They will try to conquer the entire region.'

'Your brother speaks wisely,' the Catechist said.

'No, no, this is madness, pure and simple,' Moichi said. 'Any escalation of the feud between Iskael and Aden is unthinkable.'

'I have had enough of your attitude!' Hamaan shouted, pulling him up by the front of his shirt. 'Who are you to come back here and begin giving orders? We are not in the family villa and you are no longer Father's surrogate. Feud? Listen to yourself. You are describing an old women's altercation. We are speaking of basic rights now: to be free. The Adenese want to enslave us, as it was in the beginning. We cannot allow that.' He was shaking with rage. 'What you have uttered here is treasonous.

I am Qa'tach. I could order your incarceration or your execution and none would gainsay me.'

His eyes blazing, Moichi said, 'We are not in Iskael now, or in the Mu'ad. In Mas'jahan your rank is meaningless.'

'Freebooter, anarchist, traitor! Even the avowed neutralists know when to take sides. But not you.' Hamaan drew a weapon. 'I will teach you the importance of earned rank.'

'That is enough, both of you!'

Vato-mandry stood, his legs spread, his arms thrown wide. The long sleeves of his robe had been thrust back and they could see the welter of runish tattoos wound around his arms like the coils of a serpent.

'You are not here to bury one another, but to bury a common enemy,' he admonished them. 'You must discover the trader Yesquz's source for White Lotus. It is imperative you sever the ties Al Rafaar have with the Shinju.'

'Even you must agree with that, brother,' Hamaan said disgustedly.

'I do.'

'Then it is agreed,' Vato-mandry said, looking hopefully from one brother to another for any sign of a truce.

Hamaan nodded. 'We will see him immediately.'

'Yessir!' The Fe'edjinn snapped to attention at their arrival. 'The prisoner is resting.'

'Resting?' Hamaan said, as they marched down the hallway. 'Has he had his meal?'

'He indicated that he was not hungry,' the Fe'edjinn said crisply.

'I left strict orders that he should not be deprived,' Hamaan said, annoyed.

'Yessir, but I did not believe that meant force-feeding the prisoner.'

180

'He is not a prisoner, Third Darman. At least, not yet.'

'Yessir.'

The hallway in which they found themselves was part of a vast labyrinth of like-looking corridors – a veritable warren in one of Mas'jahan's myriad pleasure palaces. But since sex and religion were deliberately intertwined among the Catechists, there were as many dervishers as there were half-naked women there. Many, Moichi saw, appeared to be both.

'In their endless proselytizing, the Catechists believe that sex is the lure and religion is the hook. They are quite right, often enough,' Sardonyx whispered.

Another Fe'edjinn guarded a locked door at the end of the corridor. He, too, was at attention before they arrived in front of him.

'How is your charge, Second Darman?' Hamaan asked sourly. 'Still starving himself?'

'Yessir!' the Fe'edjinn replied. 'That is, I believe so. I have not heard a word from him since he refused his food.'

'Open the door,' Hamaan said impatiently. 'And see that we are not–'

'What was that?' Moichi pushed the guard aside, put his ear to the door.

'What did you hear?' Hamaan said.

'I do not know,' Moichi replied, 'but it sounded like a chair being kicked over.'

'Open the door!' Hamaan roared.

While the startled guard fumbled with his keys, Moichi took a step back, smashed his bootsole just above the door lock. It shattered and the door swung wildly inward.

Inside, the room smelled of sweat, blood and fecal matter. It was a small beamed cubicle furnished with the bare minimum: a mattress on the floor, a nightstand with a pitcher of water, a chair and rickety table. Tatty curtains billowed about an open window in the far wall.

'Chill take it!' Hamaan cried.

For Yesquz, his face sickly and bloated, hung from a rope that had been tied to the center rafter. Below him, a chair on which he had been standing had been kicked over, perhaps by him. Perhaps not.

Moichi ran to the open window, looked down into a narrow gray alley. A Fe'edjinn lay on the ground, one floor below, either unconscious or dead. Behind him, he could hear Hamaan bellowing at the top of his lungs, and there was the martial sound of booted feet coming at the double. He levered himself through the window, dropped to the ground.

Crouched beside the Fe'edjinn for a moment, he took his pulse, then turned his head. Throat slit neatly and expertly. He looked around. Sand had built up in the alley and he could see the faint outline of footprints. Large ones. He took off after them.

The alley debouched on a crowded street that led to the spice market. He saw a big man in a d'alb hurrying into the closest edge of the stalls and he headed that way, shouldering people aside. He moved quickly and efficiently past the tented awnings beneath which were heaped aromatic bins filled with star anise, cardamom, leaf sage, orange pepper, along with a cornucopia of other spices, familiar and alien. The voices of the proprietors filled the air like the braying whistles of bright-plumaged macaws and cockatiels. Haggling was expected and intense, a way of life for the traders.

Moichi, on the lookout for the big man, glimpsed him again, the d'alb's cowl concealing his face, and, bowling over a pair of spindly traders, he raced toward him.

His burly arms burnished bronze with cinnamon, the big man turned as he heard Moichi approach. Dujuk'kan looked into Moichi's face. He stuck his left hand into the pile of cinnamon, then took off.

His girth belied his quickness. Besides, he was thoroughly familiar with the citadel and he slipped through the throngs like an eel through a coral reef.

Moichi lost sight of him, then, putting on a burst of speed, found him again. He was obliged to leap atop a spice bin to round a corner in time to see Dujuk'kan pass behind a cart full of whole nutmeg kernels, veined with red mace.

He followed, closing the gap somewhat. But Dujuk'kan had thrown a handful of the nutmeg on the ground and Moichi slipped on one, skidding painfully against the wall of a building.

He saw Dujuk'kan's grin as he picked up steam, heading away. But as Moichi rose, Sardonyx appeared at the other end of the street. He shouted, racing toward her and the Adenese. Dujuk'kan came to an abrupt halt, seeing her. Of course, he did not recognize her, having seen her only as Aufeya, but from her drawn weapon and the manner in which she advanced on him, he gathered her intent.

He looked once over his shoulder at Moichi coming on, then back at her. He whirled and disappeared into the doorway of a building on the left. Moichi and Sardonyx arrived at the doorway at almost the same time. He gave her a quick smile and they headed through. It was another sex palace, another warren of narrow corridors, small rooms and back entrances.

'Clever bastard,' Moichi said. 'We will never find him in here.'

A Catechist approached them and told them they were disturbing the patrons. When they told him their intent, he politely but firmly ordered them to leave. They had no choice but to comply.

Outside, in the street, Sardonyx pulled him into the shadows of a doorway.

'Turn and face the door,' she said, and when he looked

at her she put a hand on his shoulder. 'Do you trust me?'

He did as she asked. Later, he would swear that his eyes were open, but a shadow so deep passed before him that it was as if he had fallen asleep. There was a brief sensation of falling but not falling, as if in a dream. Then he felt her hand turn him around.

He was looking into the face of a male Fianarantsoa. He was about to open his mouth in protest when he looked into the Catechist's clear blue eyes and saw Sardonyx. He was getting a measure of proficiency at this. On impulse, he put his hands up to his face, pulled at the full beard that now covered his face, touched the brimless leather hat on his head. He looked down at his striped robes.

'We will try this again,' Sardonyx said, and as two Fianarantsoa elders, they re-entered the sex palace.

This time, the Catechist bowed in respect and gave them no second glance. They had free run of the place.

'Where shall we begin?' Moichi asked.

'Begin at the end,' Sardonyx said, leading him up a set of well-worn sandstone stairs. 'I have divined Dujuk'kan's whereabouts.'

Oiled women, their flesh gleaming in torchlight, slipped through the corridors like fish in a stream. Their long hair fell free – the only place a female Catechist was allowed this freedom – swaying across the indentation of their spines, alternately revealing and concealing bare hips and buttocks. They carried with them like pilot fish cut-throats and murderous traders, embezzlers in flight and con-men of every description. It was like diving into a bay full of sharks.

Though she had never been here before Sardonyx guided him unerringly through the noisome warren. Eventually, the corridor gave out onto a large room filled with people. These were clustered around a circular stage made of fragrant oiled cedar that ramped up from the floor.

Half a dozen women in unclasped robes and nothing else danced in the centre of the stage. In their circular movements and the tilts of their torsos Moichi recognized elements of the dervish – yet this could not be because, as Sardonyx had pointed out, there were no female Fianarantsoa.

'This is the Ambaranata,' Sardonyx said. 'Like the dervish, it is a form of dance which induces an ecstatic state. This one, however, is a prelude to sexual ecstasy and is the sole province of Catechist women. The men – and sometimes women – standing around will pick their favorite and bid on her. Highest bidder wins. The Catechist we saw earlier collects the take and it is added to the Catechist coffers.'

Moichi watched, fascinated, as the women whirled and swooped. In this way, they seemed to lose all sense of themselves. It was as if they whirled toward a primeval core where differences in personality and even flesh were exchanged for an irresistible erotic energy. Dipped into this living flame, the Ambaranata lifted like wings striped robes, animated oiled flesh, revealing in brief stunning bursts breasts and groin, thigh and hip, shoulder and buttock beneath which well-defined muscles rippled like running animals. These dancing creatures lived now on the prayer formed with each whirl and swoop of their bodies, and the aura they exuded was a heady musk that could drive a man – or a woman of that sexual persuasion – wild.

'Compelling, isn't it?' Sardonyx said, pulling him into the crowd. She put her lips against his ear. 'Dujuk'kan is on the other side of the stage. You go left, I will take the right.'

'What about this form?' he asked. 'I am an old man. I will be unable to force Dujuk'kan to do anything.'

'But you are Fianarantsoa,' Sardonyx said. 'Your word

is law in Mas'jahan. Even Dujuk'kan must obey or risk being forever expelled.' Her tongue licked the edge of his ear. 'But I will give you a choice. If at any time you wish him to know who you are, merely think it and you will return to your form as Moichi Annai-Nin. But be very careful, for once returned you cannot go back to the Fianarantsoa form and you will forfeit a great advantage.'

Moichi nodded, setting off through the throng of avidly bidding brigands, mustachioed traders and bearded mercenaries. This was as evil a bunch of humanity as Moichi had ever encountered, even along the foul late-night dives of Sha'angh'sei's rat-infested waterfront. He was obliged to keep his attention tightly focused on the crowd, to ignore the incessant siren call of the Ambaranata.

The bidding had reached a fever pitch, the brigands and freebooters shoving and screaming out their bids, threatening their competitors, when Moichi spied Dujuk'kan. He had stuck himself in a corner, surrounded by a phalanx of mercenaries whose spirited gesticulations and cat-calls served as an effective screen.

Dujuk'kan's eyes slid across the face of the approaching Fianarantsoa, then slid past. He was on the look-out for Moichi and Sardonyx; as far as he could see neither of them were here.

As the moments slipped by, Moichi could see him relaxing more and more. All the better. He shouldered his way through the mercenaries, amazed how easy it was. Even though these men were rapt participants in the Ambaranata they did not fail to mark a member of the Fianarantsoa and give way to him. Moichi began to understand the enormous advantage he would give up were he to return to his own form.

He looked for Sardonyx, but could not see her in the milling crowd. When he was close enough to the Adenese to be assured he would be heard, he said, 'Dujuk'kan, you will come with me.'

Dujuk'kan's head swung in Moichi's direction. 'Why, Reverend Father? What have I done?'

'Nothing,' Moichi said, not wanting to alarm him. 'I merely wish to speak with you about a . . . delicate matter of trade.'

'Ah.' An avaricious smile spread across Dujuk'kan's face. 'When it comes to business, I am always at the service of the Fianarantsoa. But could we wait until the Ambaranata is concluded? I have a great deal of money in the air.'

Moichi, needing to herd the Adenese out of this very public place, said, 'I am very much afraid the Ambaranata women will have to wait.'

Dujuk'kan raised his eyebrows. 'I am shocked, Reverend Father. That is quite an un-Catechistic desire you express.' He shrugged. 'But I believe in business over pleasure any day.'

The Ambaranata was reaching its climax. Moichi led him through a crowd overheated to boiling point. Still no sign of Sardonyx. Where was she? They went along a corridor that was nearly deserted.

'May I ask where you are taking me, Reverend Father?'

No, you may not, Moichi thought. 'A place where we can speak in private,' he said. He had no idea where he was going in this labyrinth, which was why he was desperate to find Sardonyx. On impulse, he turned left, headed down a flight of steep, sandstone stairs. Were these the ones they had used to get up here or another flight altogether? In any case, it was a mistake.

'Private? You mean, you and me?' Dujuk'kan said. 'But that is illegal. Worse, it is antithetical. Wait a minute.' He put a heavy hand on Moichi's shoulder, spun him abruptly around. 'Who in the name of Chaos are you?'

It was a mistake using the stairs because they were in

a narrow, defined spot with no room to maneuver. The huge Adenese towered over him, his face filling with rage.

'You are not even a Fianarantsoa, I'll warrant!' He drew a short-bladed scimitar. The perfect weapon for hand-to-hand combat.

Moichi, mindful of Sardonyx's warning, knew he had no choice. He could keep the form of the old Fianarantsoa no longer. He thought of Moichi and became Moichi.

Dujuk'kan sprang backward up the steps. 'What sorcery is this?'

In answer, Moichi drew his dirks, lunged at the Adenese. But Dujuk'kan was ready for him and, reversing the small scimitar, he launched it, butt first down the stairwell.

There was no time to duck. It smashed into the side of Moichi's head, sending him tumbling backward down the stairs. One weapon flew from his grasp but he managed to hang on to the other even as he fetched up painfully against the wall of a landing.

His head was filled with a titanic roaring and by the time he realized that it was the sound of Dujuk'kan clattering down the stairs, the Adenese had kicked the remaining dirk from his hand. Reaching down, Dujuk'kan fitted his scimitar into its scabbard and, clutching one of Moichi's own dirks, put it to his throat.

'You have more lives than a marshcrow. Now I'll finish off what I had meant to do in Jailor's prison.'

Moichi, still half-dazed, his head throbbing with pain, still managed to smash the heel of his hand into Dujuk'kan's eye socket. The Adenese screamed, lurching back, and Moichi was on him. But he lacked his full strength, and Dujuk'kan jammed an elbow in his solar plexus, robbing him of breath. He fell and, bellowing in rage, Dujuk'kan came after him. Moichi saw his fallen dirk not more than three hands-breadths away and desperately reached out for it.

He shouted in pain as Dujuk'kan trod hard on his hand.

'No reprieve this time,' the Adenese said, kicking him hard in the ribs, then flipping him over on his back. 'I am going to slit you from throat to abdomen and watch your life come sliding out.'

The dirk's blade flashed as it came down toward Moichi. Then, in mid-flight, it paused, trembling in mid-air.

'No! Noooo!'

It was Dujuk'kan screaming. His face had drained of blood and his eyes were wide as moons.

'You are dead! You cannot be here! Impossible!'

Moichi turned his head, saw the hideous bulk of the Jailor sidling up the stairwell. His pincers opened and closed as if in avid anticipation. Of course it was impossible. The Jailor was dead; Moichi had killed him. Besides, by his own admission, he could not survive outside the tunnels of his own manufacture. Not that any of this mattered in the moment. The moment was mad, utterly insane, and Moichi used the advantage.

He drew the double-bladed push-dagger the Fianar-antsoa had given him in the Mu'ad and, gripping it with white-knuckled strength, launched himself at Dujuk'kan.

The double blades pierced the Adenese just beneath his sternum, plunging to their full depth until they punctured his heart. Dujuk'kan was almost lifted off his feet by the tremendous momentum generated by the missile of Moichi's entire body. His eyes blinked as if he could not believe what was happening to him. He looked directly into Moichi's eyes, but Moichi could find nothing there, no regret or hate; certainly no fear. Then the eyes rolled up and death clouded them with his veil.

With a grunt, Moichi pulled the push-dagger free, and the corpse of Dujuk'kan slumped to the landing. Then Moichi turned to face the advancing Jailor.

He smiled into the awful visage and said, 'Didn't your

mother ever tell you not to make faces like that? You could stay like that for ever.'

The Jailor shimmered, the outline flickering, contracting, metamorphosing until Sardonyx stood before him, hands on hips, legs spread. 'Ungrateful wretch, I just saved your life.'

'And a damn fine job of it you did,' he said, kissing her on the lips. He retrieved his dirks, but when he bent the throbbing in the side of his head became almost unbearable. He staggered and Sardonyx caught him around the waist.

'How white of face you look,' she said. 'You are frightening me.'

While they stood very close together, she put the flat of her hand to the wound, and gradually the pain ebbed.

'The worst of it is gone,' she said. 'But you still need time to heal completely.'

His head was beginning to clear. 'Thank you,' he said. Then he took her hand as they headed down the stairs.

On their way back to Hamaan and the hanged Yesquz, Moichi stopped at the cinnamon stall. Over the merchant's bitter protests he thrust his hand into the spot he had seen Dujuk'kan make use of. His fingers burrowed into the spice until it covered his entire forearm. Then he felt something and gingerly he pulled it out.

'What is it?' Sardonyx said as he blew it free of clinging cinnamon.

'It is a ring.' Moichi's stomach contracted. He turned it around and around, just to make certain. But he needn't have bothered; he had recognized the star sapphire the moment he had pulled the ring free. He stared into its deep-blue and pale gold depths. 'It belonged to my sister Sanda. My father gave it to her when she turned thirteen.'

190

Sardonyx peered at it. 'What is that engraved on the sides?'

Moichi looked closely. 'Why, it's a bear,' he said, thinking of the riddle verse Sanda had recited in his dream.

'The bear in the stone?' Sardonyx said.

'What was Dujuk'kan doing with this?'

'You mean what was Yesquz doing with it,' Sardonyx said. 'I think Dujuk'kan took it from him before he killed him.'

'Why?'

'Perhaps it is the key,' Sardonyx said. 'The connection we have been looking for. Did the Makkon kill Sanda for it? Or, as Hamaan is convinced, the Al Rafaar? But she had given it to Yesquz or he had taken it from her. Remember what your sister said to you in your dream. *"When the spirit flies above marsh and chasm."'* She looked at him. 'Perhaps you misheard her, Moichi. I believe that instead of *chasm* Sanda said Khashm.'

ELEVEN

EVE

Chiisai was dying, slowly and painfully, as Kaijikan had predicted. Without the magus's protection, the invisible energy of the ancients was seeping into her bones, intent on eating her from the inside out. On the other hand, it was more than likely that the wounds inflicted by Kaijikan would kill her first.

Chiisai opened her eyes. The reed torch had burned itself out, but fitful illumination was provided by the veins of the white metallic substance in the earth floor of the cavern. She knew she had lost a lot of blood; she had trouble breathing. Her lungs felt full and there was a pink froth at the corners of her mouth.

Death crouched beside her, stinking, its bones bleached a hideous yellow-white, cracked with age. It hunkered close to her, her sole companion. She was a warrior, and death did not frighten her. But she had never imagined dying, lost and alone, life seeping from her, second by agonized second. Defeat in battle, an honorable death, was one thing. This was quite another.

She felt the fear creeping through her as death spread its clanking arm across her shivering shoulders. *No!* she thought. *I cannot allow this! I* will *not!* But she knew there was no way out for her. She had neither the strength nor the stamina to crawl her way out of the cavern. And even if by some miracle she managed that, then what? She did not know how long she had been unconscious and by the time she made it out of the mouth – if she could – she would no doubt be so saturated with the death in here, she would die anyway.

Oh, it was cold! She could feel death's chill breath on her cheek and she shivered, then coughed, hacking up blood. This frightened her even more and she determined to move. Where? Anywhere; do anything but sit here and wait for death's icy kiss.

She turned her head convulsively away from her companion and that was when she saw her dai-katana stuck horizontally in the fissure.

The Bridge.

An idea was forming in her mind. It was so lunatic that for an instant she thought surely the invisible energy was already destroying her from within. Then she threw her head back and laughed. *Why not try it?* she told herself. *What did she have to lose – her life?* She laughed again, a harsh, sardonic noise that rattled through the cavern like the last wheeze of the damned.

Terrified, she pressed her back hard against the cavern wall and tried to stand. She cried out more times than she cared to count and, more than once, her breath failed her and the cavern spun around crazily. She concentrated on breathing, spitting blood, and going on, moving on rubbery legs along the wall, until she could reach out and grab the hilt of her dai-katana. Then, she climbed upon the flat of it.

What she was about to do terrified her to such an extent that she had to shut down all thought, moving as an animal did, out of pure instinct while the autonomous nervous system kept her alive.

Out along the swordblade she crept and now the darkness of the fissure was all she could see, a blank wall, a rock face that would surely stop her progress. And still she crept forward like a snail along the edge of a razor, unmindful of the madness of its actions.

But the rock face did not stop her. Instead, the fissure opened up like an oriel or the iris of an eye. This had been her mad notion: that in order not to die she had to be somewhere where the normal human laws of life and death did not apply.

She felt as she had when Phaidan was coming through, as if oxygen were no longer of use to her, as if gravity had ceased to exist, as if colors, sound, scent, sensation had all been whirled down a drain.

And, of course, they had, because she was crossing over to the dread place where flesh met the spirit world – the first human ever to have done so – using the Bridge to move from the realm of man into the dimension of Chaos.

Evening in the Khashm was the worst, Vato-mandry had told them before they left Mas'jahan, and he was not lying. The brackish water of the fens – actually a vast network of interlinked swamps, unexpectedly deep catch basins and treacherous tidal pools – stretched out before them, reflecting the dying colors of the day. At that moment, there seemed no distinction between water and sky, and any dry and passable land masses were totally obscured. These land masses – narrow spits and oval pads – certainly did exist; the Shinju seemed at home here. But they were inconstantly situated and, often, between them lay passages of deep-water sink holes and well-camouflaged meadows of what appeared to be solid ground but were, instead, quicksand that could draw a man under within seconds.

It was little wonder that the Syrinxians abandoned efforts to expand into the Khashm. From all accounts they were, like a majority of the more successful warlike races, a practical people. Harvesting the White Lotus might have been the ultimate prize but they saw in the massive loss of life, the sapping of their ethnological energies, a hint of their own demise. And so they had left the Khashm.

Had they been other than warlike they might have decided a peace treaty with the Shinju would have been to their ultimate advantage – the Shinju would have harvested the root for them. But treaties were not the Syrinxian way. *Conchius Altere Urbeun.* Conquest Above All. That was their motto, tattooed in paint and lacquer, etched with acid or chiseled by hand into the stone monuments that adorned their cities.

But they had been unable to conquer the Khashm.

Moichi, Sardonyx and Hamaan crouched beneath the inadequate cover of a marbatt tree, its low, twisted trunk shaped by the winds that eternally scoured sky and marsh. These trees were the only vaguely vertical objects as far as the eye could see. Otherwise, the expanse was as flat as an ocean becalmed.

They had left their co'chyn tethered at the eastern edge of the Barrier, as the Tsihombe had called it, God's creation at the moment of Shinju retribution against the Syrinxians. A week across the blistering Mu'ad had led them to a dead and crumbling city strangled by strange, creeping vines snaking through sand-streaked streets. Not even ghosts seemed to inhabit the desolate place. It had about it a sense of utter abandonment, as if God had turned His face from this place a long time ago.

Uneasy, but unable to say precisely why, they spurred their mounts on, and just beyond the ruins came upon a river. A few hours' exploration produced a fordable section and, after refreshing themselves, filling their water bladders and washing they crossed over to the far bank.

Scrubby trees like hunchbacks grew out of the sandy

mineral-poor soil, but soon the vegetation became more plentiful until the Mu'ad was but a memory.

The Khashm began almost without warning, and Moichi was reminded again of what the Tsihombe had said, for there was indeed a profound barrier sense about it. It was as if the hand of God had sliced down, turning verdant plain and rolling hillside into flat and aqueous swamp. Flashes of light played upon the still, sticky waters, and the eerie sounds of unseen marsh birds echoed across a vast purple sky.

The nights were very cold and, coming from the Mu'ad, the group were unused to the temperature. But not unprepared. Vato-mandry had had warm clothes waiting for them, along with backpacks well stocked with food, water and such equipment as they might require.

At first, Hamaan had balked. He had no intention of heading off into Syrinx without his platoon of Fe'edjinn warriors. Vato-mandry had soon disabused him of his position, pointing out that the Khashm was no place for a large group – this was one of the facts the Syrinxians had failed to grasp. Also, the Fe'edjinn were trained desert fighters. A land of marshes was not a good place for them.

At evening, the Khashm sparked with encroaching starlight. The sky and water was the color of dried blood, deep purple in the shadows. Craans, the long-necked marsh birds skimmed the water, plucking with their long beaks bony fish with flashing, oblate eyes. Like almost everything in the Khashm, the craans looked benign enough with their apricot-colored feathers and wide, elegant wingspan. In fact, they were not only predators but omnivores, fearless when it came to confronting any prey including man, who, it could easily be imagined, might prove a tastier treat than the mud-colored fish.

Moichi caught several of these eely creatures, roasting

them over a fire, only to find them so oily and bony as to be virtually inedible. The piscine oil, Sardonyx eventually discovered, proved remarkably proficient at healing the small but inevitable wounds inflicted on them daily by the low, heavily thorned gorse that grew in bewildering profusion throughout the Khashm.

What insects thrived here were out of all proportion. Their first night, Sardonyx discovered a glossy, humped-back beetle the size of her hand happy to share her tent. She was hardly so inclined and missed by a fraction being stung by a pincer. Where the end of the pincer struck a small stone, a yellow-green vapor with a caustic odor rose up, choking her. She used the blade of her dagger to hurry the creature along, and only afterward noticed the tiny series of pits in the hardened steel. Not surprisingly, she developed a healthy respect for the beasts. Once, making camp on a dank spit of land in the sea of marshes, she discovered a dead one, and spent the better part of the evening dissecting it and extracting its peculiar liquids.

Hamaan, crouched and chilled, put his hands to the fire, did not look up when Sardonyx went off to the privy. It was after the evening meal; the Khashm seemed somehow even vaster in the starlit night. Insects whirred and sang and, occasionally, the flap of a nocturnal predator's wings could be heard. Nothing else.

'Why did you bring her?' Hamaan said.

'Do you have something against her?'

Hamaan shook his head. 'Not *her* personally. I hardly know her. But women – especially your women, Moichi – always seem to get in the way.'

'I suppose that is because all my women have minds of their own.'

To his surprise, Hamaan smiled. He could not remember the last time he had seen his brother smile.

'Yes. I suppose that is true.' Hamaan rubbed his hands

together. 'You did a fine job tracking down Yesquz's murderer.'

'Would that I had brought him back to you alive.'

Hamaan shrugged. 'From what you have told me of the fiend I doubt very much whether he would have allowed that.'

Moichi, wanting to take advantage of his brother's uncharacteristically accommodating mood, said, 'Have you heard of a man named Bjork?'

'Bjork. That is neither an Iskamen nor an Adenese name. A Catechist?'

'No. From what Sardonyx tells me the name is alien to their language.'

'That name is unfamiliar to me.' He paused for a moment, staring into the fire. 'Moichi,' he said at last, 'I know we have had our differences before, but on the eve of our holy war with Aden, I have no wish to extend our quarrel. On the contrary, when I go into battle I would wish for there to be peace between us.'

'That, too, is my wish,' Moichi said. 'Jud'ae has been dead a long time, Hamaan. So should our rivalry for his affections.'

They gripped each other's forearms across the fire.

'We could use you in the Fe'edjinn,' Hamaan said, the flames sparking his eyes. 'What a team we would make, brother! What a fearsome swath we would cut through the Adenese troops.'

Sardonyx returned then, and Moichi was grateful. At the moment of his reconciliation with Hamaan he was unwilling to renew his arguments against the war.

Exhausted by their trek, they slept soundly. Moichi, wanting to dream again of Sanda, was instead stalked by owls, swivel-headed beasts with the bodies of dragons, whose improbably slender legs propelled them across the marshes with astonishing speed. He spent the night tossing and turning, attempting in his dreams to catch and harness such speed.

He awoke before dawn with a foul taste in his mouth. His body seemed a sea of pain from the recent wounds and bruises inflicted upon him. Stifling a groan, he rose and went silently to the area they had chosen as a privy. He relieved himself, staring into a distance unbroken save for the orange oblate of a slowly rising sun. At which point he became aware that he was being observed he could not say. But some instinct caused him to turn with extreme slowness.

Past a small fortress of thorny gorse he saw a pair of eyes. They were inhuman – that is, the eyes of a beast. This was his first thought. But, again, instinct kept its hold on him and he made no overt offensive motion. In fact, he made himself move not at all.

He was looking at something with a triangular head. Reddish fur plumed up the center of the face and between the large triangular ears. The muzzle was white, the inquisitive nose black. The beast was sniffing the wind for some scent of this unfamiliar being.

Now it moved and Moichi saw that it was a long-backed creature with, much to his astonishment, the improbably spindly legs of the curious beast of his dream. Its body looked perhaps most like a deer or a luma, although it was covered in the same fine reddish fur.

'You are not Shinju,' the beast said. 'Can you give me a reason not to kill you as you stand?'

Moichi was so astonished that for a moment he could say nothing.

'Not as dumb as I appear, am I?'

Was it smiling at him? He asked the only question that might save him. 'Have you a name?' he said. 'Mine is Moichi Annai-Nin. I am a native of Iskael, a land far to the southeast.'

'Return, then, to Iskael, Moichi Annai-Nin,' the beast said. 'No doubt your people look for you. Here you have neither dominion nor concern.'

'But I do,' Moichi said, and in sudden inspiration, produced Sanda's ring.

The beast, who had started at Moichi's movement, now craned its neck above the thicket of gorse. 'Myttali, can it be? You hold the Ring.'

'You know this ring?' Moichi asked, holding it out as if it were an offering.

'And so I ought,' the beast said. 'It is Shinju.'

Moichi was stunned to silence. How had his father come to acquire a Shinju artifact? Through one of his trader's deals? Obviously.

'May I come forward?'

It was only then that he realized the beast's demeanor had reversed itself. 'Come ahead,' he said. 'How may I call you?'

The beast used its slender legs to pick its way unharmed through the dangerous gorse, and Moichi saw just how long they were. This creature was fabulously made to move through marsh and fen.

'I am known as Ouwlmy,' it said. 'A female of my species, the Shakra.'

As she negotiated her way through the gorse Moichi saw how beautiful she was, slim and graceful yet, beneath the rippling coat of fur, lithe and powerful. She stood near him, peering at the ring, and he caught her scent, sweet as freshly mown hay, tart as citrus.

Her eyes, round as moons and close to its color in harvest summer, regarded him. 'Who do you seek in my domain?'

Moichi opened his mouth, prepared to damn Dujuk'kan, but instead he said, 'Bjork.'

'Ah, Bjork, the Shinju saiman—'

200

'Saiman?'

'You do not know the term? Bjork is the most powerful enchanter of the Shinju.' Ouwlmy looked from Moichi to the ring. 'This is his, you know.'

'The ring belongs to Bjork?'

Somehow, the moment the words passed his lips, Moichi knew they were the truth. But then from the moment he began to dream last night this entire episode had about it a sense of having lived it before.

'It was made by Bjork. Have you come to return it?' Ouwlmy turned those huge ingenuous eyes on him, but Moichi was not fooled. Instinct told him that she would instantly know whether he lied or told the truth.

'I would speak with Bjork about the ring and other matters,' he said. 'This ring was given to my sister by my father many years ago.'

'And she is now dead,' Ouwlmy said without missing a beat.

'How would you know that?' But in his heart he knew, and he was already weeping all over again for Sanda.

'Because,' Ouwlmy said with infinite sadness, 'she would never have parted with it otherwise.'

I am that I am.

That was, in the end, all that was left Chiisai. She felt as if she had been turned inside out, as if her skin now lay at the core of her, while her organs, blood vessels and viscera pulsed on the outside.

She wanted to see but she was blind. Deaf, dumb and blind.

She could feel nothing but the odd pulsing of her own body, not breathing precisely, because she had ceased to breathe the moment she Crossed Over. There was no oxygen – no atmosphere at all, as humans know it – in the dimension of Chaos. God only knew how these creatures sustained themselves. But they existed, all the same.

I am that I am.

It was all that stood between her and absolute oblivion. She had known this risk from the moment the insane plan had been born in her mind: that the inimical world into which she would crawl would swallow her whole, that she would cease to exist – not merely the death of her corporeal body, which was already a foregone conclusion – but *everything*, whatever it was that made her unique, that made her Chiisai.

Now it was about to happen.

I am that I am.

Was it a prayer or a mantra? What matter, as long as it kept her safe from utter dissolution?

Night was like brilliant noontime compared to the darkness that surrounded her. She might have been lost in the vastness of space for all the sensation that came to her. The pulsing of her own body continued on, inverted and distorted out of all reason, yes, but she abided, and that was something. On the Other Side where home and hearth lay she would have already expired, so she had something to be thankful for. Life continued, although its form had yet to be determined.

Contact with the dimension of Chaos had not killed her – as it had not killed her when Phaidan had come crawling through and she had felt the change shocking her through the conduit of the Bridge. Why hadn't it killed her? She had no idea. Perhaps it was because there was so much death inside her. Death was life here.

But what would she become here? A creature of Chaos? A profound sense of dread threatened to overwhelm the one tiny spark of hope that had been kindled in her core.

I am that I am.

But what if she could not live with what she had become?

She listened to the pulsing and gurgling of her newly exposed heart, lungs and stomach and, as she did so, she thought she discerned a kind of language. And, if she was right, that new-found language was telling her the toxins were being purged from her system. Exposed to the non-atmosphere of Chaos, which ate poisons as if they were exquisite delicacies.

I am that I am, but what is that?

She yearned for comfort but there was none; she ached for even a single spark that life as she knew it might still exist for her but darkness persisted; she longed for companionship with such torment that eventually even the prospect of a companion such as Phaidan or some monstrous thing like him became acceptable.

Perhaps that was not a wise thought, and she moved to strike it from her mind when she heard something. Heard? That was the wrong term for she had no ears with which to hear and, in any event, what sound could carry in the non-atmosphere of Chaos?

No, what it was was this: she became aware that she was not alone.

Deaf, dumb and blind she nevertheless saw in her mind the image of a woman, diaphanous gown flowing about her, tattered, ripped and shredded yet beautiful still. Her golden hair and blue eyes peered up into a sun that could not exist here. She was bound to a living tree from which had been stripped all leaves, branches, and bark, revealing naked cambium grown hard and wizened from exposure to the non-elements of Chaos.

This woman, at once beautiful and familiar, seemed blind in a way that Chiisai herself was not. Thick tears of blood leaked from her eyes, and her mouth was open in a soundless scream. Except that Chiisai, like some primordial sea creature, was aware of those screams. They fell upon her inverted form like waves upon a shore, and they pained her in a way she was unable to describe. It was a horrible feeling, like watching one's own death in a dream, slipping off a cliff and falling, falling . . .

Except this beautiful and familiar woman was not Chiisai – she was Sanda, Moichi Annai-Nin's sister. Chiisai had never met her but during her adventures with Moichi he had spoken of her often enough so that she could imagine she had. The truth took a moment to register: Sanda was also in the dimension of Chaos. And yet, this vision was subtly different.

Chiisai struggled to turn the vision in her mind, to see it at different angles. In succeeding, she discovered her answer. Unlike her face, Sanda's form could not be defined. In fact, Chiisai became aware that beneath the shredded gown it did not exist. Then what was here, in the dimension of Chaos? Was it Sanda or . . . ?

And then she knew and her heart contracted with sadness. Sanda was dead. At least, her corporeal body was gone. Yet she remained, a wraith, a ghost bound and chained, her spirit imprisoned within Chaos. What mad beast had done this to her? It could have been any of the minions of Chaos, and that meant there must be at least one other Bridge to the world of man than the one she had crawled through. What unthinkable horror was being readied against mankind? Was Phaidan only a part? It would seem so.

Now Chiisai knew what she must do at all costs, even if it meant becoming one of Them. She had knowingly entered the realm of Chaos and she had not perished as it had long been believed a human would. She did not want to ask why. She knew instinctively that no answer would be tolerable. She needed to act, and for that she needed to become – what? In the end, it mattered very little. Life as she had known it was finished. But existence, that was another matter.

So slowly that at first it was undetectable, she began to revolve, to break the stasis that had bound her healing form, to create her own gravity where before none had existed, to create her own form of physics, a world of chemical reagents and chimerical reactions, a biological fluorescence neither of man nor of Chaos.

Something was coming.

She was emerging like a sun being born out of the starfield, out of the sea of night.

Soon . . . Soon . . .

It was only to be determined now what that Something was.

I am that I am . . .

TWELVE

BJORK

Moichi, clinging like a lover to Ouwlmy's furred back, sped across the evil fen of the Khashm.

'I want to get the others,' he had said, but the Shakra had shaken her long, triangular head.

'I can take only you to see Bjork.'

'But these people–'

'This is not a negotiation,' she had said.

The wind brushed the hair back from his face. He could feel the play of muscles in her withers and croup and he closed his eyes, dreaming. It was a delicious sensation to be borne across inimical terrain by so powerful an engine, to lose oneself in the effortless motion, to lie down upon gravity as if it were an eiderdown bed, to drift away from the myriad aches and pains of the body, to drift . . .

And in his languor, the bear came to him. Its predatory head, with haunted eyes that chilled chickadee and rabbit alike, was striped black and white. And its arms, when it opened them, seemed to encompass the entirety of the Khashm. Then Moichi became aware of encroaching flames, rising high enough to engulf an entire city. As powerful as the bear was, it did not move. Even when the flames licked and singed its fur, it seemed incapable of movement. Instead, it opened its mouth, canines glowing, and cried out, and he knew that it was speaking directly to him.

'Ouwlmy,' he said, opening his eyes. 'What beast was that?'

'The master of the Khashm and its prisoner,' she said enigmatically.

'I do not understand.'

'It is significant that she came to you in the drift-stage,' Ouwlmy said. 'I was right to insist on transporting you alone. How many intruders Bjork has bade me destroy in order to maintain the sanctity of the Khashm.'

'The Shakra do Bjork's bidding?'

'The Shakra do as the Shakra may,' Ouwlmy said. 'Bjork knows this. Just as he knows that each action we take has a reaction. For what we fulfill there is a price.'

'Would you do the bidding of others – for the right price?' Moichi asked, alarmed.

Ouwlmy tossed her magnificent head. 'You mistake us, but do not anger us. Special you may be, but I still have the power to trample you underhoof if that is my desire. The Shakra belong to the Khashm, just as the Shinju do. A subtlety the Syrinxians never appreciated. Thus, in their arrogance, they perished. There is a connection between each and every species of the Khashm. We are it and it is us. Inseparable for eternity. This is our life and our power. Those who ignore this immutable fact do so at their extreme peril.'

Moichi stroked her long, powerful neck. 'Would you truly trample me underhoof?'

Ouwlmy's lips pulled back from her muzzle revealing three rows of formidable teeth. She began to laugh. 'I am an unforgiving master,' she said. 'You have only to ask Bjork. But the truth is I like you. Inside your strange form, your power meridians are accurately aligned. That is in your favor, so worry not.'

'Good,' Moichi said. 'I like you, too.'

The sun was already a white orb in a yellow and red sky filled with scudding clouds as long as war streamers of the gods. The horizon remained an unbroken line in all directions. Below, Ouwlmy's slender hooves made almost no splash as they moved in and out of the sluggish water. Moichi, who had fallen into that strange dreamish languor, had no idea how far they had come from the camp he had made with Sardonyx and Hamaan. He wished he had been able to leave a note for them so that they would wait for his return and not worry. He wondered if Sardonyx could locate him as she had done with Dujuk'kan in the Mas'jahan sex palace.

'Hold tight now.' Ouwlmy's voice broke into his musing. 'We must cross a large sink hole. The water is very deep here and on either side are wide bars of quicksand.'

The sink hole opened up with breathtaking quickness, and they were plunged into deep water, black as night. Moichi, fully alert now, noticed swarms of white flowers floating upon a surface so dark it reflected the sky as accurately as a mirror. A pair of swooping craans left a visual trail in the water, then were gone across the fen.

'Is this the White Lotus?' Moichi asked, pointing to the floating flowers.

'A harvest yet to be,' Ouwlmy said, but when Moichi reached over and began to pluck one, she cried out, 'Keep your hands to yourself! It is forbidden! You are not a harvester!' The tension in her normally calm voice caught his attention. The blossom he had touched had begun to shiver as with an ague.

'Ah, too late,' she said almost as a lament.

Ahead of them, the still surface of the sink hole had begun to pearl and swirl. Then, quite frighteningly, it lifted up in a huge egg-shaped mound. More swiftly than the eye could follow, the mound became a knoll and then a hill off which cascades of water sluiced.

'Râs Gharib!' Ouwlmy said.

Rising from the depths of the sink hole was an armor-plated leviathan with a long snout, three-foot jaws and tiny evil eyes glittering the color of emeralds. These double-lidded orbs with gold vertical iris slits peered at them in cold-blooded calculation as the leviathan catapulted through the water toward them.

The massive jaws opened wide, and now Moichi could see its thick tail acting as a rudder to guide it. Ouwlmy leapt forward. Moichi leaned down, putting his mouth against the Shakra's twitching ear.

'Ouwlmy,' he whispered, 'can you get around behind this beast?'

The Shakra did not bother replying but instead put on a burst of speed, surprising even the implacable six-legged Râs Gharib. Moichi drew out his push-dagger.

'Closer,' he whispered, observing the thickness of the beast's armor plate. He prayed for strength. 'Closer.'

Râs Gharib was closing the circle, propelled by its six legs and its powerful tail, closing the gap between them until Moichi could scent an odor that reminded him of the camp's privy.

'Closer,' he urged, leaning over. 'Closer!'

The tip of the leviathan's tail rose out of the water, and Moichi divined the Râs Gharib's intent. In a moment, it would swing its tail sideways like a scythe, sweeping Moichi off Ouwlmy's back and ripping the Shakra in two.

Now!

The moment they were in range, he plunged the narrow blades through the armor plating into the base of the monster's tail. As he suspected, there was a major nerve cluster hidden beneath the scales.

The Râs Gharib rose up, its six short legs thrashing

water in all directions, then plunged back into the sink hole. Ouwlmy took off, the re-emerging monster swinging its head around, those evil eyes tracking the Shakra and her rider. It propelled itself forward with a furious leap, but almost immediately foundered. As Moichi had suspected, it relied on its powerful tail not only for direction but for balance in the water. Without the use of it, it beat itself around a small circle, snapping its jaws and wailing in a high-pitched tone.

At the far side of the sink hole, Ouwlmy fairly leapt out of the water into the shallows of a fen. 'What you did showed courage and resourcefulness,' she said. 'It has been such a long time since I have been impressed I had almost forgotten what a pleasant feeling it is.'

Hearing something in her voice, Moichi said, 'You took me through the sink hole deliberately, didn't you?'

'I beg your pardon?'

Once more, they were moving swiftly through the fen. Craans and somewhat larger birds, darker and more sinister-looking passed by overhead.

'Tell me, how would you have summoned the Râs Gharib if I had not disturbed the White Lotus blossom?'

'Whatever do you mean?' Ouwlmy said with that smile of hers. 'However, I will grant that the blossoms of that particular sink hole are in need of harvest. They are so thick I fear you might have inadvertently brushed your leg against one.'

'So it *was* a test,' Moichi said. 'And a rather dangerous one, at that.'

Ouwlmy tossed her head. 'Not by any means.' She bared her triple set of teeth. 'Often enough I have had occasion to bite Râs Gharib where it will hurt him most.'

'An evil creature, to be sure,' Moichi said.

'Unthinking, perhaps. Single-minded, yes. But not evil.

The Râs Gharib is governed by only two imperatives: food and territory.'

'Ouwlmy, I think you are a born philosopher,' Moichi said.

'Philosophy and physics rule the universe,' the Shakra said. 'Together, the two disciplines make a whole.'

'And what of magic?' Moichi asked. 'At the end of the Kai-feng, I had believed – hoped – that the age of magic was done; that the age of mankind was evolving.'

'Do you fear magic, Moichi? It is but the perfect blending of philosophy and physics, the one used as a foil against the other. Do you know what magic is? Have you seen light refracted through a prism? Magic is only that: philosophy employed to flex the laws of physics a bit more than is usual.'

Moichi considered this as they raced across the Khashm. He glanced up at the sky and saw that the sun was still near the eastern horizon. It appeared to have moved not at all from the last time he had checked, and he realized that from the moment he had mounted the Shakra time seemed to have ceased to exist. He mentioned this to Ouwlmy.

'I see I do not need to remind you to be observant,' the Shakra said. 'Contrary to common belief, time is not linear, but rather a sea into which we are all plunged. I have met you before, Moichi. You know me, do you not?'

Moichi thought about the profound sensation of déjà vu he had felt ever since setting foot in the Khashm. He could not recall ever having been here. And yet . . . 'It would seem that I *do* know you, Ouwlmy.'

'Yes. We have made this journey many times before. Time finds a way to repeat that which it deems most significant.' She raised her head. 'We are almost there. We have only the Bay of Demons to cross.'

Moichi gazed out across the fens. At first, he saw nothing

remarkable, but as he looked more carefully he began to discern a slight difference in the color of the water just ahead of them. Instead of reflecting accurately the hue of the sky, creating one seamless and disorienting whole, there seemed a slightly lighter shimmer to the water.

'That comes from the quicksand plains just beneath the skin of water,' Ouwlmy explained. 'Bjork created this bay – a barrier within the Barrier of God's construction.'

'How will we get across?' Moichi asked. 'It appears as if the quicksand plain is too vast to circumvent.'

'It is,' Ouwlmy confirmed. 'But we are going directly down its middle.'

'How do you propose to do that?'

'Watch,' the Shakra said, coming to a stop at the edge of the Bay of Demons. Lowering her head, she extended a pale green tongue from between her lips. It was thick at its base, wedge-like at its tip. And from that tip a thin, glistening strand was extruded. It was soon followed by others. These strands wafted on the wind, intersecting again and again until they made a close-knit web that floated further and further over the quicksand plain until the far edge was out of sight.

Ouwlmy coughed, raised her head, and said, 'Hang on tight.'

Moichi did as he was told and it was a good thing, too, because the Shakra took off in a manic burst of energy. Moichi, glancing down, saw her delicate hooves treading the skein she had constructed with such delicacy that the web barely gave, even with their combined weight.

In this enchanted manner, they fairly flew across the Bay of Demons, leaving untouched what evil remains might lie beneath, pulled down to an eternity of darkness, drowned and suffocated all at once.

All around them, as the quicksand plains gave way, the

Khashm was like a mirror in whose reflective surface they no longer appeared. It was as if they had crossed over into another dimension where light – a corollary of time – was a fixed point or, as Ouwlmy had pointed out, a vast sea within whose depths they were submerged.

'We have reached the other side,' Ouwlmy said, as if confirming Moichi's thoughts. 'Bjork is waiting for us.'

'Where is he?' Moichi asked. 'I see nothing but the Khashm.'

'That is as it should be,' Ouwlmy said. 'Bjork will be seen when it suits him.'

The Shakra at last came to the end of the skein she had made and stepped lightly off it. Here, the vast fen had given way to low, earthen spits, like fingers thrust out into the dark water, and quicksand. Soon enough, these fingers came together in what might be termed the palm of the hand. Here rose a circular copse of triple-canopied trees that Moichi, for reasons he could not understand, had not noticed before. And yet the trees were enormous, with reddish-gold trunks and spreading, thickly foliated boughs that, clustered, rose in graceful fan shapes. A light breeze rippled through the treetops and from somewhere Moichi could hear music being played on a pipe-like instrument.

Now he was aware of Ouwlmy's extreme pleasure. The Shakra pranced, fairly dancing along the finger of land toward the copse of trees. And as they approached, Moichi saw that the trees were something more. They formed an odd kind of dwelling, an immense house that rose hundreds of feet into the air. The music was louder now, a beautiful melody in a minor key. It appeared to be emanating from within the trees.

Slipping off Ouwlmy's back, Moichi discovered a keen sense of anticipation and, with the Shakra at his side, he strode toward what he perceived to be a dark opening, what in this form of abode might serve as a doorway.

The sweet music stopped and a deep, rich voice said, 'Welcome to my castle. Enter if you will.'

Moichi stepped through the doorway with Ouwlmy just behind him, and found himself inside a cathedral-like bower that rose in emerald splendor towards the very clouds. In the center of this space he saw what appeared to him to be a bear. Except that it stood very comfortably on its hind legs. Its fur was the same beautiful reddish-gold as the tree bark and it held in its right hand – yes, hand was a more appropriate word for the appendage than paw – a triangular instrument, a set of pipes. It was the bear who had been making the music.

Moichi looked around for Bjork, but he saw no one save the bear.

'Ouwlmy, my good friend,' the bear said. And the Shakra snorted, bobbing her head in delight.

Moichi stared wide-eyed at the bear. 'Bjork?'

'The very one.' The bear grinned, revealing heavy canines. 'I should bring you a mirror so that you might see your own expression.'

At his side, Ouwlmy snickered.

Through Moichi's mind came the enigmatic words spoken to him by Sanda in the dream: *'Time is of the essence/When the spirit flies above marsh and Khashm/Take care to bury past heart/And seek out the bear in the stone/ Not to possess/But to be possessed.'*

He had come through marsh and Khashm and was now confronting a bear, but as the Tsihombe had predicted, this was not the kind of bear he had been expecting. *Take care to bury past heart* – what did that mean? And the bear in the stone?

'Do not take it personally,' Bjork said. 'All are surprised who see me, though nowadays they be few enough.' He gestured, putting aside his pipes. 'You must rest and

214

refresh yourself. You have had a long journey through the Khashm.'

'And encountered the Râs Gharib.' Ouwlmy snickered again.

'Successfully, I see,' Bjork said, as he led them deeper into the bower. 'That beast needs a bit of discipline now and again.' He was obviously pleased.

They sat beneath the cool shade of a tree and, as songbirds flitted this way and that high above their heads, drank a heavy, sweet, fermented beverage while Bjork laid out plates piled high with smoked meats, aged cheeses, fresh fruit and shelled nuts. It was a veritable feast and Moichi, suddenly famished, set upon it with gusto.

'I have many questions for you,' Moichi said around a mouthful of delicious food.

'Really?' Bjork glanced at Ouwlmy. 'I did not realize that you had heard of me.'

'Your Jailor provided me with the basic information,' Moichi said, and related the story of his encounter with Bjork's creature and Dujuk'kan in the Mu'ad.

'Not one of my more successful creations,' Bjork said mournfully. 'Still, he was one of my first so I had a special fondness for him.'

'I am sorry I was obliged to kill him.'

'Don't be,' Bjork said bluntly. 'He overstepped his mandate. That was his choice and he had to pay the consequences for his actions . . .' Another quick glance at Ouwlmy. 'As we all must.'

'I am here for a purpose,' Moichi said, setting aside his plate. 'White Lotus is being sold on the other side of the Khashm. A trader named Yesquz is said to be dealing the drug. As a Shinju I think you must know him. He is a dark-complexioned Iskaman who lives and harvests the herbs and spices near the slopes of the Mountain Sin'hai.'

'Yesquz and I do business,' Bjork said. 'I have known

215

him for a long time. I would trust him with my life.'

'Yesquz married my sister. She is dead now and so is he. She was killed by the Makkon, a Chaos beast and he was hung by the slave trader, Dujuk'kan. And all because of White Lotus.'

'Calm yourself,' Ouwlmy said, nudging Moichi's hand from his weapon with her muzzle. 'You are among friends here.'

Moichi looked at the Shakra. She had the extraordinary ability to tell the truth with instant believability. No mean feat in a world where truth and lies were often indistinguishable.

'I know Sanda is dead,' Bjork said. 'But Yesquz.' He shook his head. 'May I have that which belonged to me?' He extended a paw.

Moichi hesitated, but looking into the bear's eyes he could find no malice, and at length he handed over the Shinju ring. At once, Bjork closed it in his fist and turned away from them both. While Ouwlmy pawed and stamped the ground with distress Moichi stared implacably at Bjork's back. Among friends he might be but they still had a great deal to answer for.

When Bjork turned back, Moichi could see that his eyes were red. He had been weeping silently. 'Come with me,' he whispered.

Moichi followed him further into the tree-castle, surprised that the Shakra did not accompany them. He found that he had grown used to her company, her philosophical wit, and he already missed her. At length, they came to a series of wound vines and Bjork began to scramble up them. He paused, looking down at Moichi. 'Come on,' he said. 'The climb is not difficult, even for a human.'

Moichi ascended hand over hand. Bjork was right, the vines were wound in such a manner that they provided non-slip purchase for both hand and leg. They were high up in the canopies when Bjork swung off the complex of vines. He turned and, reaching down, helped Moichi into what could only be termed a tree-house.

From this lofty perch could be seen the curving line of trees and Moichi realized that they were near the far edge of the castle. Looking out, he saw that they had come to the edge of the Khashm. He faced a sprawling savannah, bisected by a wide river of clear turquoise, beyond which midnight-blue slopes reached upward until they rose blackly into the sky.

'The Mountain Sin'hai,' Bjork said. 'Magnificent, isn't it?'

Moichi almost trembled to be in such close proximity to the sacred Mountain of God. Upon those slopes God had made His indelible mark. Within the swirling clouds and fulminating ice-storms of the summit He dwelled, though none would ever dare climb the Mountain Sin'hai's face to find Him.

'I have been living in its shadow for centuries.'

'Centuries?' Moichi looked at him.

'Yes. I am singular among Shinju,' Bjork said with the kind of infinite sadness that gave Moichi pause. 'Just as I am alone among the ruins of deserted Syrinx, a ghost walking a ghost-filled land. I am the last of the Shinju.'

Moichi looked at him. 'Your magic has kept you alive,' he said.

'If one thinks of biology as magic.' Bjork gave an ironic grin. 'Yes, I am a mage of some considerable expertise. But it is also true that the Shinju are – *were* – an exceptionally long-lived race. We kept this freak of nature a dark secret because we felt other races would feel threatened. For us, eight hundred years is a normal life span, but there were certainly those who lived considerably longer.'

'Eight hundred years!' Moichi tasted the number on his tongue as if it were a spice.

217

'Yes. That is why it was strictly forbidden for us to intermarry with other races.'

Thinking of the Shinju Miira marrying the Syrinxian minister Bnak, Moichi said, 'I do not understand.'

Bjork sighed. 'Think for a moment. Can you imagine yourself growing older while your wife barely ages? It would be utterly disastrous. Besides, no one could know the traits of the issue of such an intermarriage, what freak of nature might be born.'

Moichi rounded on him. 'I require answers, not a history lesson.'

Bjork, staring down at the ring in his paw, said, 'I am afraid you cannot have the one without the other. I first met your father many years ago when he was a man of middle years. He was an extraordinarily ambitious man – a visionary, really. His fervent desire was to connect the world – the cultures that had, over the centuries, fallen in upon themselves, shunning the outside world. Trade, he believed correctly, was the universal commodity. Every race needed something, every race would want more as soon as it was exposed to the range of treasures the world has to offer. In that pursuit he traveled widely.'

'I know.'

'No doubt. But what you may *not* know was just how widely he traveled. On one journey he crossed the Mu'ad and came to Syrinx.'

Moichi stared at Bjork. 'My father met you *here?*'

'Yes. As you have been told, there are spices and herbs here unavailable elsewhere. In pursuit of trade and profit he journeyed here – and he stayed for a time.'

At once, Moichi made the connection. 'That year when I was fifteen and we were sent word that he had broken his hip in Kintai and could not be moved.'

'Precisely,' Bjork said, pleased again. 'We struck up a strong friendship, your father and I. He was an exceptional man, as I have said. And he fell in love with Syrinx. Unlike others, he was enchanted by the ruins and the ghosts rising each night like mist off the Khashm. Together, we roamed the Syrinxian capital, observing sad and disfigured faces drifting past us like clouds. And, at dawn, we listened to the soft explosions as the ghosts vanished into the sunlight.

'Of course we did business.' Bjork fingered the ring, turning it over and over. 'That was why he had come here. I had no illusions about that. But it did not matter because he chose to stay for very different reasons.'

'Did he . . . ?' Moichi felt an unpleasant pressure in his throat. 'Did you sell him White Lotus?'

'Your father was a trader, Moichi, not a criminal. White Lotus is a dangerous drug. He knew nothing of it until he came here.' Bjork looked up into Moichi's face. 'But by the time he left he knew more about it than he ever wanted to.'

'What do you mean?'

Bjork stared up at the blue slopes of the Mountain Sin'hai. 'I said before that every action has its consequence. And, like ripples in a pond, those consequences may have effects that echo on and on.' He raised his hand, leading Moichi down, out of the protection of the tree-castle. They went across a field of blue-green grass that sloped steadily down to a stony embankment beyond which rippled the swiftly flowing river that snaked through the savannah toward the slopes of the looming Mountain Sin'hai.

Bjork sat on a pink granite rock, throwing a handful of pebbles one by one into the river. Perhaps a hundred yards away, Ouwlmy cropped contentedly at the grass. 'When I was a boy,' Bjork said, 'I used to come here. That was a long time ago, when the Syrinxians thought they ruled the land. We let them cling to that belief; it was easier that way.' A pebble plunked into the water, vanishing. 'It was so peaceful here, just the sound of the wind and the water, whereas elsewhere the eternal bustle of the ever-industrious Syrinxians was unavoidable.'

He cast the last pebble into the river, then brushed his hands. 'Now even this peace is no longer granted me. Perhaps that is as it should be. I – like all Shinju – have done terrible, questionable things.' He glanced up at the wreathed summit of the sacred mountain. 'Something is dreadfully amiss up there.'

'How do you know that?' Moichi asked.

'Because of the Makkon. The Chaos beast you encountered. It had no tongue, isn't that correct?'

'Yes.'

'It came down from the Mountain Sin'hai, and when it tried to come here to get White Lotus, I cut out its tongue to teach it a lesson. And I sent the tongue on a long journey as proof of my continuing control over the beasts of Chaos.' His head swung around, the eyes catching Moichi in their gaze. 'Because, Moichi, there are those among the races of man who have allied themselves with Chaos in order to further their own power. These people, too, must be taught a lesson.'

'Listen, Bjork, it isn't that I disbelieve you, but I know what I know. I saw what that maimed Makkon did to my first mate. It did the same to my sister. And where my first mate died, a berserker on White Lotus had trashed the place. My brother Hamaan believes it was a member of Al Rafaar. He captured your friend Yesquz in Mas'jahan. He was in possession of White Lotus, so I know–'

'What you say is impossible.' The bear looked at Moichi, his liquid brown eyes curiously sympathetic. 'Yesquz had no interest in White Lotus, and he never got any from me.'

'You have ceased to harvest the drug, then?'

Bjork said, 'Ouwlmy already indicated to you that White

Lotus is still being manufactured. Is that not so?'

'It is. But I thought it prudent to see what you would say.'

Bjork turned to Ouwlmy. 'Do you like this fellow, or what?'

The Shakra gave him an enormous grin. 'Quick on his feet.'

'So you *do* harvest it.'

'Strictly speaking, no. Ouwlmy and her Shakra harvest the root. They pluck it and chew it into a pulpy paste. Something in their saliva activates enzymes otherwise locked in White Lotus. Then they turn it over to me.'

Moichi said, 'Now that we have established the existence of the harvest, who do you sell it to?'

When Bjork hesitated, Moichi added, 'It was wise not to have allowed my brother, Hamaan to come here. He is not an understanding man. You are selling the root to Al Rafaar. This is why we have come. If he finds you he will kill you the first chance he gets and I am not certain that I will stand in his way.'

'I do not believe that. But, yes, Hamaan is another matter entirely.' Bjork looked up. Ouwlmy had come over, silently high-stepping through the blue-green grass. Now she put her muzzle against his side until he bent over and kissed her between her ears. 'Yes,' he whispered, 'I know. But, you see, I must. I have no choice. And he is the right one, the only one.'

Putting his arm across the Shakra's croup, he said to Moichi, 'My client – my *sole* client for White Lotus is Chaos. All Chaos feeds on it. I promise you that neither I nor Yesquz has had any dealings with Al Rafaar.'

'I do not believe you,' Moichi said. 'I saw what the Makkon did to my first mate. The manner was absolutely consistent with how Sanda was killed.'

'You saw her, then.'

'No. Her corpse was described to me by a member of the Fe'edjinn.'

Bjork stared silently at Moichi for a long time. 'The Makkon did not kill your sister, of that I have no doubt. For expediency's sake, her death was made to look like the work of a berserker.'

'You mean Hamaan was right? It *was* Al Rafaar?'

'Did not her death galvanize the Iskamen populace? Did it not bring even the most recalcitrant into the Fe'edjinn's fold?'

'Yes. It was like a lightning rod.' He stared at Bjork, his mind numb with the implications. 'Are you implying that the Fe'edjinn had my sister murdered?'

'It is the only answer that makes sense, Moichi. The Fe'edjinn were the only ones to benefit from her demise. She became a rallying cry, a martyr the Fe'edjinn could take into the final battle for which they all ache.'

'What of the Makkon? What was it doing in Ala'arat? Why did it trek all the way across the Mu'ad to Mas'jahan?'

'For this.' Bjork held out Sanda's ring. 'I gave this to your father when he left here as a keepsake. But it also had a far more significant purpose. It is my talisman. The being that possesses it has the power to summon me wherever he or she might be.'

He stared at the ring as he turned it around between his fingers. 'Perhaps it was weak of me. I suppose that only proves I, too, am human.' He gave an ironic laugh. 'Your father meant so much to me I could not endure the thought of never seeing him again. So I manufactured this ring and he took it with him. Before he died, he gave it to Sanda but never told her of its power. She thought of it only as one of his most prized possessions.'

'How do you know this?' Moichi asked.

Bjork smiled. 'Your father summoned me one last time. Just at the point of dying.'

'But I was there? I was with him!'

'Yes. I know.'

And then Moichi remembered that he seemed to have fallen asleep at the moment his father had died. Sitting by his bedside Jud'ae had been alive one moment, dead the next and Moichi had no memory of what had transpired in between.

He looked at Bjork. 'Yes. I believe it possible you were there.' He thought a moment. 'One thing I do not understand. Ouwlmy told me she knew Sanda was dead because I had the ring. Ouwlmy said she would not have given it up otherwise.'

Bjork heaved a long sigh. 'Strictly speaking that is true. However, not in this case. Do not think ill of Ouwlmy; she omitted the truth only to protect me.'

Late afternoon light played off the facets of the ring as he turned it. 'Moichi, your father . . .' His voice drifted off. 'How shall I put this? How *can* I put this? There are many things about me that make me unique, that other races would find strange and, perhaps, abhorrent.' He took a breath and, as he did so, the outline of the bear shimmered and collapsed in upon itself.

Moichi blinked, for in the bear's place was sitting a beautiful golden-haired woman. 'I know what you are thinking,' she said in a soft, melodious voice, 'but I assure you this is not an illusion. The truth is I am both male *and* female. And when your father arrived here he saw not the bear, not the male, but I, Bjork, the woman.'

Moichi felt a brief constriction of his heart. 'And you fell in love.'

Bjork nodded. 'That is why he stayed so long, why I felt such pain at his leaving.'

'Why you gave him the ring.'

The woman's eyes closed briefly. 'I think he might have

stayed had I asked him to, but I had no desire to imprison him here. Besides, his family needed him.'

'So you did the next best thing. You were able to come to him whenever–'

'Oh, do not think ill of him, Moichi.' She leaned over, touched Moichi's wrist. 'He was such a wonderful man, and he loved his family so. He spoke of his children so often that I felt I knew them.' She looked away for a moment, out across the brilliantly lit savannah. 'And he did not call me often. It was painful for both of us, you see.'

After a long while, Moichi said, 'Yes, I think I understand.'

She bowed her head. 'Thank you for that.'

'So the Makkon was after the ring.'

Bjork nodded. 'I had maimed it and it wanted revenge.'

'Then it would seem logical it killed Sanda.'

'No. Sanda had long before given the ring to Yesquz.'

'But why?'

Bjork rubbed her forehead. 'They were in love, of course. But the marriage never should have been. Yesquz made sure to tell me only after the fact. I flew into a rage and, finally, I convinced him to tell Sanda the truth. You see, their marriage was an abomination. He was her half-brother.'

Moichi sat in stunned silence for some time. When he was able, he said, 'Yesquz was your son?'

'Yes.' She could only manage a whisper. Her liquid brown eyes pleaded silently with him for understanding.

'And my father was . . .'

She nodded. 'Yesquz's father.'

Moichi put his head in his hands. He heard the purling of the water, the calls of the birds overhead as if from a great distance. There was a roaring in his ears he could not control. He gasped once, then said, 'I want to hear the history now.'

'Moichi–'

'No!' He pulled away from her. 'No more of this. Tell me about the Shinju.'

Ouwlmy made a sound deep in her throat and Bjork shushed her.

'Consequence, Moichi. In the end, it all comes down to that. You may wonder why I am the last of the Shinju. What happened to my people, if we were so long lived?'

She waited for a response, but when none came, she went on, her heart heavy, 'Legend has it that the Syrinxians killed us off, but legends are often simply common knowledge distorted to serve the common good, to assuage the fears of mankind. But they are just as often lies. You see, uncounted millennia ago the Shinju made a pact with Chaos. We would provide them with White Lotus if they would extend our longevity.'

'How is any of this possible?' Moichi lifted his head. 'Chaos is not of this world. In fact, all the Makkon I have encountered, save the one in Ala'arat, were not even fully in the world of man. They belong to Chaos and their incursions here are for the purpose of expanding Chaos – a dimension inimical to man – into our world.'

Ouwlmy made a high keening sound and Bjork kissed her again. 'I know, but all must be told now. It is fated.

'Moichi,' she said, 'I make it known that I am breaking the most sacred vow of the Shinju. I do it now because I must. Because the Makkon came down from the summit of the Mountain Sin'hai. Because I am the last of the Shinju and as such my one desire before I die is to expunge for ever the sin committed so long ago by my people.'

She stood up and they began to walk by the side of the river. 'Remember what I said about the common good. It is mankind's most widely held belief that Chaos is its most implacable enemy, that all Chaos desires is to invade the world of man and make it its own. In a way, this is true. But it is also untrue.

'Once, the dimension of Chaos did not exist. Then, this world of man was eclectic enough to encompass all of God's children – mankind and Chaos creature alike. Together, they dwelled here, if not in complete peace, then in a kind of balance.

'But the ends of mankind and those of Chaos are different. Mankind must constantly change. It is a relentlessly restless creation, warlike, possessive, territorial. Whereas the Chaos beings are more like us – they prefer stasis. Chaos does not change – it is enough that it abides. Mankind could neither understand nor tolerate this, and so a war ensued in which the mages of mankind managed to banish Chaos, sealing it in another dimension.'

Moichi said, 'I still cannot imagine mankind and Chaos living in one world.'

Bjork said, 'If you understand that man and Chaos were born as one being then all becomes clear.'

'What are you saying?'

'I think you know perfectly well,' Bjork said. 'Ouwlmy tells me your meridians are in alignment, therefore deep down you understand. Give it time; let it surface.'

She scratched the Shakra's head as they walked along. 'It has probably occurred to you that the Shinju are both more advanced and more primitive than most of mankind. Certainly your father understood this in the most primal way. That is, I believe, what drew him to this place – and to me.'

They paused on a knoll that overlooked the savannah. There, all manner of wildlife could be seen dwelling in natural balance under the shadow of the Mountain Sin'hai.

'This is where the last ancient battle was waged, close to where the mages of mankind created the Portal into

Chaos and sealed it for what they believed was all time. I know this because the Shinju are closer to Chaos – to the way things used to be – the integration of man and Chaos, the light and the darkness, a whole that is now unimaginable – than any other race.'

She turned to Moichi, those liquid brown eyes boring into his brain. 'And, even more unimaginable, a fundamental shift has recently occurred in the dimension of Chaos. It advocates change. In short, it wants back what was taken from it.'

Moichi's scalp was crawling with a peculiar and unpleasant sensation. 'What does that mean?'

'Chaos wants you, me, everyone. It wants to *reintegrate* – to quite literally crawl inside each of us and take up residence.'

'God of my fathers!' The thought was so abhorrent that for a moment Moichi's mind went numb.

Beside them, Ouwlmy's ears pricked up, swiveling, and she lifted her head. 'They are coming,' she said to Bjork. 'I told you they would.'

Bjork turned her beautiful head. 'If that is so then it, too, is fated.'

'What will you do when they come?'

'Shhh,' Bjork said, soothing the Shakra with her long, delicate hand. 'This matter must be finished before they arrive.'

'Who is coming?' Moichi said, his hand on the hilt of a dirk. 'Is there danger?'

Bjork gave him a strange smile. 'Apparently, your companions have followed you here. And at the moment I cannot say what danger awaits. You know your brother better than do I.' She shrugged. 'I will tell you this, however. Whatever Hamaan has told you, Yesquz possessed no White Lotus. Do I make myself clear?'

'I–'

'Come. Hamaan is almost upon us,' she said abruptly. 'There is little time to finish what I have begun.' She pointed. 'Up there, on the summit of the Mountain Sin'hai is the Portal into Chaos.'

'Impossible,' Moichi said, staring at the cloud-wreathed mountain. 'That is a sacred place. It is the home of God.'

'And God made all of us: Shinju, Shakra, human, Chaos.'

'Wait a minute. Something is very wrong.' Moichi regarded her. 'Where are the cruel highlands, the mountain goats from which you manufactured fantastic garments lighter than air?'

'What are you talking about?'

'The legend of Miira's Mirror,' Moichi said. 'I have heard it told so many times I can recite it by heart. The Syrinxians swept through here, decimating the Shinju, driving the remnants into the cold highlands.'

'As you can see, there are no cold highlands here,' Bjork pointed out, 'save the slopes of the Mountain Sin'hai itself. But no, when the Syrinxians came we allowed them the land they wanted. They seemed to have more need of it than we did. Our home has always been the Khashm, and it was only when they wanted this, too, that they were stopped.'

'You slew them.'

'We did no such thing,' Bjork said. 'That form of violence does not come easily to us.' She smiled, a secret light in her eyes. 'But we had the Khashm itself, its sink holes, quicksand plains, its Râs Gharibs, its craans, its Shakras. Nature took care of our land, Moichi. We had need to do nothing at all.'

'Then how did the Shinju die out?'

'We did not die out,' Bjork said. 'We were slaughtered by the legions of Chaos who streamed through the Portal atop the Mountain Sin'hai. It was our punishment for feeding them for millennia, for keeping the tenuous connection open between the two worlds.

'As I said, Chaos is our brother; we are stasis creatures. But when Miira used her mirror to destroy every member of the Syrinxian inner council she set in motion an irreversible chain of events. The Syrinxian capital was thrown into anarchy. A fearsome reign of terror spiraled outward until it engulfed the entire population.

'A Shinju became an agent of change. It went against Nature. But then Miira was always a rebel. She married a Syrinxian and became an outcast from her own people. She was despised by her husband's race and could never return to her own.'

'This is very different from the legend.'

'I am afraid the truth was too terrible to be supported by the common good, so the legend arose, based on fact, yes, but distorted so as to be palatable, inspiring, even.'

'How do you know all this?' Moichi asked.

'In the worst way possible,' Bjork said, scratching Ouwlmy behind her ears. 'I, Bjork, am Miira's child.'

A thick silence now engulfed them. Every other moment, it seemed, Moichi was having to readjust his sense of reality. At last, he said, 'But you were murdered by Bnak's enemies. They left the body–'

'But it was not my body,' Bjork said. 'My mother saw to that. Do you think she did not know what was happening, what was to occur? She was Shinju – and more, she was herself a sorcerer. She looked into her mirror, into the ocean of Time and saw the possibility of my murder. Therefore, she took steps to ensure my safety. She hid me and substituted another in my place.'

'She sacrificed a child?'

'To save me, yes.' Bjork looked at him evenly. 'She was no saint. Far from it, in fact. But I wonder – and I beg you to consider this before you condemn her out of hand

– would your own mother have done less to save you?'

'How can I answer that?' Moichi asked.

'How can anyone?' Bjork confirmed.

Moichi considered this for some time. He thought of what Bjork had said regarding an offspring of a Shinju intermarriage: *no one could know what freak of nature might be born.* Bjork was the result, the progeny of a Shinju sorcerer and a brilliant Syrinxian minister. And what of Yesquz? At length, he said, 'But you yourself said that she was judged to have sinned because Chaos was loosed from the Portal.'

'As an agent of change, she sinned. It is not in our nature.'

'But what kind of a God destroys almost an entire race?'

'By her actions Miira disturbed the delicate balance between the world of man and the dimension of Chaos. God – Nature, the Eternal Force, whatever one wishes to call it – had no choice but to restore that balance.' Bjork's eyes played over Moichi's face. 'You remember what I said about action and consequence.'

'Yes. Then what is happening? Why is the Makkon here? I thought that Chaos's destruction of the Shinju restored the balance.'

'So did I,' Bjork said, 'until the coming of the Makkon and the Dolman. Now, in seeking the overthrow of stasis, Chaos has begun to take on the characteristics of mankind. This is an absolute impossibility. Chaos was created to be the dark side – the exact opposite – of mankind. If this should change, as it is beginning to do, all lifeforms – mankind and Chaos alike – are threatened with extinction.'

'If all you say is true then you must close the Portal,' Moichi said.

'I cannot. Unlike my mother, I am incapable of being an agent of change.'

'But by what you have revealed to me you have broken your stasis.'

Bjork shook her head. 'No. I have been a facilitator only. I have taken no overt action as my mother did. I will not do that.'

So that was it, Moichi thought. Here was the bear in the stone, caught like a prehistoric fly in amber.

Bjork's eyes glowed. 'That is why you have come, Moichi. You are the agent of change. It is you who must journey to the summit of the Mountain Sin'hai and there confront whatever may await you.'

The Kaer'n speaks:

I have never been to Sin'hai, but for myself I admit to some anticipation. For millennia – perhaps ever since our creation out of the cosmic Dark and Light – Sin'hai has been a subject of intense debate among my kind, for Sin'hai is the one place on the planet where we have been enjoined from going.

Understandable, perhaps. To be in Sin'hai is to acknowledge Syrinx, and we could never exist alongside the Shinju; we would remind them far too much of their eternal enslavement. Also, we would remind them of what, perhaps, they once aspired to be but could not be.

And, I suppose, it is just as well. We have had no designs on Syrinx. On the contrary, I doubt we could live comfortably among the ruins of the inhumanity of the races. What is Syrinx, after all, but a monument to cruelty? The blood-soaked earth is good for nothing now but growing rank foliage that is fast sweeping through the cyclopean buildings erected by a long-dead race.

They may be dead, but as we are taught as infants, their legacy infects the races of man with a tenacity that is appalling. War, power, greed, envy – these evils will outlive the abandoned stone edifices of Syrinx, and do far more damage.

For there is blood-lust still staining the waterways of the Khashm, and the proximity of holy Sin'hai has made it prey to the malevolence there. Perhaps, after all, Sin'hai will prove itself as abandoned as the land below it. I hope not. I hope the God of this Universe is still there. But I have my doubts. Every day now I feel the evil growing, and it is a desecration for any wickedness to exist on Sin'hai.

Each sunrise, when I make my prayers, I include one for Sin'hai, because as its light goes, so goes the fate of the world . . .

PART FOUR
SIN'HAI

THIRTEEN

DRAGON

Chiisai, searching for all that remained of Sanda, could not find her. The transformation was over. Chiisai had become whatever it was she was destined to be. She did not yet know what that was as there were no mirrors, rivers, no reflective surfaces of any kind in Chaos in which she could see her reflection. In fact, there were no surfaces at all, just an endlessly gyring vortex broken only by great bouts of energy, erupting at random intervals, in random directions. In other words, Chaos.

It might bear a resemblance to some religions' concept of hell, only it was much worse.

Perhaps, Chiisai thought, in the very process of transformation, while she was being born, something had been lost. Why else had she been able to find Sanda's essence before and not now? She closed her eyes, searching for Sanda amid the constant roar of Chaos but she had been cut off from her.

She looked straight into the vortex and it was like staring into the eye of the sun. How was it that she hadn't been aware of the vortex before? She had floated in a void. Deaf, dumb and blind. Now she could see and hear. Did this mean she had become part of Chaos, a beast more at home in this dimension than in the world of man?

But, no. She felt herself crawling on the edge of the

vortex. Something inside her warned her not to get nearer to it lest she get sucked in, never to take a breath of air again. Crawling on a sliver of gold, a strand of hair, a filament so fine it often seemed to disappear. Crawling onward.

And at its end was a great eye that opened as she approached. She held neither hesitation nor fear but was, rather, motivated by an elemental need to move forward, ever forward. Through the eye of the lens . . .

. . . Onto the flat of her broadsword which stuck horizontally from the crevasse in the cave in the bluff overlooking the sea of Ama-no-mori. Home.

Yet not quite, not anymore. Home and yet strangely different, like returning to the place where her ancient ancestors dwelled, memories surfacing she never even suspected existed inside her. She *knew* this place, and not merely from recent memory. Echoes of voices, strange yet oddly familiar, filled her skull with a feast of remembering. Home for them in a way she was just beginning to envision.

I am the first, she thought. *But am I the first of many, or the last of my kind?*

She dropped off the blade and, mindful of the glowing white metallic veins in the floor of the cavern, made her way as quickly as she could to the mouth. There, she stood upon the escarpment looking out at the water. Where had Kaijikan taken the reanimated Tokagé? He had begun his merging with the Chaos satellite Phaidan, and might already have reached his full potential, unless she had been successful in stopping it. What terrible plan had the revenge-bent Kaijikan in mind? Surely it must involve the death of Chiisai's father, the Kunshin, for it had been he who had killed her sister. Or so Kaijikan believed.

I must away to the capital, Chiisai thought. *To Haneda.*

And, without conscious thought, she spread her enormous armored wings, the air beneath them levitating her so that she hovered for a moment, as astonished as anyone could be. She looked down upon the rocky scree up which she had labored, ungainly earthbound being she had once been.

She had a moment of pure panic, seeing nothing but air between her and the crashing ocean. Then, instinct took over, and she wheeled into the sun, flexing those powerful wings.

Over the creaming waves she soared, arcing back over the land as it swept down the snowy scree into the lowlands where their luma had been tethered. The mounts were gone, no doubt taken by Kaijikan and Tokagé. Overcome by a fierce elation, she swung upwards in a series of loops, rolling over so that sky and earth followed one after the other in a tumble of blue and green and silver-white.

When she came out of her last roll she was far away from the scree upon which the deadly cavern resided, and she scanned the countryside leading toward Haneda. Her keen eyes picked out a figure astride a luma. Behind, a riderless luma – no doubt the one she had ridden – trotted docilely, tethered to the leading luma's saddle by its reins.

Chiisai made for the figure. Her speed was such that almost immediately she recognized Tokagé. But where was Kaijikan? Perhaps she had used her powers to transport herself to the Kunshin's moated castle in the heart of Haneda.

Chiisai changed the angle of her wings and she swooped down toward the warlord. Tokagé, seeing her shadow or merely sensing danger, turned in his saddle. He lifted one armored arm while drawing his longsword.

'Kaer'n!' he cried as Chiisai extruded her talons and, beating her powerful wings in rhythm, struck him across the helm. The golden talons of her forearms scored deep gashes across his salamander helm, knocking it askew. Parallel lines of blood oozed across his scalp.

He swung at her with the longsword but Chiisai found it ridiculously easy to avoid. She struck again, drawing blood again, and Tokagé screamed in unearthly rage. Had Phaidan completed its possession of the warlord? Chiisai recalled the halo of Chaos energy swirling around Tokagé's head when she had stabbed him in the neck. Kaijikan had obviously healed the wound but what had happened inside him?

Then, as Tokagé reared back to attack again, she saw the filmy reddish vapor leaking from between the neck-plates of his armor. So I *did* damage him, she thought. Perhaps, knowing this, Kaijikan left him here, ill and dying.

Tokagé swung at her with his longsword, the blade's edge cutting along one wing as she dived in again, bloody talons extended. They slashed across his breastplate with such force that he was flung clear of his luma, who reared up, baring its teeth in terror. One of the warlord's ankles was caught in his leather stirrup and as the luma wheeled, galloping away from its attacker, it dragged him along the ground until, as it leapt a line of stones, his ankle came free.

Tokagé lay on his back, his scored salamander helm askew, the armor plates across his torso pried apart. Still, even half-stunned, one leg fractured in several places, he had the presence of mind to wield his sword. Chiisai, screaming as she came in for the kill, was almost sliced in twain, but she twisted at the last instant, and the point of the sword punctured the membrane between two wing bones.

She landed upon Tokagé with all her fore-talons fully extended. With the force of her dive behind her, they pierced damaged armor, plunging into skin and flesh. Tokagé screamed, arching up as the talons went clear through him. His face was a rictus of agony and his arms beat a tattoo against the ground.

Now Chiisai's wings beat in rhythm – the kill-rhythm she had heard the Dai-San speak of when describing his Kaer'n. The tempo increased as shivers went through the dying warlord. His face was drained of blood, his black eyes rapidly losing focus. Chiisai tightened her grip upon him and his body shook in its final death-spasm.

At the moment of his passing, there came an evil hissing from the rent in his throat, and the reddish vapor began to coalesce. Phaidan, the satellite of Chaos was materializing.

The vapor had become a colloid – particles suspended in a kind of liquid – and these particles were colliding, merging, doubling and redoubling, forming clusters, colonies, countries, continents of substance that, abruptly, startlingly became solid, three-dimensional.

And, as Chiisai watched, transfixed with horror, this red substance crouched upon the corpse of the traducer, Tokagé, feeding upon its flesh and bones like a berserk cannibal until there was nothing left of the warlord save tattered banners of sere skin, which shriveled up and blew away like tumbleweeds along the black, rocky earth. The empty armor squealed and groaned beneath the weight metastasizing upon it.

'O, *the agony!*' Phaidan cried and, turning its baleful gaze upon her, said, '*I will return the favor – now!*'

And it leapt upon her. The old Chiisai – the Bujun warrior, though virtually fearless – would have been helpless before the Chaos satellite's attack. But the old Chiisai was dead, shed like Tokagé's wrinkled skin in the eternal maelstrom of Chaos. She was part Chaos now, and she used that part of her, lifting her long, horned head, baring long, pearl-colored fangs, that clashed and sparked as Phaidan hurled its chimerical form against her.

Fifty tentacles, then one hundred more erupted from the shifting body, curling around and around her, pinioning her wings to her scaly sides, holding her rear legs so that her talons extruded into the chill black earth. Chiisai struggled with her forelegs, working to get them inside the snaking tentacles, the razor-sharp talons severing them as she went. But for every one she sliced, two others appeared to take its place until Phaidan appeared as an enormous head from whose scalp sprang a forest of tentacles, thick as hair.

Then these tentacles themselves began to metamorphose, ophidian heads emerging from their ends, jaws opening wide, fangs bared, forked tongues flicking out to taste the scent of the prey. Chiisai ignored these, focusing on the head itself, trying to lay it open with her talons. Instead, more and more serpents writhed upward from the scalp, to be slashed in two, and to rise again three- and four-fold from the ball-like head.

She was tiring and the serpents were tightening their grip upon her wings, preventing the kill-rhythm. And now, here and there, in increasing numbers, the serpents' fangs sank into her flesh, trying to suck her life-force. When that failed to weaken her further, six of them twined together above her head, spiraling upward, stiffening, until they formed a great sword that began to slash down at her skull.

Chiisai opened her mouth and a tongue coated with glittering fire stabbed out, cutting through serpent and vein, plunging directly into the core of the Chaos beast.

As one, all the serpents screamed, their heads arcing back into a kind of protective sphere. But it was too late and in clusters they slithered away to a jelly-like substance, then returned to the red vapor, wisps taken by the wind.

Who are you? Phaidan cried. *I know all Kaer'n but I know you not.*

I am that I am, Chiisai said, driving her tongue deeper into its core. *You know me.*

Who? Who? Phaidan shrieked as it writhed, impaled.

I am that I am.

Pale fire rippled from Chiisai's tongue, engulfing Phaidan piece by piece, incinerating it in sections, an excruciating way to die – if, indeed, death was the correct term for the termination of a Chaos creature.

There was a leathery rustling as Chiisai's wings unfurled and, fluttering in the wind, beat the air in the instinctive kill-rhythm. So that is what I have become, she thought. A Kaer'n.

So she rested, the wind rustling along her wings as it did through the nearby cryptomeria. Tokagé's fantastically worked armor had rusted away as if it had been left to rot for a century. It lay like the skeleton of a time-ravaged beast, rattling and moaning as the wind swept through it.

Chiisai closed her eyes. It was difficult adjusting. For one thing, she no longer had lungs; she breathed via capillary action through the complex pores of her hide. For another, her blood – more accurately, her life's fluid – was pumped by a triple heart, encased within a well-protected bone cavity at the back of her long skull, and she still found the rapid beats of it disturbing. The list was virtually endless, and each change took painstaking accommodation.

A shadow passed over her and she looked up. Clouds were occluding the sun and the chill was back in the air. Perhaps another snow squall was on its way in off the ocean.

'So this is how it has ended for you.'

Chiisai turned her head on her long, articulated neck, saw Kaijikan floating toward her. She was smiling. 'When I set the trap, when I used the damaged Tokagé – the

Tokagé *you* made useless – as bait I must say I never expected a beast to take it.'

'I am not a beast,' Chiisai said.

'No, of course not,' Kaijikan said as she approached. 'Four legs, a tail, a dragon's head, scales and horns wherever you look. Not a beast at all.'

'What beast speaks?'

Kaijikan's smile widened into a grin. 'My dear, all *my* beasts are as articulate as I am.'

'What beast thinks as a human?'

The Keeper of Souls stood in front of Chiisai and laughed in her face. 'Is that what you believe? How naive. How could you when you are no longer human?'

'I am that I am.'

'That kind of mumbo-jumbo might have worked with Tokagé – what was he anyway but a receptacle? It might even have worked with Phaidan – what was it anyway but a satellite? But it will not work with me. I know who and what you have become, and believe me when I tell you that you are a beast, an evolutionary dead-end that cannot reproduce. Like all your kind you are useless; neither of one world nor another.' She made signs in the air. 'You have cheated death once, I will give you that. But I promise you, you will live to regret that feat.' Runes building in the ether. 'Because whatever life remains to you is *mine*.'

Chiisai, who was sick of this arrogance, tried to move against Kaijikan. To her astonishment, she remained immobile. Neither muscle nor nerve would respond to the commands her brain sent out. She was stuck, rooted to the black ground, a dragon set in stone.

Kaijikan, grinning still, took her time walking around Chiisai. 'You see, I will not regret Tokagé's demise, after all. Because now I have you – my own personal Kaer'n – to do my bidding. I had planned to use the reanimated

242

warlord to murder the Kunshin, but think, my dear, how much more delectable will be my revenge when his daughter does it instead.'

'Welcome,' the bear said, its fur bristling. 'We have been expecting you.' Bjork had transformed into the male ursus as Sardonyx and Hamaan had come over the rise.

Moichi, wondering how they had ever traversed the dangers of the Khashm without the help of a Shakra, said, 'I hope you were not worried about me.'

'I wasn't,' Sardonyx said softly. 'I knew where you were and whom you were with.' She rubbed Ouwlmy between the ears just as Bjork had done. 'How are you, sweetheart? Isn't Moichi wonderful?'

'He is the one,' Ouwlmy said.

'Yes. He is.' Sardonyx bent down, kissed the Shakra on the cheek. 'I have missed you, beautiful one.'

As Ouwlmy tossed her head and snorted in pleasure, Moichi said, 'You know each other?'

Sardonyx threw her arms wide and spun like a giddy little girl. 'This was where I learned my sorcery, Moichi. It is Shinju magic I perform.'

Moichi turned to Bjork. 'Is this true?'

The bear nodded. 'I do not practice my mother's art but I passed it on to Sardonyx.'

So that is how they passed unscathed through the treacherous Khashm, Moichi thought.

'What is all this?' Hamaan said, striding up. 'Dragons in the fen, talking luma, all manner of sorcery flying about? And now an intelligent bear. Who – or more accurately – *what* are you, sir?'

'I am Bjork,' the bear said. 'Last of the Shinju.'

'A Shinju!' Hamaan's eyes lit up. 'If I am dreaming, do not wake me up!' He took Bjork's paw in his hand, pumped it enthusiastically. 'You are the answer to all my prayers!

And, so hard by the Mountain Sin'hai, the home of the God of all Iskamen, it is fitting that you come to our aid.'

'I beg your pardon?' Bjork said.

'White Lotus, man!' Hamaan cried. The light of the fanatic had once again taken possession of his eyes. 'You are its guardian, you know all its secrets. You will turn the tide for us!' In an instant, a small skinning knife was in his hand, its blade held across the bear's throat. 'I'll warrant you will cease trading with the Adenese now, won't you?'

'I imagine so,' Bjork said calmly. But his liquid brown eyes warned the others not to make a move. 'Especially since I have done no trading with the Adenese.'

'No? Then who do you sell your harvest of White Lotus to?'

'I cannot continue to talk at the point of a knife.'

Hamaan moved the edge of the blade inward a fraction. 'You will do what I say, when I say. Is that clear?'

Hamaan gasped as the massive ursine outline wavered, collapsing in upon itself. In his place stood a beautiful woman with flowing red hair. Her eyes staring into his, she grasped his wrist, flipping it over so that Hamaan was bent over double, and kept on twisting until the knife fell to the ground. Then she let go.

'Yes,' Bjork said. 'It is very clear.'

'What madness is this?' Hamaan said, rubbing his wrist. 'Are you man, beast or woman? Or is all this an illusion?'

'In point of fact,' Bjork said, 'I am half-Shinju and half-Syrinxian. This is the truth, Hamaan.' She lifted a long arm toward the storm-wreathed summit of the Mountain Sin'hai. 'Now, before us and before your God, it is time you spoke the truth.'

'What are you talking about?'

'Did you think I would not find out? Did you think that

the death of a Shakra would go unnoticed? Or unpunished?'

Hamaan's face screwed up as if he were inhaling a foul stench. 'What nonsense are you spouting?'

'Tell him, Ouwlmy,' Bjork said. 'Tell them all.'

'Since summer, two raids have been made to the same White Lotus harvest ground, on the extreme eastern edge of the Khashm,' Ouwlmy said. 'After we masticate the root to paste, it must dry in the sun for forty-eight hours. Two such harvests were taken before full refining could be done. In the second raid, a Shakra was slaughtered.'

'And who was responsible for these raids? For the death of the Shakra?' Bjork said as she stared at Hamaan. When he remained silent, she pointed. 'Fe'edjinn carried out the raid. Elite, highly skilled shock troops under this man's direct command.' Bjork stood in front of Hamaan. 'The truth, man. Before God and your brother.'

'Lies.' Hamaan coolly turned to Moichi. 'Can't you see he is covering his dealings with the Adenese?'

'Oh, Al Rafaar got their White Lotus, all right,' Bjork said, 'but it was a Fe'edjinn operative who sold it to them.'

'What?' Moichi cried.

'Talk about outlandish accusations,' Hamaan said. 'No one would believe that.'

'Just as they would not believe you had your own sister murdered.'

Hamaan's face drained of all color. 'I will kill you for that.'

'I know you will try,' Bjork said. She held out the ring that she had given to Jud'ae Annai-Nin so many years ago, the ring Moichi had returned to her today. 'Take this, Hamaan. Hold it tightly in your right fist.'

Hamaan stared at it as if it were a poisonous serpent. 'I will do no such thing.'

'Yes, you will,' Bjork said. 'For in a moment we will be

confronting the truth. If, as you say, I am lying then you have nothing to fear. Quite the contrary, you will be exonerated.'

Moichi took a step toward him. 'Do it, Hamaan.'

'This is a trick, an illusion. She—'

'No illusion,' Sardonyx said. She turned to Moichi. 'I guarantee it.'

Moichi nodded. 'Take the ring, brother.'

Still, Hamaan hesitated. Then he snatched the ring from Bjork, enclosed it in a white-knuckled fist.

Almost immediately, a man appeared. He was garbed in the black robes of an Adenese Al Rafaar. He stood, looking around him for a moment, then, spotting Hamaan, he made a tiny genuflecting bow. 'Qa'tach,' he said. 'Where am I? What has happened to me?'

'Never mind that,' Bjork said. 'Tell us who you are. You need fear nothing. We are all Iskamen here or allies of Iskael.'

'I am not in Aden,' the man said. 'Qa'tach?'

Hamaan, ashen-faced, had dropped the ring. 'No, you are no longer in Aden,' he said in a voice at first shaky but quickly regaining strength. 'Tell these people who you are.'

'I am Kh'aligg,' the man in Al Rafaar robes said. 'I am a member of the Fe'edjinn.'

'And who is your direct control?' Bjork said.

'Qa'tach Hamaan,' Kh'aligg said. 'He trained me himself.'

'To do what?' Bjork asked gently.

'To infiltrate the Al Rafaar.'

'And . . .'

He looked at her in confusion.

'What has been your specific mission most recently?'

Kh'aligg looked at Hamaan, panic-stricken.

Hamaan, staring into Moichi's eyes, said, 'Tell them, Kh'aligg. There is no shame in it. You are a patriot.'

246

'I became a kind of middle-man,' Kh'aligg said, licking his dry lips. 'I sold White Lotus to Al Rafaar.'

'And where did the White Lotus come from?' Bjork asked.

'I do not know.'

'Tell them,' Hamaan said.

'It . . . it came from you, Qa'tach. You led two parties into Syrinx in order to obtain it.'

Moichi, stunned, said, 'Hamaan, have you lost your mind? *Why?*'

'You know why,' Bjork said briskly, picking up the ring. Kh'aligg vanished. 'The Qa'tachs believed that Al Rafaar berserker attacks inside Iskael's borders – within the capital itself – would win them unanimous support for their holy war against Aden.' Bjork leveled her gaze at Hamaan. 'But the plan did not go as you envisioned, did it, Qa'tach?'

'Hamaan,' Moichi pleaded. 'Tell them this is all a lie.'

Now Hamaan's eyes seemed to glaze over. 'We were almost there,' he whispered. 'Our avowed goal was just within our grasp. The Qa'tachs met in secret and it was decided that a more specific, more horrific goad was required. They allowed me the grace of abstaining.'

Moichi, his voice seemingly squeezed out of his mouth, said, 'Did you?'

'I did my duty.'

'Your *duty?*' Moichi felt the rage building inside him. Could this actually be the man with whom he had reconciled? The brother with whom he had agreed to forget the past? What kind of monster had he become?

'I am a patriot!' Hamaan cried. 'My sacred duty as Fe'edjinn is to make Iskael safe.'

'And you did this by providing Al Rafaar with White Lotus?' Moichi said incredulously.

'It was not fully refined,' Hamaan explained. 'I knew this. The Adenese who ingested it died within a week.'

'And how many innocent Iskamen were murdered in the interim, while you let the Al Rafaar berserkers loose inside Iskael?'

'It was a distasteful but ultimately necessary step in order to achieve our goal.' Hamaan's face was flushed with fervid emotion; at this moment he seemed incapable of remorse. 'Brother, listen to me, we have never been free of the Adenese yoke. Not really. You have been away a long time. Decades, centuries have passed since God let us through the Mu'ad. But always the Adenese have sought ways to punish us, closing down our trade routes, undermining our negotiations with other countries, destroying our wide-ranging caravans. It has been war by attrition ever since they realized we had not died in the Mu'ad. And then we began to terraform Iskael with such success that their jealousies were aroused. They have coveted the port of Ala'arat for decades. Don't you see, we are locked in a death-spiral? It is us or them. That was why the Fe'edjinn came into being.'

'No,' Moichi said. 'The Fe'edjinn were created by a small cadre of warriors chafing under the burden of peace. They no longer knew what to do with themselves and, worse, in peacetime they discovered that their powers had eroded. What status can a warrior expect when the one thing that gives him power no longer exists?'

Hamaan shook his head. 'You do not know how wrong you are.'

'The proof of what I say, brother, is right here, right now. Look at what you have done. You have put your own country at risk, allowed your citizenry to be slaughtered, to live in fear of Al Rafaar terrorists.'

'All for the glory of the God of our fathers, who brought us through the Mu'ad.'

Moichi slapped his brother so hard across the face that Hamaan staggered. 'Do not use God's name to legitimize your foul work. The Qa'tachs usurped power, fed on it like Chaos beings, until they – like you – have become unrecognizable.'

'We did what we had to do. We–'

'You sick bastard, have you any idea what you've done? You murdered your own sister!'

Moichi struck Hamaan again, but this time it was with his fist. Hamaan stumbled backward, blood flying from a split lip, and went down on one knee. Immediately, he picked up his knife, brandished it, point first. 'Come on,' he said, spitting out a tooth. 'Come on, brother. Why do I even bother with explanations? I always knew deep down that this was the way it would end for us. It was inevitable, wasn't it? You never understood me. You never understood that the Fe'edjinn's ministry of fear was necessary to keep Al Rafaar at bay. At least I know what I stand for. You have nothing. You *are* nothing.'

Moichi drew a dirk. Sardonyx, seeing this, took a step toward him, but a warning glance from Bjork caused her to stay her hand. 'This must be played out,' Bjork said, 'to the very end.'

'But they both might die.'

Bjork nodded. 'So be it, then. It is not within our purview to intervene.'

Sardonyx threw her a stricken look, but she shook her head firmly.

Moichi struck first, slashing open an oblique line across Hamaan's shoulder. Hamaan leapt to his feet, kicking out. The heel of his left boot caught Moichi on the side of the knee and he went down. Immediately, Hamaan was on him, maneuvering for position and leverage. Moichi slashed upward, but this time Hamaan was ready for him. He parried the blow with the guard of his knife as he smashed the edge of his hand into Moichi's windpipe.

Moichi convulsed. Black lights pulsed behind his eyes

and there was a terrible roaring in his ears. His lungs fought for breath as he struggled to keep conscious. Dimly, he saw the knifeblade stabbing down at his shoulder, and he jammed an elbow into Hamaan's ribcage, succeeding in deflecting the strike just enough so that the blade punctured the meat of his arm and not his shoulder. He cried out, slammed the heel of his hand under Hamaan's chin. But his brother twisted away, stabbed him again and again in the muscle of his right arm.

Red rage now supplanted the pulsing black spots and in a titanic adrenaline surge Moichi managed to heave his brother off his chest. They rolled over and, as they did so, Moichi hammered the knife out of Hamaan's fist with the copper butt of his dirk. Then he threw his own weapon away and, using his hands, beat Hamaan insensate.

He crouched over his brother, panting and bleeding. Rage and the rush of endorphins pulsed a strong tattoo through his body. At length, he became aware that Bjork was holding out his dirk to him. As he took it, she said, 'Will you kill him now?'

'I do not know.'

'He slaughtered a Shakra, murdered his own people.' She bent over. 'He gave his consent for the assassination of your sister.'

'Bjork, stop it!' Sardonyx said. 'This has gone on long enough. How can you torture him so?'

She would have gone on but Bjork held up a hand in warning. 'Remember,' she said softly, 'who is the master and who the pupil.' Then, turning back to Moichi, 'Well, what are you waiting for? He has been accused, tried and convicted by his own words and independent corroborating evidence. Pass sentence, Moichi. It is your duty. Your responsibility.'

Moichi held the dirk above Hamaan's throat. Then, reversing it, he slammed it home into its sheath. 'No,' he said, rising and pulling his brother up beside him. 'If, as you say, I am fated to journey to the summit of the Mountain Sin'hai then Hamaan will accompany me into the House of the Holy. Let God pass what judgement He may on my brother. That is His province, not mine.'

FOURTEEN

CLOUDLAND

It would have been painful to climb this multi-spined volcanic rockface under the most ideal conditions. The fact that both Moichi and Hamaan hurt from a host of wounds only exacerbated the fact.

Sin'hai had always been an intimidating mountain, but never more so than when one was assaulting its ebon basalt slopes. Some were almost vertical, rising like icy spires into a cloudland so dense the climbers could already feel the weight of the storm-charged atmosphere, an acrid taste at the back of their throats from the ozone thrown off by the pink lightning that forked high over their heads, rumbling down the mountain face with the force of an avalanche.

Bjork and Sardonyx had worked hard overnight to stanch, disinfect and cauterize the combatants' wounds, but Bjork had been meticulous in remaining aloof from the tension that wreathed both brothers.

Once, while both Moichi and Hamaan tossed in dream-laden slumber, Sardonyx had asked, 'What was the point, Bjork? Their hatred is alive and breeding like some kind of hideous animal.'

Bjork looked off to the fulminating summit of the Mountain Sin'hai, alight and alive with the pink lightning so powerful it pierced even the heavy cloud cover. Three or four major earth temblors had shaken Syrinx in the hours following twilight. 'For the moment, the hate is fuel that will serve them well on their ascent.' Her gaze swung to Sardonyx. 'I have grave misgivings about you accompanying them. Even I do not know what they will encounter at the summit. It is more than possible that they will not survive to make the journey back down.'

Sardonyx allowed Bjork's words sufficient time to sink in before she answered. 'I made up my mind a long time ago, when Moichi first came to the land of the Opal Moon.'

'I do not have to tell you the consequences of your decision.'

'No,' she said quietly, glancing briefly at Moichi, placing her hand alongside his cheek, calming him in his restless sleep. 'But what else can I do? My heart surely turns to stone when I am not with him. For good or ill, he has become part of me.'

'Have you told him about yourself?'

'He knows most of it,' Sardonyx said. 'He does not need to know it all.'

'At some point, perhaps sooner than you think,' Bjork said with no little gravity, 'he will.'

They began their assault at first light. Bjork provided Moichi with a map of the lower part of the eastern face up which they must climb. She had also provided such equipment and foodstuffs as they might require. She estimated three days to Cloudland; then they were in terra incognita, on their own to the summit.

The black basalt of the Mountain Sin'hai was without erosion. Though it had existed for millennia still the myriad peaks and rills were as sharply defined as they had been the moment it thrust itself out of the molten mantle of the earth below. This was both good and bad. The face was studded with excellent hand- and foot-holds for their ascent but the mountain possessed none of the weather-smoothed areas of other peaks so that, without respite, they were obliged to climb up vertical rock chimneys and traverse treacherous rifts that plunged thousands of feet past ragged outcroppings into blue shadow so deep it was impossible to discern the bottom.

The higher they climbed, the more often they were obliged to pause to catch their breath. It would have been far more prudent, Moichi knew, to stop and make camp more often to allow them to accustom themselves to the rarefied atmosphere, but he chose to push ever upward, driven by his fears of Chaos streaming through the Portal, marching into the world of man to reclaim what it believed belonged to it. The thought of being possessed by some Chaos creature like the Makkon or, God forbid, the Dolman was enough to keep him awake and sweating at night.

For his part, Hamaan had said almost nothing since they began. He had taken his defeat like the good soldier he was. 'I consider myself a prisoner of war,' he said, stolidly refusing to look his brother in the eye. 'I will follow your orders but I consider you the enemy and I will escape as quickly as I am able.'

Moichi tried to talk him out of this rigid mind-set of military code, but all entreaties proved useless. Therefore, he was obliged to tie Hamaan up at night to ensure that he would not escape or slit Moichi's throat. Moichi no longer knew what he thought of his brother. He had returned home to a waking nightmare. Aufeya was dead and Sardonyx had taken her place. Then, he had discovered that his brother Jesah was Fe'edjinn and henceforth known as Hamaan, a Qa'tach responsible for unspeakable crimes committed in the name of patriotism and God. At night, when he knew he would not be seen, he sat facing the sheer drop-offs that were never far from them and, putting his face in his hands, tried to blank his mind from the horror.

On their second night on the Mountain Sin'hai, while he was thus occupied, Sardonyx checked Hamaan's bonds for any sign he had been trying to loosen them. Since he always was, she retied some of the knots more tightly then, stepping over him, stood for many minutes looking at Moichi's bowed back.

At length, she crossed the narrow rock ledge on which they had made cramped camp and, putting her arms around him, crouched behind him. For a long time, they remained in that position. Then Moichi sighed. 'How is it, after all that has happened, I still want to love him?'

'Because he is your brother.'

He shook his head. 'That is not enough.'

'But it is. And it is a very human emotion.' Sardonyx stroked his hair. 'I know I would love you no matter what you did.'

'Easy to say. Neither you nor I are criminals.' His tone was bitter.

'But you have done the right thing. You made the decision Bjork was determined you should make. You did not judge him. Bjork did not judge him and neither did Ouwlmy, though he committed crimes against them. They allowed you to take him.' She glanced briefly over their heads at the sparks of lightning. 'To have God judge him.'

'God. I have to laugh,' Moichi said. 'If God existed He would not have allowed such atrocities. He would have saved Sanda.'

'Why, Moichi? Is she so special that she should be exempted from God's plan?'

Moichi turned his head. 'Is that what you think? That all of this is some kind of plan? Chill take it, if so, it is an unconscionably cruel one.'

'Any more cruel than the Iskamen suffering for centuries at the hands of the Adenese?'

Moichi was silent; he had no answer for that. But he put his hands on her arms. As they held each other, they felt the deep rumble as another temblor shook the mountain. Just below them, a chunk of rock split off, went crashing down the face.

'Lord, what is happening up there?' Sardonyx said. 'It looks like the storms are increasing in intensity.'

'Soon enough,' Moichi answered her, 'we will find out.'

The next morning, they breakfasted lightly, untied Hamaan and performed their abbreviated ablutions. Then they broke camp and were on their way. Mist closed over them almost at once so that the hypnotic panorama of Syrinx, the Khashm and, beyond, the walls of Mas'jahan were blotted out in a swirl of pearlescent sheen.

Moichi thought of the enigmatic Bjork – the self-described freak of nature, Sardonyx's sorcerous mentor. And he thought of Ouwlmy, whom he missed with an almost tangible pain. He missed Bjork, as well, but in a way that was unclear to him until Sardonyx said to him, 'Do you see now why I did not tell you where I learned my sorcery?'

'No,' he said. 'I would have appreciated knowing about Bjork in advance.'

'Is that so? Tell me how you would describe her to someone who had never met her.'

Moichi considered for a moment as he double-checked the line. 'I don't even know whether to call Bjork a "he" or a "she."'

'Neither do I,' Sardonyx said, coming up beside him on a narrow ledge. 'So isn't it better that I let you form your own opinion?'

'Bjork called herself a freak of nature. What do you think?'

Sardonyx paid out the line so Hamaan could follow them up. 'When it comes to Bjork it isn't important what I – or anyone else besides you – think. *She* thinks of herself as a criminal – not by any man-made law, but what difference does that make?'

'She collaborated with Chaos, mankind's enemy.'

'But you already know the falseness of that,' Sardonyx said. 'Chaos is mankind's shadow-self, banished by ancient mages who may or may not have had the good of mankind in mind. Remember what you said about the cabal of Fe'edjinn Qa'tachs. That form of usurpation of power is, I will warrant, older even than mankind. The gods themselves fought over issues of power.'

Hamaan came up beside them and, for a moment, the three of them shared the precarious perch. Hamaan's eyes locked with Moichi's for what seemed an eternity. Then, Moichi launched himself upward.

'Don't bother,' Hamaan said to Sardonyx. 'He has trouble with commitment of any kind. He will never understand you or me.'

'Save your strength,' she said, shoving him against the rock face. 'We have a long way yet to travel today.'

As the day progressed, the mist grew thicker, lodging in their mouths and throats. Around them, now, the pink lightning danced, crackling like logs being felled in a forest. At midday, they paused to refresh and relieve themselves.

'I want to warn you of something,' Sardonyx said. 'Before we set out, Bjork told me that the higher we climb the less I will be able to work my magic. We must be careful to use it sparingly – only twice, Bjork warned – because Sin'hai has the ability to sap that form of energy. And even then there is no surety it will function properly.'

'Noted,' Moichi said. After a moment, he added, 'Will it work at all on the summit?'

'No one knows, but I have little doubt that is where

we will have need of it most.' She took a swig of water. 'Ready?'

Just past mid-afternoon, they found their way blocked by a massive rockfall. The vertical chimney – the last landmark on the upper reaches of Bjork's chart – had been almost completely filled in. Moichi looked up. The outside of the chimney bulged from the face of the mountain. Worse, this piece must have been born in one long thrust because it was almost glassily smooth without a foot- or hand-hold to be seen.

'Is there a way around this?' Sardonyx asked.

'Not according to Bjork's map.' Moichi was studying the almost unnaturally smooth face. 'No help for it but to attempt an assault.'

He drew out a pteron, a thick spike-like implement with a loop at one end which he hammered into a small stress-fracture zig-zagging up the rock. He stepped up onto it, hammered home another. The safety line trailed down behind him as he ascended. But by the time he had hammered in the fourth pteron, he knew they were in trouble. The stress-fracture petered out an arm's length above his head. From then on to the top of the bulge, the rock appeared absolutely seamless. There was no place to hammer in another pteron.

He glanced down. Hamaan was already on the second pteron and Sardonyx was readying the lines to go up herself. Moichi looked upward again, searching for a way to traverse the outside of the chimney. He thought he spotted something and, climbing onto the last pteron, he stretched himself to his limit.

There!

The face was not absolutely seamless after all. A stress fracture – to be sure, thinner than the vertical one they were now on – snaked its way almost laterally, more or less bisecting the chimney. But would it lead to a way off?

Moichi, with little to lose, reached up and hammered in a pteron. He threaded the lines, moved upward. Behind him, Hamaan and Sardonyx followed. He paid his brother scarce attention. Here, at the edge of an almost sheer drop Moichi did not have to concern himself with Hamaan trying to escape. They were all bound together by the safety lines, and there was nowhere for Hamaan to escape to.

Methodically, like a spider over glass, he moved across the sheet of smooth rock. A chill wind fostered mini-whirlwinds of mist and damp, brushing his cheek and swirling down the collar of his tussah-silk vest. Without perspective, it was impossible to judge how far they had come and, worse, how much farther they had to go. Tension sang in the lines, was marked in the concentration on their faces, the hard bulging of muscle, the stretch of sinew.

After he drove in the fifth lateral pteron, he called a rest period. Despite the efficacious ministrations of both Bjork and Sardonyx his wounds pained him fearfully. One of them had opened up and he was obliged to wipe the blood away every few minutes. When they made camp tonight – if they got off this Godforsaken chimney – he would have to get Sardonyx to cauterize it anew. He could not risk the onset of an infection at this point.

They hung by their safety lines, clinging to the rock that bulged out from the mountain-face. Winds, rising, buffeted them as if they were ships on the ocean. Moichi was never so aware of the distance between himself and Sardonyx. He wanted to reach out and take her hand but she was too far away and, in any case, Hamaan was between them.

He called them out of their reveries and he swung to the left, onto the next pteron. And so it went. Sardonyx was obliged to pull up the last pteron and, as they moved pass it forward to Moichi to reuse. There was no turning back.

Moichi counted twelve pterons he had driven into the slender thread of a fissure. He climbed onto it, stretched himself out to drive in the thirteenth. Day was ending. Even at this altitude, where the sun hung in the sky very late, it was obvious in the change in hue in the mist. It became more and more pink, like blood in water, as the sun slid beyond the horizon and the main source of illumination became the flickering pink lightning from the ice storms above in Cloudland.

Moichi knew that he was exhausted and that was why when his fingers searched along the rock face for the continuation of the fracture and found only smooth stone he checked three times. Nothing. The fissure ended eighteen inches from where he had driven the thirteenth pteron. Now what? Even, if by some freak chance, there was another parallel fissure the low light made it all but impossible to pick it up.

So there they hung on the bulge, with night fast encroaching, with nowhere to continue on. Moichi turned to Hamaan and Sardonyx and passed along the bleak news. It was suicide to attempt to continue the assault in twilight. They decided to spend the night suspended where they were and hope for the best tomorrow. They ate a spare meal of dried meat, fish paste and water. Then they slept. Or, at least, tried to.

It was evil time.

Bjork had said Syrinx was filled with ghosts and, suspended on the mountainside between sleep and waking, Moichi could believe it. Once, the black earth had run red with the blood of Syrinxian and Shinju alike. So much death. No wonder the atmosphere, even this high up, was rank with it. Souls stalked the night in the fitful wind, the intermittent icy rain showers, the pink lightning, flickering like a reptile's forked tongue. They sang in the blood, carried inside by inhalation, then inward on each double-pump of the heart, each rush of blood through artery and vein. They told their tales of misery and death, of life cut short, of deprivation and warfare.

Moichi, sleeping and dreaming, guided by these lost souls, fought Syrinxian wars, felt Shinju deaths, experienced the retribution of Chaos. His muscles jumped and popped in galvanic response, and when he awakened at first light, he felt as if he had not slept at all.

Trying to stretch his aching muscles, he craned upward, then to left and right and, finally, desperately, below them. Then, seeing that the others were awake, he told them the news. 'We are stuck,' he said. 'There are no more fissures anywhere to be seen. The pterons will not go into solid rock.' He looked past Hamaan to Sardonyx. 'We need you now,' he said. 'It is the only way.'

She looked at him and he knew what was in her mind: Bjork's warning of using her sorcery only twice. And he knew she wanted to save both for what might be waiting for them on the summit, where the Portal into Chaos somehow had been opened. 'There is no help for it,' he said. 'Without you we will never even reach the summit.'

She nodded, closed her eyes. Once again, as he had in Mas'jahan when she had transformed him into a Fianar-antsoa, he was aware of a profound sensation of slumber, and then a dreamlike falling, falling . . .

He opened his eyes to find himself wedged into the center of the vertical chimney. 'Almost there!' he cried, glancing down at Hamaan and Sardonyx climbing the chimney just below him. 'Six more feet and that rock slide we passed down below would have filled this chimney and made it impassable.'

As he said this, as the reality of it permeated him, he was also aware of an odd sensation, as if his voice was coming from some distance, had been spoken by someone else inhabiting his body. He broke out into a cold sweat. Then, the eerie sensation passed and he banged in the last pteron, threaded the line and levered himself up through the hole in the chimney.

Looking around while he caught his breath, he found himself on a snow-covered ledge that sloped upward to the left almost like a natural path. Hamaan, then Sardonyx emerged from the chimney and when they were all on the ledge, they brought up the remainder of their equipment. Darkness was falling along with snow as dry as sand. It clung to every non-smooth surface, settling on their equipment, their eyebrows and lashes, the men's beards.

As they set up camp, Moichi said softly to Sardonyx, 'What happened?'

'Time and the future,' she said. 'This was Miira's special gift – the sorcery she passed on to Bjork and she to me. Time and the future are both, in small, incremental ways, mutable. In fact, there are many futures, just as there are many currents in the ocean. What comes to pass can sometimes be . . . manipulated.'

'You mean you can create your own?'

'No, no. Perhaps not even God has that power any more,' Sardonyx said. 'Futures at any given moment are multiple. So many factors go into creating the future out of the past and the present, a human would go mad trying to categorize them let alone count them. But sometimes I am able to reach out into the currents of time and pick *another* future, make it come to pass.'

'Like now.'

'Yes. Here, in this future, the chimney was passable and there was no need for us to head onto the outside.' She stopped what she was doing, clutched Moichi's arm. 'But this is a dangerous occupation on the Mountain Sin'hai. So close to both God and Chaos, such sorcery can be distorted. That was why Bjork warned me. Remember, I can only use my power once more.'

She was about to turn away when he said, 'What happened to us in that . . . other future?'

She put her hand to his cheek. Her eyes glittered darkly. 'Don't *ever* ask that question because you do not want to know the answer. *This* is our only reality now. Be satisfied with that.'

After dinner, she tended to the men's wounds. She was not happy to see the fresh blood on Moichi's face and she cleaned the wound as best she could, then cauterized it. Hamaan carefully observed the entire procedure. Even when white-hot blade tip pressed against his brother's skin his eyes revealed nothing, but as Moichi squeezed his eyes against the agony he breathed a tiny sigh.

The next morning, taking the icy ledge upward, they entered Cloudland. Even Bjork, who had apparently roamed the lower slopes of the Mountain Sin'hai, had never ascended to this height. The thick clouds tasted of antimony and copper. The storms were constant, lashing the travelers with a combination of sleet, hail and the same dry snow they had experienced last night.

Even so, it was an enormous relief not to be hanging on to sheer rock with fingernails, boot toes and tied-off lines. It felt good to use the legs again as they had in altitudes below, before they came to Sin'hai. Even Hamaan came to recognize that they were no longer a part of the old world – the world of Iskael and Aden, of the Mu'ad and even the Khashm. This was terra incognita for all of them.

In a way, Moichi felt sorry for him. Hamaan was a warrior, and such people had no business being prisoners, though often enough that was how they ended up. Part of the process, one could even argue, but there was something about it that struck Moichi as akin to placing a magnificent wild animal in a six-by-six cage. They needed to be free or be dead. But not this.

At night, he lay awake, listening to the tick of his own body as if it were some instrument he had been brought in to study. In his exhaustion, he longed for Sanda to come to him again, in a dream or in any other way. For perhaps it was her judgement rather than God's that he awaited. His own judgement, so distorted by complex emotions, he did not trust in this matter. He thought of Sanda's spirit held somewhere in a curious prison and the pain in his body was overcome by the ache in his heart. *I want you back*, he thought, clenched fists pressed tight to his eyes to stop the hot tears from forming. Why couldn't Sardonyx's magic bring her back? Why couldn't she reach into the stew of Time and choose another future, one in which Sanda lived? It was too late. Even sorcery could not resurrect the dead. But he found that the mere knowledge of it made his sister's death all the more difficult to bear.

When he slept, only the rough souls of Syrinx chased themselves across his dreaming mind, reliving for the span of a blink of an eye an entire lifetime.

The icy rock of Cloudland was on the whole easier to negotiate than the sheer, vertical face of the lower levels. How this could be Moichi never could quite figure out, since the interminable ice storms made even a mental mapping impossible. As soon as they passed through a certain section it vanished from view in a welter of ice pellets and bitter wind, and it was as if it never existed.

They pushed on, bent into the wind, ascending through ice fields, across glacier-like floes. Once or twice a day they were obliged to break out the pterons and, hooking their safety lines to them, begin a vertical assault. But, though often difficult, these vertical sections were never large enough to leave them stranded on the smooth face of . . . *Forget that!* Moichi admonished himself. *That particular reality belongs to another future.* Or was it by now the past?

Often, he wondered what it must be like to be able to peer into the ocean of Time and see the swirl of multiple futures and to pluck one out like a bright-scaled fish. Just like a god. And that, perhaps, was why Bjork had warned Sardonyx to keep her sorcerous profile low. Up there, somewhere, was the House of God, and no other power could stand before Him.

At night, it was so frigid that the material of their tents froze into stiffened corpses. Accordingly, Moichi instructed them to carve out blocks of ice with which they built small conical structures, which they found protected them from the elements better than the tents ever had.

But their sleep was interrupted by strange howlings that chilled them as even the cold could not.

'What is that?' Moichi asked.

'Wolke'en,' Sardonyx replied. 'They are large snow-white predators with ice-blue eyes. They live in Cloudland and above, but occasionally Bjork would glimpse them on his journeys across the lower slopes. Even he gave them a wide berth; they are said to be very clever, relentless killing machines once they are on a hunt or smell blood.'

'I will remember that,' Moichi said, tucking his head into his arms and trying to close his ears to the eerie cries.

Daytime came as a pale wash, but since the night-time was bright with sparking lightning the differences were negligible, and they were obliged to rely on their own internal rhythms to identify the demarcation between the two. When they were tired, they slept. Otherwise, they plodded on.

Hamaan, living his whole life in the desert, suffered the most. At least Moichi and Sardonyx had lived in colder climes when winter came without mercy. Still, neither of them had experienced such bone-chilling temperatures and inhospitable weather. Hamaan's wounds, which seemed to be healing well, were chafed by the heavy exertion and they opened, suppurating.

When they broke at midday, both Moichi and Sardonyx worked on him, cleaning the wounds, making sure they were well padded. But he nearly froze to death while he was uncovered and they knew that they could not expose him to these harsh elements again.

'This is the way the world is at night,' he said, his head tilted back against an outcropping of ice. His eyes were slits so that the snow and hail would not blind him. 'We are surrounded by dreams.' So he felt them, too. 'And the dreams are given presence – a life – by us.'

'They are the souls of Syrinx,' Moichi said, binding a wound.

But Hamaan shook his head. 'For you, perhaps. But for me these dreams are familiar. At night, they come to feed off me like sharks.' Moichi gave Sardonyx a quick glance. 'Oho, brother, I know what is in your mind. You think I am being haunted by those I have murdered or have ordered murdered. You think that here, on the Mountain Sin'hai, a miracle will occur.' He grinned through teeth gritted with pain. 'God is showing me the nature of my sins so that I may repent.' His torso shot forward suddenly and he gripped Moichi by the front of his vest. 'That is what you think, isn't it, brother?' Nose to nose, they glared at one another. 'But I am incapable of repentance. I am like a shark, myself. A predator. I go forward, ever forward. I do not look back. I despise the kind of contemplation that is your weakness.' He dropped his hands, lay back, panting. 'I am weak now and so the nibbling begins. When I die other predators will know and they will feed off my corpse.' His own breath drifted from between his lips like smoke. 'That is the way of it; the way I wish it.'

He seemed stronger in the morning, as if spitting his

bile into his brother's face had energized him. They performed their brief morning rituals and struck camp. The way became steeper again and they spent the better part of the day slung in their gear, Moichi hammering pterons through ice and rock. This was an increasingly dangerous task because as they ascended into the upper reaches of Cloudland there were larger patches of black ice – ice that had been made part of the rock face for so long it took on the color of the mountain beneath and so was virtually indistinguishable. But unlike fissured rock it would not hold the weight of one person, let alone three.

More than once, the deeply sunk pteron broke free beneath the testing weight he put on it. Worse, once it held solid for the test but gave way as he climbed onto it. The ice face rushed by him as he fell. Then the safety line brought him up short and he swung from the end of it eight feet below where Hamaan clung.

'Pull on the line!' Sardonyx called to Hamaan, as she began the process of reeling Moichi back up the mountain.

Hamaan staring down at his brother did nothing, until Sardonyx said, 'Start pulling now, Qa'tach, or I will put a knife between your shoulderblades.'

Hamaan shrugged without taking his eyes off Moichi. 'If you kill me, lady, who will help you haul your beloved to safety?' He paused a beat. 'I want a concession.'

'What kind of concession?' Sardonyx asked just as Moichi was shouting, 'No bargaining, chill take you!'

'I want to sleep unfettered,' Hamaan said. 'I weary of being treated like a tethered animal.'

'That was your choice,' Moichi shouted, working to stabilize his swinging. 'Not ours.'

'If we free you at night you will try to escape,' Sardonyx pointed out.

'I give you my word I will not escape.'

'What is your word worth, brother?' Moichi called.

267

Sardonyx looked at Hamaan for a long time. 'All right,' she said. 'Now do as I say.'

Hamaan worked in perfect concert with her, hauling away, bringing Moichi up the mountainside by increments. As the two brothers came abreast of one another, Hamaan said, 'One day you will thank me for my generosity, brother.'

Moichi said nothing. He was angry with Sardonyx for making the deal even while he was grateful to her for bargaining in a situation where he could not. He understood the necessity of what she had done but he did not have to like it.

Some time later, a fierce snow and ice storm swept over them. This one was the worst yet, a stinging white blanket falling across the world, making it impossible to see more than a hand's breadth in front of the face. Virtually blind, they struggled on up the ice face, making slow but steady progress.

At last, Moichi reached up for a spot to hammer in the next pteron and his fingers encountered a horizontal ledge. He called down to Sardonyx and Hamaan, then levered himself up.

He could sense almost immediately that this was more than a mere narrow ledge. They were on the edge of an ice field of some sort. It sloped upward, to be sure, but the angle was not particularly steep. When all of them were up, they started off up the slope. They had to be careful, for though much snow had already fallen up here, their weight often brought them down to the ice beneath and if their weight wasn't directly over their lead foot, they could take a painful spill.

Heads down to protect themselves against the storm, they plodded forward for several hours. They were obliged to stop more frequently now because of the increasing intensity of the earth temblors. Several made them feel as if the mountain was trying to shake itself apart. In the distance they heard, like echoes, the deep rumbling of rock slides and avalanches.

It was still light when Moichi called a halt in the lee of a jumble of ice-encrusted rocks. Something in those sounds, those eerie echoes, sent a warning bell ringing in Moichi's head.

'We will make camp here,' he told them.

'But why? The storm is rising and we are so exposed here,' Hamaan said. 'We still have several hours of light left.' He looked around. 'By then we might be off this Godforsaken ice field and in some decent shelter.'

Logically, Moichi knew he was right, but his decision had nothing to do with logic. Those echoes, still resounding in his head, caused him to sweat despite the extreme cold. Something was out there and he had no intention of facing it blinded by a snowstorm.

They made camp as best they could. They tried to hack off blocks of ice, but it clung to its stone base with an unnatural tenacity and all they came away with were long icicle-like shards.

As had been agreed, they did not bind Hamaan's wrists or ankles. He curled down in a ball, covered himself in his stiff tent and was instantly fast asleep. Moichi and Sardonyx took turns sleeping. He stood guard first. It was dark and close. The wind howled but otherwise the storm made it seem as if he were locked in a small closet. The earth trembled and was still, but those echoes continued, filling Moichi with fear. What was out there in the darkness?

He closed his eyes, trying to calm himself, and was soon asleep. He was startled awake by a human scent. He opened his eyes to see Hamaan crouched beside him. He held the point of an ice shard to the soft hollow of Moichi's throat.

'I want you to know I kept my promise,' he whispered

harshly over the wind. 'I said I would not try to escape but I made no mention of not killing you.'

Moichi stared into his face without fear. 'Did we come from the same parents?'

At almost the same instant the two brothers saw a movement in the night. They remained silent and still, listening to their instincts. A moment later, it appeared as if a mound of snow were moving. Then, the head came up and they saw a pair of piercing ice-blue eyes.

Wolke'en!

The beast, its thick snow-white coat dusted in snow, stared at them. It was as big as a man, perhaps six feet long. Its four legs looked powerful and its long bushy tail flicked nervously back and forth. Hamaan moved and its ears flattened back and it went into a crouch. Both men were sure the Wolke'en would leap at them, but it did not budge. The staring contest continued. They could see the tiny clouds of its exhalation staining the night. The ice-blue eyes did not blink. At last, so slowly that at first they were unsure anything was happening, it backed away, until it was outside the perimeter of their camp. Then it vanished altogether.

For a time, neither man spoke or moved as the built-up tension gradually evaporated. Slowly, everything came back to normalcy and the brief moment when the brothers had been locked together against a common antagonist vanished as completely as the Wolke'en.

'Oh, yes.' Hamaan returned his attention to his brother. 'Can't you see father in both of us?'

Moichi felt the makeshift weapon still at his throat. He closed his eyes. 'Yes, kill me. Make the deed complete. Murder all your siblings.'

Nothing happened, and when he opened his eyes, he saw Hamaan had returned to his place beneath his stiff tent, curled in a ball, already asleep.

The next morning, as they were striking camp, the storm abated and by the time they were ready to set off, it was gone altogether. A rare glimpse of sunlight illuminated the snow-covered ice field. Above, blue sky glittered like an unattainable grail.

They moved up the slope of the ice field, crunching through the virgin snow. But directly ahead Moichi could already see a thin gray line, that became thicker and deeper with alarming rapidity until it resolved itself.

The trio stopped in their tracks. Even Hamaan was struck dumb. Now Moichi understood the unconscious warning of the echoes of the rock slides and avalanches. Had they continued on yesterday, as Hamaan had suggested, they would be dead now.

There before them, not three hundred yards from the spot where they had made camp, lay a yawning rift in the ice and rock face so deep and wide it could have been made only by the hand of God.

FIFTEEN

THE GREAT RIFT

'Can you feel anything when I do this?'

Kaijikan pursed her full lips and held her hand aloft. In it, encased within a shimmering transparent ball, swam a tiny Kaer'n.

Chiisai.

Kaijikan, laughing, shook the ball as a child would a toy, and Chiisai tumbled snout over tail.

'How does it feel to be powerless, my dear?' Kaijikan chuckled, sucking in cheeks with an unhealthy pallor. 'Get used to it.'

In truth, Chiisai could see nothing at all. From inside, the sorcerous ball was utterly opaque. But she could hear Kaijikan's voice as clearly as if she stood next to the Keeper of Souls. The vertiginous sensation that had overtaken her when Kaijikan had made the second runish pass in the air had not abated. Sick to her stomach, Chiisai could do nothing but float docilely and pray this state would soon pass.

Soon enough, it did. But when the opaque bubble broke and the fluid in which she had been immersed drained away, she wished she were back inside the sphere for she saw they were within her father's private chambers, at the center of the Kunshin's castle in Haneda. How Kaijikan had transported them here she had no idea, but they were already beyond the moat, the bristling armaments, the

Kunshin's specially trained elite guards. Somewhere here her father, the leader and spiritual power of all the Bujun, lay unsuspecting and vulnerable to attack.

'Even that hideous Kaer'n face possesses expression,' Kaijikan said. 'And I like what I see.' She circled Chiisai. 'Your fear excites me. It is like an exotic spice tasted on the tip of my tongue.' She stepped closer and her tongue flicked out, licking Chiisai's scaly skin. 'Mmmm.' She closed her eyes as if in ecstasy.

Then her eyes snapped open, and they were steely hard. 'Time,' she whispered, 'for retribution.' She beckoned for Chiisai to follow her.

'I cannot move,' Chiisai said. 'Not even one muscle.'

Kaijikan turned back. 'Is that relief I hear in your voice?' She smiled that altogether wicked smile. 'Surely we cannot have that.' Her long fingers made signs in the air, releasing Chiisai from her stasis. 'Understand me, child, you move now at my behest,' Kaijikan said softly. 'You have no choice. You *will* do as I tell you.'

'You are mistaken,' Chiisai said. 'I will prove–' Against her will she lurched forward. She peered down at herself walking behind Kaijikan. Her mind was totally detached, floating in layers of fog. She tried to give her nerves and muscles direction but it was as if she had forgotten how. Nothing happened, except that she continued through room after room, heading deeper into her father's world. If her triple-hearts could have constricted with dread they would have, but she no longer had any connection with her physical body. She was like Sanda, her essence trapped in the ghastly limbo of Chaos.

But she could still speak. 'Why are you doing this?' she asked.

'I told you,' Kaijikan said irritably. 'My sister–'

'Your sister's death had nothing to do with you making an unholy pact with Chaos.'

Kaijikan paused, smiling thinly. 'You know, it really is a shame that you will have to die. In a way, it is a sin against nature to destroy that lightning-quick brain of yours.'

'Chaos is a crime against nature.'

'Ah, there you are wrong, young lady. And I am astonished that you who have Crossed Over could still believe that very human lie. You are no longer human, Chiisai. In fact, I daresay you are now more like me than the father you will soon murder.'

'How can you make such an outlandish statement?'

'Because it is the truth.' Kaijikan looked her in the eye. 'Look at me, child. What do you think I am? A human being? Could you mistake me for Bujun or Kintai? I think not.'

And it was true. Ever since she had met the Keeper of Souls, Chiisai had wondered at her origins.

'I am Shinju. Do you know that race, child?'

'I have heard of them. I know the legend of Miira's Mirror.'

'Miira!' Kaijikan almost spat out the word. 'It is so unjust that the legend should have grown up around *her*. *I* should be the subject of legend.'

'But the Keeper of Souls—'

'Is, as you say, a frightening fable meant to keep children obedient.' Kaijikan seemed truly sad. 'I have been reduced to being an ogre in a children's story. What a pathetic cliché! Miira's legend, meanwhile, had panache, style. Everyone admires her.'

'Perhaps if you had not made a pact with Chaos you, too, could—'

'You stupid, stupid girl. Don't you understand? *All* the Shinju made a pact with Chaos, even the heroine, Miira. Do you think she was any different because she had the exceedingly poor judgement to run off with a Syrinxian

274

politician? And now her half-breed child lords it over the Khashm, thinking rebellious thoughts just as Miira did. Don't you think I know it was he who cut the tongue from the Makkon and sent it to me as warning? My God, the whole mess makes me sick.'

'Then what is it you want?' Chiisai said.

'I want what all of Chaos wants because it is right and just. Reintegration. Chaos wants what rightfully belongs to Chaos. The piece of this world denied it when it was banished aeons ago.'

'You cannot mean that.'

Kaijikan's face was an anguished mask. 'Oh, but I do. I want to be whole again, as you are now – part of this world and part of Chaos. But you already knew this, didn't you? You just wanted to hear me say it. Now that I have, are you satisfied?'

Chiisai, her essence locked away by Kaijikan's sorcery, quailed at the truth. The thought of every being on the planet being possessed by the essence of a Chaos beast was too terrible to contemplate for long. She was a different case – perhaps unique. Her life in this world was coming to an end. She took the only route open to her and by some alchemical process had been transformed. Perhaps it was once true, as Kaijikan said, that man and Chaos had existed as one, but that time was long gone. Mankind had evolved while Chaos had not. Man was now well beyond the stage when reintegration would work. She knew that if Chaos were allowed its desire the end result would be nothing short of disaster. Humans could no longer tolerate the sight of Chaos, let alone its presence.

'No, no,' Chiisai cried, 'you must see how misguided the notion of reintegration is.'

A terrible, livid color suffused Kaijikan's face. 'I see nothing of the kind,' she raged. 'I am damaged, don't you understand. I *need* what only Chaos can provide. They are sworn to cure the disease that has ravaged me from birth in return for my help. All Shinju are born part Chaos. That is our inherited affliction. Our power began to wane when Chaos was banished through the Portal; I want it back.'

'What Portal?' Chiisai asked. 'The only Portal I know of I made with my sword in the cave fissure.'

'That is an adjunct, a mere pinprick hole,' Kaijikan said. 'I have been working for years with Chaos to weaken the fabric between their dimension and this world. But the main Portal is on the summit of the Mountain Sin'hai beyond the Khashm of Syrinx.'

'That is how the tongueless Makkon came through?'

'Yes. I have given Chaos everything it needs to succeed. My sorcery has at last unbolted the Portal on the summit of the Mountain Sin'hai so that Chaos may re-enter this world. And through the same method I delivered to Sakkourn, the new Chaos-master what it wanted most – the soul of a certain human. That was why the Makkon was loose in Iskael.'

Immediately, Chiisai thought of Sanda, trapped in Chaos, and her heart despaired. They were both helpless prisoners of Chaos.

She watched bleakly as Kaijikan made signs in the air and Chiisai saw her own body moving from one room to the next, passing through chambers familiar to her from her childhood. Each artifact, decoration and piece of furniture had a history, a purpose, and she knew them all, recounting them to herself like a child's invocation against evil.

But evil was coming, implacable and menacing; the malefic force was at her side, guiding her every move, and she despaired for her father's life which, she was quite certain, was about to end by her own hand.

* * *

The great rift ran to left and right as far as they could see in the swirling mist that was, once again, closing in on them. Already, the patch of blue sky was fast disappearing and the mountain trembled. A new storm must be on its way.

'What do you think?' Sardonyx said as the three of them stood on the brink. 'An eighth of a mile across?'

'At least,' Moichi said.

'We will never make it,' Hamaan said, but they paid him scant attention.

'See there.' Moichi pointed. 'Though the rift is very deep there are series of formations thrust up from the bottom. The spaces between them are not so great. If we can fasten the line to one, we can swing from one to another.'

'They are fingers. Some are as thin as stalagmites,' Hamaan said. 'What if they cannot take our weight?'

'Let's get ready,' Moichi said, and pointed again to a formation several yards to their right. 'We will start there. The rock finger looks closest.'

Moichi got the line around the tapering top of the rock finger on the second try, pulled it fast. 'Hamaan is right, these formations are suspect,' he said. 'It's only fair that I go first.'

'Moichi—' Sardonyx's face was filled with trepidation.

He smiled at her. 'Have faith. We are in God's domain now.'

He gripped the line with both hands then, taking a deep breath, launched himself out into the rift. Vertical fields of ice- and snow-covered rock rushed by below, and he could hear the wind moaning through the depths of the rift. He came up on the rock finger with appalling speed and, twisting his body, just missed being slammed belly-first into it. Instead, he swung around it, his fingers slipping for a moment on the icy surface, then catching hold.

For a moment he clung to the icy rock, hanging in the

middle of nowhere. It was almost like being suspended in space. His heart hammered painfully in his chest and he fought to regain control of his breathing.

Then, he set about work, choosing an appropriate spot to hammer in a pteron, running the second line he carried through the loop end, securing it. He waved to Sardonyx and Hamaan and, taking aim at the second finger, swung toward it. When he had safely made it, he turned in time to see Hamaan swinging out toward the first finger.

So it went in laborious fashion until in intense concentration a certain rhythm was achieved: swing, grapple, hammer, sling, check, rest, re-check, swing again as the entire process repeated itself. There was a kind of joy in the rhythm, in successfully completing one job after another, that took the edge off the terror of the rift yawning at every moment just below where they hung.

Storm clouds swept by overhead, and the deep-throated rumbling was now an all but constant reminder that they were closer to their objective than they had realized. They had successfully negotiated more than two-thirds of the rift when the pteron on the finger toward which Hamaan was swinging gave way.

Hamaan cried out as he fell through open space. Twenty feet down, the safety line came up taut, jerking him out of free-fall. In doing so, he was propelled into an ice outcropping. He went into it head first.

'Hamaan!' Moichi called.

'He is hurt, badly,' Sardonyx, who had a better angle, shouted across the rift. 'He is either unconscious or dead.'

'Stay where you are,' Moichi called, 'I'm going back for him.'

'But Moichi—'

'I need you to stay in place, Sardonyx. If I go down you are the only anchor we will have.'

He dug the heels of his boots into the ice finger, flung

himself back across the rift. Catching hold of the icy rock, he searched for the spot into which he had sunk the pteron. Black ice! No wonder it had given way. A six-inch chunk had simply sheared off under the pressure.

He looked directly below him, saw his brother hanging bloody head downward, banging slowly against the ice outcropping. 'I'm going down,' he called to Sardonyx, 'but I don't know whether I have enough line to reach him.'

Down he went, hand over hand, the toes of his boots digging for purchase along the slick ice. Now that he was lower, he could see the problem clearly. The ice outcropping was part of a shorter rock finger, so a gap remained between the formation he was on and the one from which Hamaan dangled.

'Come back!' Sardonyx shouted. 'You are not going to be able to get to him.'

Perhaps she was right, Moichi thought. But he could do nothing else save try. He continued downward, then, at the right instant, kicked outward. For one breathless instant he was suspended in space, then he dropped into what seemed like dizzying infinity. The minor finger loomed in front of him and he grabbed onto its summit. Now he could see Hamaan more clearly. There was a large gash in one temple that was bleeding profusely. Sardonyx was right: it looked very bad.

'Hamaan!' he called. 'Hamaan, I am right above you!'

'Moichi,' Sardonyx shouted. 'He cannot hear you!'

'Hamaan!' he continued, ignoring her, 'Just reach up and I can grab your hand!'

There was no response; the body continued to bump-bump-bump against the side of the rock finger. Moichi let himself down, down until he reached the limit of his line. He could go no further without completely disengaging himself from the harness and then he would have no way back up.

'Hamaan!' he cried one more time in despair. Then he looked up at Sardonyx and said, 'Do it!'

'No,' she said. 'Absolutely not. If I engage my power now that will be the last time.'

'I cannot . . . I *will* not leave my brother.'

'Moichi, we will be utterly helpless once we get to the summit.'

'So be it, then,' he said.

'You know, he may already be dead. In that case . . .'

'I know. You will have used your magic for nothing. You cannot bring him back from the dead. But we don't know that he *is* dead, do we?'

Sardonyx looked at him. 'Pull yourself back up,' she said bleakly.

Moichi did as she bade him. As he reached the upper finger he felt an overwhelming desire to close his eyes. The world spun and he dreamed he was falling, falling . . .

And when he opened his eyes, the three of them were sprawled on the far side of the great rift. Hamaan lay between them, curled into a ball. Moichi pawed through the ice and snow to turn him over.

'Hamaan.'

His brother opened his eyes. Seeing Moichi, his mouth curved in a peculiar smile. 'You owe me now, brother.'

'I . . . what?'

Hamaan sat up. 'For saving your life out there in the rift. Or have you conveniently forgotten?'

The horror of it was that he hadn't. After that disconcerting moment when two realities overlapped, the new one rushed in on Moichi and he remembered everything in gory detail: the pteron pulling out of the black ice, him tumbling downward, and Hamaan swinging immediately to grab him around the waist before his head smashed into a buttress of ice.

Moichi looked wordlessly across at Sardonyx, who was

reeling in the last of their lines that had stretched across the rift.

She shrugged. 'It was the only future where the three of us made it across unscathed.'

'What the chill is she talking about?' Hamaan said irritably. 'We make our own futures.' He grinned into Moichi's face. 'Isn't that so, brother?'

The Kunshin relaxed alone in his royal bath. The bathing chambers were extensive for, it was said, he often loved to bathe with a number of nubile young women who did considerably more than run invigorating sponges over his shoulders and back. And yet the truth was far more mundane. For the Kunshin the bath had always been a time of solitude. The scalding water, the herb-infused mist rising from its surface, served to distance him from everyone and everything. In this manner he was best able to formulate policy, deliberate reforms, conquer whatever problems might arise.

So this was how his daughter found him, eyes closed, hairless body floating in an octagonal tub of polished cedar slabs and black jade, his mind a thousand miles away as he turned over some weighty matter affecting the Kunshindom.

As in a nightmare, Chiisai watched herself creep closer on ten-inch golden talons, across the damp cedar planks, past neat and homey piles of towels, washcloths and all manner of freshly laundered raiment that the Kunshin might require following his bath.

She wanted to call out to him, to raise her voice in warning, but it was no longer her voice, and she was no longer his child. He could not possibly recognize in this great winged beast the woman who had been Chiisai.

Some finely honed sixth sense made him turn as she approached.

'Kaer'n?' he said, seeming not at all surprised. 'Is my presence required?'

Chiisai's body kept coming on, but her detached mind wondered what was going on. He should have been stunned by the presence of a Kaer'n in the castle, let alone in his private bath chambers, and yet he took it as an altogether common occurrence.

He levered himself out of the water, wrapped a thick towel around his torso, rubbing briskly. 'It will take me but a moment to dress and then we can be on our way.'

'You are going nowhere, Kunshin.' Kaijikan stepped out from behind the bulk of Chiisai's body. 'Except to each one of the ten thousand hells I designate.'

The Kunshin blinked, peering at her in the low light. 'Who are you? How did you get in here?' Now he did seem startled.

'I came with the Kaer'n,' she said, not altogether truthfully.

The Kunshin nodded distractedly. 'That explains it then.' He was looking through his selection of clothes.

'I am afraid it doesn't,' Kaijikan said. Chiisai had stopped a short pace from where her father was climbing into loose silk trousers and shirt. 'Do you remember Ulrika?'

At the name, the Kunshin paused momentarily, then he continued dressing. 'I know no one by that name.'

'Liar!' Kaijikan screamed. Her clawed fingers performed arabesques in the air and Chiisai stumbled forward, her forearm reaching out, the taloned hand wrapping around her father's waist.

'What is the meaning of this? How dare you touch the Kunshin's person!' he sputtered.

His protestations only made Kaijikan laugh. 'Men! How ineffectual you all are, in the end! How different this land would be had there been a woman on the Dragon Throne.' She closed her lifted hand into a fist and Chiisai felt her own hand closing painfully around her father's torso. The Kunshin gasped and grimaced in sudden pain.

'Now does the name Ulrika sound familiar?' she asked.

'Y-yes.' The Kunshin's face was pale, but Chiisai could see his eyes darting around the bath chamber in an attempt to identify some weapon or implement he could use against his attackers. 'Ulrika was a mistress of mine. But that was some time ago, before I ascended the Dragon Throne.'

'Tell me about her,' Kaijikan said.

'She was beautiful,' the Kunshin said. 'Delicate and pale, almost like a spirit.'

'Go on.'

'Is it prurience you are after?' the Kunshin said stoically. 'I have no intention of—'

'She was mute, wasn't she?'

The Kunshin seemed shocked by the violence of her words. 'Yes. She was without words. But it did not matter; we found other methods to communicate.'

'Yes, indeed,' Kaijikan said. 'Over and over, you climbed upon her body and had your way with her.'

Quite unexpectedly, the Kunshin smiled. 'Actually, it was pretty much the other way around.'

'Liar!'

'You asked me to tell you about her and I am. She was quite a sexual hellion.' He cocked his head. 'You mean you did not know this about her?'

'My sister was chaste when you as much as abducted her. You raped her, kept her pent up like an animal.'

The Kunshin frowned. 'You are Ulrika's sister? Ah, yes, I see a resemblance now. But what gives you the idea that I raped her and kept her a prisoner? Nothing could be further from the truth.'

'Then why did she stay with you?' Kaijikan shrieked. 'She never came home. She abandoned me!'

'Yes, I believe she did,' the Kunshin said. 'She hated her family, and especially you. You bullied her, berating her every waking moment to work on learning how to speak. To make her more like yourself. That became your sacred quest, didn't it? And you never bothered to discover that she did not want to speak. As I said, she had other methods of communication. And, believe me, they were often far more profound than mere speech.'

'You killed her.' Kaijikan fairly spit in his face. 'Murdered her in cold blood.'

'Nonsense,' the Kunshin said. 'Why would I do such a thing? Ulrika died among her beloved Kaer'n.'

Kaijikan staggered backward a step. 'What?'

'It was she who introduced me to them. She could speak to them, you see. They require no words. It was with the help of the Kaer'n that I became Kunshin. Why do you think the highest office in Ama-no-mori is called the Dragon Throne? It is no coincidence. The Kaer'n are the true power behind the Kunshin. They have kept the peace here for millennia. All Kunshin have been their partners – and their most loyal allies.'

'I will hear no more of this slander against my sister,' Kaijikan raged. 'I know the truth. It *must* be the truth!'

So saying, her hands flew through the air and, to Chii-sai's horror, she saw her own Kaer'n body betray her, betray the ages-old alliance between Kaer'n and Bujun. As her father's face became bloated, as he tried to twist this way and that to escape, her grip tightened on him until her long golden talons began to sink into his flesh.

On the far side of the great rift the clouds were lowering. The mountain trembled, periodically sending cascades of rock and ice hurtling into its depths. Moichi thought it providential that no such avalanches had occurred while they were traversing the rift.

Pink lightning streaked through the billowing clouds, so close overhead that one could make out their crimson centers. Bursts of icy snow, increasing in intensity, fell in oblique sheets, their strength cutting through the howling wind.

'We had better keep moving,' Moichi said, hoisting the last of their gear onto his back.

'Let me go,' Hamaan said. 'A life for a life. That is God's way, you know it. You owe me as much.'

'Is that why you saved my life, Hamaan, with this calculation in mind?' He shook his head, answering his own question. 'No, it all happened too fast for that. You acted out of instinct. You *wanted* to save me.'

'I cannot think why,' Hamaan said dourly. 'Each hour that goes by I am more convinced that you march us to our doom.'

'If that is your conviction,' Moichi said, 'then I free you. Go back down the Mountain Sin'hai.'

Hamaan laughed sourly. 'Is that some kind of joke? Alone, I would not last half-a-day. For starters, how would I traverse the great rift?'

Moichi shrugged. 'In the same way we came across.'

They all turned as the earth shook and, with a great roar, a thick shelf of icy rock collapsed into the abyss.

'That is not a comforting thought, brother.'

'Then continue on with us,' Moichi offered.

'To be offered up to God like a sacrifice.'

'I have freed you of all obligation,' Moichi said. 'Do as you will.'

He signed to Sardonyx and they set off away from the great rift, on the last leg of the journey to the summit. Hamaan stood staring after them. Then, with a muttered, 'Chill take him!' he strode after them, hurrying to catch up. He had no desire to be alone in this wilderness.

'I hope you know what you have made me do,' Sardonyx said.

'You have saved a life,' Moichi replied.

Sardonyx shook her head. 'Perhaps so, but in so doing we have left ourselves far more vulnerable to whatever might be waiting for us on the summit.'

Moichi grunted. 'What will happen if we run into terminal trouble and you attempt to use your Shinju sorcery?'

'Truthfully, I cannot say. I only know that Bjork warned me against using it more than twice.'

The way was becoming steeper and narrower all at once. A form of ice fog hung in the air like chill cobwebs, forcing them to slow their pace. With the weather so bad it was impossible to judge the time of day but Moichi, anxious to reach their objective, pushed them to pick up their pace. Ahead of them, the pink lightning looked like streaks of blood upon the ice, and now it was possible to see that they all appeared to radiate from a central point that was directly ahead of the travelers.

'The summit,' Moichi said, pointing. 'We are almost there.'

'Moichi,' Hamaan said, coming up at his side, 'what happened back there in the rift? When I think about it sometimes I remember it one way, and other times . . .' He paused and a quick shudder went through him. 'I don't know, it's as if I was dying.' He gave a sharp uncomfortable laugh. 'But I'm not, am I?'

'No, Hamaan. We are all alive.'

'Then what am I feeling inside?'

'Why pursue it?'

'Because I find it disturbing,' Hamaan said. 'I have never had thoughts like these. Am I going mad?'

'No.' Moichi turned to his brother. 'No matter what you have done, no matter what you say or think, I was not going to let you die. You are my flesh and blood and by God I will hang on to you come what may.'

Hamaan was ashen-faced. 'So it was not a nightmare. It really happened.'

'Forget it,' Moichi said. 'What happened was that you saved my life, remember?'

'I remember them both,' Hamaan said, dropping back a pace in order to be alone with his thoughts.

'What has happened?' Sardonyx asked him a moment later.

'He remembers both realities,' Moichi said, 'and it has rattled him.'

Sardonyx gave him a brief glance. 'Good. Perhaps now there is less chance he will stab us in the back.'

The path they had chosen up to the summit quickly became a narrow defile. Above them on either side, great conical rock formations rose into the icy mists. The wind howling through them created the semblance of speech, heavily tremoloed and distorted beyond comprehension. And yet it fostered the notion that they were entering a place where life existed all around them, in objects and elements normally without consciousness. It was as if the very air was possessed of spirits that rose and fell, gyring on treacherous currents.

It seemed now as if they ascended a cyclopean staircase hewn from the living basalt for they rose in precise increments, passing from tread to tread, rising toward what could only be their objective: the summit of the Mountain Sin'hai.

The bolts of lightning clashed constantly, illuminating everything in a feral glow. The basalt formations became larger, more massive, until they rose on every side, a mountain atop Sin'hai. And at their very peak a red glow burned through the icy mist like a massive lantern hung at the apex of a lighthouse.

As they watched, the swirling sheets of ice metamorphosed. As they struck the rock formations they did not bounce off but, rather, accreted onto the rock, becoming one with it. Lower down, enormous boulders that hung like goiters from the nearly vertical formations quickly broke down, dissolving into liquid that rose into the air, transforming into more sheets of ice.

This was the House of the Holy, where dwelled the God of Iskael, where, it was said, roamed the living God of the Catechists, where, so Bjork had told them, the Portal into Chaos had been created and sealed uncounted millennia ago.

Which part was the truth and which legend? Moichi, gazing up at that red glow, had the distinct feeling that they had entered a whole new universe, that the best they could hope for now was to adapt to the laws that pertained to Sin'hai and to no other place in the world.

But what were those laws? Clearly, the first one was fluidity. What was immutable in all other parts of the world of man was mutable here. States of being mutated as quickly as the eye could follow.

Moichi was still trying to figure out how to use this to their advantage when the ice storm lifted off the summit to rage high overhead. As it did so, the source of the feral red glow was revealed and Moichi knew that all of Bjork's worst fears had been confirmed.

The Portal to Chaos had somehow been opened and, even as they watched, transfixed, the first of its monstrous creatures emerged with a blood-curdling howl into the world of man.

SIXTEEN

HOUSE OF
THE HOLY

'Die! Die!' a half-maddened Kaijikan shrieked.

And, as if acquiescing to her demented demand, the Kunshin's head ballooned outward and exploded like a melon dropped from a rooftop.

But there was no blood and, as Chiisai watched in paralytic awe, her grip upon her father – or, more accurately, what had once been her father – was pried loose. In place of the docile Kunshin, loomed the armored and intimidating form of the Dai-San.

'NO!'

All the legendary creatures embossed upon the articulated plates of his armor seemed to writhe as he strode toward Kaijikan. His hand, heavily encased in the six-fingered gauntlet manufactured from a Makkon's hand, closed around her neck.

She stared up in terror at his crested visage, surmounted by his high helm. 'No,' she cried, 'I sent you away. I made certain the bones of the snow-hare foretold the future as I would wish it. You should be on the other side of the world.'

'But I am here.' The Dai-San's voice rumbled through the chamber, echoing painfully against the walls. 'And I gave you your opportunity to embrace the truth, to remember and to mourn your sister as she had been. Your chance at repentance is gone.'

Kaijikan goggled at him. 'But how did you know? I planned everything so carefully.'

'Your ignorance of the Kaer'n was your undoing,' the Dai-San said. 'Had you been able to see your sister for who she really was you would have come to understand the Kaer'n and their mystical relationship to this island. You would have known that they are the guardians of the delicate balance between mankind and Chaos.' He shook her until her teeth rattled. 'Now, largely through your perfidy, that balance has been severely disturbed.' He drew her upward until her feet dangled off the floor. 'Now you will help me ensure that it has not been irreparably ruptured.'

He threw her into a corner of the bath chamber, where she huddled, talking gibberish to herself. Then the Dai-San turned and, walking up to Chiisai, slid his hand out of his Makkon-hide gauntlet, gently stroked the side of her long, curving neck. 'Have no fear, your father is safe with the Kaer'n, guarded from her sorcery.'

Chiisai, who was slowly regaining control of her nerves and muscles, said hoarsely, 'You know who I am.'

'I know everything,' he said. 'Had I such power I would have intervened to save you, but not even the Kaer'n possess the wherewithal.' He smiled the smile reserved only for her. 'You see, I have a special kinship with the Kaer'n. I am, in essence, one of them. I was made so through Bujun sorcery. They determined that a *human* champion was required to deal with Chaos. The Kaer'n have no desire for their ... *consequence* in the scheme of things to become public knowledge.

'As you know, they – and, to the same extent, I – have some of the essence of Chaos inside them. That makes them averse to change. We are true guardians – facilitators rather than agents. They have me – and I have Moichi. By virtue of my human form I have the power to do more than the Kaer'n; and Moichi has more power to enact change than do I.'

Then he did something quite extraordinary. He leaned forward, kissed her lovingly. 'Do not despair for your humanity, my darling Chiisai. You are truly blessed. Like Eve, you are the first of your kind: a female Kaer'n. Until now, the Kaer'n have been unable to breed because there were no females. But now a new day is dawning for them – and for you. If you choose to help them, they, too, will have a chance at life.'

Chiisai was about to tell him that she did not mourn for her old life, when she saw Kaijikan's fingers making signs in the air. She felt the first tuggings of her mind being separated from her body, and she did not think, merely reacted. She opened her mouth and her tongue shot out. Flames rippled along its length and they began to burn Kaijikan as Chiisai wrapped her tongue around the Keeper of Souls.

Try not to kill her. She heard the Dai-San's voice in her mind. *She will be of use to us where we are going.*

But he did not know what it was like to have your mind locked away behind glass while someone else manipulated your body. She was terribly frightened and, besides, even as she burned Kaijikan would not give up her spell-casting. And so Chiisai did the only thing she could to stop her. She rolled up her tongue and Kaijikan with it. Then she bit down very hard, turning her mind far away as she masticated. She felt the hot squirt of Kaijikan's blood, the crunch of her bones. The spell disintegrated with her death. Chiisai swallowed again and again. Then she turned her head toward the Dai-San.

I did what I had to do, she said in his mind. *What needed to be done.*

Do not worry, he said. *We will find a way.*

Where are we going? she asked.

The one place I never thought I would see, he replied. *Chaos.*

The entire mountain-top resounded and shuddered to the howling of the Chaos beast. Behind them, rock slides and avalanches rumbled and crashed like an ocean in storm-tossed torment.

'God of my fathers!' Hamaan cried. 'What monstrosity is that?'

Terrifyingly, it looked human. It stood upright on two sturdy legs, had two powerful arms emanating from its massive shoulders, but that was where the resemblance ended. The head was a mass of writhing tentacles. A series of chilling, ophidian eyes ringed the crown, hidden and then revealed by the restless mass. Its howls of pain or terror or aggression increased, each echo feeding on itself exponentially.

The Chaos beast came through the Portal bleeding – or, at least, trailing the liquid stuff of Chaos. Clearly, it had not been an easy crossing. It took a step onto the mountain, its clawed feet digging into the icy rock, creating a mini-avalanche. All around it, rubble clattered in a fine icy haze. They could see its tail, slapping this way and that, balancing it on the way down.

It regarded them implacably with a baleful hostility more chilling even than the rarefied atmosphere of the summit.

'Which one?' it shrieked, its eyes looking from one to another. 'I was promised reintegration. Which one of you is for Lorcun?'

'Get back!' Moichi called, but it was already too late. With incredible speed, Lorcun had gripped his wrist and was drawing him toward the writhing nest of tentacles.

292

'Reintegration!' It shrieked. *'Now!'*

Moichi hacked at it with his dirk to no avail. And as he watched in horror, he saw the tentacles elongating like liquid as they snaked toward his face.

'No!' Sardonyx cried.

Moichi felt the eerie sensation of slipping off the edge of the world, and his eyes closed though he struggled to keep them open . . .

The formation kept shifting. First, it appeared to be a mountain, complete with rills and ridges, the next instant, it presented itself as a conical staircase hewn out of red obsidian. In fact, the only stable element was the hue – a deep blood-red that shimmered and throbbed in the non-light of Chaos. All around them came the bellows and trumpets of an aural cacophony.

'There are two Portals now,' Chiisai said again. She had told him this as they had raced across Ama-no-mori toward the lethal cave set high in the snow-covered scree. 'The one we entered in Ama-no-mori is one Kaijikan forced me to open.' That was where they had stationed one Kaer'n to seal the Portal after all the rest of them had gone through. 'But the main one – the one Kaijikan unlocked – is on the summit of the Mountain Sin'hai.'

'That is where Moichi is,' the Dai-San said as they maneuvered through Chaos. 'And I fear for him be-cause–'

The spiral staircase – for such it appeared at the moment – shuddered beneath them and an abrupt downdraft threatened to hurl them – powerful wings and all – over the side.

'What is it?' Chiisai cried, struggling to regain her balance.

'Someone has been very foolish,' the Dai-San said grimly. 'Dark sorcery is at play on the summit of Sin'hai,

293

and no one may know the outcome of it now. What long-hidden powers may be released we cannot even guess.'

'Let us make all haste, then.' Chiisai glanced back over her shoulder at the host of Kaer'n who most willingly followed her and the Dai-San.

'That would be wise,' the Dai-San advised. 'Show us the way to the Portal on Sin'hai.'

'No problem, I–'

Then, in the wink of an eye, the blood-red staircase was gone, and so was the mountain. They flew through darkness.

'Something has happened; I cannot see,' Chiisai cried. 'I have lost all sense of direction.'

'The sorcery is affecting us here in Chaos.' The Dai-San cursed. 'Why can't people do as they are told?'

'I must orient myself,' Chiisai said, 'but I can find no landmarks.'

And then out of the utter blackness of Chaos, she heard a voice: *I am here. Can you hear me?*

Yes! Chiisai said in her mind. *I hear you.*

By the God of my fathers, I thought surely I had lost you forever!

Sanda!

Yes! I know the way to the Portal. It was how I was brought through by the Makkon.

Just a moment, she said and, turning to the Dai-San, told him, 'I have found our path to Sin'hai.'

She was using her sorcery against Bjork's warning. He wanted to tell her to stop but as in a dream he was mute. Lorcun's foul stench rolled over him and he gagged. The tentacles were almost at his face. Then one brushed his skin in a cold kiss and he jerked his head away. But they were coming on. In an instant they would suck him in and Lorcun would begin the process of reintegration, his gelatinous essence absorbed through Moichi's skin. If only Sardonyx's sorcery could stop him.

He felt the sensation of dislocation, of falling, falling in a dream. Then, in a sudden quake, he was jolted to full consciousness. His eyes flew open in fear. What had happened?

He saw Lorcun throw its head back and howl in glee. 'Power!' As it began feeding. 'Yes, yes! More power!'

When Sardonyx realized that it was absorbing her power as quickly as she manufactured it, she quit, understanding Bjork's warning. In despair, she watched the Chaos beast dragging Moichi toward it. She swung her katana at it again and again until she was sobbing with the effort and frustration. She swung her weapon over her shoulder preparatory to striking it again, when she was pushed roughly aside.

'Stop it!' Hamaan said. 'Can't you see that has no effect? There is only one way . . .' And so saying, he rushed at Lorcun, shouldering Moichi aside with such startling power that Lorcun's grip was momentarily loosened. Hamaan used the opportunity to hurl his brother away into the snow. Then he leaped to embrace the Medusa's head of the Chaos beast.

'No!' Moichi shouted.

But Lorcun wasted no time, engulfing Hamaan within a sea of tentacles. Moichi rose to his feet, heard his brother's screams of outraged pain and fear. Moichi stood beside Sardonyx. Both held weapons that were useless. But he had to do something. He could not stand helplessly by while his brother absorbed Lorcun's essence.

Overhead, lightning forked and cracked, spilling all across the sky, turning it the color of blood, running like ribbons in the rain. Above them, the Portal was flickering as it filled with restless shadows. It appeared as if more Chaos beasts were making the crossing, and his soul was filled with dread. Not for himself – he could deal with his own demise, and perhaps that of Sardonyx, but what would happen to the world after they were gone? Who would protect mankind? Not Bjork. How he wished his bond-brother, the Dai-San were here. How he needed his strength and power now.

But you have your own power, a voice said in his mind. He looked to Sardonyx but she was concentrating on Lorcun's reintegration with Hamaan. Who had spoken then?

At that moment, a titanic bolt of lightning struck the towering rock formation just to his right and he saw, instead of the kinetic energy dissipating into the ground, a bright shower of azure sparks. Lorcun, busy with his ritual, yelped as several of the sparks burned his hide.

His heart rate quickening, Moichi ran to the spot the lightning had struck and saw laid bare a patch of dark gray metal. He hacked at a newly made fissure, saw that the entire formation was riddled with the metallic substance. It was this that was attracting the lightning. Everything is transmogrified here, he thought again and, calling to Sardonyx, bade her break off as much of the fissured rock façade as she could to expose the metal.

The lightning forked and boomed. It streaked down, attracted by the exposed patches of metal ore. Sparks bloomed and faded all too soon. Moichi knew he must risk everything to get Lorcun closer to the formation – even death.

He launched himself at the Chaos beast, catching it in the middle of reintegration. His shoulder struck Lorcun in the side, staggering the beast. It used its tail to balance itself and, as it did so, Moichi recalled in a flash the spot where the Râs Gharib was vulnerable. Syrinx was closest to Chaos, as Bjork had said. Perhaps its creatures, too, possessed some Chaos attributes.

Pulling out his copper-handled dirk, he plunged the tip

of the blade into the base of Lorcun's tail. The beast howled even as the edge of the blade glanced off the scaly hide, and Moichi used his shoulder again, kicking out with his back leg. Lorcun lurched heavily toward the rock outcropping.

Sardonyx leapt back as yet another lightning bolt cracked, shooting downward to strike the exposed ore. A great flash of sparks shot upward, this time inundating Lorcun.

It shrieked in pain, collapsing to the snow. Moichi fell upon it, digging the point of his dirk into its cold black eyes one by one. Lorcun writhed and screamed and almost threw him off it. But another bolt showered it with sparks and it began to convulse. Moichi knelt, hauling on Hamaan's shoulders, trying to pull him away from the Chaos beast.

But Lorcun's tentacles were tenacious and, unlike the base of its tail, they were impervious to Moichi's attack. Then Sardonyx's booted foot came down upon the back of Lorcun's neck. A heavy snapping sound caused the beast to arch up. It was stinking from its many burn wounds. The sparks had burrowed their way beneath the hide and were eating into the thing's viscera.

When Lorcun rolled over, Hamaan came free.

'It is dead,' Sardonyx said.

Moichi cradled Hamaan in his lap. His brother's face was a mass of red sores, suppurating a liquid Moichi did not recognize. Hamaan jerked and spasmed even while Moichi tried to comfort him. His eyes, frightfully wide and staring, were focused on something far away inside himself.

'You must kill him,' Sardonyx said, kneeling beside Moichi.

'No, no.'

'But you must,' Sardonyx said gently. 'Look how he

297

suffers. The process of reintegration has gone too far. You cannot bring him back, and neither can I.' She rose, looking down at him. 'You know what is best for him now.'

Moichi was grateful, at least, that she turned her back. Everything she said he knew to be true. He only need use the evidence of his eyes. How Hamaan was suffering! It would be a mercy to kill him, the quicker the better.

'That is not a comforting thought, brother, to be offered up to God like a sacrifice,' he had said.

'I have freed you of all obligation,' Moichi had replied. *'Do as you will.'*

That Hamaan had done. Moichi freed a dirk from its scabbard – the one he had not used on Lorcun and, saying a prayer for Hamaan's soul, plunged it to the hilt through his brother's heart. Immediately, the spasms ceased, and Hamaan released a long-held sigh. His eyes fluttered into focus for an instant.

'Hamaan,' Moichi whispered. 'You saved my life again.'

Hamaan's bloodless lips opened as if to reply, but they froze in that position. His eyes were fixed in their stare up at his brother.

From behind him, Moichi heard Sardonyx's voice. 'More of Chaos is coming through the Portal.'

He looked up. It was true. The flickering shadows had darkened and now that horrific howling they had heard when Lorcun Crossed Over reverberated anew among the shattered rock formations. And now, out of the Portal emerged the warriors of Chaos, each bent on reintegration. They crowded out of the Portal, shrieking long pent-up rage for retribution. Such a horde as Moichi had never before seen, even on the bloody plains before Kamado at the Kai-feng. He stood up, holding Sardonyx's hand. How were they to stay this torrent of Chaos when they were all but done in by a single beast?

'*WE WANT WHAT IS OURS!*' the host of Chaos bellowed as one. '*GIVE US OUR DUE!*'

And at the head of this malefic army strode a creature of singular countenance. While the rear of its torso was carried horizontally on four fleet-hooved legs, the front part rose vertically like a human being's, from which a pair of powerful arms extended, bearing claws the length of a warrior's sword. Its head was horizontal, long and as scaly as the hide of Râs Gharib, save that these plates rose up and out in a vicious curve that was razor sharp at its edge. Its eyes were faceted like a startled insect, and they peered at the brave new world into which it had entered with a terrible avidity, as if it harbored a burning desire to consume all it beheld.

The profound chill creeping down Moichi's spine told him he was looking at the new Chaos-master, heir to the power of the Dolman.

'Yes, Sakkourn!' a voice resounded from behind the Chaos-master. 'You will get all that is rightfully yours!'

And through the Portal burst the Dai-San, cape billowing. He was riding a Kaer'n and behind him, emerging in great numbers, were more Kaer'n. As they came, the warriors of Chaos turned and, stumbling, slipped down the icy slope. They cried out as one when they saw the Kaer'n and its leader, brandishing his longsword, *Aka-i-tsuchi*. The weapon sliced the head off one Chaos beast.

As if that were a clue, the Kaer'n broke off into well-disciplined twos and threes, attacking the Chaos horde. Leading them, Moichi saw, was not only the Dai-San, but a Kaer'n that was subtly different from the rest. Its eyes were long and almond-shaped, and the mane that grew from just behind its ears was plaited in a Bujun warrior's queue.

Just like Chiisai, Moichi thought.

Sakkourn whirled and, in a stunning burst of fury,

clawed down the nearest Kaer'n. Its great talons impaled the Kaer'n and when it turned its head to bite, it sheared the Kaer'n's head from its neck.

A blood-curdling cry went up from the assembled host of Chaos, and they redoubled their efforts against the Kaer'n. The shout came again as Sakkourn broke the Kaer'n's back and flung the carcass high into the air for all to see.

Moichi broke toward the beast, hurling a dirk toward one of its eyes. The blade clattered against the armored scales along the ridge-line of Sakkourn's cheek and it swung its baleful head in his direction.

That was when the Dai-San leapt from his position astride a Kaer'n. He landed atop Sakkourn. The Chaos-master reared upward, its head swiveling one hundred and eighty degrees. Its jaws snapped shut on the Dai-San's shoulder and began to grind down through the armor into skin and flesh.

Moichi leapt onto one of Sakkourn's legs, plunging his remaining dirk toward its eyes. The beast's protective lid closed down, and Moichi's thrust glanced harmlessly off it. The Dai-San began to pant from the grip Sakkourn was exerting on him, as the beast's fangs penetrated deeper, spurting toxins as they did so.

Moichi had drawn back his arm for another attempt, when he felt a presence beside him. Sardonyx, he saw, had climbed up beside him. Now she jammed the point of her sword through one of the beast's unprotected nostrils. Sakkourn screamed as a fountain of powdery blood spurted upward.

Freeing his arm, the Dai-San drove the point of *Aka-i-tsuchi* into the base of Sakkourn's neck. The sorcerous blade pierced the armored hide and plunged inward. Sakkourn screamed so that the entire summit shook. In so doing, it released the Dai-San's shoulder.

In a flash, the Dai-San grasped its neck between forearm and fist, forcing it backwards. Sakkourn's body thrashed and whipped from side to side. Sparks flew as its long talons scored down the Dai-San's armor, searching for a weak spot. Its jaws clashed and snapped, attempting to regain its grip, but the Dai-San continually smashed his Makkon-gauntleted fist into the Chaos-master's snout.

For a long moment, the two antagonists were locked in what seemed a timeless struggle. They barely moved, but the intensity of their conflict could be measured in the grinding of metal upon metal, the crackling of bone joints brought to maximum strength and beyond. Sakkourn yowled and roared, its outline shimmering and pulsing as it brought all of its power to bear against the Dai-San.

The sky was aflame with blood-red lightning bolts, an inferno of kinetic energy, bursting so quickly that it seemed the entire summit was bathed in its fiery heart. The ground shuddered and shook and, once, an entire rock formation peeled off, thundering down in an immense cloud of icy crystals and metallic fragments.

Moichi was high enough to see the Dai-San peering down into the beast's eyes. What was it he was looking for there? he wondered.

Then, with a fierce multiple cracking, Sakkourn's vertebrae sundered, splintering beneath the inexorable pressure. Moichi and Sardonyx had the good sense to leap free as the beast's body convulsed, its arms and legs flailing about with stupefying speed.

Now the Kaer'n drove into the Chaos horde with true fury, ripping and rending, consuming beast after beast as they went. It was a sheer feeding frenzy. They clawed great gobbets of viscera from the Chaos warriors, chomping down with sharp-toothed mouths, beheading and dismembering, then ravaging the torsoes, cutting a swath through the monstrous legions.

'God of Iskael,' Sardonyx breathed, 'what is happening?'

'This is truly the wrath of the God of my fathers,' Moichi said in wonderment. 'Or the return of the balance between man and Chaos.' He wished Hamaan and Sanda were here to see this because, each in his or her own way had played a hand in this future that had now come to pass.

All around them, the feeding had come to an end. The Kaer'n swooped and played like innocent children, gliding delightedly between the bolts of pink lightning which were now diminishing into a rather mundane ice storm.

The Dai-San guided his Kaer'n to the snow-packed rock in front of Moichi, Sardonyx and the fallen Hamaan.

'Bond-brother,' the Dai-San said, reaching out to grasp Moichi's forearm in the traditional Iskamen manner. 'Again we meet upon the field of battle.'

'It is always the way with us, Dai-San.' He introduced Sardonyx but was too preoccupied to notice the penetrating look the Sunset Warrior gave her. He was already entranced by the Kaer'n who had led the pack. He watched it closely as it arced down across the Portal. One of its wings entered the Boundary and all but disappeared, becoming insubstantial. A moment later, another Kaer'n bounded through, this one even more familiar than the first. The two of them made a series of complex passes across the Portal. A deep, almost subliminal rumbling filled their minds and, instantly, the red beacon-like light was extinguished.

'The Portal has been resealed,' the Dai-San said, as the two Kaer'n landed beside him. They flanked him like guardian angels, their heads bobbing, their nostrils wide as they snorted with excess energy. One of them stuck its head out, lowering it until it was just above Moichi's.

He took a step forward but Sardonyx held his arm. 'Be careful,' she said under the Dai-San's scrutiny, but Moichi shook his head. He felt the ice crystals dancing on his face and the wind that blew through the summit of the Mountain Sin'hai was fresh and invigorating.

'There is no danger here,' he said, and he reached his hand up, touching the muzzle of the Kaer'n. 'I have met you before,' he said in some wonderment. 'I know you.'

The Kaer'n's head bent further and he held on to one of its curving horns so that he could look into one immense eye. What he saw there sent a shiver right through him. He turned his head to his bond-brother. 'Dai-San, can this be so?'

The Dai-San's high helm glittered as he nodded his head. 'It can, Moichi, and it is.' He gestured to the Kaer'n. 'This is Sanda, transformed, yes, but still your sister.'

'Sanda,' Moichi whispered. 'You came to me in a dream I had in the Mu'ad. You told me to find Bjork, the last of the Shinju, and I did.'

Beloved brother, do not weep for me, the voice came in his mind. *My spirit lives within this new body. Now Chiisai and I have a chance to change the old order.*

'Chiisai?' He turned his head to the Kaer'n on the other side of the Dai-San, the one with the warrior's queue. 'What happened?'

She told him briefly of her encounter with Kaijikan and the reanimated Tokagé. He nodded dumbly, too stunned to speak. The wind blew soft petals of snow through the peaks of the summit and no one said anything for a long time. At last, Moichi stirred and, still holding on to Sanda, took her to where Hamaan lay, cold and dead.

'I was asked to judge him, Sanda, but his crimes were too many, too intimate and I could not. I prayed for you to come and do what I could not.'

God will judge him now, she said, lowering her head to press her muzzle against Hamaan's shoulder. *We must bury him here on the summit of Sin'hai.*

303

Moichi took his brother's corpse in his arms and climbed upon Sanda's back. The Dai-San came up to him, offered up his sorcerous longsword.

'It will make your work that much easier,' he said.

'My thanks, but no,' Moichi told him. 'This is one task that should not be made easy.'

Near the great rift, he dismounted. Snow was swirling in great plumes toward a green sky. Sunlight reflected off uncounted ice crystals, making the light prismatic.

Sanda and Moichi began to excavate, pushing snow aside, hacking through the dark ice beneath. Despite the cold, he began to sweat.

They had dug down perhaps three feet when he saw something out of the corner of his eye. He looked up to see the long predatory muzzle of a Wolke'en. It was, like all its kind, snow-white. Its ice-blue eyes watched them with canny intelligence. Could this be the same one that had come into their camp the night Hamaan had threatened to slit Moichi's throat? It was Moichi's opinion that Hamaan had seen something in the Wolke'en that had made him change his mind. Staring fixedly at the corpse it licked its chops.

Noticing where he was looking Sanda said, *Under the circumstances I think it best we bury Hamaan very deep.*

But Moichi shook his head. 'This is wrong. I knew it from the beginning.' He sheathed his dirk, began kicking chunks of ice back into the grave they had been digging.

What are you doing?

'When I die,' Hamaan had said, 'other predators will know and they will feed off my corpse. That is the way of it; the way I wish it.'

He told her what Hamaan had said. 'Leave him here, back away now.'

When they were five hundred yards away, the Wolke'en began to circle in. It was wasting no time, Moichi saw.

Perhaps the severe cold had made food scarce, or perhaps it recognized a fellow predator.

'He had a warrior's death,' Moichi said, his eyes on the Wolke'en. 'Now he will have a warrior's interment.' The Wolke'en, one eye on them, tore into the corpse. 'His last remains provide sustenance for another warrior.'

The ceremony – for such, Moichi realized later, it was – was over in an astonishingly short time. As Sardonyx had said, the Wolke'en was a prodigiously efficient killing machine. Just as Hamaan had been.

They returned to the site of the continuing celebration in a sober frame of mind. 'It is done,' Moichi said solemnly to the Dai-San and Chiisai. He looked at them. Considering they were such strange creatures he felt peculiarly comfortable with the Kaer'n. Chiisai, returning his gaze, knew his thoughts; knew, also, why the Kaer'n should be so familiar to him. As the Dai-San had told her, he and Moichi were inextricably linked, one the extension of the other. *I have the power to do more than the Kaer'n; and Moichi has more power to enact change than do I.* Perhaps somewhere deep in his unconscious Moichi understood this. If not, she was not the one to tell him.

The Dai-San, divining Moichi's mood, gestured toward the summit. 'Come with me,' he said.

Together, they climbed the steep snowy face, crunching, now and again, on the remnants of the Chaos horde. Moichi felt his mind clear. It was good to be with his bond-brother. After so many cataclysmic changes there was particular comfort in this old friendship.

'Who are they,' he said after a time, 'these Kaer'n?'

They had reached a stout rock lip that overhung the entire face of the Mountain Sin'hai. Through a brief break in the clouds he could glimpse the high walls of Mas'jahan and, beyond, the Mu'ad. Somewhere in that vastness men were preparing to go to battle and he knew that in order to stop them he could not long tarry in Sin'hai. In a swirl of snow, the scene was completely obliterated.

The Dai-San considered before speaking. 'It is right that you know their secret, Moichi. The Kaer'n were born millennia ago as part of a secret experiment. After the Shinju mages of mankind sealed Chaos away on the other side of this Portal they discovered, to their dismay, that certain elements of Chaos had remained. They tried in every fanatic way to purge these few elements from the world of man – to no avail. These elements belonged here and here they would stay despite all the sorcery then at mankind's command.'

The Dai-San put his gauntleted hand out to touch the sealed Portal which glimmered and glistened like sunlight on ice. 'So these mages began experimenting with the Chaos elements to see if there was some use for them, after all, in the world of man. The Kaer'n were the first result. They thought them crude and so frightening they tried to kill them off. When this did not work, they altered the Kaer'n, made sure that they were all males. With no females, they could not reproduce; therefore, eventually – though no one knew the lifespan of a Kaer'n – they would die out.'

He banged on the Portal with his mailed fist and a dull throbbing echoed through the formations of the summit. For a moment, the Kaer'n ceased their ecstatic dance. Then they resumed it as if nothing untoward had happened.

'Fear makes men foolish because it impedes thought,' the Dai-San continued. 'And so it was with the Shinju mages. They never bothered to understand the true nature of their creation, they never knew that they were meant to manipulate the elements of Chaos just as they had, that they were meant to create the Kaer'n – the guardians of the balance between mankind and Chaos.'

He looked at Moichi. 'Now, two female Kaer'n have been

created in the cauldron of karma and Chaos. Now Chiisai and Sanda may – if they so choose – go on to found a dynasty of Kaer'n for the future.'

He lapsed into an uncharacteristic, contemplative silence. Above them the Kaer'n still swooped and called to one another. And still the silence of the place overarched everything. Snow filtered down, blowing into their faces every so often, borne on gusts of wind.

Moichi took a step toward the Dai-San. 'What is it, my friend?'

The Sunset Warrior did not answer for a long time. 'The irony is that I love her, Moichi. I would have made Chiisai my bride.' He swiveled his head, impaling Moichi with his formidable gaze. 'No one – *no one* – knows this secret.'

'Even Chiisai?' Moichi said softly.

The Dai-San's eyes picked out the Kaer'n among all the others. 'Especially her.'

'Perhaps that is a mistake.'

Still following her flight, the Dai-San shrugged. 'Mayhap it is.'

Moichi, so close to the Dai-San after so long a time, suddenly realized how isolated he must be from everyone and everything, and he was overcome by a sense of melancholy. Even the one woman his bond-brother loved was unavailable to him. What could life be like for him? This was not a question he had ever thought to ask and, frankly, now that he had he could see that it did not bear scrutiny. Any one of ten thousand answers was equally painful. In that moment, he felt closer to the Dai-San than he ever had before, certain that their bond was more profound than even he could know.

Slowly, as he came back to himself, he took time to turn something over in his mind. 'Down below in Syrinx, Bjork, Miira's child, told me that all Shinju had within them some Chaos.'

307

'It is true.' The Dai-San came out of his reverie. 'But the Shinju were fatally flawed, and in some ways weak. They were tied to Chaos in a singular way through White Lotus. They could not be trusted with such guardianship.'

'Then who – or what – caused the elements of Chaos to be left behind? The way you speak of this history makes it sound as if there was a master plan in place.'

'Yes. It does appear so.'

Moichi looked around the summit. 'My people believe that this is the House of the Holy, Dai-San. The Catechists, as well. They say Zarathus, their living God, walks these slopes.'

'And, in a way, he does,' the Dai-San said. 'Just as he sometimes walks the streets of Mas'jahan.' He smiled at Moichi. 'Did not Bjork tell you she roams the face of the Mountain Sin'hai? She is sometimes lonely for the company of man. Sometimes she wraps herself in her mother's cloak and does the same in the citadel of the Catechists.'

Moichi was aghast. 'Bjork is their god?'

'If the Catechists see Bjork as such then it must be so.'

This sent a sudden chill through him. 'What of my God, Dai-San? The God of the Iskamen?'

The Dai-San looked out over Sin'hai. 'As you say, my friend, something – or someone – created the master plan.' He put his hand on Moichi's shoulder. 'Many men have spent their entire lives searching for God. Perhaps it is not an apt occupation.'

'For a human, you mean.'

'For anyone.'

ON THE SEA
OF NIGHT

He awoke to the sound of the scream. It was a mortal scream and he leaped up with his dirk already drawn. Beside him, Sardonyx, deeper in sleep, was rolling over.

He had been dreaming of his last moments on the summit of the Mountain Sin'hai. Night had come down with the abruptness usual at such altitudes. He and Sardonyx were gazing skyward at a galaxy of new stars – the Kaer'n as they began their long journey back to Ama-no-mori. They had no wish to overstay in the land of the Shinju, and since the Portals had been sealed they were obliged to fly halfway across the world. Moichi raised his arm in salute to them, and in a more private salutation to the Dai-San, who rode upon Chiisai's broad back. Who knew when they would see one another again, such close friends whose karma kept them so much apart?

The galleon moon, riding high in the sky, was eclipsed by the fleet of Kaer'n as they rose as one and, wheeling playfully across the heavens, began their flight homeward. It was a magnificent sight, one Moichi would not soon forget, and he promised himself that before his time in the world of man was over he would visit Ama-no-mori.

Beside them, Sanda stirred. She had stayed behind to transport them back to Syrinx where Bjork and Ouwlmy were no doubt anxiously awaiting them.

She nuzzled his side. *Time to go. The temperature is dropping precipitously.*

She lowered her head and Moichi swung onto her. Sardonyx followed suit, seating herself in front of him but, as comfortable as he was astride the Kaer'n she was ill at ease. He put his arms around her waist in silent reassurance.

Upon Sanda's back they rose into the night skies, through the storm clouds, the gusts of snow and ice pellets, until the moon broke through. Away to the east they could see the fleet of Kaer'n, tiny now, glittering with pale and ghostly moonlight, like stars themselves. And then, as Sanda banked steeply, the sensation of falling, falling . . .

Into the mortal scream.

Moichi was up and running across the embankment on which they had made their bed. They were within Bjork's cathedral-like tree-castle on the inner edge of the Khashm. All about him loomed the enormous arboretum that Bjork had made into a singular home. But now, the spectral network of branches had taken on a sinister aspect, catching the scream and bouncing it back upon itself. It was a scream of pain and, more, of mortal fear.

Moichi felt rather than heard someone running behind him. Sardonyx? There was no time to look back and see, but his mind was unaccountably filled with her. She had seemed peculiarly cool to Sanda, and again her unease astride the Kaer'n played in his mind like a scene stuck in time. For her part, Sanda, loving Sanda, whom he had not seen for so long had flatly refused his invitation to stay with him a while in Syrinx. Perhaps it was not so surprising; no Kaer'n cared to tarry in that land where they had been created, misunderstood and abused by the Shinju mages. Still, she was his sister and he longed to spend time with her, to get to know her all over again. But he had a certain duty to his country, and they both knew that if the war Hamaan and the other Qa'tachs had so cleverly

310

sought was to be avoided he would have to return to the Mu'ad with all due haste. Revealing the Fe'edjinn plot to the Iskamen populace was paramount, and Moichi knew he was the only one to do it.

The mortal scream resounded again through the latticework of branches. Moichi sped onward, through the flickering moonshadows, through odd patches of cold blue light.

Several times before they had made ready for sleep, he had obliquely asked Sardonyx why she had been so cold to Sanda but she had given him no good reply – no reply at all, really. Finally, he had shrugged and given it up. If she did not wish to speak of it he could not make her tell him. But, at dinner, he noticed all of them – Sardonyx, Bjork and Ouwlmy – were uncharacteristically unresponsive. This was not the scene of triumphal return he had imagined as he had flown down the Mountain Sin'hai on Sanda.

Amid the chiaroscuro landscape, he could see figures struggling. The high scream came again and now, this close, he recognized the voice – Ouwlmy!

Something huge and menacing gripped the Shakra by the throat, and as Moichi raced across the last of the terrain he could see that it was prying open Ouwlmy's jaws. She was fighting as hard as she could, using her hooves and her powerful flanks, but the being that held her fast was obviously far stronger. In a silent rage, it shook her, making her teeth rattle. Then, as Moichi looked on, horrified, it reached between her open jaws and slowly extracted her tongue until it was stretched to its full length.

God of my fathers, Moichi thought, it's the tongueless Makkon, seeking revenge. He drew both dirks as he raced toward the Makkon, knowing full well that here he had no chance against a Chaos beast. On the opposite side of the clearing, he saw a figure step out of the shadows.

'Bjork,' he cried, 'the Makkon you maimed is about to cut out Ouwlmy's tongue!'

To his astonishment, Bjork did nothing, merely stood still, staring out across the clearing, past the antagonists.

'Bjork, are you deaf or mad?' Moichi shouted, rage boiling in him. 'You have the power to stop the Makkon! Why don't you? Would you sacrifice Ouwlmy? For what? Chill take you, answer me!'

The Makkon, enjoying the terror it saw in the Shakra's eyes, continued to play with the tongue, pulling it, tugging at it, at length clamping it between two talons.

Dear God, Moichi thought. He ran the remaining distance, swung one weapon at the Makkon. Almost casually, it sideswiped him with the back of its six-fingered hand, and he went sprawling head over heels.

When he came up, he saw what Bjork was staring at. Behind where he had emerged, Sardonyx was advancing across the greensward.

At last, Bjork broke her silence. 'You know what you must do.' Sardonyx said nothing. 'Precious Ouwlmy will die unless you act.' Still, Sardonyx came on, passing Moichi, heading toward Ouwlmy and the Makkon. 'I don't have to remind you of what Ouwlmy has done for you. She was your firmest advocate even while I was unsure whether or not to train you.' Sardonyx seemed in a trance, as if the scene playing out before them, combined with Bjork's words, had cast a spell over her. 'Act now or she *will* die.'

Now, not more than three feet from the Makkon, Sardonyx came to a halt. She looked back over her shoulder at Moichi but when she spoke he knew it was not to him but to Bjork. 'I prayed this moment would never come. It is the one nightmare that has haunted me from the moment you began the initiation.'

312

'You are what you are,' Bjork said. 'You *must* accept that if you have any hope of surviving.'

Sardonyx nodded, a quick, reflexive action and she turned back to where the Makkon was about to pluck Ouwlmy's tongue from her throat. But not before Moichi saw a look in her eyes that chilled him. It was as if they were hollow, and he could see down into a void beyond his imagining.

Then, she raised her hand, made a series of vertical signs in the air. A wind began to rise, rustling through the cobweb of branches, turning the leaves over so their silver undersides sparkled as if the stars had been flung down from the very heavens.

The Makkon, alerted at last, lifted its hideous head and began to turn around. But it was already too late. Sardonyx had drawn her sword and, plunging it into the center of a giant root that arched out of the grass, she murmured an invocation in a language whose syllables hurt Moichi's ears.

He clapped his hands over his ears lest the unspeakable sounds render him numb. But he could not avert his eyes. What he saw rooted him to the spot. A pale green light began to shimmer and then, in a roar, poured upward from the spot where Sardonyx had buried the sword point. A hot wind began to howl, sending up tiny leaf-storms all through the tree-castle.

The storms converged upon the Makkon, who tried to keep its grip on Ouwlmy. The green howling was too powerful, and it slid away, tumbling head over heels along the ground, sparks and billows of smoke spurting in its wake.

Moichi ran to where Ouwlmy lay upon the ground, sobbing. He cradled her head in his lap, but still his eyes refused to leave the nexus of the green storm which now held the Makkon in its grip. The Chaos beast, its fists clenched and beating the ground in rage, was hurtled feet first into the dark heart of that sorcerous storm. Down the beam of light it flew, dwindling as it did so, its outline becoming indistinct, flickering like a candle's flame in a tempest.

Then it was gone, vanished in a black-green flash. The green windstorm followed it down, and so, too, the beam of light. At length, Sardonyx wrenched the blade out of the root, and the night regained its senses.

'Moichi, I am all right. Just a little sore,' Ouwlmy whispered. 'Please help me up.' He kissed her on the cheek and together they rose.

Bjork was coming toward them from the far side of the clearing. Sardonyx stood as still as a statue, clutching her unsheathed sword, staring fixedly at nothing.

'What is going on here? What happened?' Moichi asked.

Bjork came up beside Ouwlmy, and the Shakra said, 'Tell him, Sardonyx.'

'She is right,' Bjork said. 'The truth has already been demonstrated.'

'Only because you forced it,' Sardonyx said hotly. 'You could have dealt with the Makkon yourself.'

Bjork nodded. 'Perhaps so. But that would have done you no real good. Quite the opposite, in fact.'

Sardonyx shot her a venomous look, which she cheerfully deflected. 'Sardonyx opened a Portal into Chaos,' Bjork said as matter-of-factly as if she were reporting on the month's crop totals.

Moichi looked at Sardonyx and she nodded.

'It is true,' she said. 'I was born in Aden, as I told you, but I am Shinju.'

'*Pure* Shinju,' Bjork interjected, 'unlike me.'

'But why didn't you tell me?' Moichi asked. Now he understood the antipathy between Sanda and Sardonyx.

'Because,' she said defiantly, 'we are all traitors to man-

314

kind. Ever since the Shinju mages locked Chaos away behind the Portal atop the Mountain Sin'hai there remained a way to undo what they had done. Even we do not know much about our own mages. What drove them, for instance? But surely since they kept the secret of access into Chaos they must have lusted after power.

'The Shinju continued to harvest White Lotus long after the Portal had been sealed. Why? Because the Shinju – certain Shinju who passed the secret down the generations – continued a clandestine relationship with Chaos. Why? I do not know. No one, I think, does. Perhaps we are like moths to a flame; perhaps we cannot survive without them.

'They, on the other hand, despise us. We knew their weakness for White Lotus and over the course of the centuries we played upon that weakness, exploiting them.'

'Until they had had enough,' Bjork said. 'And then they streamed through the Portal and all but destroyed the entire race.' She looked at Sardonyx with great compassion. 'Not that we did not deserve such a fate. We were greedy and avaricious and arrogant. We sought to make the Kaer'n our slaves. We ignored the laws of God and Nature. And how we were punished for our sins!'

'Why did the Shinju treat the Kaer'n this way?' Moichi asked.

'I can only speculate,' Bjork said slowly. 'I think they must have been frightened of what they had created. You have only to look at the Kaer'n once to understand that. And then, I believe, they were jealous. All along they had believed themselves to be mankind's sole link to Chaos. This made the Shinju special; unique. Now, along come the Kaer'n to make a mockery of that notion. Once, I imagine, the Shinju considered themselves mankind's shepherds, keeping them safe from Chaos. But with the advent of the Kaer'n deep down they knew they were only the creators of man's guardians.' She sighed. 'The Shinju hubris – I am afraid we were quite the egotists.'

There was silence for a long time in the glade. Nocturnal birds flitted from branch to branch but knew better than to sing their songs. Now was not the time.

'Ouwlmy . . .' Bjork reached out an arm into which the Shakra nestled. Before they left, Ouwlmy lifted her head, kissed Moichi tenderly.

'Goodbye, Prince of Iskael, long life to you!'

'And to you, dear Ouwlmy,' Moichi said. He was quite moved. 'But you are mistaken. I am no prince; I am but a ship's captain.'

The Shakra smiled a most enigmatic smile. Then, snorting once, she trotted off with Bjork at her side and Moichi was left alone with Sardonyx.

Moonlight continued to stream down through the arboreal cathedral, cascading over her in ribbons and pinpoints, hiding her as much as it revealed. Standing there with her naked sword still gripped tightly, her eyes downcast, she seemed as sad and alone as had the Dai-San on the summit of Sin'hai. Moichi ached to reach out to her, to reassure her, but keen instinct held him back. He knew she needed to divulge one last thing, buried deeply, and he could not help her in this difficult exorcism.

'Guilt,' she said at last. 'I think more than anything my life has been molded by guilt. Guilt as to what I am, what my people have done and are capable of, has set me to reinventing myself. You know, it's curious; when you are not the real thing, when you expend so much energy making yourself *seem* genuine, then you wind up being *more* genuine than the real thing. Being so self-conscious you can weed out the flaws you recognize in others.'

She was silent for a long time. At last she said, 'Are you listening to me?'

'You know I am,' Moichi said.

'I wonder.' She sighed. 'After all this time, I wonder what you must think of me. Perhaps you don't believe anything I've told you.'

'Sardonyx–'

'No, no. I would not blame you, certainly.' She turned to face him squarely. 'Perhaps you even harbor a suspicion that I killed Aufeya in order to be with you.'

'I believed you when you told me she slipped and fell while I was dealing with the Firemask.'

She took a step toward him and he could see the pain and longing in her beautiful, scarred face. 'I could have lied.'

'What difference would it make now?'

She was astonished. 'Why, all the difference in the world!' she cried.

'By that answer alone I know you told the truth.' He smiled at her and took her hand. 'It's over now. Don't you see? All the running, the hiding, the – what did you call it? – reinventing. I, at least, can accept you for what you are. So, I suspect, can many others, including my sister.'

'No.' Sardonyx was shaking her head vehemently. 'The Kaer'n will never forgive what the Shinju did to them.'

He held her close. 'By thinking that aren't you perpetuating what your race did to them – dismiss them, denigrate them, abuse them?' And in his own words he saw the true ending to the centuries-old war between Iskael and Aden; the kernel of an understanding.

She appeared to think about what he had said for some time. Then she buried her head in his shoulder. It might have been the wind through the trees but he thought he could hear her weeping. He put his arms around her and, after a very long time, she let go of the sword. It fell at her feet, lying there, gleaming dully as a ghost of moonlight fired its edge.

Finally, he pulled her thick hair back from her face,

kissed her temple, but he made no effort to move. He thought of Bjork and Ouwlmy. He was enveloped by a sense of serenity he could not explain. Perhaps, so close to the Mountain Sin'hai and all its secrets – known and unknown – he could allow himself the notion that the kinship he felt so profoundly for these folk was not merely psychological. Could it be that somewhere inside him a bit of Shinju or – like the Kaer'n and the Dai-San – Chaos still abided? He remembered what Bjork had told him of his father's fascination with Syrinx.

He held Sardonyx more closely, feeling a sense of calmness gradually steal over her. She was right: from the moment they had met in her castle in the land of the Opal Moon it was clear they were meant for each other. No one else, he knew, could have saved the sorceress from her own spell. He kissed her again, heard her sigh as she clung to him.

Time enough after he defused the holy war to explore his own nature. He was quit running away to sea – at least for the time being. The oceans of the world – such old friends! – seemed remote to him now, almost dreamlike, much like his journey astride his Kaer'n sister upon the sea of night.

He looked upward, through the latticework of the leaves, to the clear sky filled with clusters of stars so bright they seemed burned into the velvety blackness like suns. Somewhere, up there, he knew, the joyous host of Kaer'n was flying homeward. As if he were there, he saw Sanda catch up with them, flying alongside Chiisai and the Dai-San. Part of him was with them.

I am but a ship's captain, he had said so ingenuously to Ouwlmy. Only now was he beginning to understand the nature of her enigmatic smile.

318

Dragoncharm
Graham Edwards

The ultimate dragon saga

THE WORLD IS TURNING

The bones of trolls are turning suddenly to stone as nature draws apart from the Realm, the mysterious source of charm. It is a young world, but soon it will be old, and no magic is strong enough to resist the onset of a new era.

Instead, a young natural dragon named Fortune, with no fire in his breath nor magic in his power, holds the key to the survival of charm.

The malevolent Charmed dragon Wraith knows this, and he awakens the basilisk in a desperate bid to gain power over Fortune . . .

Myths handed down since the dawn of time tell of dragons, the most strange and magnificent creatures of our mythical prehistory. In this glorious epic fantasy, Graham Edwards captures the terror and the beauty of the days when dragons roamed the sky.

ISBN 0 00 648021 7

Magician
Raymond E. Feist
New Revised Edition

Raymond E. Feist has prepared a new, revised edition, to incorporate over 15,000 words of text omitted from previous editions so that, in his own words, 'it is essentially the book I would have written had I the skills I possess today'.

At Crydee, a frontier outpost in the tranquil Kingdom of the Isles, an orphan boy, Pug is apprenticed to a master magician – and the destinies of two worlds are changed forever. Suddenly the peace of the Kingdom is destroyed as mysterious alien invaders swarm through the land. Pug is swept up into the conflict but for him and his warrior friend, Tomas, an odyssey into the unknown has only just begun. Tomas will inherit a legacy of savage power from an ancient civilisation. Pug's destiny is to lead him through a rift in the fabric of space and time to the mastery of the unimaginable powers of a strange new magic. . .

'Epic scope . . . fast-moving action . . . vivid imagination'
Washington Post

'Tons of intrigue and action'   *Publishers Weekly*

ISBN 0 586 21783 3

Only Forward
Michael Marshall Smith

A truly stunning debut from a young author. Extremely original, satyrical and poignant, a marriage of numerous genres brilliantly executed to produce something entirely new.

Stark is a troubleshooter. He lives in The City - a massive conglomeration of self-governing Neighbourhoods, each with their own peculiarity. Stark lives in Colour, where computers co-ordinate the tone of the street lights to match the clothes that people wear. Close by is Sound where noise is strictly forbidden, and Ffnaph where people spend their whole lives leaping on trampolines and trying to touch the sky. Then there is Red, where anything goes, and all too often does.

At the heart of them all is the Centre - a back-stabbing community of 'Actioneers' intent only on achieving - divided into areas like 'The Results are what Counts sub-section' which boasts 43 grades of monorail attendant. Fell Alkland, Actioneer extraordinaire has been kidapped. It is up to Stark to find him. But in doing so he is forced to confront the terrible secrets of his past. A life he has blocked out for too long.

'Michael Marshall Smith's *Only Forward* is a dark labyrinth of a book: shocking, moving and surreal. Violent, outrageous and witty - sometimes simultaneously - it offers us a journey from which we return both shaken and exhilarated. An extraordinary debut.'
Clive Barker

ISBN 0 586 21774 6

The Master of Whitestorm
Janny Wurts

'Janny Wurts is a gifted creator of wonder'

Raymond E. Feist

Everyone knew there was no escape from the slave galleys of the Murghai: but Korendir, a man whose past was shrouded in mystery, recognized no impossibilities in life.

After leading a desperate and successful revolt, he frees the prisoners and sets out on a series of remarkable quests; battling the sorceress Anthei to lift the curse on the blighted land of Torresdyr; challenging the elemental Cyondide to win the lost hoard of the dragon Sharkash; travelling to far Northengard to save its people from a plague of poisonous wereleopards.

Always Korendir's goal was treasure; but never for its own sake. His ultimate aim was to build a fortress at Whitestorm, impregnable against all comers, be they mortal or supernatural, to protect himself, its Master, from the dark secret of his ancestry. . .

'Pace and fire . . . Janny Wurts writes with astonishing energy'

Stephen R. Donaldson

'Powerful . . . epic grandeur . . . magnificent!'

Anne McCaffrey

ISBN 0 586 21068 7

Red Mars
Kim Stanley Robinson

WINNER OF THE NEBULA AWARD

MARS. THE RED PLANET.
Closest to Earth in our solar system,
surely life must exist on it?

We dreamt about the builders of the canals we could see by tele-
scope, about ruined cities, lost Martian civilisations, the possibil-
ities of alien contact. Then the Viking and Mariner probes went
up, and sent back - nothing. Mars was a barren planet: lifeless,
sterile, uninhabited.

In 2019 the first man set foot on the surface of Mars: John
Boone, American hero. In 2027 one hundred of the Earth's finest
engineers and scientists made the first mass-landing. Their
mission? To create a New World.

To terraform a planet with no atmosphere, an intensely cold
climate and no magnetosphere into an Eden full of people, plants
and animals. It is the greatest challange mankind has ever faced:
the ultimate use of intelligence and ability: our finest dream.

'A staggering book . . . The best novel on the colonization of
Mars that has ever been written'   *Arthur C. Clarke*

'First of a mighty trilogy, *Red Mars* is the ultimate in future
history'   *Daily Mail*

'*Red Mars* may simply be the best novel ever written about Mars'
Interzone

ISBN 0 586 21389 9

The Broken God
David Zindell

'SF as it ought to be: challenging, imaginative, thought-provoking and well-written. Zindell has placed himself at the forefront of literary SF'   *Times Literary Supplement*

Book One of David Zindell's new epic trilogy is set in Neverness, legendary city of Light, where inner space and outer space meet . . . where the God program is up and running.

Into its maze of colour-coded streets of ice a wild boy stumbles, starving, frostbitten and grieving, a spear in his hand: Danlo the Wild, a messenger from the deep past of man. Brought up far from Neverness by the Alaloi people, neanderthal cave-dwellers, Danlo alone of his tribe has survived a plague – because he is not, as he had thought, a misshapen neanderthal, but human, with immunity engineered into his genes. He learns that the disease was created by the sinister Architects of the Universal Cybernetic Church. The Architects possess a cure which can save other Alaloi tribes. But the Architects have migrated to the region of space known as the Vild, and there they are killing stars.

All of civilization has converged on Neverness through the manifold of space travel. Beyond science, beyond decadence, sects and disciplines multiply there. Danlo, his mind shaped by primitive man, brings to Neverness a single long-lost memory that will challenge them all.

ISBN 0 586 21189 6

Take Back Plenty
Colin Greenland

Winner of the Arthur C. Clarke and British Science Fiction Association Awards for the best science fiction novel.

Tabitha Jute was in trouble on Mars.

It was Carnival time and everyone was partying except her. Up against the law, penniless and about to lose her livelihood and best friend, the space barge *Alice Liddell* – Tabitha needed some luck. Fast.

Then along came the intriguing gloveman Marco Metz. He needed a lift to Plenty to rejoin his bizarre cabaret troupe – and he would pay. Tabitha knew Plenty was a dodgy place since its creators had been exterminated by the Capellans, the masters of the Terran system. But she didn't have any choice.

What should have been a simple five-hour journey and some quick cash turned into a chaotic chase from the orbital tangle into the depths of hyperspace, with the cops on her tail.

And that was only the start of her problems . . .

'A great, big, magnificent, galaxy-shaking plot that will make you forget to eat and sleep.'   *Michael Moorcock*

'A masterpiece. If you ever wondered why you began reading science fiction this book answers that question. *Take Back Plenty* is fun.'   *Interzone*

ISBN 0 586 21339 2

Curse of the Mistwraith
Janny Wurts

The first volume of Janny Wurts' new and
exciting epic fantasy

Two brothers worlds apart, their fates interlocked in
enmity by the curse of the Mistwraith . . .

The world of Athera lives in eternal fog, its skies obscured
by the malevolent Mistwraith. Only the combined powers
of two half-brothers can challenge the Mistwraith's stranglehold: Arithon - Master of Shadows and Lysaer - Lord of
Light.

Arithon and Lysaer will find that they are inescapably
bound inside a pattern of events dictated by their deepest
convictions. Yet there is much more at stake than one
battle with the Mistwraith - as the sorcerers of the
Fellowship of Seven know well. For between them the
half-brothers hold the balance of the world, its harmony
and its future in their hands.

'Astonishingly original and compelling'   *Raymond E. Feist*

ISBN 0 586 21069 5